Ex Libris

Gabriel Murray

A THOUSAND KISSES DEEP

The love story between Leonard Cohen and Marianne Jensen.

GABRIEL MURRAY

Copyright © A Thousand Kisses Deep, 2021. by Gabriel Murray. All rights reserved. No part of this publication may be reproduced, distributed, or transmitted in any form or by any means, including photocopying, recording, or other electronic or mechanical methods, without the prior written permission of the publisher, except in the case of brief quotations embodied in critical reviews and certain other non-commercial uses permitted by copyright law. For permission requests, write to the publisher, addressed;

Dun Emer Press, 2, Flr, 13 Upr Baggot St, Dublin 4.
Contact; pegasusagent123@gmail.com

Acknowledgements; Many thanks for their commitment to this project. Mark Heaton, Phd, Proofing and Editing, Typing. Kersty Evans,

Gabriel Murray was born in Ireland. He is an award winning screenwriter, and has been a delegate at Cannes Film Festival. He is a member of; The Alliance Francaise, The Courtauld Institute, The Society of Authors, The English Writers Guild, The Royal Historical Society and the Irish Film and TV Network. He originally studied Fine Art at the National College of Art. He also studied English contemporary fiction at Oxford University; and creative writing at The Irish Writers Centre in Dublin. He was awarded a Masters in History from Dublin City University.

By the Same Author.

Novels
The Golden Flame
Flag of Freedom.
Cherokee Nation
The Lost Diary of Betsy Ross.

Novellas
Radclyffe Hall.
The Rebel Countess
The Sound of Silence

Non Fiction.
The Spielberg Files
The Lost Homeland
The Countess of Desart

"I fell in love with her courage, her sincerity, and her flaming self-respect. And it's these things I'd believe in, even if the whole world indulged in wild suspicions that she wasn't all she should be. I love her and it is the beginning of everything."
— F. Scott Fitzgerald

The beat scene was beautiful. It was live jazz and we were just dancing our hearts out for hours on end, happy on very little. I mean we were living, most of us, on a shoestring. Yet, there was always so much to go around, if you know what I mean.
You know, there was so much energy and sharing and inspiration and pure moments and quality times
together on very little or no money.
-Susanne Verdal

I will willingly abandon this miserable body to hunger and suffering, provided that my soul may have its ordinary nourishment."
- Saint Catherine Tekakwitha

This book is dedicated to three women
;Susanne Verdal,
the woman that inspired the song;
that saved and launched
Leonards career as a poet and songwriter.

;Saint Catherine Tekatwaia the
Mohawk, Indian who also
inspired Leonard; for her, sacrifice, virtue,
and vow of poverty.

;Marianne Jensen, for her devotion to
Leonard, in his struggles to
create his novels, poems and songs.

Leonard Cohen, Sept 21, 1934-Nov 7, 2016.

Introduction
Forgotten Words and Bonds.

A Thousand Kisses Deep is a fictional work based on some of the events of Leonard Cohens life on Hydra from 1960-1967. Much has been written about Leonard Cohen and the expats that lived on the island of Hydra, in Greece. However, only few writers knew Leonard and his circle on Hydra. As a result, there are certain gaps in the story of what their lives were like there from 1960-1967, that this novel explores. The book examines for the intellectual and emotional lives of the many artists and writers that Leonard knew there, in order to establish a clearer idea of the world they lived in. I first visited Hydra on the invitation of Timothy Hennessy at his villa. I first met Leonard at my birthday party, that Hennessey had organised for me there. In that circle was Anthony Kingsmill, who was a close friend of Leonard, but little has been written about him or Hennessy. I met Leonard at various times in Bills bar and at Hennessy villa, where we discussed they period that this book explores.

In 1989 I was in Paris for the celebrations to mark the two hundred years of the French revolution, and met Anthony at Shakespeare and Company. He had lost his home on Hydra weeks before and made his way to Paris by boat and train. I invited him to stay with me in London. He had not lived in England for over forty years. During these months Anthony recounted his time on the island and his time with Leonard. The notes I took helped me in writing this novel.

A few years later Timothy Hennessey moved to Ireland, and lived on the top floor of the Castletown House, house on the invitation of the Guinness family. He later bough Prospect House, Co Kildare in 1990 and lived there with his second wife Isabel Hennessey, who worked as a fashion accessory designer for Yves Saint Laurent. I visited him there many times and we spoke about his time on Hydra and his circle of friends there. He also gave me access to his archives that included albums of photographs. In 1997 tragedy struck Hennessy wife Isabel when she choked on a chicken bone. They were unable to save her.

Hennessy told me that he buried her in the local graveyard without inscribing her name on the tombstone. I assumed that it was his way of not been able to accept his death. I have since learnt that parents of children that commit suicide, cannot do the same often for many years after their passing. Hennessy moved to Avignon to Rue De la Croix to a villa behind the Bishops Palace. I visited him there a year before he died with Peter Calderon my lawyer friend.

This book is written to pay homage to lost friendships and the artist and writers that I once knew in a formative year of my life. It was important for me at that time to meet those that engaged in creative lives. They made it seem possible to live such a life whether you were a poet, songwriter, painter or a novelist. In a time now where the world has become more cynical and more and more people reject engaging with the arts, in the search of more conventional occupations; this book becomes more relevant for those who want to take an alternative path.

***

Leonard Cohen is a world-famous poet and songwriter. Yet his early years between 1960-67, were a struggle for some form of literary success. This is a novel about his journey in search of a bohemian world from Montreal, Paris and to Hydra, an island in Greece. Cohen left Canada in search of people who were involved in musical, artistic, literary, and spiritual pursuits; that were wanderers, adventurers, and vagabonds. Cohen grew up in French speaking, Quebec.

His first novel, The Favourite Game sold very a few copies. His second book Beautiful Losers, explored Quebec separatism with France, and his fascination for the Canadian Indian Saint Catherine Tekakwitha, and her virtues. He lived on Hydra for seven years as a struggling poet and novelist. But the idea that Hydra was paradise, or a theatre for dreamers, was not an accurate one. Some of the island's population had died from starvation during the Nazi occupation of Greece during the war. There was no electricity, and water had to be imported from the mainland. Many of the expats had to live on food credits including Leonard, from the local store. Their lives were in stark contrast to the various members of the jet set that arrived there in search of this 'lost paradise'. It was a hand to mouth existence set against the various social conflicts among the local and ex-pat community. Life was not a bed of roses for a struggling writer. Leonard fell in love with a married Norwegian woman named Marianne, whose husband Axel had engaged in 'free' love and new age philosophies. In 1967 the military took over Greece, and Leonard escaped the island. With the lack of success and interest in his novel, Beautiful Losers, Leonard turned to song writing.

His friendship with Susanne Verdal in Montreal; inspired his first deeply spiritual song. It was this song that saved his career and brought his music to a worldwide audience, and established him as a major poet and songwriter. The novel is an exploration of this journey, and the trials and tribulations of Leonard Cohen's struggles, in the early days of his career. What emerges is a man that had enough faith love and hope to pursue his vision in his poetic quest. It is the story too about the song Susanne and the belief in Saint Catherine, the Canadian Indian Catholic - that saved him!

***

Cast of Characters and Locations.

Montreal, New York, London, Paris, Venice, Athens, Hydra. Dublin, Losangeles.(1960-1967).
Leonard Cohen – novelist, poet and songwriter.
Marianne Ilhen Jensen – Norwegian actress.
Axel Jensen – Norwegian novelist husband of Marianne.
George Johnson – Australian novelist.
Charmian Clift - Australian novelist. Wife of George.
Anthony Kingsmill -English painter and poet.
Timothy Hennessy -American artist
Susanne Verdal – Friend of Leonard Cohen.

Contents;
Foreword. Forgotten Words and Bonds.
Prologue; Ink Stains Upon Some Lines.
Chapter 1. A Child in the Crystal.
Chapter 2. Madame Libertine.
Chapter 3. Poems of Flaming Red.
Chapter 4. The Flamingo Club.
Chapter 5. Susanne Takes You Down.
Chapter 6. He Who Tires of London.
Chapter 7. Shakespeare and Company.
Chapter 8. Hellas.
Chapter 9. My Dear Friend Anthony.
Chapter 10. The Count and Countess.
Chapter 11. The Doors of Perception.
Chapter 12. My Angel Marianne.
Chapter 13. Icarus and the Hermit.
Chapter 14. An Angel at my Table.
Chapter 15. The Wild Duck.
Chapter 16. George.
Chapter 17. Island of Hunger.
Chapter 18. Ramblin Jack.
Chapter 19. Priam's Gold. Sat
Chapter 20. Lorca's Ghost. Sun
Chapter 21. Pain and Pleasure.
Chapter 22. Ghika's House.
Chapter 23. The Stormy Seas.
Chapter 24. Boy on a Dolphin.
Chapter 25. The Venetian Ball.
Chapter; 26. I Loved You in the Morning.
Chapter 27. The Seventh Seal.
Chapter 28. The Queen of Persia and America.

Chapter 29. Peal Me A Lotus.
Chapter 30. Rimbaud word.
Chapter 31. The Death of Lorca.
Chapter 32. King Constantine.
Chapter 33. Jesus was a Sailor.
Chapter 34. My Indecision is Final.
Chapter 35. Rivers of Memory.
Chapter 36. By Grand Central Station I Sat Down and Wept.
Epilogue; The Innocent and the Beautiful.
Postscript; In Search of Lost Time.
Copyright and Credits.
Photos.
Acknowledgements.

Prologue
Ink Stains Upon Some Lines.

Paris, Sept 28, 2012.

The early morning sun streams through the clouds over the city of Paris. At that time of the morning the light was liquid and translucent, shining upon many of its facades. Leonard arrived at the Hotel Crillion as part of his 'Old Ideas World Tour'. His secretary had stolen over five million dollars from his bank account; while he was studying Buddhism in a monastery in California. He was forced on the road again to pay his bills. He remembered the lines from the bible; 'The first shall be last, and the last shall be first'.

He passed the ballroom. It was like a scene from his song 'Take This Waltz'. He could see young men in black suits and dickie bows dancing with young women in long dresses. The porter concierge informed him that he was preparing for the Bal des Débutante's.

He headed for the Ambassador's bar and ordered a glass of red wine. He sat alone in this elegant space, just beside the Baccarat crystal sculpture of an elephant. He thought back to the first time he had been in Paris and bought a book by the French poet Rimbaud. His words, had exited him then. They were words of passion for life and for poetry. He always carried the little book with him. Its pages were frayed with the passage of time. He began to read Rimbaud's own words from a letter he had written in 1871.

'The first task of any man who wants be a poet is to know himself completely; to seek his soul, inspect it, test it, and learn from it. He must develop it as soon as he's come to know it; this seems straightforward: a natural evolution

of the mind; so many egotists call themselves authors; still others believe their intellectual growth is entirely self-induced!

I mean that you have to be a seer, mould oneself into a seer. The poet makes himself into a seer by a long, involved, and logical derangement of all the senses. Every kind of love, of suffering, of madness; he searches himself; he exhausts every possible poison so that only the essence remains. He undergoes unspeakable tortures that require complete faith and superhuman strength, rendering him the ultimate invalid among men, the master criminal, the first among the damned, and the supreme specialist, for he arrives at the unknown!

For, unlike everyone else, he has developed an already a rich soul! He arrives at the unknown, and when, bewildered, he ends up losing his understanding of his visions, he has, at least, seen them! It doesn't matter if these leaps into the unknown and it kills him: others will follow him; they'll will stare at the horizons where the others have fallen! This language will be of the soul, and for the soul, encompassing everything, scents, sounds, colours, one thought mounting another. At its root, there will be something of Greek poetry in them. Eternal art will have its place; poets are citizens too after all.'

Where had this journey begun why had he taken this path like Rimbaud, Verlaine, Yeats, Lorca and many others, who now belong to the pantheon of the world's greatest poets. Leonard's eyes closed and in the rivers of memory - he recalled his childhood.

***

A Child in the Crystal
Chapter 1.

Montreal, Canada, 1959;
The city of Montreal in French Quebec, was covered in a white blanket of snow. The white crystal snow shone and shimmered in the early morning light. The shadows were blue, not grey. It was as if the city had been enveloped in a crystal white-blue blanket. But this crystalline snow had been deceptive. This was because it always brought with it the deep freeze of winter, where temperatures plummeted to minus thirty degrees. He longed for the sun, and the warm summer breeze, and the rays of light touching his skin.

The dream to escape haunted him at night as he lay in bed in his father's house. The moonlight at times illuminated his room. He thought of poetry, of love and a place like Arcadia, that the ancient poets wrote about. He knew he had to escape and to live his dream, to pursue it, to live it, to search beyond the cold horizon of Montreal; to a warmer world that did not threaten his existence. Perhaps he thought he could escape to a place where he could write those lines. There he could discover the poetry in his soul. Words and phrases raced across his mind in a wondrous pattern. He knew he had to give some form to them, and summon words and images within the depths of consciousness.

He had read many of the great poets, Yeats, Byron, Shelley. Their words had inspired him. He had not sought fame or fortune, but only the beauty of a line, its meaning, and a search for a new philosophy; and the words that had elevated the human mind. It was a thing of beauty, and held the mystery of a greater purpose. Sometimes he felt that these great poets were close to him, like ghosts that were always with him. As he dreamed, he saw that the spirits of the dead called to him in the darkest night just, before dawn illuminated his lonely world. He felt restless and some days he would write a poem or part of one. He knew he needed inspiration.

His mother was a Russian Jew, who had escaped, like many of her friends during the pogroms. She had sweet face, and black hair that fell down her shoulders, like waves in the ocean. Her eyes were tilted, and was part of her eastern heritage; and had deep penetrating eyes and long eye lashes. She always wore white lace collars and velvet dresses. It was a dress that belonged to another age, far beyond in Russia, where she had been born. She had a dignified air about her. His mother would cook for him, and sing an old Yiddish folk song called Oyfn Pripetchek, that belonged to her childhood. The song was about a Rabbi teaching his young students the alphabet, that was sung in all Jewish schools in Russia.

> *'In the heart a fire burns, and in the house it is warm, and the rabbi is teaching little children the alphabet. See the children, remember dear ones. What you learn from here, learn children, don't be afraid. Every beginning is so hard. When you grow older, children, you will understand by yourselves. How many tears are in these letters?'*

His mother was always filled with many emotions, that echoed the melancholy and sentimentality of her lost homeland. She had an operatic voice that echoed throughout the house. Sometimes the words of her songs would bring tears to her eyes. All the wealth that she had now, could not hide her past struggles, the pain of emigration, and the dislocation from her village thousands of miles away that she knew she would never see again. She had found a place, a refuge among Protestants and

Jews here in Montreal. Regardless, it did not dull the pain of her dislocation from her country.

He recalled how his mother had spoken about her journey from Russia by train to a port in Germany. The great ship, fleeing with thousands of Jews, docked in London. But the laws had changed, and immigrants were not allowed to stay. However, the few days she spent there in this wondrous city had enchanted her, with its ancient buildings, and great parks.

She inspired him and with her fascination for this city. Leonard vowed that one day he would visit there. He was born in the new world, but in some way, as he got older, he knew he was part of the old world. He knew that many immigrants felt that way, dislocated from their past.

Leonard recalled when he was a boy, his mother kissed him warmly in bed at night. It was a consolation to him. He awaited her kiss. He could hear the sound of her dress that rustled as she climbed the stairs and along the corridor to his room. It was a nightly ritual that he would always remember. He longed for her, long after her kiss. It was a longing he would always have, as the years rolled by. The love of a woman, whomever that might be. He recalled her warm face, her sweet lips, and her gift of love from her sweet soul. Her presence comforted him in his moment of need.

In the morning he had breakfast with his mother. He spoke to her about his restlessness. The table was always laid with a white linen and the cups and saucers were perfectly aligned, along with the knives, forks and spoons. There was a symmetry about her world that was perfect in that breakfast room. On the walls hung many photos of her relatives from Russia, Poland and Lithuania. It was a far-off place that his father also had spoken about. He had passed away and they now lived there with his sister, Ester, who was always late for breakfast. She was older than him, with a sweet face, bobbed hair and eyes of great beauty.

***

Leonard recalled being driven through the streets of Montreal by his father. He was nine years old and his eyes just reached the lower line of the car window. Outside he remembered the perfectly manicured lawns, and the houses of red brick and well cut grey stone. His house had a white veranda with white trellis of interlocking woodwork. Beyond the house were the lawns of Murray Park. It was covered in trees and flower beds with all the colours of the rainbow. The streets were clean and well cared for by their rich residents and the city's fathers.

He was a privileged boy, born into a special world that had an order to it. The car climbed the hill and stopped at 599 Belmont Avenue. His father wore large round glasses, and had slicked black hair, that had that oil known as brylcreem, to make it shine. He had a broad round face and sported a moustache. He also wore a blue pinstriped suit that was a perfect fit. Leonard often visited his father's factory, where the suits were made by the best Jewish tailors one could find in Montreal. Leonard wore the best of clothes too; a cobalt blue jacket with a white stripes and buttons on the cuffs, and short pants of the best grey wool.

Leonard was close to his sister, Esther. She was older than him. Her hair was cut short and she always wore a ribbon in it. She wore black shoes in contrast to his white shoes; and a blue coat like Leonard's, that all children wore in the winters of Montreal. Esther was always kind to him. She mothered him and helped him with his school work and smiled at him a lot. She gave him love when he needed it, and he soon learned in childhood that the love of women, whoever they might be, was a comfort to his soul and his mind.

Another woman in his life was a maid named Mary. She was an Irish Catholic, who like his mother had immigrated from Ireland, escaping from poverty and revolution. He called her

Nursie. She had dark red hair and a face that had freckles in places. She would sing Irish songs to him, and read him from a book of Irish poetry that she had brought with her from Ireland. One poet that she always read to him was the Irish poet W.B. Yeats. She would read to him at night before he went to sleep. He always remembered of her poems by him.

'Down by the Sally Gardens.
My Love and I did meet,
She passed the Sally Gardens,
With little snow-white feet,
She bid me take love easy,
As love grows on the tree,
But I, being young and foolish,
With her would not agree.'

Their gardener had emigrated from the Caribbean. He tended the flowers and cut the lawns while Leonard watched nearby. He always sang Caribbean songs that had a rhythm to them. Leonards house, was a house of immigrants. It was what they had in common. As he grew up, he learned of his father's family homeland was in Lithuania. His grandfather Lazarus was a teacher of the Torah. He had come to Canada, to try and find a new life. When he arrived in Montreal there were few Jews there. There, he helped build a synagogue and assisted with new immigrants arriving there. Leonard learned that he belonged to a family of Jewish leaders and rabbis. They had the gift of tongues, and they spoke at Jewish meetings and at times of prayer. Leonard smelt the incense, as the Jews huddled together in the cold and the snow outside. He remembered sitting close to his father. He wore a cap and woollen gloves. His face felt cold at times and when he breathed, a little fog it appeared beyond his

lips. The chanting of the Rabbi comforted and consoled him, and the rituals of worship that they engaged in.
Chapter 2.
Mademoiselle Libertine

His cousin Edgar was a man who wrote books. He had given him a copy of one. Its title was 'Mademoiselle Libertine – A Portrait of Ninon de Lanclos'. It was the kind of book that all French Quebecian's loved. Inside its crisp white pages was a portrait of a beautiful woman named Ninon. He observed the soft curls on her forehead, her long nose, full lips, and her high rounded cheeks that were tinted red. She wore pearl earrings and necklace.

She became a friend of Moliere, the French playwright. She believed that one could live a good life without religion. This angered the French bishops and she was sent to gaol. It was Christina, the Queen of Sweden, who obtained her release. She was a friend of Voltaire, who criticised Christianity, and promoted the freedom of speech, and of religion and the separation of church and state. Edgar and Leonard were close and he encouraged him, with the idea that an independent mind and a voice was something important to aspire to. It was an idea that had been given birth to in seventeenth century France among the great writers. Edgar was an admirer of this independent spirit.

***

Leonard had learned from an early age, like many children, that even in a perfect world all things could come to an end; and that the glass would shatter and the pieces would lie on the floor. When Leonard was five, his father had arrived early to tell his mother that there was an anti-Jewish march in Saint Lawrence Boulevard, led by French nationalists who hated Jews. It was an anti-Jewish movement that was deeply influenced by the French government that now collaborated with Pétain's anti-Jewish Nazi regime, and the German dictator, Adolf Hitler.

He was too young to realise its implications. He just remembered his parents, aunts and uncles sitting up all night and listening to the radio. The anti-Jewish meeting was not banned, and they agreed that it was a disgrace how the government had handled it. They felt threatened for the first time in their chosen homeland. Windows of Jewish owned shops and restaurants were broken and racist slurs of graffiti were daubed on the walls. It was Canada's 'Kristallnacht', known as 'The Night of Broken Glass'.

There were accusations too, that Jews had taken control of the clothing business. His father felt threatened that his livelihood and his business would be destroyed. They felt isolated and their lives threatened. They rarely went out now. His mother became more reserved among the Protestant community they lived with. Her prominent Russian accent was covered up, when she spoke to her neighbours. His parents tried to blend in and become more unnoticeable, and hide their cultural origin as a Jew.

Leonard did not like this, even his cousin Edgar felt they should not have to hide their identities. They attended the synagogue quietly and prayed that they would not be attacked. They read that the Jews were now moved to a camp known as Drancy in Paris, and later they were sent to the gas chambers in Poland. Their world and their kind were being murdered for no good reason, based on a bizarre theory of racial purity and hatred.

As their Jewish world collapsed, his father's health deteriorated and two years later he died at the young age of fifty-two. Mary, his nurse, told him the news. Leonard held his sister's hand. She told him softly that they would not be going to school that day. The funeral, the following day, took place on Esther's birthday. The cake that was covered in candles was replaced by a silver seven-branched candelabra on the dining room table. His mother wore a black dress and a lace veil that concealed her face. Suddenly his whole world was plunged into darkness and a melancholy enveloped him.

In the morning six men carried the great oak coffin into the living room and lay in its centre. People arrived and the entire Jewish community was there. They spilled out into the back gardens. It was the first time that Leonard saw many different Jewish people together. Some were Ashkenazi, from central Europe, and also Sephardic Spanish Jews from Spain. But the ones he found most fascinating were the Hasidic Jews, who wore large fur hats and long black coats. They were many people from his father's clothing factory. They were faithful and hardworking, who he had helped and gave a job to them in a time of need.

Leonard's grandmother Rachel consoled him. Her hands touched his face. She kissed him and consoled him. She placed ten Canadian dollars in his hand and told him to buy some sweets. Leonard peered into the coffin. He could see his father's face flickering in the light. He wore a tallit, a prayer shawl that was striped. His father's face was a pale white, in deep contrast to his black moustache. His uncle Horace arrived with snow on his shoes. Leonard could see a blanket of snow outside, as pale as his father's face. He looked up at his uncle's face and he whispered to him; "You have to be like a soldier now. You have to be strong!" Mary read a poem to him that night after the funeral by Yeats titled; Under Ben Bulben.

'Many times, man lives and dies.
Between his two eternities,
That of race and that of soul,
And ancient Ireland knew it all.
Whether man dies in his bed,

Or the rifle knocks him dead,
A brief parting from those dear,
Is the worst man has to fear?
Though grave-diggers toil is long,
Sharp their spades, their muscle strong,
They but thrust their buried men
In Drumcliff churchyard Yeats is laid,
By the road an ancient cross,
No marble, no conventional phrase,
On limestone quarried near the spot,
By his command these words are cut,
Cast a cold eye,
On life, on death,
Horseman, pass by!

    His father was buried that day in a cemetery covered in snow. Only a red rose on the green wreath on the coffin, that was lowered into the grave, bore any colour. When he got home, he went to his father's room and opened his drawer, where his shirts were neatly folded. There he found his black dicky bow. He wrote his first poem with some words to his father's memory words of love for his dear father, who had died so young. He buried this poem and the dicky bow, in the garden in the flower bed beside the red roses. It was a mystical secret ceremony for him.

***

Chapter 3.
Poems of Flaming Red

One of his uncles told him that the Cohens belonged to a great line of rabbis who believed in the spoken, the written word and the gift of tongues. He knew that he would pursue this craft, even at a young age. Months after that, he became more aware of his father's loss. It was like a crack had appeared in his world and the darkness seeped in. He now became the little man of the house at the age of nine. He felt that his sister and his mother were in his care now. He somehow had to protect them. His father's death had brought them closer together.

***

A few months after his father died, he met another Jewish boy named Mort at school. They spent the summer together at a lake north of Montreal. He swam with Mort in its cool waters. He loved diving, to see the fish and the waving green ferns, and the pools of light that penetrated the surface. His father was also dead. Mort was also Jewish, and they attended Westmount High, a school where a quarter of the students were Jewish. When he was thirteen, he read the Torah to everyone at his Bar Mitzvah.

There were few rules in his house now without his father's presence. Leonard at the age of thirteen began wandering through the streets of Montreal. The St Lawrence river and the harbour fascinated him, where he met immigrants just after they had arrived. He stood observing the harbour of the Saint Lawrence river, and watched all the lights glittering on the water's horizon. They danced before him like a strange kind of ballet of light. Boats took cargo up to the great lakes. At night, he came across many sailors, docker's and passengers that just had disembarked from ships.

There he also found people lingering on the sidewalk; pimps, prostitutes, and drunks - people who lived for the night. One could find them in the streets late at night in the many bars. There were clubs, where one could listen to country music, jazz, blues, and the traditional music of Quebec. There were places, too, where he found juke boxes with new tunes from beyond Montreal.

He wrote about his night journeys across the city in his diary. He went out alone until Mort joined him. He learned that a lot of these bars were controlled by the mafia and the underworld of Montreal. It was a world as a child that he was protected from. He began to explore this hidden world, its rights and wrongs, and learn about the people he came across.

Leonard played the saxophone in the Westmount High student band. Mort also played the clarinet. He played the records of Benny Goodman, known as the 'King of Swing'; to his new friends at college, and at tea parties at home, organised by his sister Esther and his mother Masha. Mort was a fan of the great trumpeter Louis Armstrong nicknamed Satchmo. 'Mack the Knife', was his favourite that Armstrong sung. The words echoed across his house.

> *'Now on the sidewalk on a sunny morning,*
> *Lies a body just oozin life,*
> *And someone's sneaking 'round the corner,*
> *Could that someone be Mack the Knife? '*

***

The great discovery of his youth, Leonard recalled when he was fifteen, was in a second-hand bookshop. Browsing through the old frayed books, he found the poems of Federico Garcia

Lorca. He opened the pages and found the poem 'The Morning Market'.

> *'Under the arch of Elvira,*
> *I want to see you pass by,*
> *To know your name,*
> *To drink in your eyes,*
> *And make myself cry.'*

The poems excited him. It was a moment of revelation. There was sensuality and beauty about his lines. The lines had a directness that he had not read before. Leonard had experienced the loss and loneliness after his father's death, the poems seemed to fill this emptiness. His heart and mind were filled at times with loneliness. Somehow the poem elevated him to another world, and another understanding of life's meaning.

Lorca loved old Spanish folk songs. His poems were filled with melancholy sadness, and emotions that were deeply honest. Lorca loved flamenco. It was a proud, dignified music of the gypsy. After reading Lorca, he seriously began writing poetry. He wanted to respond to Lorca's poetry; to somehow parallel Lorca's pleas, emotions and his voice. He never tried to copy Lorca, but to find his own voice now was his quest.

***

One day, while walking down Craig Street, he stopped at a pawn shop. He knew what it was as three balls hung outside, that was traditional symbol of pawner. Inside, he bought a Spanish guitar for twelve dollars. He began to learn some chords. Leonard had a ukulele, that his uncle Lazzy had given him after his father died. He knew how to play a tune. He remembered his kindness to him. He became like a father to him and helped him through moments of sadness and solitude.

He brought him to a hotel where the great musician Roy Smeck performed. He was known as 'The Wizard of Strings'. He wore a well cut suit, a waistcoat with a gold watch on a chain, a colour tie covered in squares, and a straw hat with a red bandanna. Roy greeted Leonard and played the banjo for him. The song was the 'Foggy Mountain Breakdown' that was first recorded by Flatt and Scruggs and the Foggy Mountain Boys. Leonard was fascinated by Smeck's five string banjo, and the strong metal sound of the plectrum striking the metal strings, that was a new kind of music to his ears.

Leonard travelled with Mort one summer to a Jewish community camp. He played his guitar and sung from 'The People's Song Book', a socialist song, like 'His Truth Goes Marching On'. It was a popular American patriotic song written by the anti-slavery writer Julia Ward Howe, that echoed in Leonard's mind.

> 'Mine eyes have seen the glory of the coming of the Lord;
> He is trampling out the vintage where, The Grapes of Wrath are stored,
> He hath loosed the fateful lightning of his terrible swift sword,
> His truth is marching on,
> Glory, glory, hallelujah!
> His truth is marching on,
> I have seen Him in the watch-fires of a hundred circling camps,
> They have built Him an altar in the evening dews and damps,
> I can read His righteous sentence by the dim and flaring lamps,
> His day is marching on,
> Glory, glory, hallelujah!

*His truth is marching on,
In our hands is placed a power,
Greater than the hoarded gold,
We will give birth to a new world, From the ashes of the old.'*

The word Halleluiah echoed in Leonard's mind. He promised himself that someday he would write a song about that word someday. When he returned home that summer, he discovered some more records in a shop on the St. Lawrence Boulevard. He found Woody Guthrie's record 'Bound for Glory', and his dust bowl ballads. He loved one of the tracks and sung it all the time.

*'This world is not my home,
I'm here for a moment,
It's all I've ever known,
The fight is not my own,
These burdens aren't my future,
The empty tomb has shown,
I am free because I'm bound,
I am bound for heaven's gate,
Where my feet will stand on holy ground,
I am bound for glory.'*

***

His mother sung in the house, sometimes to a record by Nat king Cole. He had grown up with her voice, which was a beautiful falsetto tone. She would visit the cafes and clubs on St Laurence with him after his father died. He used to go there to sing and play his guitar in a club there. His mind reflected back to those days as he lay on his bed.

He remembered a girl called Claudia that wanted to be with him. She had dark hair and beautiful eyes with fake eyelashes. She had long red fingernails and wore a dress of crimson red and had heels of gold. Around her neck was a string of pearls which she told him were made of plastic. She told him that she wanted to leave that place to be with him.

Leonard told her he wanted to leave Montreal. She told him that she wanted a man to look after her, and that the new feminism for her meant nothing. Her face was filled with an expression of sadness and she attempted to touch Leonard's hand. Leonard remembered Claudia. He remembered her standing beneath a street light, that he called Boogie street. He began to write a poem about that world. Her remembered kissing his lips, the pleasures they shared, and how he was enchanted by her beauty. He had to leave Claudia on Boogie street. It was a place he wanted to leave behind. Even for the comforts it had given him.

Leonard visited the local chemist with his mother. He observed the small glass bottles lined up in rows, with strange names like a museum to the medical world. It had a long-polished cedar wood counter. At large desk sat a rather distinguished man sporting a dicky bow and a white starched shirt with pointed collars. On the desk was a stiff card printed with the name Harold Ostrow. He reminded Leonard of his father. He had the same black hair and moustache. He was a sweet man and always treated him and his mother with kindness. Later he discovered that his mother and Harold had developed a romantic relationship and some months later they were married. Leonard had to come to terms with the new romance and a stepfather of sorts. He felt he was of an age now, at twenty-five, where he did not need a step-father. He felt that his beloved father could not be replaced.

He realised that people moved on and that love lost can be found again. Somehow among the ashes something can be reclaimed; and that something can be found among the ruins of one's life. Even on the edge of loneliness there is a new life, there is redemption. It was a reality that he had begun to learn about, that people can have many marriages, many loves, whether by desire, divorce or death. Nothing was forever, nothing was complete. He remembered another poem that Mary, their maid, had recited to him from the poet W.B. Yeats.

> *'Things fall apart, the circle cannot hold,*
> *And all about us the ceremony of innocence is drowned.'*

Leonard attended the synagogue and the marriage ceremony. There was chanting and singing as the ring touched her finger. It was a moment in time, when his past life came to an end and a new world for him began. His mother had made choices. He was free now to make his.

***

Chapter 4
The Flamingo Club

    Mort arrived with a new Cadillac. It was painted white and had long wings on each side as if it could fly. Mort would arrive late after midnight. Leonard was fifteen and Mort sixteen. They went in search of beautiful girls. They cruised down to the old part of the city. They stopped at cafés and clubs and engaged in conversation with whoever was on the sidewalk. Sometimes they got lucky and found two girls to talk to. They bought them coffee and if they were up to it, they brought them to the Flamingo Club that played jazz. He longed for love and he expressed his longing in his new poems; like his great inspiration Lorca. Their great poems and their influences, had begun to bear fruit.

    Mort and Leonard motored over to a park called Vieux-Moulin, that was located on the banks of the St. Lawrence river. This historical site is set around a windmill dating back to 1720, with a magnificent gazebo overlooking the river. It had a pavilion, with some band playing. They could see people dancing beneath a large white tent. Mort recognised his sculptor friend Armand dancing with a girl.

    Later Leonard was introduced to Armand and the girl, whose name was Susanne. Leonard though that she was enchantingly beautiful, with her dark eyes. She had long black hair that floated over her shoulders. She wore long skirts covered in flowers in many colours. She also wore feathers in her dark hair, with Indian beads, necklaces and large earrings and ballet shoes. She made some of her clothes and wore scarves of red and magenta. She wore beads of many colours, that he had bought in the

Salvation Army store on Rue Notre Dame. Leonard thought that her clothes made her look like a gypsy girl.

She wrote poetry, but her dream was to be a dancer. She read books about the Russian dancer Nijinsky. She wanted to dance in the Bolshoi Ballet, in Moscow. She lived in an old warehouse, and Mort and Leonard were invited there, whenever they wanted to visit her. He could see that Armand and Susanne were in love.

***

Leonard graduated from high school that year. He wrote in the year book:
'We cannot conquer fear, yet we can yield to it in such a manner as to be greater than it.' At Mc Gill University, Leonard avoided many lectures, but poetry lectures was something he never avoided.

It was a form of expression that the secretary embraced. It was his secret passion. He also studied books about the Russian revolution, and the murder of the Tsar and his family in a cellar in Siberia. He read also about Russian dictator Stalin who had passed away in his dacha, and was found dead on his couch, but no one would assist him. He had been dead for three days, but no one would touch him. He read about the thousands like his mother, who had fled Russia to avoid a very bloody revolution.

Leonard studied French and English and began to learn that French speakers in Montreal belonged to a secret underclass that many refused to recognise. He met many of the French Canadian girls and boys, that arrived each week from the countryside. Leonard heard French spoken in the cafés, but a secret apartheid operated. French speaking teachers could not work in French schools and English teachers could not work in French schools. The French schools were Catholic, while the English schools were Protestant. The Jews attended the Protestant schools. Leonard became president of the university debating society, and his gift as a great orator emerged. He also became President of the Jewish fraternity house. Leonard had begun to keep a journal of all his new poems. He bought his first typewriter and for the first time his words appeared in print.

***

His uncle, the rabbi Solomon Kline, visited his house. He read to him from the Book of Isaiah. The book sets out the themes of judgment and the restoration of the righteous. 'God has a plan which would be realised on the 'Day of Yahweh', when Jerusalem will become the centre of his worldwide rule, and on that day all the nations of the world will come to Zion.

Rabbi Kline told him about the Russian, Hasidic school of the rabbi Nachman of Breslov; the great-grandson of the Baal Shem Tov, the founder of the Hasidic movement. He had a following of thousands in the Ukraine, Belarus, Lithuania and Poland. Rabbi Nachman emphasised the study of both the Kabbalah and the Torah, to his disciples. His teachings also differed from the way other Hasidic groups were developed, as he rejected the idea of hereditary Hasidic dynasties and taught that each Hasid must search for the 'tzaddik', a saintly righteous person.

At his classes at Mc Gill University, it was Professor Dudek's lectures that were most engaging for him. The professor was a Polish Catholic, who exposed him to all the great writers and philosophers of Europe and Russia. He lectured on the German writers Goethe, Schiller and Mann; the French writers Rousseau and Proust; the Russian writers - Tolstoy, Chekhov and Dostoyevsky; the English writers Eliot and Lawrence, and the Irish writers Joyce and Wilde. His agenda was to introduce Canadian students to the great wealth of European and Russian literature.

Europe is where the great poets, the great writers came from, he would say to his class. It sometimes made Leonard feel inferior, that he belonged to a culture that had not produced such great works. But he felt that he belonged to a great culture already, of the Jews where ancient poems and prayers were celebrated. However, his professor had introduced him to something new, poetry and prose that had pushed boundaries of the expression of pain, suffering, fears and desires. It gave him a foundation, a benchmark, and a standard to aspire to.

Leonard formed a band and invited friends to his house. His mother sometimes sang an old Russian song, while his sister Esther made sandwiches and tea in the kitchen. He invited his Professor Irving Leyton, who would become a great friend and mentor. Leyton was larger than life, like a lion that liked to roar. He was a man filled with fire and a passion for poetry. Leyton was not Canadian, but Romanian. He was Jewish, too and his real name was Israel Lazorovira. Many of his relatives were murdered by the Nazis. They came from the opposite side of the tracks. Irving was a working class Jew, while Leonard was from the rich middle class.

Irving hated Canadian conservatism. He would say to Leonard. 'My battle is against the world, the narrow minds, the people who seek to destroy liberalism.' Leonard sat with him often in the coffee shops of the St. Lawrence Boulevard talking about poetry. Irving told him that poetry could change the world. If Irving could not achieve that, maybe Leonard wondered if he could.

However, after the war people felt that this was impossible. The glass had been broken and shattered and millions had died, both Christian, Protestant and Jew. Millions had died in a great sacrifice against the Nazis, and their world was lost. Leonard wrote a book of poems 'Let Us Compare Mythologies' about this state of mind.

Leonard began to see that this life and the civilisation he was part of, was frail, fractured and vulnerable. There was no true democracy and the truth became a myth. Leonard felt that life after this terrible war was fractured and disturbed, like a bunch of crushed flowers on the sidewalk.

Leonard had one consolation, the love of his mother, and had developed a respect and love for women, because they can be gracious and kind. "Go for long walks," his mother said, "long walks and fresh air will do you good," she said, as she poured him some tea from a Dutch delft blue tea pot. "Yes, I need to visit the park. There is a beautiful park so close to us." replied Leonard.

Leonard left the house and headed for the park. As he approached it, he heard the sound of a guitar. The light streamed through the trees, the leaves shimmered with thousands of green shades and were covered in intense patterns of white, yellow and lemon. He opened the iron gate of the park and entered. Beyond the tennis court where many people, that came to watch the players enjoy their sport.

He saw a young man playing a guitar on a park bench. He looked up and smiled, and gazed into his eyes. He had an intensity about him. He was playing flamenco, and he was surrounded by some girls that were listening to him. Leonard loved the way he played. It was the way he wanted to play. He had long hair and wore a leather jacket and had a purple scarf around his neck. His fingers were elongated, as if they had been stretching for many years. He played and sung a tune that he had not heard before.

"What was that song?" asked Leonard.

"Guantanamera," he replied, with a Spanish accent.

"It's a beautiful song."

"Yes, it is. It's a Cuban song. Where are you from?

"Spain, Andalucía," he said rolling his fingers across the strings, like a conductor in charge of his orchestra.

"What's the song about?"

"The Cuban writer Joseíto Fernández, wrote this beautiful song. It's about the woman, from Guantánamo. Some of the lines are also written by the Cuban poet Jose Marti. In that town you can find a statue to the Cuban poet. He was the great liberator of Cuba. He died fighting the Spanish. It's about a poet who, before dying, wanted to tell us about his poetry. he words go like this.

'I'm an honest man,
From where the palm trees grow,
I'm an honest man,
From where the palm trees grow,
And before I die I want,
to let my verses out of my soul,
My verse is clear green,
And burning red,
My verse is clear green,
And burning red,
My verse is a wounded deer,
That seeks refuge in the mountain,
I cultivate a white rose,
In June as in January,
I cultivate a white rose,
In June as in January,
For a true friend,
Who gives me his honest hand,
And for the cruel one that tears away from me,
The heart with which I live,
And for the cruel one that tears away from me,
The heart with which I live,
I cultivate neither thistles nor nettles,
I cultivate the white rose,
With the poor people of the earth,
I want to make my destiny,

With the poor people of the earth,
I want to make my destiny,
The mountain stream,

Leonard asked him if he would give him guitar lessons. Leonard pointed to his mother's house, which they could see from the tennis court; and made an appointment to meet him there the following day.

"What is your name?"

"Pablo."

"Mine is Leonard, can you teach me how to play guitar."

"Of course." Then Pablo turned and crossed the park and vanished into the deep green horizon beyond.

***

Pablo came to his mother's house the next day.

"Let me hear you play something," said Pablo. Leonard tried to play.

"Let me show you some chords," he said, taking Leonard's guitar in his hands.

Pablo then played a sequence of chords.

"Now you do it."

Leonard began to play.

Pablo invited him to a club he was playing at on St Laurence Boulevard that night. A few hours later Leonard sat watching Pablo perform with a Cuban five-piece band. The club was dark and only the spotlight illuminated the stage. The air was filled with smoke and the light penetrated, and the faces of the performers appeared like ghosts in the night.

***

Leonard woke late and observed the time on his watch. It was two o'clock. He put on his clothes and hurried downstairs. A note from his mother was on the breakfast table. "Len, I've gone shopping." Leonard remembered that he had agreed to call to see Pablo at his hotel located on the other side of the St Lawrence river. He called the number. The phone rang for ages. Someone eventually answered it. The line was not a good one. He heard a woman's voice and he asked if Pablo was there. She said nervously: "Come quickly," and put the phone down.

Leonard left the house immediately. He knew something was wrong. He wondered had something happened to Pablo, and what could it be? He called a taxi and ten minutes later he was speeding across the city towards Pablo's hotel. He entered to find a woman behind at reception desk with a police officer.
"Is Pablo here," said Leonard, looking at their saddened faces, that seemed to be filled with fear.
"Who are you?" asked the police officer.
"My name is Leonard. I was with Pablo at the Cuban bar last night."
"He's dead," said the police officer.
"Dead?" said Leonard, in shock as the words sunk in.
"Come with me," said the officer. "You can identify him?"
Leonard followed the woman and the police officer up the stairs. They entered Pablo's room and found him lying on a bed. His face was as white as a sheet, and his eyes were staring at the ceiling.
"Yes, it's true, he is as dead as a door nail. I found him in his room an hour ago." said the woman. Beside him lay his guitar. Leonard could see the sheet music from the song, 'Guantanamera', lying beside him.
"How did he die?" said Leonard in deep shock.
"I think it was an overdose. I found pills lying on the bedroom locker.
"Sleeping pills," said the old woman, casting her eyes to the ground.
"May the Lord have mercy on his soul."

***

Three days later, Leonard attended the funeral along with his mother and the Cuban band. Leonard's mother wore a black hat, with lace that hung down over her face. His mother paid for the coffin that was made of oak. A priest read from the bible.

> *'He restoreth my soul; he guides me in the paths of righteousness for the sake of his name. Even though I walk through the valley of the shadow of death, I will fear no evil, for you are with me. Ashes to ashes, dust to dust.'*

***

The death of Pablo had struck him like a bolt of lightning. The sheer pointlessness of suicide depressed him. It filled his heart with emptiness. He could not understand why anyone would, make that decision. He felt a coldness inside him, and was deeply saddened by this event. What was the point of suicide, and of this young to taking his own life? It sunk him into a deep dark depression for weeks. He sat in his room writing poetry and he reflected on his life. Leonard's recalled his encounter with Pablo and his enchanting song and the words of the Cuban poet Jose Marti.

> *'I'm a truthful man from this land of palm trees.*
> *Before dying I want to share these poems on my soul.*
> *My verses are light green, but they are also flaming red.'*

His poems too could be *'flaming red'*. These words, for Leonard, were profound words. They sounded in reflection to be a suitable epitaph for Pablo's death and his own poetry. He looked out the graveyard and reflected. Pablo's song echoed in his mind. The words haunted him.

> *'I cultivate a rose in June for the sincere friend who gives me his hand. And for the cruel one who would tear out his heart.'*

***

Chapter 5
Susanne Takes You Down

Leonard decided to go see Susanne Verdal. He had heard from Mort that she had a café now in the same warehouse, on the St Lawrence river. Suzanne greeted him with a kiss and a smile. She was warm and enchanting. Susanne was pleased to see him and showed him around her new café. It had stained glass windows with angels and cherubs, where the light shone through and cast shapes on the floor. Suzanne served him tea with mandarin oranges, lychees and nuts by candlelight. They talked about the spirit of poetry. They were joined together in this great quest. It was a special moment, spiritual, and transforming to have another person that understood him.

Leonard and Suzanne walked along the harbour and watched the ships sail downriver. They visited the Notre Dame Bon Secours chapel, located on St. Peter Street. Susanne told him it was where the sailors were blessed by a priest before heading out to sea. It had a beautiful green copper spire that shone in the sunlight. On two of the churches domes there were angels with their wings proudly standing upright. On another dome stood the nun who founded this church. Susanne told him that her name was Saint Marguerite, the founder of the congregation of Notre Dame, in the colony know as New France, in 1658.

"It's a very spiritual place," said Suzanne. "It was here in this very place that Canada was born. It was a religious community of women. They could live and work outside the convent. The nuns educated these women."

The altar was framed beneath a Roman arch. It was made of white marble and the arch was filled with rays of gold, as if a burst of spiritual energy had come from the painting of Saint Marguerite, who wore a long blue and white cloak. Beneath her were seven angelic cherubs that seemed to float in space.

"Eight hundred French girls were sent here by Louis the sixteenth, the king of France, to marry the colony's men," said Susanne.

"Maybe some of their descendants are here today," said Leonard with a smile.

"They were known as the king's daughters Yes, they are. I see their faces in many of the women in Montreal."

"Maybe you are descended from one of them," replied Leonard. "Verdal sounds French to me."

"I like to think that I have been descended from a special one; that I am connected with the past," said Suzanne approaching the altar and lighting a candle. Then she handed one to Leonard. He lit it and placed it in a brass holder. They said a few prayers and they both felt that time was suspended. Even though he was Jewish, praying in a Catholic church seemed natural to him. It was a moment in time that Leonard would never forget.

Suzanne had touched him with her revelations and with her mind. He wanted to write a poem about Susanne and her inspiration. Some day he knew he would do it. Susanne stopped in front of a picture of a woman framed in gold. She stood there motionless, and she wiped a tear from her eye.

"Who is it Susanne, why are you crying?"

"It is someone who my grandmother spoke about and prayed to. It is the Canadian Indian who converted Catholicism. Her name was Kateri Tekakwitha. In 1943, Pope Pius XII declared her venerable, she will become a saint someday, I am sure of that."

"Tekak...witha," said Leonard, trying to pronounce the words.

"When she converted to the Catholic faith her name was changed to Catherine."

"She was a Mohawk Indian who was baptized as a Catholic. She was known as Lily of the Mohawks. She died in 1680. They want became a Roman Catholic saint. She was a woman with a pure heart, and a pure in spirit. She converted at the age nineteen. She refused to marry. She left her village and moved for the remaining five years of her life to the Jesuit mission village south of Montreal. Saint Catherine took a vow of perpetual virginity and poverty. She helped the poor. When she died at the age of twenty-four, witnesses' said that minutes later her scars vanished, and her face appeared radiant and beautiful. For some time after her death, she was considered an honorary yet unofficial patroness of Montreal and the Canadian and American Indians. She was a woman that sacrificed her life for others."

"She was a brave soul, I wish I had that kind of faith", said Leonard.

"You must find it Leonard, even in your darkest hour," said Susanne in deep thought for a moment.

"Sometimes the price is too high. Saint Catherine believed in the value of suffering. She did not eat very much and she would lie on a mat of thorns. There was a custom among some native American peoples at that time of piercing themselves with thorns in thanksgiving, or of offering for the needs of one's self to others. Knowing the terrible burns given to prisoners, she burned herself." Said Susanne.

***

Leonard knew that he would never forget his meeting with Suzanne. He would always remember her and her love and her kindness to him, and her spiritual values. She had an understanding with him that he had found nowhere else. Suzanne had a wonderful energy about her, a beauty that Leonard had admired. She had a wisdom, too. She was a magical woman in the rivers of his memory and she touched her perfect mind with his. Leonard searched for a book on the saint. He found only one in a second-hand book shop on the St-Laurent Boulevard titled; 'An Iroquois virgin. Catherine Tekakwitha, The lily of the banks of the Mohawk and St-Laurent. He read about her sacrifice and her vows of chastity and poverty. The book was written by Édouard Lecompte, who was a Canadian Jesuit historian. His books were devoted to telling the story of the Jesuits in Canada. He died in 1929.

He also found another book titled; Kateri of the Mohawks by Marie Cecilia Buehrle, that dramatized the story of how she ascended in a few short years, from paganism to a holy and radiant and Christian death.

Leonard also read the poem by Henry Longfellow; The Song of Hiawatha written in 1855. It was an epic poem about the adventures of an Ojibwe warrior named Hiawatha; and the tragedy of his love for Minnehaha, a Dakota white woman. Leonard read the lines.

> 'Farewell forever!
> "Farewell, O Hiawatha!
> And the forests, dark and lonely,
> Moved through all their depths of darkness,
> Farewell, O Hiawatha!
> And the waves upon the margin,
> Rising, rippling on the pebbles,
> Farewell, O Hiawatha!
> And the heron, the Shuh-shuh-gah,
> From her haunts among the fen-lands,
> Farewell, O Hiawatha!
> Thus, departed Hiawatha,
> Hiawatha the beloved,
> In the glory of the sunset,
> In the purple mists of evening,
> To the regions of the home-wind,

To the Islands of the blessed,
To the Kingdom of Ponemah,
To the land of the hereafter!'

***

Leonard had made a decision, that he wanted to leave Montreal. This decision was made easier by the arrival of a cheque of $2,500 from the Canada Council, to travel abroad and write a novel. His plan first was to head for London. He would have to tell his mother, his sister Ester; and his friends Mort and Irving about his decision. Leonard sat with his mother one morning over breakfast. When he told her, there was a cold silence. He understood her, she was losing a son, but not maybe for long she hoped.

He called Irving his professor at Mc Gill university, one morning and told him about the grant and asked him to call over. Irving arrived when Leonard was upstairs packing his old suitcase

"I'm leaving," said Leonard.

"Why?" said Irving.

"I want to escape; I'm heading for London.

"Leonard, you were one of my brightest students."

"I write a poem at least once every day. Maybe it's because of all that chanting I heard in the synagogue in Romania. It's in the blood, we Jews just pray a lot. Poetry is like a prayer," said Irving who had energy about him that was infectious.

"You write a lot of poems, Irving, but it's quality not quantity," said Leonard, smiling at him. Leonard lifted his book of poems on Lorca.

"Let me read you one of Lorca's poems, called Its True." Irving listened intently.

"It's True

Ay, the pain it costs me, to love you as I love you!
For love of you, the air, it hurts, and my heart,
And my hat, they hurt me.
Who would buy it from me,
This ribbon I am holding,
And this sadness of cotton,
White, for making handkerchiefs with?
Ay, the pain it costs me, to love you as I love you!'

"He was so truthful," said Leonard as he paused and looked out of his window past the trees, that had lost their leaves now. Beneath they lay rusting, in a desolate in the frozen landscape.
"I'm searching for something. I am a poet, like you are a dreamer. I don't want to be part of this normal world. I want to be part of the beautiful losers, that are not in search of money or fame. I am in search of the truth, whatever that truth may be." said Leonard in deep reflection. Then he threw the book into his suitcase.
"There are many truths, you just have to find them," replied Irving.

***

Leonard said goodbye to his mother, who held him in her arms for a while, and wondered if she would she ever see him again. She touched his face and kissed him on the forehead. He assured her that he would write to her, and let her know where he was. Their parting was difficult. Ester was sad too. Leonard gave her a present of some money, to buy some new clothes with. Leonard's mother had given him a pair of leather gloves that belonged to his father. He was travelling lightly, and carried his small suitcase and a guitar.

Then it was Irving's turn. Irving for him was his buddy, his poetic twin, his mentor, and he would sorely miss him. Mort called to his house to say goodbye and wish him well. He was a dear friend and he would miss him. He took him to the airport as snow was falling. They both shivered as they reached the terminal. He said goodbye to Irving, and he felt, that he would not be seeing him for a long time.

***

The plane crossed the frozen landscape covered in a white blanket of snow and headed out across the Atlantic. Leonard rested for the first time since he had begun his adventure, and thought about the novel that he wanted to write, 'Beauty at Close Quarters'. He had another title called 'The Favourite Game', but he was not so sure about it. He was filled with a sense of excitement, but it was shadowed by certain fear, a fear of the unknown. However, he had summoned up the courage to undertake this journey. A shaft of light pierced through his window. He could see the great constellations above and Orion stars to the north. Out here the sea had a vastness to it. Only the moon hung like a giant orb over the gleaming sea beyond Montreal. In the vast Atlantic Ocean, he felt as if one was suspended between heaven and earth, as he peered out into the night.

***

Chapter 6
He Who Tires of London

Early the following morning Leonard looked out the window. He could see land, that was like a green island in the vast blue sea. It must be the shores of England, he thought. A few hours later they approached the runway at Heathrow airport.

Leonard took a train into London's to Victoria station. The green English countryside, was filled with many shades of green. The fields were smaller than Canada, and were surrounded by hedgerows. He could see no skyscrapers, only white Edwardian and Georgian façades and red brick houses. Leonard thought to himself how ancient London looked compared to Montreal. Every building looked so solid to him, as it was built from brick and stone, in contrast to the timber buildings of Canada. This landscape for him was rooted in a history that stretched back many hundreds of years. He felt hungry and stopped at a café to eat a sandwich. London was another world to him. The accents were different and the clothes. With the help of a conductor, he located a taxi rank.

Irving had given him the name of a bed and breakfast in Hampstead, run by a woman called Stella Pullman. One of his students Nancy Bacal was staying there. When he arrived, it was raining and the sky was overcast. It was December, and he could see Christmas decorations of holly and ivy and gold garlands in the shop windows. He could also see angels and cherubs and a baby Jesus lying in a manger. Like the little boy Jesus, he thought to himself, he had no place to stay. A door opened and a woman wearing a flowery dress, with bobbed blonde hair and a warm face greeted him.

"I am looking for Stella Pullman," said Leonard.

"That's me, I have no rooms today, come back tomorrow!" she said in a deep east-end Cockney accent.
"I'm looking for my friend Nancy Bacal, is she staying here? It's kinda wet out here." Stella looked at Leonard up and down as if it was a military inspection. Then she thought for a moment.
 "Yes, she is. You can sleep on the sofa in the front room until a bed is free. Come inside, or you will catch a cold."
Leonard hurried into the hallway, covered in a warm green carpet. The sitting room walls were covered in old prints of Buckingham Palace and the Tower of London. Leonard sat on the large sofa, covered in cushions. In the bay window there was a table with a large bowl of flowers.
"What's your name?" said Stella, sitting on an armchair in the corner.
"Cohen, - Leonard Cohen."
"Where are you from?"
"Canada – Montreal."
"Let me give you the house rules. It's two pounds a week in advance. You have to be up before the others at eight, to light the coal fire. The bathroom is down the hallway. I'll bring you a blanket and a pillow. There is no drinking or staying out late. I have a curfew of twelve o'clock. If you're not in by then, I will lock you out."
Leonard handed her two pounds. She wrote out a receipt with her phone number on it and handed it to him.
"And one more thing! No drugs, no hashish or whatever they call it. Now let me get Nancy for you."
Leonard lay back on the couch and reflected on his new home. A tall dark-haired woman entered the room. She wore glasses that were perched on a long nose. She had high cheekbones and dark brown eyes. It was Nancy.
"Irving gave me your address."

"How are you, Leonard? Yes, I remember you from Mc Gill University. Welcome to London."

Stella peered her head in the doorway.

"I have to go to work early. I'm a dental assistant. Do you need any teeth done Leonard?"

"Well, I have a problem with one," said Leonard, feeling his jaw.

"Ok, I'll take you to see the dentist tomorrow. I'll leave you to chat. Remember breakfast is at nine." Then Stella disappeared.

Nancy sat down on the couch and gave him a warm smile.

"What are you doing in London? " said Leonard.

"I'm studying journalism. What brings you here?"

"I got a grant from the Canadian government to write a novel," said Leonard, putting his guitar and suitcase behind the couch.

"That's so cool. You're like me, you wanted to escape Montreal. We can explore London together."

When Nancy went to bed. Leonard lay on the couch in the sitting room, covered with a warm blanket. He could see the wooden beams and a picture of an old landscape. It was an image of cows drinking water at a small pond beside a timber thatched house. He felt at home here. London was a place of history, and all around him he felt the ghosts of its great poets.

***

The following day Leonard visited Highgate cemetery, with Nancy. Its entrance reminded him of an Egyptian temple. It was an enchanting place. It had many Gothic crypts and sculptures of angels, dogs and cats carved on its tomb's. Many famous people were buried there. Nancy told him that the Communist Karl Marx, the Pre-Raphaelite poet Christina Rosetti, the novelist George Eliot, and the infamous lesbian novelist Radcliffe Hall graves could be found there.

"The Victorians liked to have picnics beside the graves," said Nancy, as she approached Karl Marx's statue.

"Marx said, religion is the opium of the people. Maybe there is some truth in that," said Leonard. They read the inscription under the plinth in gold: 'Workers of all lands unite.'
"What do you think about religion?" asked Nancy.
"I'm a Jew. I was brought up a Jew. I cannot reject my religion. I will always be a Jew, even if Marx claims it is just an opium for the people. It's in my blood. My grandfather was president of a synagogue. He could recite every line of the Torah."
"I understand it's part of your life," said Nancy
"Life is about searching for the truth, in whatever way we can. Religion binds us together, but it can also tear us apart," said Leonard looking at the large imposing granite statue of Marx that towered above him.

***

Leonard and Nancy went later to the Spaniards Inn for a drink. A plaque over the door recorded that it was built in 1585. The highwayman, Dick Turpin, was a regular, and Charles Dickens had mentioned this inn, when he wrote the novel 'The Pickwick Papers'. It was frequented by the poets, Byron and Keats, that Leonard greatly admired. Nancy told him that the poet Keats house was nearby. He visited the house with her. Inside, was a glass case with his poem; 'Ode to a Nightingale':

> *'Thou wast not born for death, immortal bird!*
> *No hungry generations tread thee down,*
> *The voice I hear this passing night was heard,*
> *In ancient days by emperor and clown,*
> *Perhaps the self-same song that found a path,*
> *Through the sad heart of Ruth, when, sick for home,*
> *She stood in tears amid the alien corn,*
> *The same that oft-times hath,*
>   *Charm'd magic casements, opening on the foam,*
>   *Of perilous seas, in faery lands forlorn,*

*Darling, I listen and for many a time,
I have been half in love with an easy death.'*

***

Leonard took the underground to the centre of London with Nancy, and emerged at Piccadilly Circus. He observed the sculpture of Eros hovering above Leicester Square. This was the city he knew had given birth to the Beatles and the Rolling Stones. It was this music that had recently exploded upon the world. It was a city where the youth had emerged from suburbia into the city centre, that was recovering from the war. Leonard observed the Napoleonic neo-classical façades of the buildings. He passed by the Criterion Theatre where the Agatha Christie play 'The Mousetrap' was on. They observed some buskers playing music. Then they walked through the many pigeons and crossed over to Shaftsbury Avenue, where they took a turn that brought him past the famous 'Windmill Club', with erotic dancing girls. Within minutes they were in Soho with its many cafés.

Nancy knew of a place called the Sunset Club. It was a racially mixed club, where jazz was played until six in the morning. Its name was surrounded by lights and a pink flamingo hung over the doorway. They descended down a darkly lit stair. They entered a basement, filled with many people. Leonard and Nancy observed its walls, that were covered in posters of jazz and calypso bands, with names like 'The Jamaica Kings', 'The Mamba Boys' and the 'The Havana Trio'. The club began to fill up with all nationalities. The Caribbean band played some calypso and Leonard and Nancy soaked up the atmosphere over a bottle of wine. Leonard could smell the whiff of hashish, in this dark cavern of music. It was another world, far away from the world he had left. London was a melting pot, for emigrants in search of a new place to survive in. Poverty had driven them there, from a beautiful world of crystal blue waters and white sandy beaches

The ticket seller told them that the Trinidadian musician Rupert Nurse was the bandleader that night. Rupert introduced a calypso band, led by a by a Caribbean man from Trinidad, called Lord Kitchener. The waiter told Leonard that that he had arrived a few months before, on the emigrant ship - The Empire Windrush. He sang a song about racism in England and what he had experienced from the English teddy boys.

> *'The only thing to stop those teddy boys,*
> *From causing panic in England,*
> *They need another kind of punishment,*
> *I say one thing to cool down this crime,*
> *Is to bring back the old-time cat-o-nine.'*

.
***

Nancy knew about another club in Soho called 'The Colony Rooms', that was run by a French woman called Muriel Belcher. They located the club in 41 Dean street and rang the bell. A doorman opened it and let them in. Inside the walls were painted in deep green. Nancy told him that it was a mecca for bohemian artistic London. In this small space some of the great figures of art, writing, theatre and photography graced this space.

They observed three men sitting at the bar. Behind them stood a woman with bobbed hair. She had an oval face and deep, dark, piercing eyes and a long-curved nose. Behind her was an eclectic collection of glasses, statues and memorabilia. They glistened in the light. There were many works of art on the walls, of people that frequented the place, including a mural by the painter John Andrews; and prints of paintings by Francis Bacon and Lucien Freud.

"Can I help you?" asked the lady behind the bar, as she lit up a cigarette.

"Yes, I would love a beer, and red wine for Nancy," said Leonard.

"You have an American accent," replied the woman.

"No, we are Canadian."

"Welcome, we are a private members club. Do you want to join? The membership fee, is only ten pounds. My name is Muriel."

"Yes, I would love to," said Leonard.

"It's a perfect place for misfits and outsiders," said Muriel, pulling him a pint of Pilsner and Nancy a glass of the house wine.

"Sounds like what I'm looking for," "I write poetry. Have you any poets in the club?" said Leonard.

"Yes, we have many poets here. Hopefully they will not die of alcoholic poisoning, before they produce some great lines," said Muriel with a shriek of laughter.

"Then why are you selling them alcohol, Muriel, dear?" said one of men with a large bulbous nose.

"Shut up, you old tart, and order some more champagne!" shouted Muriel, glaring at him.

"Ian, cut the crap!" she said, with a sharp tongue, to a man with a rather large bulbous nose, caused possibly from drinking spirits.

A distinguished man entered, in a large white hat and a red striped tie. His suit was pale blue and was creased in all the right places. Leonard's eyes travelled downwards towards his shoes that were covered in white spats. In his right hand he held a leather case.

"George, great to see you!" This is the great musician, George Melly," said Muriel."

"A double whiskey for me."

"We have a new members."

"What's your names?"
"Leonard Cohen and Nancy Bacal."
"He's Canadian."
"We all have some cross to bear," said George rather sarcastically. He gulped down the whiskey and opened his case; and took out a brass saxophone that glistened like gold in the light. Leonard observed George's lips wrapped around the mouthpiece. He played a wondrous tune that echoed across the room. Then he began to sing.

> *'South of the border, down Mexico way,*
> *That's where I fell in love, and where stars above, came out to play,*
> *And now as I wonder, my thoughts ever stray,*
> *South of the border, down Mexico way,*
> *She was a picture, in old Spanish ways,*
> *Just for a tender while I kissed the smile, upon her face,*
> *For it was fiesta, and love had its day.*
> *South of the border, down Mexico way.'*

***

Leonard and Nancy also visited the famous French House pub with George. He introduced them to the owner, a Belgian called Victor Berloment and his son Gaston. Victor spoke in French to Leonard. He was fascinated by Victors moustache known as a 'handlebar'. It was the largest one he had ever seen. A French restaurant was opened in an upstairs room, where Victor told him that Lord Beaverbrook was a frequent diner.
"He was always presenting me to a niece who was with him," He had more nieces than any man I've ever known". Gaston said. He had wondered if the women were 'ladies of the night', or one his

mistresses. Gaston said that it was a French tradition that the English seemed to have adopted.

Downstairs in the cellar a ring was installed, where Leonard and Nancy watched a boxing match, with the French boxer called Carpentier. He was a regular visitor to Soho. George, was also an actor, a vaudeville song and dance man, and a former World War I pilot.

Victor told him how he had acquired this pub in 1914, and he was the first foreigner to be granted a full English pub licence. He took over the pub when it was called 'The Wine House', from a German called Herr Schmidt, who was threatened with internment during the war. The pub was patriotically renamed the York Minster, but was soon known as "The French" by virtue of Berlemont's tenancy, although he was in fact Belgian.

Victor told them that during the Second World War the place became popular with the Free French forces. Charles de Gaulle was supposed to have visited there. It was also home from home for the 'Fifis', who were Frenchwomen that made made up most of Soho's prostitutes, and were known as 'street walkers'.

"They used to come in here and have a half bottle of champagne, a Pernod or Ricard," said Victor. "And, if anybody approached them, they'd yell for help. In here they did not want to be disturbed. This place was sacred to them. They had my protection."

Victor told them that the pub had a liberated European ambience about it, at a time when in Europe, this was unattainable. It attracted people who worked in the film and publishing industries. Victor rattled out the list of famous people who had visited there. He had pictures of them in black and white on the walls. Among them was; Stephen Spender, Brendan Behan, and Dylan Thomas, and the occult writer known as 'The Great Beast.' Alister Crowley, who also drank there. Gaston told Leonard that many people, treated him like a banker. But if they drank all their credit, they were barred from the pub with the lines, 'One of us will have to go and it's not going to be me.'

Leonard and Nancy had to push through the crowd of sailors, prostitutes, airmen, and sailors to get to the bar. People stood close to them and whispered to each other like monks in a church. There was warmth and sweat everywhere and conversations that sounded like poetry. It was a classless, timeless, cave like place that was full of pleasures, like an opium den, Victor would whisper in Leonard ear as he passed, the words by the 17th century writer Samuel Johnson; 'When a man is tired of London, he is tired of life; for there is in London all that life can afford.'

***

One morning Leonard woke feeling cold. His feet were like ice and it was raining heavily. Nancy arrived in the sitting room, with a cup of tea. She told him to get dressed quickly, as she intended to bring him shopping to Burberrys, for a raincoat that morning.

An hour later, he was trying on a blue raincoat in front of a long mirror. Leonard bought it and strolled down the street with her. He was so happy to have this raincoat, that he thought someday he would write a poem about it.

Nancy reminded him that he had a missed appointment with Stella's dentist in the afternoon. By three o' clock his tooth was being extracted. He could see Stella and the dentist peering over him. Landlord and dentist all at the same time - he felt trapped!

Later, Leonard and Nancy stood in the rain outside. He saw a sign opposite with the name 'The Bank of Greece'. He remembered that he has a cheque that his mother had given him, and he wondered if the bank would cash it for him. Inside the bank he could see a floor of white marble and walls covered in pictures of ancient Greece. Leonard approached the bank teller that has a deep tan, and handed him the cheque. The teller looked at him intently.

"I can cash it if you open an account here. Have you a passport?" Leonard nodded and took it out and handed it to him.

"Where did you get that tan from?" said Leonard.

"I have just come back from the island of Hydra in Greece," said the teller handing him a form to sign and stamping the cheque, and cashing it.

"Where is that?" said Leonard quite curious.

"One hour from the port of Piraeus, near Athens the capital." said the teller beaming him a smile and pointing, to a large framed map of Greece, on the wall. "With that kind of weather, I want to go there?" said Leonard. The young man smiled at him.

"I am Canadian and we have always been in search of the sun. What part of Greece are you from?" asked Leonard, while drawing on his cigarette.

"I think it's the place for me," said Leonard with a smile.

"You should try it, as it is cheaper than London and has lot of great food, and the Greek drink called ouzo and of course the hot sun."

"I think I will give it a go." Leonard thought to himself, this was the escape that he was in search of. He remembered that the poet Byron, had escaped to Greece. He had gone there in a heroic quest to fight the Ottoman Turks. He assembled a small army, but tragically, before he could lead in it, he died of malaria in a town on the coast called Missolonghi.

"If you go there, just ask for Bill, he owns the bar there," said the bank teller.

Leonard returned home that evening, with only one thought in his mind. He would escape to Greece and get away from the English weather and the big city of London, to live a simpler life, and write his novel and his poetry.

***

Nancy heard about the launch of a book by the English travel writer Patrick Leigh Femor at the publishers. John Murrays, Their offices were in Dover street near the Ritz hotel. The current owner's great ancestor was a close friend and correspondent of Byron. Murray published many of his major works, including Childe Harold's Pilgrimage, which sold out in five days, leading to Byron's observation. 'I awoke one morning and found myself famous'.

Sir John Murray told them that his grandfather had participated in one of the most notorious destructive acts in the history of literature. Byron had given his grandfather, the manuscript of his personal memoirs to publish. Together with five of Byron's friends and executors, he decided to destroy Byron's manuscripts, because he thought the scandalous sexual details would damage Byron's reputation. With only Thomas Moore objecting, the two volumes of memoirs were burnt in the fireplace at Murray's office. Sir John looked over at the fireplace where a fire was still burning. Leonard and Nancy looked at the flames with a sense of disbelief.

They met Patrick Leigh Femor, a tall handsome man with dark wavy hair. He told them that the age of eighteen he decided to walk across Europe, from the Hook of Holland to Istanbul. He set off in December 1933 with a few clothes, a volume of Horace's Odes. He slept in barns and shepherd's huts. He was lucky, as he was invited by farmers and the aristocracy into their country houses across Europe. He experienced hospitality from the monks too, in many monasteries along the way.

In January 1935, after two years travelling, he toured around Greece. In Athens he met Balasha Cantacuzène, a Romanian noblewoman who he fell in love with. They lived in an old watermill outside the city looking out towards Poros, where she painted and he wrote. Patrick spent two years there, writing a large part of his book; Mani, travels in the Southern Peloponnese and translating the Greek Resistance memoir 'The Cretan Runner'.

He fought in Crete during the German occupation. He parachuted, with the British Special Operations Executive (SOE), who were posted there to organise the island's resistance to the Nazi occupation. Disguised as a shepherd he lived for over two years in the mountains. With Captain Bill Stanley Moss as his second in command, Leigh Fermor led the party, that in 1944 captured the Nazi Commander Major General Heinrich Kreipe.

Leonard and Nancy also met Baroness Barbara Rothschild, who told them that she had just divorced her second husband Nathaniel Rothschild and had acquired his name. Leonard though she was very beautiful. She had bright clear pink skin, and had deep dark eyes and hair like silk. She could have been a Hollywood star. He could see why she had so many husbands. She was now was engaged to a Greek painter called Nico Ghika, who had a large villa on Hydra. She told Leonard that if he ever got to Hyda, that he should visit him there. Nico always offered artist and writers a room there.

***

Sir John Murray gave Leonard a map of Greece, and a copy of Bradshaw's travel guide. Inside he learnt that it was written in 1839; and had all the information about boat and travel times, with details of the many towns and cities on these routes.

When he got back to Stella's place, he laid the map on the dining room table. Nancy and Stella studied the map with him. He opened Bradshaw's book and found the section on Greece, and the island of Hydra. He read it out to them.

"Hydra, Ydra or Idra is one of the Saronic Islands of Greece, located in the Aegean Sea. It is separated from the Peloponnese by a narrow strip of water. In ancient times, the island was known as Hydra a reference to the natural springs on the island.

Occupied by the Ottomans and liberated by the Greek in 1821. It was the Home of artist's writers and painters."

"Make sure you write that novel. I want to see you finish three pages a day," said Stella, with assurance, like a professor at Mc Gill university.

"Don't worry I will," said Leonard closing the book.

Leonard and Nancy took a taxi to Victoria. The station was filled with hundreds of people looking at a large sign with the train timetables. Leonard destination for the ferry to France was Dover. A few minutes later it appeared, and he said goodbye to Nancy. Leonard hurried down the platform and beckoned to the conductor to let him on the train. Ten minutes later, he looked once again, upon the English countryside. His plan was to take the ferry and then the train to Paris. Then onward, on the Orient Express across France, Switzerland, Austria and down through the Balkans.

Two hours later he boarded the ferry to Calais. He sat back in the ferry's bar and drank a glass of French wine and reflected. Then he opened his book of poems by Lorca and read his poem; The Wounds of Love.

> 'This light, this flame that devours,
> This weight of sea that breaks on me,
> This scorpion that lives inside my breast, are a garland of love,
> A bed of the wounded, were dreamless,
> I dream of your presence among the ruins of my sunken breast,
> And though I seek the summit of discretion in your heart,
> Grant me a valley stretched below, with hemlock,
> And passion of bitter wisdom, it is the wounds of love.

***

Chapter 7
Shakespeare and Company

The train arrived after midnight at Gard du Nord in Paris. The lights of Paris appeared. They shone and lit up the shop fronts in an orange and yellow glow. Leonard crossed the street to a café and ordered omelettes and fries. The walls of the café had flowered wallpaper and prints of Monet's impressionist landscapes. He could smell the coffee and the fresh bread from the café.

He rented a cheap room above the café. His cigarette gave him some solace in the loneliness of the night. His spirits were raised when he heard that beautiful song by Edith Piaf 'La Vie en Rose', on the radio, that was to him like a voice as pure as a nightingale. He could hear the words.

> *'Hold me close and hold me fast.*
> *The magic spell you cast.*
> *This is 'vie en rose'.*
> *When you kiss me heaven sighs.*
> *Though I close my eyes.'*

***

The following day Leonard went to see the cathedral of Notre Dame. It soared above him. He could see the great rose windows with their great array of colours. The light streamed through the glass, red, blue and yellow, and cast a coloured mosaic on the floor. He recalled the faith of his father and his Jewish roots.

He wondered why the two great religions had been torn apart - Jew and Catholic. Then he remembered that Irving had explained it to him. For the Catholics, Jesus was the messiah, but for the Jews he was one of many such prophets. He could see a shaft of light striking a statue of Jesus. His face glowed as it had come alive. He remembered the poem 'The Second Coming' written by the Irish poet W.B. Yeats.

> 'Surely some revelation is at hand,
> Surely the Second Coming is at hand,
> The Second Coming! Hardly are those words out,
> When a vast image out of Spiritus Mundi,
> Troubles my sight: somewhere in sands of the desert,
> A shape with a lion's body and the head of a man.'

He passed over a bridge in front of Notre Dame, then down by the Seine, where traders sold rare second-hand books. He did not stop, as there was another second-hand bookshop he was looking for. He crossed the street to the left bank and the home of bohemian Paris. He entered a bookshop called Shakespeare & Company. It was here that James Joyce had published Ulysses with the help of Silvia Beech, the owner of the shop in the 1920's. This book was banned in many countries. The place was filled with books from floor to ceiling. He could smell the old books – the leather, the paper and the ink. Sitting at a desk was a man with a grey moustache and goatee beard. He had bright eyes and a domed forehead.

"Good day to you," said Leonard. "I am looking for some poetry books."

The man got up from his desk and walked over to a shelf.

"Let's see, I have some books by the poets." Verlaine, and Rimbaud - visionary poets who transformed French poetry. He had a scandalous love affair with Paul Verlaine". He said, lifting up a book and gave it to him. Leonard observed the face of Rimbaud on the book cover.

"You're American?"

"No, Canadian."
"I am George Whitman," he said, shaking his hand.
"Are you related to Walt Whitman?"
"Yes, literature runs in my blood. I bought this place after the war. I can offer you a coffee, if you like. I'm having a poetry reading here later."
"I write poetry."
"Good, welcome aboard."
George boiled a kettle and made him a coffee. "I've been here since 1951. I came here after the Nazis left," said George looking up at a sign over the door. Leonard read it. 'Be not inhospitable to strangers, lest they be angels in disguise.'
"That's a good motto to live by," said Leonard sipping his coffee.
"All the best writers have been here: Ginsberg, Corso, Burroughs, Joyce, and Hemingway. It's a socialist utopia masquerading as a book store," said George, running his hands through his whiskers.
"You can stay here if you want, if you can prove to me that you are a writer. I've got guests who blow in every day on the winds of chance. But the Beat Hotel may be a better place for you. All of my beds and couches are full up tonight. Read me a poem from Rimbaud," said George sitting back and fondling his whiskers. Leonard flicked through the book and began to read the poem called 'Being Beauteous.'

> *'Against a fall of snow, a being beautiful, and very tall,*
> *Whistling of death and circles of faint music,*
> *Make this adored body, swelling and trembling,*
> *Like a spectre, rise,*
> *Black and scarlet gashes burst in the gleaming flesh,*
> *The true colours of life grow dark, shimmering and separate,*

In the scaffolding, around the vision,
Shivering's mutter and rise,
And the furious taste of these effects is charged,
With deadly whistling and the raucous music,
That the world, far behind us,
Hurls at our mother of beauty,
She retreats, she rises up,
Oh! Our bones have put on new flesh, for love.'

***

Leonard said goodbye to George and walked over to the Beat hotel, on No 9 Rue Gît-le-Cœur in the Latin quarter. George was right it was the cheapest hotel one could find. It was known as class thirteen hotel, where it was only required by law to meet the minimum of health and safety standards.

The owner Madame Rachou, greeted him and showed him his room. The room had windows facing the interior stairwell and had not much light. Hot water was available only on Thursdays, Fridays and Saturdays. Madame Rachou informed him that the hotel had only one bathtub, situated on the ground floor. If he wanted a bath, he would have to reserve it beforehand, and pay the charge for the hot water. Curtains and bedspreads were changed and washed every spring. The linen was changed every month. Leonard wondered if they were bedbugs there.

She was impressed by Leonard's French. He told her he was from French speaking Quebec. Madame Rachou, told him sadly that her husband had passed away after a traffic accident in 1957. Besides letting rooms, she had a small cafe on the ground floor. She told Leonard that she had worked at a bistro frequented by artists, that included the impressionist painters, Claude Monet and Camille Pissarro. Because of this, she encouraged artists and writers to stay at the hotel, and at times permitted them to pay the rent with paintings or with poetry.

Leonard lay in bed and he could see the lights of Paris across the Seine and the street lights seemed to float like green orbs in the liquid blue cobalt sky. There were framed photographs hung on wallpaper covered in flowers. Paris by night was a place that Brassai, the Hungarian photographer had recorded, a Paris of silhouettes, of prostitutes lingering on the sidewalk on Rue St. Germain. It was a city of ancient neo-classical buildings built by Hausmann; a city like a living museum that was another world for Leonard.

Madame Rachou talked that evening of the old Paris, of a lost world that she felt had disappeared. She told Leonard that Parisians had grown to love their new city and forgotten about the old Paris, that had disappeared beneath the earth. For her the old Paris was the real Paris. Madame Rachou gave him the book of poetry, by Baudelaire, The Flowers of Evil, that was published in 1857. She told him that Baudelaire criticised 19th century French modernity and Haussmann's renovation of Paris. The poem dealt with the feelings of isolation that people felt in a newly rebuilt 'modernized' city. Baudelaire was critical of the geometrically laid out streets of Paris, and how the old street laneways had vanished forever. He remembered the alienated and the forgotten anti-heroes of Paris who served as his inspiration. There were the; beggars, blind, workers, gamblers, prostitutes, and the old people of Paris. She felt that Before the war, Paris was a city of brothels and night clubs, now it had been destroyed by the well-meaning bourgeoisie, who had shut down these palaces of sex and seduction.

Leonard read Baudelaire's poems late into the night. He could see that Baudelaire was fascinated by the underdog, and the poor of this great city, and not its rich exalted citizens. For Baudelaire, the city has been transformed into an anthill of identical streets, with facades that looked like a badly designed wedding cake. A city that he could no longer recognize. Baudelaire and his publisher were prosecuted under the regime of the Second Empire as an outrage known as 'aux bonnes mœurs'; an insult to public decency, and was fined three hundred francs. Victor Hugo said that Baudelaire had created 'un nouveau frisson,' a new shudder and a new thrill in literature. In the foreword of this book, Baudelaire's boredom of the new Paris outlines its worst miseries. Leonard began to read the introduction titled as 'Au Lecteur', 'To the Reader' of this poem and admired Baudelaire's passion for Paris.

'If the rape, the poison, the dagger, the fire,
Have not yet embroidered their pleasant designs.
The banal canvas of our pitiful destinies,
It is only our soul, alas! is not bold enough.
If rape, poison, dagger and fire,
Have still not embroidered their pleasant designs
On the banal canvas of our pitiable destinies,
It's because our soul, alas, is not bold enough!
It's Ennui! —The eye charged with an involuntary tear,
He dreams of scaffolds while smoking his hookah.
You know him, reader, this delicate monster,
Hypocrite reader! -my similar, -my brother!
It's Boredom! —Eye brimming with an involuntary tear
He dreams of gallows while smoking his hookah.
You know him, reader, this delicate monster,
Hypocritical reader, my likeness, my brother!'

In contrast to the new world of Canada, Paris had a surreal landscape. He felt alone, but within that aloneness there was a kind of exhilaration. He was seized by a sense of his own destiny. He had been inspired each day by finding new poems. He knew he wanted to craft them and sculpt them into a form that would bring a perfection of emotion to his poetry and to his prose.

***

The next morning, Leonard took a taxi to Gare de l'Est, in South Paris. He observed its beautiful neo-classical Napoleonic façades. Once inside he bought a ticket to Venice and had breakfast on the Belle Epoch café upstairs, beneath the beautiful murals of a bygone age were painted on the ceiling.

He boarded a train, on the final leg of the journey. The train he took was the Orient Express. Leonard spent most of his time in the restaurant carriage, where he had coffee while writing his novel. Now and again he would look across the landscape, as the train crossed the countryside towards Switzerland. He could see a landscape filled with vineyards, and grapes hanging from the vines. Leonard had a couchette with a single bunk bed.

He read a book about the French writer Francoise 'Bonjour Tristesse' Sagan that he had found at the train station in Paris. Her quotes were so profound and so true. She wrote about love that she felt that lasts about seven years. She had loved to the point of madness; which she felt was the only sensible way to love. She felt too that men refused all ideas of fidelity or serious commitments.

***

The train rattled across eastern France. He slept lightly that night in his couchette on starched sheets. The light from the road near the empty train stations would peer through the small curtains from time to time. He looked at his watch it was 2.30 am and he could hear dogs barking. The conductor knocked on his door and asked for his passport. He had arrived at the Swiss border. He peered outside and observed a border guard checking travellers paperwork. Soon they were on their way again and he went back to sleep. When he woke, he hurried to his window to observe the snow-capped Alps soaring majestically into the sky.

He looked like he had been sculpted out of shards, of blue and grey rock. The train sped on.

***

Later that morning the conductor knocked on his door shouting Venezia!' Peering outside he could see a long bridge that stretched towards Venice. This ancient magical city that appeared like a mirage in the distance. The train sped along the bridge towards the Mestre on Venice's mainland.

Venice had a charm about it, Leonard thought. It's classical Romanesque facades, were of an elegance that he had never seen before. He took a river boat down the Grand canal and observed the buildings of ochre, yellow and pure white. There were many shaped windows in the style of gothic, classical and oriental. Their panes of glass and the stonework had many shapes and designs, that spoke of a great bygone age.

He found a cheap hotel near St. Mark's square and later went for a stroll there. There he could see the majestic Doge's Palace, with beautiful copulas and domes. Beside it stood in red brick tower called the Campanile, topped by four arches and a green roof.

He had a coffee at Café Florian situated in Piazza San Marco, that was established in 1720. Possibly the oldest coffee house in Italy, and perhaps the oldest in the world. The waiter told Leonard that the cafe was patronised in the past centuries by; Goldoni, the Italian playwright and librettist from the Republic of Venice; Wolfgang von Goethe the German poet, playwright, novelist, scientist, statesman, theatre director, critic, and Giacomo Casanova the Italian adventurer and infamous playboy. The great lover was attracted by the fact that Caffè Florian was the only coffee house that allowed women to sit there. Lord Byron, Marcel Proust, and Charles Dickens were also frequent visitors.

***

Leonard bought a cheap second-class ticket and boarded the train for Greece. He could see the many islands that dotted the Venetian harbour and the evening mist as it descended. Flocks of birds climbed to the sky as the train passed. The train sped past Trieste where James Joyce had once lived. The landscape became whiter and less greener. The air grew drier and the sun loomed higher in the sky. After a day travelling, the train sped past Belgrade, then Zagreb and headed for the Macedonian border. Leonard could feel the heat and the warmth of the sun.

***

Chapter 8
Hellas

A day later the train stopped at Thessaloniki station in the north of Greece. Leonard stepped onto the platform and stretched his legs. The train headed on. He knew he was deep in Greece now. He could see that the houses and the pavement stones were painted white and blue. He could smell fresh roses and see grapes dangling from branches. The light became sharper and less translucent. It flooded the landscape and the sky became paler. The deep greens had vanished. He observed paler shades of green that emerged along with yellows, greys and iron oxide across the landscape.

Athens appeared and Leonard could see the classical ruins of the Acropolis perched on a hill. This was the city that he had read about in Bradshaw's Guide; the city of Socrates, Plato, and of the heroic Greeks. Modern civilisation had encroached upon it and he could see a sprawling city of new houses and offices shining white in the intense sun. Things had changed since Bradshaw had published his book in 1913.

The train came to a halt in Athens Station. Leonard stepped off the train. He could see that Greece was another world compared to northern Europe. The faces of the Greeks looked weathered by the sun. He observed old women, some carrying baskets of fruit and flowers, dressed in black. He would later learn that widowed women always wore black after the death of their husbands – many for a lifetime. The Greek features looked darker and more classical with high foreheads and strong aquiline noses. Many men wore beards and moustaches. The women had a dark mysterious beauty about them, with deep black eyes, long eyelashes and long black hair. Leonard walked out of the station

into the piercing midday sun, and observed a taxi parked outside that was painted in bright yellow. Leonard greeted the taxi driver who leaned out and beckoned him to get in.
"Where to?" asked the old bearded Greek with curly hair streaked with grey.
Around his neck he wore a gold necklace with a pendant in the shape of a cross.
"I want to go to Hydra," said Leonard putting on his sunglasses.
"You've got to go to Piraeus, on the coast," replied the taxi driver.
"I take you; I give you a good price."
"Okay," said Leonard, throwing his suitcase and guitar case into the back seat and jumping in. The Greek engaged the clutch and put his foot down and sped off.
"We Greeks play hard and drive hard," he said, laughing out loudly. "Your first time here?"
"Yes," said Leonard a little nervous and holding on to his seat.
"Where are you from?"
"Canada."
"Yes… moose and big bears."
"Ha-ha yes." said Leonard laughing and observing the Athens buildings, speeding past him, as he held onto his seat.
"You will love the ouzo here."
"What's is that?"
"It's the Greek's national drink. It's great…it will put fire in your blood." The taxi driver turned on the radio and the sound of a bouzouki player filled the taxi cab.
"Who's that?" asked Leonard.
"It's Milkis Theodorakis."
"No, I have not."
'You're heading for Hydra; my father was born there. Hydra is a magical place, built by Greek and Venetian pirates. You will love it there." The taxi sped through the streets to the edge of the

city. Then it reached the main road to the coast, and very soon Leonard could see the thin blue line of the Mediterranean.

The taxi screeched to a halt in Piraeus harbour. Leonard could see a myriad of yachts, boats and ships, large and small, tied up at the jetty. He could see also one large boat named the 'Argos' moored and with people entering it via a gangplank. It had two large funnels painted black with a red stripe. The ship was painted white with parts of it also painted blue. At the rear there was a large Greek flag blowing in the breeze. The taxi driver shouted. "Two drachmas!" Leonard told him that he only had dollars, but he gladly accepted.

"Ok give me two dollars."

"The dollar is like gold dust here," said the taxi driver roaring with laughter.

Leonard grasped his guitar and case and hurried to the ticket office. A few minutes later he climbed up the gangplank. Many Greeks rushed about, some with baskets of melons, grapes and apples. There were baskets containing live chickens. Many wore straw hats to hide from the sun. Some old women sat in solitude clutching rosary beads, praying Leonard though in memory of their dead.

Leonard's eye caught sight of a Greek sailor climbing to another level. He followed him and found an empty seat at the rear. The foghorn sounded and the boat's giant ropes were cast off. The boat headed out across a calm, light blue sea. Only the white crests of small waves broke gently on its surface. It was a serene place to be. It had an extraordinary calmness about it, and was such a contrast to the Atlantic Ocean.

He looked at the map that the ticket office had given him. Hydra was not too far away now. One of the waiters told him it was two hours by boat. An island appeared to the left. From the map he knew it was the island of Spetzes. It was in the heart of the Sardonic gulf like Hydra. Leonard realised that he was now sailing across the Aegean Sea. Leonard lay back in the sun and tipped over his eyes a straw hat, that he had bought from a Greek boy on deck. Then he thought of some words from the poem that he wanted to write about Suzanne and Saint Catherine.

> *'Jesus sailed on the dead sea. One day he walked upon the water. He spent a long time searching from his lonely ivory tower. But he knew that only drowning men could save him.'*

***

Hydra appeared like a thin white filament before him on the horizon. His eyes fixed upon this until it grew larger and larger. The ship blew its foghorn as it approached Hydra. Leonard stood up and observed the wondrous sight before him. He could see the many clusters of white houses that were like perfect cubes, and also beautiful villas. The many roofs created their own patterns of reds, yellows, ochres and iron oxides The harbour was protected with two great arms, made from stone Inside their embrace, he could see many yachts and boats bobbing up and down on gentle waves. As the ship gracefully approached, he could see a promenade with many cafés and shops with seats outside. They were all sheltered under canopies of white and light blue. There was a church to the right and some buildings flew the Greek flag on their roofs.

He could see fishing boats that were painted blue and white and moored to the harbour walls bobbing up and down. Leonard could see whitewashed stone houses that ascended up the hillsides. The wind has whipped up a little now and it felt cooler for him. There was a picture postcard quality to this place. It had all the elements of an ideal world, a place of refuge, like Arcadia.

He could see the old architecture of Hydra. Many of its walls had ancient vines that seemed to embrace and soften the architectural features. There was a reserved dignity and a majesty about this place. It seemed to him that these ancient buildings and ruins stood for a thousand years, enveloped in white, that gave it an attractiveness, in contrast to the many grey stone buildings of northern Europe. There was a scale, too, about this place, compact, cosy and much smaller than the city of Montreal that he had grown up in.

The ship dropped anchor. Leonard grabbed his suitcase and guitar and made his way down the gangplank. Leonard walked along the promenade and saw a café with name Katsikas. He was greeted by a young handsome Greek man, who introduced himself as the owner. – Nick Katsikas. He ordered a coffee. He could see an oven where bread was baked, and flames danced inside when Nick took the loafs out. In the café there sat a few old men playing chess. Leonard saw cats everywhere, some sleeping, others licking their paws and stretching their legs above their ears. He saw a small sweet kitten snuggling up to her mother.

Leonard discovered that Katsikas was also a storeroom that sold food supplies. Leonard saw boxes of oranges, bananas, and grapes. There are octopuses and pieces of meat covered in nets, and many bags of flower stacked to the ceiling. He could see bottles of wine, and whiskey. There were also household goods, baskets and cooking pots and pans.
"We Hydroite's store a lot of food, even secretly," said Nick, coming up behind Leonard. "We had a famine here during the war, a third of the population died. We Greeks have long memories," said Nick, handing him a glass of ouzo. "It's on the house?"
Leonard tasted its bitter taste like liquorice, but very refreshing.
"Thank you," said Leonard. "Tell me, do you know where Bill's bar is?"
. "Yes, Bill's bar is that way," said Nick, pointing his finger.

***

Leonard found the bar behind the harbour. A sign with the name 'Bill's Bar' hung over a doorway. Inside he found a large dark haired man with handsome features cleaning the bar top. Behind him was an array of glasses and bottles of whiskey, vodka and aperitifs, and a framed picture of the Queen of England.
"I'm looking for Bill|?" said Leonard, smiling at the barman.
"That's me. How did you know my name?"
"A Greek in London told me about this place," said Leonard.
"Where are you from?"
"Leonard my name, I'm from Canada…I'm a wandering soul," replied Leonard, with a smile.
"This place is full of wandering souls," replied Bill, cleaning a glass.
"Want a drink?"
"Sure..ouzo."
"I need a place to stay!" said Leonard. They looked around and saw a man enter with a thin frame and a weather-beaten face. He had a long aquiline nose and piercing eyes.
"George, how are you?" said Bill.
"Good Bill…bit of a hangover. I need a cure?" said George with an Australian accent.
"This is George Johnson, a journalist and novelist. He will sort you out. He knows everybody on the island." said Bill.
"You sound like an Aussie." Said Leonard.
"I am."
Bill poured George a beer. George gulped it down as if it were water. Leonard observed him George extended his hand to Leonard and he shook it.
"Leonard Cohen."
"Pleased to meet you."

"I have a place for you. You can stay with me, until you get sorted. Bill, tell Anthony Kingsmill we have a new visitor." said George.
"Who is Anthony?"
"He's an artist and poet. He knows a lot of people on the island too. He can put the word around about a new arrival. Bill if you see Anthony tell him about Leonard."
"I also write," said Leonard.
"That's good Hydra could do with a few more writers. My wife is a writer, too. We live in each other's hair."
"What are you working on?" said Leonard.
"A novel. That can be hard at times; you need stamina for a novel."
"Have you a title for your novel?"
"Beautiful Losers."
"That's a bloody good title. We are all losers in life, one way or another. We ain't leaving this place alive – that's for sure."
"I write poetry now and again."
"Stick to poetry, my son. It's an easier game. Novels can break your back and your endurance. It's not for wimps, I write them myself" said George.
"I'll keep that in mind," replied Leonard.
"This island is full of empty houses. A lot of people have moved to the mainland."

***

Leonard, George and Bill continued to talk as the evening advanced. The golden Greek sun descended and disappeared beyond the horizon. Bill played a song on his record player by Nana Mouskouri; 'The White Rose of Athens'.

> *'Till the white rose blooms again,*
> *You must leave me, leave me lonely,*
> *So goodbye my love till then,*

Till the white rose blooms again,
The summer days are ending in the valley,
And soon the time will come when we must be apart,
But like the rose that comes back with the spring time,
You will return to me when spring time comes around,
Till the white rose blooms again.'

His new found friends were very accommodating and friendly. They had experienced their own struggles and had their own hardships. They had resigned from the world, to this place of refuge far from civilisation. He felt the same way, and he wanted to belong there. The bell rung in the church on the port and he thought of his dead father, Pablo and Saint Catherine. He knew he had found the place of refuge – that he had always dreamt about.

After Bill closed his doors, they took a back street to a Greek restaurant called Douskos taverna, that George called 'The Garden of Earthly Delights'. They entered a place covered in vines, that twisted up along the walls. Leonard felt that this place had been there for centuries. Dotted across this paved taverna were tables covered in white cloths. On each table a small candle created a glow that shone in the evening light. George ordered a bottle of Greek wine. He seemed to Leonard to be an expert on the wines of Greece. He talked about the wines of the Aegean islands, south of Hydra on the island Samos, where one could find the best red and white wine. He loved wines that had been flavoured with passion fruit and lemon, to give the wine a sweet taste. The Samos Muscat was made with raisins and coca. It had the flavour of raspberry fruit and herbs. Some Greeks believed that Anthony and Cleopatra had drunk this wine. George told them that this wine was drunk by Aristotle.

As they burned the midnight oil, a bouzouki player appeared and performed some ancient Greek tune. Leonard marvelled at his delivery of the lyrics in Greek, even though they were unintelligible to him. He wondered to himself, if only he could achieve that phrasing, that measured sense of pace that all the great musicians had learned. Leonard began to feel at home. He had found new friends in George and Bill. As he embraced his glass of wine and ate souvlaki; a rice dish with skewered chicken, he knew he had found his new home.

Leonard and George said goodbye to Bill. Then George and Leonard walked down some dark alleyways that night. Leonard followed him with his guitar and suitcase. George had drunk a full bottle of wine, but he still seemed to know his way home, like a homing pigeon. He grunted some words now and again in his Australian accent, that Leonard could not understand. He could see the great Greek sky above him with thousands of stars, and out beyond the horizon hung the perfect round orb of the moon. Its blue tint seemed to fill the dark shadows that covered the passageways that they now ventured in. However, he had confidence in George.

Soon they reached their destination - a small white house near the edge of the sea. Outside Leonard could see wild roses climbing up its walls. George fumbled for the key in his pocket. turned the key in the lock. They both entered.

Inside Leonard saw an attractive dark-haired woman sitting at a table. She had arched eyebrows, high cheekbones and had red lipstick, and a hair that lay in curls at the shoulders. She wore a white blouse with an upturned collar. On her finger he could see a wedding ring and her nails were painted red. Leonard could see that she had long elegant fingers. She held a glass of red wine and beside her he could see a half empty bottle. Leonard laid his guitar on the floor along with his suitcase. Charmian smiled, as George made a fumbled introduction, even in his drunken state. "We have a guest...Leonard Cohen, ...all the way from Canada!"

"I told George not to drink so much. He never listens to me, welcome aboard!"

"You're a bad boy, I've been waiting on you!"

"This is my wife, Charmian. Isn't she a peach`, she's writing a novel too?"

"What's it called?" asked Leonard, sitting down on a wicker chair.

"Walk in Paradise Gardens." It's about a small Australian beach resort that should have been a restful place, but the human current of problems, ran deep as the ocean." George turned to Leonard and looked at him intently.

"My wife looks at the human soul in great detail," said George. "She is a good writer. She writes about the small bars, the bedrooms, the damp bath houses and beach picnics in a brilliantly vivid way. My wife's knowledge of people is so subtle, sophisticated and deep. She uncovers the underbelly of Australian society."

"You speak very highly of me, George."

"I explore human nature. It's just that I like to look into every person's soul. My books are about life and death," replied Charmian.

"What about suicide?" asked George. "You talk so much about life and death."

"Suicide is always a good way out for people that don't want to face the world".

"Suicide is never an answer," replied Leonard, and he reflected on the recent death of Pablo.

"For some it is curtains! Have a glass," said George, pouring him and Leonard a glass of wine and lying back onto the sofa. George, Charmian and Leonard drank late into the night.

***

Leonard drifted into a sleep and woke late in the morning. He saw George lying on the couch. Charmian was nowhere to be seen. Leonard could see the bedroom walls that were filled with paintings of oriental scenes and of women in veils – harems and palaces. Leonard observed ships that had triangular red sails, sailing towards the harbour of Hydra; a tranquil scene with a calm ocean that had the colour of green marble. Beside this painting was a Greek icon of the figure of Jesus in a gold halo. One of his hands was held upright and written on the palm on his hand were the letters I.H.S. He knew it meant 'I Have Suffered'. He had seen this symbol before, in a painting of Saint Catherine. IHS 'I have suffered.' was a known as a Christogram; a combination of letters that represent the holy name of Jesus. Early scribes would abbreviate the sacred names of Jesus by using the first two letters of the name, or the first and last letters, with a line over the letters. In Greece I had a special meaning. The Greek letters Chi-Rho, which looks like our English X and P, was an abbreviation for the name Christ. It was adopted as a symbol by the Pope in the Vatican. Leonard recalled seeing this symbol before.

***

Chapter 9
My Dear Friend Anthony

Leonard ran his hands through his hair and rubbed his eyes and the stubble that had grown overnight. He heard a rasping voice outside the door, a deep voice that sounded like the grinding of corn in a stone mill. He staggered over to the window and saw a man outside with a donkey. Leonard opened the door. A man with a large head of blonde hair with a smile greeted him.
"I'm Anthony Kingsmill, Bill sent me over here. Are you Leonard?"
"Yes", said Leonard, as his eyes adjusted to the strong sunlight.
"I found a house for you to rent, it is cheap, if you want it".
"That's great, come in."
Anthony tied up his donkey and came inside. He seemed to know his way around and made some coffee for them both.
"I'm from Hastings in England. I escaped here after the war. England was such a dull place then. You will like it here, it is cheap. The food and the wine, and the women are nice too," said Anthony laughing.
Leonard made them both a coffee and sat down and had a chat. Before long they were in deep conversation as if they were old friends.

"I escaped from England after the war and have been stuck here ever since," said Anthony in deep thought. "I was born, in an old mill near the battle of Senlac, near a place called Blood Lake. It was a large ditch that opened up during the course of the battle, and many soldiers fell in and were trampled to death. The result there was a river of blood as far as one could see. There was a local legend, that the soil turned red after the rain fell. The old poet Michael Drayton wrote about it. "

"Some men escape in many ways. When they are backed into a corner, they make moves like heroic warriors against life, they try to outmanoeuvre their problems," said Leonard lighting up a cigarette.

Anthony remembered the lines from Drayton.

'The Battle of Hastings, once distained with native English blood; whose soil, when wet with any little rain, doth blush, to put in mind of those there sadly slain. When Hasting's harbour gave unto the Norman powers. Whose name and honours now are denizened for ours, in that boding, ominous brook!'

'Where are your parents now?'

'I had a stepfather. I never met my real one. I remember his funeral well.

The day before my mother told me that I should go and see him in the coffin'. "I had to walk four miles to the undertakers and stopped at a cat museum on the way."

"A cat museum," said Leonard puzzled.

"Yeah, it was a barn full of dusty glass cases of cats and kittens. It was all rather surreal, some of the cats were dressed up in 18th century costume. Some wore berets, and one sat on a Kings throne. Then there were glass cases with cats that were three headed, two tails, and five footed - accidents of nature I suppose. I came out feeling sick and dazed. It did not place me in good shape to visit the undertakers, but I continued on anyway. I was greeted by an old man with a sweet nature, with a bald head."

He shook my hand and was told my stepfather was laid out for me to pay my respects. I found him lying in a coffin at the centre of a room that had six large candles in brass on each side. He wore a Victorian bonnet, and his face had shrunken, and chalky deposits of white powder lay on his cheeks and lips. The undertaker told me, that I should touch the body because then he would not haunt my dreams.

I bent down and kissed his lips, as I had often kissed him as a child. But the coldness of his lips made me realise, that he was as dead as a doornail, and my heart was shredded. I really did love him!'' said Anthony, sadly and philosophically. Leonard though for a while.

"Most men can't show that their heart is shredded. They are filled with high hopes but then despair. So, men choose the hangman's noose rather than face it. I have been filled with those moments of despair as well at times," said Leonard.

"Me too, sometimes, I wanted to throw myself off a cliff here, but I was a coward, and could and could not do it," said Anthony, laughing in an ironic way.

"Maybe it is cowardice and not heroism that saves us. Now I toil in the tower of song, writing is such a bitch," replied Leonard. "I try and put all my love and pain in my poems. It is hard, but it is all I have to give to this world."

''You write poem, I do too.''

''We will share them some day.''

''Look if you want to see this house, and have too much of a hangover, you can sit on my donkey. He is friendly.''

"What about George and Charmian?"

"Don't worry about them …let them sleep. Did you meet their children?''

" No.'' replied Leonard.

"They have three. I am sure they are sleeping too.''

Ten minutes later Leonard with the help of Anthony, mounted his donkey. Then Anthony tied his suitcase and guitar case on either side to leather straps. Then Anthony led the way across the harbour and up the backstreets, and stopped outside a small house. Then he tied up the donkey and Leonard dismounted. The house was located in a collection of houses between Hydra and the village of Kamini. It was a quiet location with a narrow street.

Anthony turned a large key in the grey door. Leonard stepped inside and Anthony showed him around. It had electricity, and a large cistern that held rainwater. Anthony told him that fresh water was delivered by donkeys, with large earthenware jars strapped to their backs every week.

It had a large fireplace. It was cool in the summer and warm in the winter. It had a terrace on top, where Leonard could place a table for his typewriter. It would be a perfect place to smoke his cigarettes. His house had a simple layout, and that was the way he liked it. There was a sitting room with traditional Greek chairs and a table. The bedroom was very cosy with wooden beams in contrast to the white paintwork. It had an ancient Greek iron bed, that looked like it was made over a hundred years ago. Only the wood frame was there. Anthony promised to find him a mattress.

Anthony knew of a woman called Kyria Sophia, who lived nearby that was looking for a job as a housekeeper. She needed the money badly, as she had two orphans that she looked after.

Leonard visited Sophia's place with Anthony. Anthony introduced Leonard to her. She was not very tall, and had grey hair and a broad frame. She wore a scarf on her hair and an apron over her flowery dress. She spoke English but not so well at times. She told them that she survived by selling flour, sugar and bread outside her house. She also sold salads with olives and feta cheese made from goats to the locals. She lived in one room that was painted in light blue. There were ancient crosses and gold icons hanging on the walls. Leonard could see a fading photo dated 1905, that Sophia said were her parents.

Sophia took care of two orphans whose parents had died in a tragic accident. Their names were Ana and Philip. The children had never been to school. She could not read or write. It was too far for them to walk at such a young age of ten and seven. Ana was very thin. Sophia said that she gave Ana three meals every day. She only spoke Greek and smiled at Leonard and Anthony. She had long dark hair and sweet eyes. Leonard held her hand.

Philippe was disabled and one of his legs was damaged at birth and he dragged it after him. Leonard touched his cheek and he smiled. Sophia said that a donkey kicked his mother's belly when she was pregnant. The local children always made fun of him and called out to him. Leonard was shocked at how cruel children could be. She agreed to come every morning to wash his dishes, sheets, clothes and clean his floors. Sophia in a way became his new stepmother. She was pleased to meet Leonard and was thankful for his kindness in offering him this job. It was a life saver for her. She knew what starvation was; as her parents had died in the famine on Hydra, during the war. Leonard knew that he would have to live on the twelve dollars cheques from his grandfather if he stayed on Hydra. So, Sophia's salary would be paid out of this.

Leonard and Anthony returned to his house. The drank some water and sat in the kitchen.

"What do you think, my friend?"

"Cosy," replied Leonard.

"Ok if you give me the money, the old Greek said I can let it to you.''

"Sophia will look after the place for you," said Anthony.

Leonard smiled. Anthony gave him a box of Greek cigarettes. He lit the cigarette and inhaled the smoke into his lungs.

"Just what I'm looking for. How much?" said Leonard, looking up at Anthony who was peering out of a window.

"Twenty dollars a month."

"It's a good deal.'' Said Leonard taking out his wallet and handing Anthony the money.

"Any commission" said Anthony smiling. Leonard smiled and handed him another five dollars.

"Thanks boss."

"Why is it so cheap?" asked Leonard, rather puzzled.

"Do you want to know the truth?" said Anthony, looking at him with a mysterious smile. "Some say this place is haunted by spirits," replied Anthony laughing.

"Spirits!" said Leonard, looking a little concerned and drawing on his cigarette before releasing a fog of smoke.

"Spirits of the past", said Anthony. "This is an ancient place. The Turks and Venetians occupied here. There is nothing to worry about, they are friendly spirits," said Anthony, looking at a golden icon of Jesus above the front door.

"That icon is a sign that this place, was blessed by a priest. It needs to be blessed again."

"We don't bless our houses in Canada," said Leonard.

"So that's why the locals don't stay here," said Leonard opening his case and taking out his typewriter and placing it on an old table.

"I believe in spirits, so long as they are friendly," said Leonard, checking his typewriter keys.

"Why do you need a typewriter?" said Anthony.

"I'm trying to write a novel - my first," replied Leonard, sitting at the table. "It's called Beautiful Losers." As he finished his sentence, the lights went out. The room was plunged into darkness. Anthony tried the light switch. Leonard opened the timber shutters, and shafts of light streamed through the window."

"I'm afraid there is no current. We can try the lamp, until it comes on again…if I can find it" Anthony looked in the kitchen and found a brass oil lamp that Leonard helped him light with matches he used for his cigarettes. Then Leonard gave him some money and Anthony went and bought him some food in the local store.

He returned with; milk, olive oil, cheese, bread, tea, coffee, spaghetti, aubergines, minced meat and tomatoes. Anthony lit the cooker and before long a flame appeared and the wood crackled. Leonard smelled the wood burning. Anthony found a Chinese wok, among all the kitchen utensils hanging on the wall among the pots and pans. They glistened in the evening light. Anthony chopped up the tomatoes, aubergines and minced meat. He poured some olive oil into the hot wok. It sizzled on the silvery surface, gold translucent, glistening in the light. He found another pot stirred the ingredients around in the vessel and within minutes along with the boiling water he dropped in some spaghetti. It began to cook and the spaghetti began to grow limp and swirl about in the bubbling hot water. Leonard watched Anthony's handy work. He knew he could call on him anytime as his chef, whenever he needed him.

"So, have you got a woman", questioned Leonard as Anthony stirred the spaghetti and added some salt.

"Yes, a wife named Christina and a daughter Emily. They are in England at the moment. You know women, you can't live with them and you can't live without them.

"Why?" said Leonard, drawing her fingers through her hair.

"Because I'm a dreamer like you. You know women rarely marry poets or artists. They are not providers or home makers. I'm not the marrying kind. I don't know why I bothered," said Anthony.

"Poetry is the highest form of art," said Leonard, blowing out some smoke and sitting down on a chair.

"How many starving artists has the world seen and ignored?" said Anthony.

"The pursuit of truth and beauty is a noble profession," replied Leonard.

"Leonard, the world is becoming more cynical. Men don't search for the truth, but for money."

"This is the sixties and there is a new way of thinking. The poet is a new radical. Ginsberg, Corso, and Burroughs, changed the world, and the way we think" said Leonard with certain assurance.

"I want to write great books and poems like them."

"A noble ambition. But is the world listening?" said Anthony smiling.

***

Anthony took out a tattered notebook that looked as if it had seen better days.

"I write poems too," said Anthony.

"Can you remember one" said Leonard.

Anthony though for a moment and stopped stirring the pot and looked up to the ceiling in thought.

> *"It's called - For All of Us."*
> *Lord I pray,*
> *Forgive my fear, that fear of vanity, and vanity itself,*
> *Not to be afraid of what is you will,*
> *In joy and in sorrow',*
> *And please Lord,*
> *Preserve me from self-pity and bow,*
> *And violin strings before the mirror,*
> *Not to jump blindly over the clift,*
> *Or too far lead astray,*
> *Even pigs with hairy snouts,*
> *Protest against the use of pearls,*
> *Politically they are right,*
> *Your prodigal son was tamed by them.'*
> *And will always come back to you."*

Leonard thought to himself for a moment. Anthony searched in his eyes.

"That bloody good" you have talent, I love your lines...the violin and the prodigal son. It's kinda close to the symbolism I use." said Leonard.

They ate the spaghetti, then Leonard gave some money to Anthony to find a mattress, blankets and some sheets. Anthony told him that he knew a woman that sold them. An hour later he returned with a mattress tied to his donkeys back. He also had brought blankets and sheets that looked like they had been starched.

***

That night when Anthony left him alone. He knew that he was lucky to meet Anthony. He was a man that certainly knew the lay of the land and how things really operated on the island. He knew many of its artistic and bohemian residents, poor or rich it did not matter to him. Anthony would be a good friend in his new adventure. The flickering lamp lit up Leonard's face, and he wrote in his diary.

> *'Would it be possible that life would offer me someone that could fill my loneliness? I need a soulmate and someone to connect with. Someone who understands me, and who believes in his poetry and its meaning; someone who believes that poetry can move mountains and can see the value in this, instead of the pursuit of money and material things. It is the ethereal things that I am in search of. The meaning I seek is to be found in the great poets I admire like Byron, Shelley, Yeats and Lorca. They had sought out this meaning, and found something important, and something valuable in the human spirit. Maybe Anthony was right, women never marry poets. It was an impossible dream, of a desire that we can never*

complete, it would all end in unrequited love. I am in search of something. I have to find love and the meaning in my writing and in life. Yeats, the Irish poet, I remember said: 'Things fall apart the centre cannot hold, and all around us the ceremony of innocence is drowned!' Sometimes I feel like a drowning man, and no one could save me but myself."

***

Chapter 10
The Count and Countess

The following evening Leonard woke from his siesta. His eyes focused on a bunch of grapes, large blue, purple, and magenta, surrounded by leaves. Anthony's eyes peered behind them.

"I brought you grapes," said Anthony, handing him some. Leonard ran his hands over his eyes.

"How is my wandering poet!" said Anthony.

Leonard sat up in bed, ate some grapes then lit up a cigarette.

"The Jew's have been wandering for generations, especially after the war. That is the ones that survived!"

"Those miserable Nazis gave you such a hard time,"said Anthony.

"It is not so long ago that we had the war; the world is still healing," replied Leonard.

Anthony headed for the kitchen. Leonard got up and put his robe on and followed him. Anthony pulled out a drawer and found a knife to cut a block of feta cheese.

"So, what other artists and writers are living on the island?" asked Leonard, pouring a glass of wine and eating some cheese.

"There is the American artist here called, Timothy Hennessy. He is married to a Venetian countess. He lives in one of the biggest villas on the island. Some say he is a count too.

"I will bring you there, if you want."

"There are also many just passing through heading for India and Kathmandu."

They are searching, just like you, for some space in their head." said Anthony.

"Beautiful losers," replied Leonard.

Anthony handed him a plate of cheese and freshly baked bread.

"It's great cheese. It's made from sheep's milk. The Greeks have been making this cheese since the time of Homer," replied Anthony.

Anthony told him that he was also a painter and invited him to his studio. They talked late about art. Anthony loved the impressionists like Monet, Van Gogh, Gauguin and the kind of realism where the image was paramount. Leonard agreed, he had similar aesthetic tastes. Anthony did concede that the human condition was drawn to the sublime and the beautiful. He was like Anthony, not a big fan of modernism or abstraction. Anthony loved Francis Bacons paintings. He was an old friend from the Colony Room in Soho. Leonard told him that he had been there and met Muriel. Anthony told him that he missed that place.

Anthony slept on the floor that night on an old rug that Leonard found in a cupboard. Anthony told him that he had slept on the beach many times when he had drunk too much, so a floor with a rug was a luxury for him.

***

Leonard walked to the harbour with Anthony to the port the following morning, to go and see his art studio. The port was calm and the boats that floated on a beautiful blue surface as smooth as glass. It was a tranquil scene. The light from the morning sun was like liquid gold that illuminated the shop fronts and the church tower beyond. In Katsikas Café Leonard took a seat and ordered a coffee and lit up a cigarette. Anthony looked over at a church tower.

"It's the Cathedral of the Assumption of the Virgin Mary," said Anthony, taking a seat.

"It's a monastery and only used for mass, but not marriages."

"Well, I don't intend getting married any time soon," said Leonard, as his coffee's were served.

***

In one of the back streets Leonard climbed a narrow stair to Anthony's studio. It was a small room with a bed a chair and a small kitchen. Not unlike what Van Gogh would have lived in he thought. He climbed another steep stair to Anthony's studio. Leonard stood before a large painting of a beautiful woman. Anthony admitted to him that he was infamous on the island, for getting advance payments for a portrait but never completing them. Most of the time he gambled or drank the money, or lost it in a poker game.

Leonard observed of the young woman sitting on an easel. She lay on a Turkish rug with cushions, and looked like an image from an oriental picture in a harem.

"This is a painting that I'm doing for Marianne."

Leonard admired her features. He observed the perfect symmetry of her lips, and her light blue eyes. She had beautifully arched high brows and blonde streaks of hair, that floated on her shoulders. There was a dignity and a perfection about her, that had echoes of a Renaissance painting.

"Does she live here?"

"Yes, she is from Norway. She is an aspiring actress. She is married to a writer."

"There is a mysteriousness about her," said Leonard looking at her eyes.

"I'll introduce you someday. She is not here in the port so often and her son takes up a lot of her time. She lives at the other side of Hydra town."

***

Anthony showed him his albums of black and white photos of his life on Hydra over the years. He had worked on the set of a movie called 'Boy on a Dolphin'. It was a film shot a few years before, in 1957, starring Alan Ladd and Sophia Loren. Anthony explained that this was a film about sponge divers, who discovered a sunken ship filled with ancient Greek bronze and gold objects. The divers discovered an ancient statue of a boy on a dolphin. Anthony informed him that there used to be an ancient Greek sport, where boys would put a harness on a dolphin and race each other. He told him that there were frescoes found at the temple of Delphi, that illustrated images of this lost sport.

Anthony spoke warmly about meeting with Sophia Loren and Alan Ladd. He told him about Alan's early and tragic life. Alan had told him about how his mother committed suicide by taking arsenic, after some relationship breakup. Ladd's mother, who was staying with him following the breakup of a relationship, asked Alan for some money to buy food at a local store. She purchased some arsenic-based rat poison, from a grocer and committed suicide by drinking it in the back seat of Alans car.

"What a way to go. She was way too young to die." said Leonard.

"Tragedy is a part of life, my friend," said Anthony, flicking through the photos.

"Yes, so true, no one gets out of here alive," said Anthony as he flicked through the black and white photos. A man with a large frame and shocking blond hair appeared in one of the photos. "That's Tim Hennessy, the artist I told you about. Do you want to meet him?"

"Sure" replied Leonard.

"He's an unusual man. He does not live in the real world."

***

Later that day Leonard mounted Anthony's donkey again. He felt more confident this time. Perhaps the donkey had gotten used to him. Anthony guided his donkey up the back street towards Hennessy's villa, that was perched on a hill, that ran along the right side of the harbour. Anthony pointed out the villa. It was the only one with archways. A villa that was certainly built by a Venetian merchant. Leonard looked up and he could see it shining in the early morning sun.

It did not take too long to reach it. It was imposing, with high walls at least twelve feet high that supported a patio above it. Above this Leonard could see arches, that were an imposing structure all on their own. It had light blue painted shutters. Anthony tied up the mule and located a bell hiding behind some leaves. On a brass plate Leonard observed the name 'Count Hennessy' in English and in Greek beneath a letter box. Beside the letter box there was a set of ten steps that were about a metre wide, that led up to a patio. The steps were cut into the patio's supporting walls, and looked like the entrance to an Egyptian pyramid. Over the patio peered a man with a great head of blond hair. It was Timothy.

"Oh, Anthony, come on in," said Hennessy, beaming a big smile. Anthony hurried up the steps, followed by Leonard. They entered the patio with the flagstones painted in white and blue. Standing before him was Hennessy, with broad shoulders and a great smile that was infectious. He had a dignified face with a short and neat curved nose like W.B Yeats. He wore a blue cravat covered in flower patterns, a pink shirt with gold cufflinks and ochre pants made from linen.

"Timothy, let me introduce you to Leonard," said Anthony. Leonard shook his hand. "Pleased to meet you."

"Come inside and have a drink."

They crossed the patio and climbed another set of steps to a balcony with three arches. Leonard observed the walls covered in gold icons and ancient paintings of Venetian boats. It was filled with Louis 16th furniture. It had a magical atmosphere. On the left wall hung a large tapestry, that depicted knights on horseback. In a white tent stood a beautiful maiden wearing a long white veil. Around her neck he could see a necklace of green pearls. Her body was covered in lace. It was scene illustrating the age of chivalry.

Leonard sat down on a large couch covered in purple linen which was decorated with French Fleur-de-lis. Anthony sat in a large armchair that had two carved lions, attached to oak arms. Hennessy sat back on a large chaise longue like Napoleon in an Ingres painting.

"Would you like some wine?" said Timothy pouring a glass of wine for them both, into the finest glasses that were covered in extraordinary patterns.

"It's Murano glass from Venice,'' said Timothy.

Hennessy was in high spirits. He had charm was very literate and talked more like a European, with Italian and French phrases. Leonard observed his features and could see his bright blue eyes, some flecks of grey in his blonde hair, and smooth pink skin, and straight white teeth that had seen the best dentists.

"Do you like my villa? I have another one in Venice. It is a pink palace with forty rooms. I am from St Louis Missouri, but it is too ugly and modern for me to live there. That's the problem for us Americans we have no history.''

Hennessey pointed to a large silk banner waving in the breeze, hanging from the roofs rafters.

"This is one of my designs, printed on silk in a factory in Lyon in France. It's neo-romantic, medieval, oriental, Byzantine, Moorish, Venetian, Zen Buddhist. It is a mixture of many influences.''

"How did come to live on Hydra? asked Leonard.

"Ghika the painter invited me to stay in his villa.''

"I have an introduction to Ghika. From his future wife Barbara.''

"Yes, I know her. Ghika has a Greek wife. I don't think she will be happy with his decision to divorce him. Greek women are very loyal, but if you reject them, they can explode, like a volcano," said Hennessy smiling.

Hennessey looks around his large room filled with antiques. Then he spoke to them in a long monologue, as if he wanted to explain his decision to become an artist.

"I did not want to be a doctor or an accountant. I thought that been an artist was more important, to bring beauty into the world, and not to make money. I was one of the lucky ones. I was born into money. So, I could pursue beauty not money. My family-owned steamboats and railroad's, and were richer than the Vanderbilt's in St Louis. I could live my dream. I was brought up in a house, with six servants. My aunt wanted me to be a banker, but when I went to her offices, and saw Egyptian column's with gold leaf and the smell of money, it made me sick."

"You were a lucky man," said Leonard.

"It was not all a bed of roses. My brother died in a Japanese concentration camp. I was thrown out of Harvard for partying too much. I got shot in the battle of Iwo Jima. It was my own fault, I was reading Shakespeare in the trenches. I realized at an early age was that it was not necessary to learn anything. Only art, poetry and Buddhism interested me. I dreamt I would marry a sea king's daughter, and I did. I am married a Venetian countess who is the daughter of the Doge of Venice."

"How is she?" asked Anthony.

"She is well. She will join us later. Are you staying for dinner?"

"Yes, I would love to." said Leonard, who was observing the other antiques in the room. They were bathed now in the golden light that shone through the windows as evening approached. Leonard could see Ming vases, dragon-inlaid brass cauldrons, Dutch porcelain; and a myriad of objects that Leonard could not comprehend where they were from.

"I brought them all from my villa in Venice," said Timothy.

"Peggy Guggenheim gave me the tapestry as a present."
"Has she still got the museum in Venice?" said Anthony in an inquisitive voice.
"I'm working on a show for Peggy. She should be here in the coming weeks.
She just loves modernism, but it's not exactly for me."
"What do you mean?" asked Leonard, drinking his wine.
"I like the old and the new. I love classicism and modernism," said Timothy.
"Is it true that Peggy has a lot of husbands?" asked Anthony. Timothy smiled in response. His blond hair shone, as he turned his head.
"She has had many affairs," said Timothy.
"But she loved my work, so I cannot talk badly about her."
"I used to share a studio with Andy Warhol. I gave him the idea for the soup cans." Leonard and Anthony laughed.
"It's such a terrible idea," replied Leonard.
"I know, but that painting is more famous now than the Mona Lisa.
"Where are you from, Leonard?" asked Timothy.
"Montreal."
"My ancestors are from Ireland?"
"I'm Jewish."
"We have something in common. The Irish and the Jews were victims of history," replied Hennessy.
"That is certainly true. The Jews have been escaping across the Mediterranean for centuries," said Leonard.
Leonard looked at an abstract painting of a mandala hanging on the wall.
"Did you paint it?'' said Leonard.
"Yes It's a mandala…a meditation," said Timothy.
"Eastern Buddhist," replied Leonard.

"Yes, we are part of the west...but we want something of the East. Hydra is a meeting of two worlds. Western civilisation is important, but we must learn to embrace something from eastern philosophy, too", replied Timothy.

Leonard's eyes wandered to another tapestry on the wall.

"It's a Fortunay," said Hennessy, sipping his glass of wine. "He was a Spanish fashion designer. He lived in Venice, where I met my lovely wife, the Countess Adriana. He was an amazing designer and also a beautiful painter. See that portrait over there? That was a picture he painted of his wife, Henriette."

Leonard observed a painting of a woman that had intense eyes, as if in a thought. She looked somewhat like a Botticelli painting. She wore a blue glass bead necklace and a dress of gold and green patterns. Her hair was flowing in waves that parted in the middle. The background was painted in cobalt blue. Leonard felt that it was a thing of beauty, and Timothy was the first man he met in his life that contemplated such beauty.

***

Chapter 11
The Doors of Perception

Leonard and Anthony followed Timothy through a doorway. They entered an arched patio filled with paintings. A shaft of light streamed through the window and cast a golden lattice across the paintings. They heard light footsteps on the Venetian mosaic tiles. From the corners of his eye Leonard could see an elegant woman wearing a long flowing dress down to her ankles that was covered in pleats. She had a noble face that was well proportioned, with a perfectly formed nose. She had a beautifully rounded chin and a jawbone, that looked like her porcelain skin had been stretched like silk over her cheekbones.

"Adriana, how are you?" said Timothy setting his eyes or her as if had seen an angel. She returned an elegant smile, that was graceful and dignified. She was poised there as if suspended like a bird standing on one leg.

"This is my wife, the Countess Marcello." The Countess smiled at Leonard, and her beautiful eyes rested on his.

"Pleased to meet you Leonard," said the countess quite formally.

"We will be having dinner at six, you both must stay. How are you Anthony?"

"Very well," replied Anthony.

"How is Christina and Emily?"

"She is fine."

"She is such a sweet girl."

"Yes, I miss her, she is in London with her mother Christina."

The countess vanished as soon as she appeared. There was a formality about her that Leonard sensed belonged to her aristocratic background. They sat on the patio chair and watched the sun set. Hennessy continued to tell them about his past. He told them that he had inherited millions of dollars upon the death of his rich aunt in St Louis. After the war he had toured Europe, to see Paris, Rome, Milan and Venice. He created collages from photographs of his grand tour. He told him that he felt like a character in a Henry James novel. His dream was to marry into and aristocratic society. It was the ultimate fantasy for the American rich like Nancy Langhorne who married Waldorf Astor, 2nd Viscount; and Grace Kelly had followed that same route by marrying Prince Rainer.

"We Americans have everything except royalty," said Timothy, casting his eyes on a painting of Marie Antoinette framed in gold.

"Does that make you a count?" said Leonard, with a smile.

"Yes, by marriage." I can use the title, if I want," said Timothy.

"Do you like my mandalas," said Timothy.

"Yes, I love Indian mandalas, the Buddhist ones."

"I like Zen, Japanese Buddhism, I want to be a monk someday," said Leonard.

"My friend Ioannis can teach you how to meditate."

"Oh, yes, Ioannis, I remember him," said Anthony, drinking another glass of wine.

"He's here for a few days. Come upstairs and meet him," said Timothy as he opened a small doorway to a hidden stairway. On its walls was attached a brass rings, with a rope that acted like a rail. They grabbed on to it, and they climbed up the steep stone stairs. They entered a room that had a ceiling that was curved inwards at four points like a dome. The walls were covered in gold paintings of Greek icons of a Madonna and a child, that were the largest that Leonard had ever seen. They rooms looked more like it was part of a church than a Greek villa. In the corner was a shrine made of brass that held at least twenty candles. Leonard smelt the scent of burning candles.

He turned on his heals as he heard the sound of steps behind him. Standing in front of him was a man dressed in a black robe.

His face was bearded and he had deep penetrating eyes. He had a long ponytail, held with a red ribbon. Leonard thought that he was the image of Jesus. On his head he wore a cap that looked like a Turkish fez, that was black with a gold tassel hanging from its central point at the top. He had a small mouth that peered through his beard, exposing perfect white teeth. "Ioannis," said Hennessy, from across the room.

"We are looking for you. You know Anthony, this is his friend, Leonard. He is interested to how to how meditate. Can you show him?"

"Ionannis looks Greek but he is in fact German."

"That is true, I discovered Buddhism by reading the German writer Hermann Hesse. His book Siddhartha explores the spiritual journey of self-discovery, of a man named Siddhartha during the time of the Gautama Buddha, in India hundreds of years ago. That is how I discovered Buddhism. Hesse wanted the western world to discover it."

"Of course," replied Ioannis in a deep Greek accent, that had a German tone to it.

"We must sit cross-legged first," said Ioannis sitting down on the large red Turkish rug that covered most of the floor area. Leonard, Timothy and Anthony followed his example. They sat opposite each other, with legs crossed in a square formation, known as the lotus position. Ioannis closed his eyes and placed his hand on his knees. He folded his fingers in a certain way and they all tried to copy this. Then Ioannis spoke.

"There is peace in a oneness with the universe; to have no desires for money or property, just to live in the moment. Hydra is the gateway to the east, everyone passes through here. We are all on the same journey," said Ioannis.

."I would love to be a monk someday," replied Leonard.

"We all have very sublime religious aspirations. But the search is not an easy one.

We must have no desire and no ego, that is the path we have to take."

"That is the secret of Buddhism." Then, Ioannis closed his eyes once again and began to meditate. Leonard could hear the slow hum of words rising across the room until they filled it. Leonard began to meditate. It seemed as if this removed his thoughts for a moment in time. It blacked out his memory, and this world of no desires for the first time seemed a possibility.

"To have no desires is the secret of living," said Ioannis. Then they all slipped into a deep meditation that went on for a long time.

***

Later they sat on the terrace at six and observed the view of the sun setting. Hennessy poured some wine. The countess Adriana appeared on the upper terrace. She was dressed in a long chain of white pearls and an elegant Fortunay dress, with hundreds of pleats. The Countess approached them and extended her hand.

"I am delighted you stayed for dinner," said the Countess taking a seat.

The dinner table was covered with a white linen lace tablecloth. It was laid for dinner by a Greek cook named Costas, who wore a white apron and a waistcoat with brass buttons. He was of mature years and had a large round belly that protruded. He also had a moustache that was short and neat. He wore neat round glasses. He had laid the table with beautiful Greek plates illustrated with Dutch windmills and churches. Beside each plate, was laid a knife, fork, soup spoon and dessert spoon. Beyond each plate were two glasses. One was for the wine and the other for water. The drinks glasses were exquisite and Leonard admired them. In the centre were two silver candlesticks with candles, that Costas had lit and were placed in the centre of the table. There were butter trays that were made of the finest silver. There were also silver bowls filled with grapes, oranges and nuts.

Timothy began by saying a prayer. Then Costas served an aperitif in small glasses filled with mint and ouzo. The countess turned to Leonard and spoke in a sweet Italian accent.
"Did you enjoy the meditation," said Timothy.
"I would love to come here and mediate again."
"You are always welcome here. So, what brings you to Hydra?"
"I wanted to get away from Montreal to write a novel."
"What are you writing about, Leonard?" enquired the Countess.
"It's a book about people in search of something, something meaningful, something pure, something beautiful."
"Like Oscar Wilde, your profession is genius," said the Countess smiling.
"I write poetry and novels."
"Hydra is a place for dreamers like us," said the Countess.
"One can lose oneself on Hydra. Hydra is an Arcadian world – there is so much beauty to be seen here, and you will find peace here too," replied the Countess.
"What exactly was Arcadia," said Anthony, looking at his first course of sliced melon.
"It's a Greek province…a place of harmony with nature. It belonged to the golden age of Greece," replied Leonard.
"I think you studied the Greek classics, Leonard."
"Yes, I learnt all about it at university."
Leonard began to eat some melon as well. Its taste was refreshing.
"In college I read that the poet Virgil wrote a poem about Arcadia," said Leonard.
"Do you know any Virgil,"said the Countess.
Leonard though for a while and began to recite.

"Amor vincit omnia, et nos cedamus amori. Translated it means. Love conquers all things, so we too shall yield to love. It's from Virgil's, Eclogues.''

"Bravo Leonard, you are a scholar,'' said Timothy smiling at him.

Leonard looked out of the corner of his eye and saw Ioannis. When he looked again, he had disappeared.

"Ioannis is like a ghost. He appears in many places. Light can play tricks with your eyes on this island, so be careful," said Timothy looking at him.

"Why?" said Leonard.

"Because it is quite easy to fall over a cliff here on a sunlit day, or at night. The shadows play tricks here - as the light changes," replied Hennessy, slicing his melon with a silver knife.

"So, tell us about Warhol? said Anthony, who was beginning his second course of chicken soup made with herbs."

"So, tell us about Warhol," repeated Anthony while looking at Hennessy.

"Oh yes, well I shared this studio with him. I could see he was struggling to come up with ideas. So, one day I was joking with him after lunch, when I saw a soup can on the table. I said to Andy why don't you paint the soup can, and he did. The rest is history. He made millions from that soup can, and changed the face of modernism. It is all such rubbish this modernism, and then the critics row in and said he was revolutionary. Andy was just interested in one thing it was the American dollar. He had no real talent; he invaded our art galleries with his rubbish. Now look at what they are showing - blank canvases and selling them for millions," said Hennessy with disgust.

"Nothing of substance or beauty," said Leonard somewhat surprised by Timothy's outburst.

"It's the emperor's new clothes," replied Hennessy.

"Indeed,'" said Leonard.

"Modernism, is such a fraud and such a disaster for the human race. They do not contemplate beauty anymore, but ugliness."

"Now I must ask that you all be silent, as we always watch the sunset at this time," said the Countess.

They all looked across the bay and saw a great golden disc descend into the sea. A golden light passed across the water. They watched the great orb of a majestic sun descending. Leonard's eyes were fixed on the liquid golden disc, that seemed to be like a halo with a glowing molten rim that vibrated. All of their faces were illuminated by this golden light, filling their bodies with its warmth. The golden disc began to melt into the deep blue sea that welcomed the golden light into its embrace. It was a magical moment. For a moment Leonard felt that he was suspended in time.

***

Chapter 12
My Angel Marianne

One morning Leonard was greeted by the sight of the blonde woman at Katsikas cafe. She was talking to a Greek woman. She looked like an angel. She was wearing a blue dress that came down to her knees, and sandals. She wore a white blouse with a lace trim, and a straw hat, that cast a deep shadow across her face. Then her face appeared. Then he realised that he had seen her face before, in Anthony painting. It was Marianne the Norwegian woman. He approached her with a sense of nervousness, that he had never experienced before.

"Hello, I have seen you before.?" said Leonard.
"Where?'" replied Marianne.
"Anthony's portrait of you."
"Oh, dear Anthony, I am waiting for him to finish it, but he never does."
"Would you like to join me for a coffee?" Leonard could see tears in her eyes. Marianne took a seat.
"You have tears in your eyes, what's wrong?'' said Leonard ordering two coffees from the waiter.
"It's my husband you see; we have been having arguments. I discovered this morning that he has been sleeping with another woman, and he wants to leave me."
"Infidelity can destroy everything. The price of love can be high,'' said Leonard.
"Love is like a pane of glass. It can break very easily into little pieces. The mirror has broken!" said Marianne.
"We escaped here with me from Norway, from the freezing winters. I have tried to save this relationship so many times. This is the straw that broke the camel's back. We have a son; he has betrayed both of us."
"Where is he now?"

"I have a Greek woman looking for him called Maria."

"...and your husband?"

"He is leaving Hydra with his new woman, on his boat soon. Our relationship meant nothing to him in the end."

"What are you going to do?" said Leonard lighting up a cigarette.

"I don't know. I will waive him goodbye. Part of me still loves him, and another part hates him! Why are you here?"

"I am writing a novel."

"He is a writer like you. He is a free spirit. He thinks that he can love every woman, but love does not work that way."

"What did you do before you became a mother?"

"I wanted to be an actress, but my parents did not approve. Then I married this crazy writer."

"How deep is your love that is the question? How far do you want your love to grow beneath the surface? How does your love touch another heart and soul?" said Leonard lighting up his cigarette.

"You have very deep thought's, I forgot to ask you. What is your name?'"

"Leonard… Leonard Cohen."

"I want to read some of your work."

"Yes, sure.''

"My baby sitter will be here soon."

A few minutes later Maria arrived with a beautiful boy Axel Junior. He had fair hair and Nordic features like his mother.

"This is Maria, she is from the island." said Marianne as he greeted Maria and Axel Junior. She kissed him on the forehead. Maria had long dark hair, and wore a blue dress covered in tulip flowers.

"How has Axel Junior been?" said Marianne.

"He has been a good boy," said Marianne caressing Axel's hair.

"Let's go to the beach, tomorrow" said Marianne, now looking calmer than she had been earlier. She told Leonard about the beach called Kamini and invited him.

***

They met the following day at the harbour, where they found boats that were covered in canopies. The hired one and the boatman guided it out along the calm blue waters, and out past the harbour wall, that sheltered the entrance on both sides. The engine chugged away as Leonard engaged in conversation with Marianne. It was a pleasant experience for him, even thought that he began to realize that her situation had many complications. She was married and in a broken relationship, that now for him could require many challenges. For the moment he did not want to consider the reality of the situation.

The boat reached the beach and they disembarked. Leonard felt the warm sand beneath his feet. It was a beautiful place. There were only a handful of people there. At the edge of the beach there was a young Greek selling coffee and ice cream. It was the kind the Italians made called gelato. There were many flavours like vanilla, chocolate, hazelnut, pistachio, raspberry, apple and lemon. They bought some, and lay on large white towels on the sand, that Marianne and Maria had taken in their baskets. Leonard rented a large umbrella to block the sun. A Greek boy assisted him. Marianne engaged Leonard in conversation while Axel played at the water's edge with Maria.

She spoke of her unhappiness and her disillusionment with her husband and here discovery of his infidelity. It was a terrible blow to her, and for the moment she could see the only way forward was to get a divorce. Marianne told him that she sensed something was wrong months ago. She could not put her finger on it, but she had a woman's intuition. It had brought her a kind of emotional chaos. Leonard decided not to be selfish and suggested to her to consider a reconciliation with Axel.

Leonard took out a book by the English poet Shelley from his bag. He told Marianne that he was an English poet, that had died from drowning in Lerici in Italy. In the book on Shelley there was a picture of the burning of his body on the beach there. It was one of the most extraordinary iconic paintings that he had ever seen. Beneath was the name of the artist by Louis Fourier, and the date 1889. Shelly was a close friend of John Keats and Lord Byron. Leonard read a poem to Marianne that Shelly wrote called; Loves Philosophy.

> *'The mountains mingle with the river, and the rivers with the sea. The winds of heaven mix forever with a sweet emotion. Nothing in the world is single. All things by a law divine in one spirit meet and mingle. Why not I with thine? See the mountains kiss high heaven, and the waves clasp one another. No sister flower would be forgiven if it disdained its brother. And the sunlight clasps the earth and the moonbeams kissed the sea. What is all this sweet work if thou not kiss me.'*

''It's beautiful Leonard.'' Marianne told him that he thought they were all victims of the sixties. The new area of free love and that everyone though had infinite possibilities. But all that was a cost to marriages and children. For Marianne, Leonard felt that her 'ceremony of innocence had fallen apart'.

Marianne told Leonard later how Axel had started sleeping with this woman called Patricia, not long after she had given birth. It was a total betrayal for her. She had seen this American woman on the harbour, and in Katsikas cafe talking to Axel. She thought it was all quite innocent at first. She discovered that she rented a room on the island. Then she realised that the romantic dream with Axel was over. Axel had found another muse who seemed to indulge in the same new age ideas. Axel told her about the relationships. It was a meeting of minds. He told her that she and Axel were now reading the Popul Vuh, a book about the Mayan Indians from central America. The book was about their rituals and a new state of consciousness. Marianne told Leonard about the sacred mushrooms that Axel had taken, and the potions made from the peyote cactus, that gave him hallucinations.

"I've heard that it's like LSD. You start seeing visions when you are on it," said Leonard. "There is a guy called Castaneda writing about it. He went into the desert with a Yaqui Indian shaman. The peyote drug is a gateway to another world. This drug is sacred to the Mexican Indians. You know they claim in a moment of twilight; a crack will appear in the universe - between night and dark another reality will be seen," replied Leonard.

"Yes, that right, he's into that stuff. Axel wants to explore this other reality with Patricia," said Marianne.

***

Leonard could see he was now observing the emotional disintegration of a marriage. Could he stay the course and would Marianne allow him to? He was attracted to her. She was an enchanting and beautiful and sweet. It was all that he had dreamed about in a woman. He was willing to engage in this attraction, but he knew it would be a difficult quest. The question was what would the price be for him?

Little Axel and Maria returned from the water's edge and they returned to the harbour as the sun was setting. They arrived at the harbour later that evening. Dancers with Greek costumes performed with bouzouki player. They watched in wonder, as if ancient Greece had come to life, and they arranged to meet again.

***

The following day Leonard sat with Antony in Katsikas. They were relaxing and watching the world go by. Leonard saw a dark-haired woman in a long dress covered in flowers walk by.

Leonard could see her intense eyes. Then she took a kitchen knife out of her bag, that flashed in the sun light. She approached a man who looked Greek, and plunged the knife into his belly. Then with the skill of a butcher or Sweeney Tod, she sliced the knife upwards towards his right nipple. The man let out a scream like an animal trapped in an abattoir. Then she ran away. The blood spurted and flowed. Leonard grabbed his white starched table cloth, and the cups and saucers fell towards the ground. He hurried towards the man followed by Anthony, and placed the cloth over his gaping wound. His gut and his intestines emerged from the gaping wound. It was a horrific sight. Nick the owner appeared.

"I'll call the hospital…Jesus Christ - Greek women are so dangerous,"said Leonard consoling the man.

"Who is she?" he said.

The man mumbled some words.

"I got her pregnant in Thessaloniki…and I left her. She never forgave … me! She has hunted me down."

With these words, the man passed out. Leonard held back the blood that was streaming down his stomach and legs. Minutes later a doctor appeared, and two men with a stretcher. They lifted him on it and hurried across the harbour, followed by the doctor. Leonard looked down at his shirt, it was covered in blood.

"I'll give you one of mine," said Nico hurrying inside.

"Heaven hath no fury like a woman scorned. Never cross a Greek woman. Remember what Hennessy said about Ghikas wife," said Anthony.'

"You right about that," said Leonard, sitting back on his seat. He was sweating heavily and in shock.

Chapter 13
Icarus and the Hermit

Leonard told Marianne about the incident the following day. She was shocked and surprised. They agreed that a woman that sough revenge, was a terrible thing. She did not want revenge on Alex. Marianne told Leonard that she had arranged to meet her husband Axel and Patricia in the restaurant later that day, called the 'The Garden of Delights'. They arrived their early and waited for them.

She told him about Axel, and how he has been to the Sahara and wrote a book about it called, 'Icarus – A Young Man in Sahara'. Leonard could see a tall blonde haired young man walking towards them. He had piercing blue eyes and high cheekbones. He looked like a Viking warrior. It was Axel, he was a handsome man Leonard thought, with beautiful classical features. Patricia was with him.

Marianne introduced them. "Meet my husband, Axel and Patricia his new woman," said Marianne, in a condescending way.

"Pleased to meet you," said Leonard. Patricia was a beautiful woman with long dark hair. Leonard greeted Axel and sat opposite him. Axel and Patricia exchanged greetings. She greeted Leonard and Marianne warmly, without any shame, even though she had stolen Marianne's husband. She told them she was a painter from Illinois, and she was into south American mythology. They talked about the Popol Vuh, and the Mayan prophecy.

"I have heard of it. It's something to do with the end of the Mayan calendar." replied Leonard.

"That is right, it comes to an end in 2012," replied Patricia.

"They say that the world will undergo a spiritual transformation," said Axel.

"Or the end of the world," said Marianne sadly.

"Let's not worry too much about that. It's over fifty years from now," said Leonard, laughing and lightening up a cigarette.

"You are both into new age stuff," said Leonard, looking at Axel and Patricia.

Axel told them the story over drinks and how he came to write his book on his journey into the Sahara. He told him he had left Norway and fled Western civilization. He flew to Algiers. He threw away his clothes and bought a kaftan, a long robe with vertical red and white stripes. He bought it in the market from a Berber tribesman. It also had a hood that protected him from the sun and sand storms. He left his book and clothes at the Norwegian consulate in Algiers. He left the big city with its crowds and headed for the countryside. He got a lift from Arab smugglers and headed inland in their truck.

The landscape was one of sand and rocky outcrops. Everywhere there were palm trees. The Arabs that he was travelling with, had shaved heads, small goatee beards and deep tanned skin, and long Arabic noses. They talked in Arabic so Axel had not a clue what they were saying. The old truck sped along the road churning up the dust. At times they had to stop and clean the window with a wet rag. He arrived in the old French Colony of El-Menia, about seven hundred miles south of Algiers in the desert. There they stopped for the night. It was the gateway to the Sahara. They slept in rooms above a small inn.

In the morning he heard the Islamic call to prayer at dawn, and looked at the sun rising across the desert. While the Arabs were sleeping, he had breakfast and was told by an old man who spoke broken English, that the tomb of the Viscount, Charles Eugene Be Fousculd, was nearby. He told him that he was a French aristocrat who had become a Cistercian monk. He lived with the Berbers there in the 1900's. He published the first Tuareg tribe French dictionary. He lived as a hermit in a small stone hut, peacefully for fifteen years, until one day he was murdered. He was dragged from his stone hut by tribal leaders, who shot him in the head. It was witnessed by an Arab slave that had been liberated. Axel visited his tomb and contemplated his fate.

***

They continued onward deeper into the desert, and stopped for the night in the town of Godea. Axel told them that he slept in a small mud house on the second floor, on a Berber rug. There was only an oil lamp to illuminate his room. It was hot outside even at night, so he had to open the small window. A mosquito net covered his bed. Then the door opened suddenly. Axel could tell from the silhouette that it was one of the Arabs. He tried to rip his shirt off, and tried to rape him. Axel punched him in the face. He saw the blood on his fist and the Arab slumped to the floor. Axel jumped to his feet and grabbed his sandals and made a quick exit down the stairs. He grabbed some gourds of water with leather straps, and slung them over his shoulder. Within minutes he was on the edge of the village, and heading out along the road, as the dawn sun was emerging, into the desert.

His plan was to travel deep into the Sahara on a six-hundred-mile journey. He looked at the map to locate his destination; that was the town of Tamanrasset which was an oasis. It was known as a paradise in the desert, and a place where one could find; palm trees, citrus fruits, apricots, dates, almonds, cereal, corn, figs, and grapes. It was a welcome break for travellers between mostly stagnant waterholes. This was the main capital of the Tuareg tribes. Axel had a long journey ahead of him and it was fortunate that he met some Turaeg tribesmen on their camels, and they provided him with food and water, who guided him across the desert.

Axel continued his story. He told them that the Tuareg were called the blue people because their clothes were dyed with the dye indigo. This material left its mark on their skin. Their adopted religion was Islam which had spread across north Africa.

Leonard questioned Axel as to why he had undertaken this journey. Axel replied that it was for an infinity of existential reasons. He wanted to leave behind westerns civilization and shed himself of its preoccupations. That was his reasoning. It was about the search for the truth.

"We live in an era of despair and we are all searching for something," said Axel pouring some wine into his glass.

"Out there in the desert among the Tuareg – there are answers to the big questions of life and death. We are also in the search of a new era, and a new consciousness."

"Did you find anything in your quest?" said Leonard, lighting up another Greek cigarette.

"Yes, a new set of beliefs. I don't want to lead a normal life. It is not the way for me." replied Axel.

"Axel has been talking like this, ever since met him," said Marianne, smiling at Leonard as if trying indirectly to explain Axel's state of mind, and what she had to endure in her marriage. She had wanted a normal life, but it was clear that Axel could not provide it.

"Did you return then to the coast?" said Leonard.

"No, I went further into the desert and found the great sands that moved in cycles with the wind. I wanted to explore the primitive and the spiritual side of this new landscape and its people.

Axel told them that he bought a donkey and travelled into the desert to his final destination, to the town of Thaza in Morocco. He took the Arabic name of Mostafia and lived among the Tuareg nomads. He also took a Tuareg wife called Tehi, while he was still married to Marianne. Marianne laughed at this, saying he had made her his 'second wife'. "Muslims can have four wives," said Axel. Leonard could see how Patricia could become now his 'third wife'.

Axel went on to explain that he visited a French mystic in an old Moroccan villa. He taught me about a new way of thinking. "I found a new understanding in this desert place." Said Axel. "He introduced me to smoking hashish from the hookah. At my feet I saw the boundary of an empty space. I saw an endless world of a ravaged man like me. I could see that the universe was indeed infinite. I came close to the miraculous!"

"How did you feel?" asked Leonard.

"I felt fear and ecstasy in that moment!"

"When I stood in the desert my consciousness was flooded by something greater and more powerful than myself. There is an unbelievable universe out there."

"That was frightening for you?" said Marianne.

"I had a sense of rebirth and of returning to being the primitive man. Like returning to a place a hundred years behind, and into another reality," said Axel, rolling his eyes.

***

Although Leonard felt deeply attracted to Marianne, he could not bring himself to dislike Axel. In a sense Axel's failure with Marianne was his opportunity. Was there anything immoral about his love for Marianne, Leonard wondered? Was there anything unethical for a man to fall in love with another man's wife? He remembered the lines from the bible, 'Thou shall not covet thy neighbour's wife.' Axel had betrayed her feelings and had committed adultery, so the idea that he was intruding upon a marriage seemed absurd, it was falling apart anyway. Axel had pushed the boundaries and lived on the edge. He had crossed mountains and deserts, and had published a novel that Leonard felt was way beyond his own achievements. He has something to learn from Axel; that was about expanding his own consciousness and his own attempts to be a writer.

***

Axel, Patricia, Leonard and Marianne talked late into the night. A friend of Axel arrived; a woman named Olivia de Haulleville. She had dark penetrating eyes and long black hair. She told them that she practiced Buddhism, and her uncle was Aldous Huxley, who had written the book 'The Doors of Perception'. She explained that the book was about a psychedelic world uncovered under the influence of mescaline. Huxley had experienced, aesthetic and sacramental visions. He later published 'Heaven and Hell', an essay which expanded on his visions. The title was influenced by the English poet William Blake's book, 'The Marriage of Heaven and Hell' published in 1793.

Olivia told him that 'The Doors of Perception' provoked strong reactions for those exploring psychedelic drugs. It was a facilitator of mystical insight for the benefit of science, art, and religion. Many did not like the fact that this drug was seen to be taken over organised religion, especially in Europe and America. Mescaline was a psychedelic agent of the peyote from the San Pedro cacti; which have been used in Native American religious ceremonies for thousands of years. Olivia told them that a German pharmacologist, Arthur Heffter, isolated the alkaloids in the peyote cactus in 1897, after the 'doors of perception' expanded in the minds of Europeans and Americans. Native American took it to obtain visions, for it's prophecy healing and inner strength.

***

Leonard invited Axel to meet him at his house to show him his novel. Unexpectedly Axel turned up at his house a few days later. There they spoke about expanding their spiritual imagination. Axel took out a jar filled with a miniature cactus plants. He placed the cactus on the kitchen table, and began to chop it up into little pieces and crush it in a stone mortar and pestle from Leonard's kitchen.

"What is it," said Leonard curiously? "It is the peyote plant that I got in Morocco," said Axel. You can also find it in Mexico, but this Moroccan man had secretly imported it into Tangier. "Do you want to try some?"

"If you want to be a great writer it is one of the ways to unlock your imagination." Like a ritual he had been through many times Axel sprinkled the dust into a glass. Leonard observed as the particles vanished in the wine. Axel said.

"Try it, it's something you won't regret. It takes about thirty minutes to take effect." Leonard looked at the glass intently wondering if he would take this opportunity; this new doorway into his mind."

Leonard took the glass and gulped down the contents and lay on his bed. Their eyes met each other in a permanent gaze and slowly, and surely his mind drifted away into another world.

***

Like a mirage Leonard could see a beach appear on the horizon that stretched beside the sea. The waves pounded shore. On the beach Leonard could see a giant bonfire and he could hear the crackling of burning wood. He approached from a distance and observed the flames dancing towards the sky; orange, red, white and purple. It was burning with the intensity of lava from a volcano. On the beach there were four figures dressed in black. One was a woman with a black veil over her face. Beside her stood a carriage and a horseman. There was also a man holding the reins of the horse. It was an image that he imagined belonged to the nineteenth century. As he approached the figures, he could see a body lying in the flames. Then he remembered that he had seen this image before of the cremation of Shelly on the beach at Lerici in Italy in the book he had shown Marianne. The woman that stood near the carriage was his wife Mary Shelly author of the infamous novel Frankenstein, while the other figure was Lord Byron, the famous English poet.

Shelly's heart was not consumed by the flames. Mary Shelley, was given his heart to bury in a casket. Her dead husband had once written a poem, he remembered about death, that echoed through his mind like the voices of angels.

> *'Dust to the dust! but the pure spirit shall flow back to the burning fountain whence it came, A portion of the eternal. Mild is the slow necessity of death. The tranquil spirit fails beneath its grasp. Without a groan, almost without a fear. Resigned in peace to the necessity. Calm as a voyager to some distant land.'*

***

Leonard woke from his dream. He saw Axel peering over him concerned by his state of mind.
"Was it a good trip?" said Axel.
"Yes, it was, it is true the doors of perception were indeed awaiting me". said Leonard with a smile. He told Axel about the painting of the death of Shelley in his book of poems, and how it had become alive. He searched for the book of poetry and showed him the painting and Axel smiled.

***

Chapter 14
An Angel at My Table

While Axel met with Patricia, Leonard met Marianne, an extraordinary situation had developed. Leonard was in love with his angel Marianne and Axel with Patricia. Marianne told Leonard about her life in Norway. She was sent to her grandmother house in Larkollen, on the coast. She told him that his grandmother always played Grieg on the gramophone. She had grown up with his music and loved it. She read the poetry of Heine and Goethe. She told him that if they ever came across a piano in a restaurant, she would play it for him. Leonard wanted to learn the piano too, and she promised that she would teach him.

Marianne told him that her small room was covered with pictures of her parents and her school. She would sit for hours at her desk and read and write. She read the books about the great Kon Tiki expedition, organized by the Norwegian explorer Thor Heyerdahl. He had sailed a balsa raft from Peru to Polynesia, to prove that ancient Indians had inhabited the western Pacific islands. She loved Heyerdahl's book also about the island of Fatu Hiva, where he lived on with his future wife Alison, in a tropical paradise. There adventures there living on an island inspired her. She also read Knut Hamsun's Victoria; a book about a woman's choice. It tells the story of Johannes a writer that falls in love with the daughter of a wealthy landowner, but in the end, Victoria is forced to marry a soldier.

In her teenage years she had wanted so much to be an actress, and she once planned to apply to the national academy theatre in Oslo. She had read the play, "The Wild Duck," by Ibsen. It was a tragic play about suicide, secret love, revolutionary politics, guilt, memory and marriage. She told him too about her failed attempt to study acting. Her mother's cousin was part of the national academy of theatre. She prepared for the exam entrance. But her parents did not approve, and she decided not to attend the entrance exam.

She also loved Ibsen's play; 'An Enemy of the People'. It was a special play she told Leonard. It's a story about a man named Stockman, who speaks the truth, about his town in Norway. He is the medical officer and learns that the town's spa water is contaminated. She loved Ibsen's honesty and his idealism. Another play she loved was Ghosts, that was about religion, venereal disease, incest and euthanasia. This play caused a scandal in Norway, when it was first performed. She told Leonard that Axel's behavior was not unlike the plot in Ibsen's play 'Ghosts'; that was about a miserable marriage, with a husband who was unfaithful. She said that Africa had changed him. The idea of monogamy and Axel's belief systems had changed after coming back.

He told him also about her grandmothers told her life's story. She travelled to Beijing in China to marry an ambassador. She took on the Trans-Siberian Express on a journey of six thousand miles. When she got there and arrived at the embassy, she was informed that the young consul has died in a car accident. She stayed on in Beijing for several months in a sad and depressed state. She visited the Forbidden City, the home of the emperor of China. The Imperial city was a vast complex of palaces. For five hundred years all the great emperors of the Ming Dynasty lived there. She told him about how she had visited many of the palaces there with wonderful names. There was; The, Gate of the Divine night, The West Glorious Gate, The Gate of Supreme Harmony, The Hall of Literary Glory and The Palace of Tranquil Longevity. She told him also about the first emperor Qin Shi Huang who was the founder of the Qin dynasty, and the first emperor that unified China. He had gone in search of the potion for an eternal life. He wanted to live forever. He met a seer that gave him mercury to take in sweet cakes, that poisoned him. She told him also about the last Emperor Pu Yi who became China's ruler at the age of twelve; but as a young man he was forced off the throne, and reduced to being a private citizen of the Republic of China. He ended up as a gardener planting flowers.

"It made me dream of far-off places," said Marianne. To Leonard's surprise she told him because of this, she became fascinated by Genghis Khan, the great Mongolian leader.He ruled an area stretching from China to the Ottoman empire, from the Pacific to the Black sea. She imagined that she was married to him, and was one of his concubines; and travelled across the vast grasslands of the Mongolian and Russian steps on his conquests. She imagined also being on horseback with hundreds of his fighters who were following their caravans and cattle. Her dreams stretched back hundreds of years.

***

It was during the Nazi invasion of Norway on April 9, 1940, that she went to Larkollen, with her father with her little brother and mother to her grandmother's place. There she felt free. She grew up in her grandmother's place beside a fjord. She was only five when the Nazis arrived in the country. It was a terrible time for the Norwegians. She also was lucky to escape the war, when millions of Jews perished in the concentration camps. She loved to explore this beautiful place with her mother; on the walks by the sea where the large waves crashed against the rocks, by the beautiful small harbor and wooded hills. There they sat beneath oak trees.

It was only many years later that she learnt about the reason why she and her family had escaped there. Marianne remembered seeing German planes flying over. She lay with her mother beneath the trees hiding as the planes sped past. Three days before the German invasion the local police had told all the villagers in Larkollen to switch off all lights. One night the German ships approached. Later they heard explosions as Norwegian missiles struck and exploded the ships. The Germans had tried to enter Oslo by ship but the Norwegian navy attacked them. They listened to the radio and learnt that King Haakon and Norwegian government had time to escape north, and to England along with all the gold from the bank of Oslo. It was a lucky escape as the Nazis wanted the King to approve their own puppet government.

***

She told Leonard about the first time she met Axel. She was nineteen and her friend Anna has just passed her driver's license and borrowed her father's car. She had remembered that evening vividly; and the sun that lay beyond Oslo and its deep blue waters. A shaft of light had broken through the clouds illuminated part of the sea's surface. They cruised past the royal palace and the village sculpture park to the district of Bygody, to the peninsula beyond.

It was a playground for the wealthy with museums and the royal estate for the King and his family. There at a party she met Axel. He was deeply tanned after crossing the Sahara. He had deep penetrating eyes and a sharp nose. His blond hair had been bleached by the sun, and his skin was deeply tanned. She had never met anyone like him before. All the Norwegian boys were so straight, so conservative and so reserved. Here was a young man who had an adventurous spirit like her. They talked all night until early morning. She realized that her life would change forever. Axel wanted to be a writer and she an actress – they had much in common.

They met again at the Theatre Café, opposite the national theatre. It had tiled flooring, white pillars and a vaulted ceiling. It was a meeting place of the great and the good of Oslo since nineteen hundred. It was designed in Art Nouveau with a

Viennese style. It had tables with white linen, and its walls one could see paintings and photos of the many actors that had been there. Marianne hoped that she would meet some actors there too. She learnt more about Axel's passions. He read many books and travelled to places that she had never heard of. He made her realize that he belonged to a world in Norway that she was trying to break out of.

She met him again at the Café Doverhallen, that had a long hall with an interior covered in pictures; and a balcony on each side, where people could see a stage where musicians performed. There jazz was played and they listened to the music of Duke Ellington and Charlie Parker. She loved to hear the saxophone and the tunes of Parker's 'Night in Tunisia.' They spent many nights there drinking and listening to musicians. She was in love with Axel and she did not want it to end.

Marianne told Leonard that she fell in love with Axel but she felt insecure. She told him that sometimes she could feel the cracks that appeared beneath the surface of a relationship, but was afraid to admit it to herself. She told him that she realized too late that they were not cut from the same block of marble. He was intense, talkative, overbearing and arrogant. She was reserved, sensitive and unsure of herself. She was drawn to his assurance and his emotional depth, and his intellectual clarity. She knew that his world of ideas had influences beyond the Lutheran culture of Norway. He gave her books to read that he assured her would liberate her; Nitzsche, Jung, and Ouspensky. They had ideas that God was dead, and the unconscious was full of symbols.

They were the biggest influences on Axel. Ouspensky believed that he was a fakir, a monk, and a yogi, who needed seclusion from the world with meditation. She read his books but did not feel the same way about them as Axel. He told her that these books would liberate her from the rules of family and society. It was only then that she could find herself. She was happy within herself, and she did not want to follow Axel's path.

Axel second book was called the 'Cross of the Animal Tamer'. It was about people who lived in harmony with their inner world. It explored how only few people are aware of the secretive symbolic language that influenced their actions. Not many understand and because of this, their sinister sickness that was eating away at civilization and the core of our consciousness.

***

Marianne continued to tell Leonard about her childhood in Norway. She went ice skating, and floated across the ice to the sound of Mahler. This was her way of feeling free. But the intensity with Axel continued. One night in a drunken rage he grabbed a knife and pierced his hand and blood appeared. He cut his hand three times. She wrapped the cuts in a bandage and calls for an ambulance. His eyes were filled with fear, sadness and loathing for the world. Had Axel's books and experiences driven him to the edge of madness she wondered. She was disturbed by his actions and his intensity, but like many women before her, she tried to cover over this nightmare. When he was like this, she would retreat to herself. She dreamed of being on the stage in the National Theater.

She loved Greta Garbo who had gone to Hollywood from Sweden. She always played tragic characters in her movies. She had seen many of her films but she retired when she was thirty-five. After that she led a lonely life. Marianne had read her letters, where she said

> *'I go nowhere and I see no one. I am sad to be alone, but sometimes it's more difficult to be with someone. But now I want be alone.'*

"She was called the Swedish sphinx," said Marianne, pouring them both a glass of wine. "I never want to be like her – to be alone."

"I have many fears now. It is the fear of being alone that grips me and creeps into my mind. It is the terrible fear of being abandoned." said Marianne nervously.

"Love can be a joy, but it can also be a burden." replied Leonard.

"Axel did inspire me when I met him. He told me that I would follow a creative path. Axel liberated me and made me see that I could have another life."

"Now you have become a victim of his liberation." said Leonard.

Marianne feared that and admitted to Axel that she had a fear of being alone, and a fear of not being enough for him.

"My heart was filled at times with angst. My feelings were buried inside me. I tried to find the meaning behind the pain. I needed to get closer to Axel. I wondered was it possible. I needed to face the music and what our relationship meant."

"You have me now Marianne, I hope we will always be together or at least friends.'' Leonard felt her warm lips touch his. "I hope so," said Marianne. "I sincerely hope so."

He kissed her lips, then her neck and his fingers touched her breast through her dress. He could smell her perfume, her face blushed. Her lips touched his warmly softly and in her sensuous embrace Leonard felt Marianne's love.

"You kisses are – a thousand kisses deep," said Leonard.

"Yes," replied Marianne, "A thousand kisses for sure."

***

For Leonard and Marianne there was sadness, but also joy, serenity and peace on Hydra. The island was always covered in a golden light, especially at sunset. The walls seemed to be covered in crystals, that were embedded in the white paint that glowed in the sunlight. It gave the interior to his house a magical feeling. From their bedroom window, Marianne could see the rooftops and the thin line of the blue sea. There were pink flowers to be seen on the eucalyptus trees. They could hear the ringing of the church bells and priests singing the Gregorian chant. Life for them seem on Hydra sometimes was a mystical place. Under the evening lamp, Leonard read his new poems to Marianne. She felt she belonged there with Leonard now. She had someone to love. There was no turning back now.

Because of their bills for food at Katsikas café, Leonard kept a record of their accounts as their money was so delicate. Marianne sewed her own dresses and obtained clothes from the other women on the island. After lunch she took a siesta in the hottest hours, when the sun was overhead. Leonard would then get up and work again until twilight and sunset. There was no rain from spring until winter. Lime was lowered in a bucket to kill the bacteria in the water cistern.

Sophia washed their clothes on a washboard in Leonard's mobile marble sink. With an old iron with hot water inside, she ironed their clothes for them. Sophia also supplied them with ice that came on a small boat from the mainland.

Every morning Leonard and Marianne were awoken with the sounds of the church bells and the people calling. Leonard and Marianne could see nuns walking down the street in their white bonnets to shop for food. Marianne cooked home baked bread and made homemade jam. July and August brought the strong winds called the' meltemi'.

It came in quite suddenly like a ninja with stealth and surprise that lasted for over a week. In the autumn came the 'sirocco' wind carrying sand and dust that came from the Sahara. Marianne and Leonard had to close the windows and the shutters, but the pink dust came in through the cracks and covered the floor and walls. They lit the fire and watched the flame dance across the walls.

***

Chapter 15
The Wild Duck

Marianne told Leonard that she would dress in the past in her finest clothes for Axel. She would put lipstick on and darken her eyelashes that were fair. She went through all of this ritual as young woman do, when they are in love. Axel had rejected society. He father was a lawyer and his clients were the rich of Oslo, who had many sons who were more suitable to marry. But her father had tuberculosis and was sent by his doctor to a hospital, where one of his lungs was removed. Her two year old brother, Nils had also caught it. They were both close to death on many occasions. Her father did not approve of Axel. He had no university education, job, or a place to live. Her father was rather conservative. He was not happy either in his marriage.

"That sounds so bad," said Leonard, caressing her hair. "He became and invalid. Her father was frail and was slowly dying. The arguments and the fractured relationship with him was over. Now love took on another dimension, replaced with duty and the care of him. The war years did him no good. He became frail and wasted away. He wrote poems like you, Leonard. I can see something of you in him."

"Now I know why you love me," said Leonard. "You really are in search of the father you lost."

"Maybe!" replied Marianne smiling.

"He gave up his law practice and in the end my mother has to go to work. That was certainly a role reversal for her."

"My mother was the daughter of the great opera singer Willam Kloed. He had a plan to build and opera house in Oslo in 1916, but it never happened. The city just never came up with the money. This is why Marianne's grandmother travelled to Germany and Italy to perform. She recalled as a young girl that her grandfather sang some arias for the opera at home."

"When did the cracks appear in your relationship with Alex?" said Leonard, while exhaling some smoke from his cigarette.

"It's just one of those things that a woman has a sixth sense of." said Marianne combing her hair. "Axel became unpredictable. He lived in the moment and on impulse. Every day he changed his plans. It made me feel insecure all the time. I loved him though he was a dreamer like me. I wanted to be a movie star like the ones you see in Hollywood, in those black and white movies," said Marianne combing her hair.

Marianne told him that her mother had a sophistication about her. She had learnt French in Paris and wore beautiful clothes from there, when she attended the local Lutheran church on Sundays with Marianne. Her mother had taught here one lesson in life which was to do your best, and put up with your sorry circumstances if you have to. This lesson now applied to Axel too. Marianne went to work selling shoes, and tickets in the local cinema. One night she saw a film starring Sophia Loren and Alan Ladd; located on the beautiful mysterious island of Hydra, titled the 'Boy on a Dolphin'. The enchanting blue cobalt sea was inviting and she wished that she could be there swimming in its blue waters, as Oslo was covered in snow.

Axel was always at his typewriter and when he found work, he saved so he could make another trip to the Sahara again. Axel encouraged Marianne to be creative. He said to her. "We are here on earth not to sleep, but to create. The act of creation is the most important in life, and when all is said and done, it is the only thing that gives existence and a kind of meaning. When you create you share yourself with all human beings? The creative power lives within you. Without creating, existence loses all meaning. "Marianne told Leonard that Axel told her that he loved her, but she must be free to live my own life too.

"He said and I must work it all out for myself."

"That is the situation you are now in Marianne; he had abandoned you," replied Leonard. Love cannot survive on freedom, it needs some rules of engagement," said Leonard blowing some smoke into the night air.

"Axel was overbearing and aggressive. He smothered me. I was too sensitive and too traditional for him. He made me understand that I could look at the world in another way. But that had its own risks. There were no limits, for him - that is why he has another woman now," said Marianne sadly.

***

The following day Leonard went to the beach with Marianne. There they found some turtles hatching eggs. It was a wonderful sight. They watched them slowly crawl towards the water. Marianne brought in her basket Axel's letters to her. She told him she read them from time to time, to experience again their emotional intensity.

She told Leonard that Axel told Marianne one day that he was going to meet the mystic John Starr Cooke in Copenhagen. He was a rich Hawaiian. He met him at a hotel there. He had a shaven head and was dressed in an Arabic black kaftan. He had a gold pendant around his neck with the symbol of the Egyptian sun god Ra. They agreed to travel together. John took out a pendant and placed it over a map. The pendant stopped over Tunisia. They agreed to travel there. Before Axel left, he had given him a gold bar to Axel, for him to pay towards his trip, and agreed to meet him later on in the city of Tunis.

With all this confusion and drama Leonard wondered how they had married at all. She told him that one-day Axel told Marianne that he had a brilliant idea to save them both from their families. He bought her a ring and suggested they should marry. "He said my home was a danger to my soul." He did not ask my father as he said he should have no say in the matter. He did not agree in formalities. I have no money but what does that matter," he said.

"I have heard that one before," said Leonard with a smile.

"So, you said yes," said Leonard looking at the moonlight.

"He was so sure of himself, but I was not. He led and I followed. I was afraid of his talk of freedom, but I went along with it anyway. It was an adventure for me."

"That's why we are here Leonard. That is what brought us here to this place, this mysterious island on this adventure," said Marianne, looking at Leonard intently. "Yes, we would never have met, even Axel would not object to us being together," said Leonard.

"We had love, it was beautiful, I was lost without him, but the freedom he wanted destroyed us."

"Love can never be free. It has to have some fidelity and some rules to survive!"

Marianne told him that Axel had finished his novel called Icarus that recorded his journey across the Sahara. Marianne and Axel were invited to a grand reception in the publisher's house in Oslo. The house had Greek columns and beautiful paintings by classical Norwegian painters. The great window had a view over the fjord. They attended a formal dinner with the great and the good of Oslo.

Axel's next novel was about the Oedipus complex, so he wanted to go to Greece to see the Temple of the Oracle at Delphi, and to visit Hydra. Marianne's parents objected to her going to Greece, as they were not married yet.

"I found it hard to leave against my parent's wishes. Axel's parents did not object and came to the station to say goodbye," said Marianne.

***

They took the night train to Hamburg. The train sped through the night and the landscape was covered in snow. It sped down from Northern Europe, and their adventure had begun. Marianne wore her grandmother's fur coat that she had given her. But there were tears in her eyes as she thought of her parents. The train passed over the Swedish border and on to Gothenburg, and then to Malmo. They passed over the great bridge that crossed over to Copenhagen into Denmark. Then the train travelled on to Hamburg.

There they rented a room in an attic and the following day Axel bought a car. It was an old Volkswagen Beetle. He drove hundreds of miles down the great autobahns, then over the Alpine pass into Austria and on to Zurich, in Switzerland, and then on to Venice. They walked among the pigeons in St Mark's square. Then they drove on to Skopje in Yugoslavia.

They travelled down long winding roads through the mountains towards Greece. The roads were icy but they soon reached the Greek border. The car ground to a halt, and they were invited to stay in a shepherd's house. The old couple looked after sheep and lived in a one roomed house with their grandson. It had an organic earth floor, one bed and an old oil lamp. They sat at a wooden table where one of the places remained empty. They told them that it was an old Greek custom. to leave a seat for one of their dead Greek ancestors.

Marianne slept with the old woman in her bed, while Axel slept on the floor. The following day, Marianne developed a sharp pain and a doctor was called. He diagnosed appendicitis; that could have been brought on by stress. She was taken to the doctor's house and placed in an old iron bed. Three Greek women all dressed in black prayed for her. The doctor operated on her. It was a makeshift operation without an anesthetic. Marianne was given strong Greek whiskey and recovered.

They travelled onwards and arrived in Athens. Then they visited Delphi, to see the temple of the Oracle. It was there that the enchantress once held court and gave predictions. It was here too that King Oedipus consulted the Oracle. They slept among its temples under the moon on this great plateau. It was a place regarded by the Greeks as the center of the world. They visited the great amphitheater and they could see the valley below, that was covered in beautiful trees. Axel shaved his head and prayed to the Greek gods. Marianne wondered if he had lost his mind.

They drove on to a village called Ermioni where they met an old man called Papadopoulos. He spent some time in California, and had become rich from selling chocolate. He brought them dinner and showed them the best way to get to Hydra. Leonard looked into Marianne eyes and he could see the pain, the distress and the abandonment that she had gone through.

"So why did you marry him if he was such a troubled soul?" said Leonard.

"I loved him, all women think they can change their men. It was a kind of a love hate relationship. We think the relationship is possible, but we realize in the end it is not possible."

"You married him and you had a baby!"

"I know; we women do strange things for love. We married in the Anglican church in Athens. I remember I was dressed in a white silk blouse with buttons up the back, and band of gold ribbon for the neck. I wore a dark blue suit that my mother had made. I wore blue gloves. I looked like some aristocratic Norwegian waiting to meet my king. That moment for me was sacred, whatever I may think now."

***

Chapter 16
George

Leonard and Anthony decided to go and see George and Charmian. Georges face was covered in foam and he held a razor up to his chin.

"I'll be with you soon," said George. "Good to see you. Leonard make a coffee." George joined them in the kitchen. "How long have you been here?" said Leonard.

"Five years," said George, drinking his coffee. "It has been a bit of a struggle, but we get by. I have three children to look after and it's all paid through writing. If I don't write, we don't eat. How about you, Leonard?"

"I'm trying to finish my novel."

"George was in the war," said Anthony.

"Yes, I reported on the Japanese invasion of New Guinea. You know it was those New Guinea tribesmen, along with the Australian army who won that war in the jungle. The called the tribesmen, the Fuzzy Wuzzy Angels. It was a tough time in the jungle for us all. That's where I really learned how to write. At six every morning, clanking on my portable typewriter; so the whole of Australia could get the news from the frontline."

George gulped down his coffee and continued talking.

"Then I went travelling. I'm a wandering soul like you Leonard. I was travelled in Burma, China, Tibet, Japan, India, Italy, and now Greece."

"He writes potboilers. He's the paperback king of Australia," said Anthony, laughing.

"It pays the rent. Not many writers can do that. I'm not Fitzgerald or Hemingway, but the books are not bad. They have stood the test of time."

George got up and returned with some paperbacks and placed them on the table. The titles appeared: Grey Gladiator, Battle of the Seaways, Australia at War, New Guinea Diary and Pacific Partner. "It's called pulp fiction!" At the doorway appeared Charmian in her nightgown.
"Gentlemen, may I join you? Anthony, Leonard - how nice to see you," said Charmian, taking a seat.
"Charmian, how are the children?" asked Anthony.
"They are sleeping."
"How many have you?" asked Leonard.
"Three – Martin, Shane, Jason. So, you see, Leonard, I write to pay the bills," replied George.
"Charmian is writing a novel. I think she is more talented than me, and more
literary."
"A book is a book, literary or not," said Anthony, pouring Charmian a coffee.
"Well, there is a lot of snobbery in publishing. What kind of writer are you, Leonard?" Leonard thought a moment and reflected.
"I like to write something that means something to me, and hopefully to other people. I never write for money. It's not my motivation."
"When you start starving, you will." They all laughed at the thought.
"Charmian used to be a pin-up girl. She won a few photo competitions," said George.
"Stop it, George, I was just a teenager. That's just George trying to make out that I'm just a stupid model, not a writer."
"That's not true," George protested. "I've always encouraged you to write."
"I became pregnant very young, so it was a struggle to be a single mother. George, saved me and I'm thankful for that."

"What about you, Leonard, do you have a woman?"
"Yes, but I don't like to talk about her."
"Are you staying for long?"
"As long as possible" replied Leonard, taking a cigarette from Anthony.
"Mind if I smoke?"
"Of course not," said Charmian, taking one also.
"How did you two meet each other?" said Leonard.
"I got pregnant in Australia, and the father abandoned me, like most men. But George to his credit, is not like that."
"I got her a job at my newspaper, as a journalist 'The Argos' in Melbourne. But when staff found out we were having an affair they disapproved. Hypocrites, the lot of them!" said George. "I was married at the time and I had not obtained a divorce."
"What happened?" asked Leonard, pulling on his cigarette.
"They fired me; can you believe it? The board of the paper had a meeting and fired me! A right bunch of hypocrites! So, we had to escape Australia, it maybe the land of sunshine, but it isn't the land of freedom! Underneath that Australian smile there is a deep conservatism. Post war Australia is a nasty place. It's all about hunting the money!"
"Yes, George is right, the new mantra is 'greed is good'. I was relieved when that boat passed Harbour Bridge. We came through London, and that's a depressing place, too. It's a grey place and overcrowded."
"That's why I'm here, too," said Leonard. "We all have escaped, for one reason or another."
"I think one can never be truly free," said Charmian, "even on this island, it has its problems."
"Yes, I have seen some already?" said Leonard.
"There is always a dark side to every place, you will find out in your own way, even Hydra has it secrets," said Charmian, lifting her eyebrows and pouring herself a glass of wine.

"I feel marooned here sometimes," said Charmian smiling. "Like Robinson Crusoe. We have begun to be invaded by tourists. I came here to find some peace."

"I think that film with Sophia Loren 'Boy on a Dolphin' has brought the tourists, here." said George. "That is not the only concern about Hydra. This is hidden paradise of many secrets. There are other darker forces. You will find out in time, if you stay." said George in a mysterious way.

"What forces?" asked Leonard.

"You will find out in your own time Leonard!"

George began to cough, a terrible cough until his face went red. He leaned over on his chair. Charmian rubbed his back.

"He's has been to the doctor George, he has T.B."

"That's bad," said Leonard.

"Yes, he has inactive TB, so you won't get infected. But if he does not get treatment it may become infectious. That's another good reason why we are thinking of returning to Australia. The treatment her is not so good. I think he picked it up in Asia".

"So, you won't be seeing much of me for a while Leonard," said George sitting up strait again.

"The doctors have given him antibiotics to take."

"I hope you will be ok George, let me know how you are."

"Our time is numbered, whether we like it or not." said George lighting up a cigarette. But Charmian grabbed it and stubbed it out in an ashtray.

***

Marianne arranged to meet Leonard at a place known as Spilia. It was a place for swimming on the west side of the horseshoe harbour, and a meeting place for Hydra expatriates. Leonard met her at Katsikas café and crossed the Agora and took the pathway there. Leonard could see twenty descending concrete stairs with platforms for sunbathing. He had bought a pair of swimming trunks and a towel made from wool, with its edges that were covered in Greek patterns. They lay their towels out and soaked up the sun. Leonard could see a number of locals diving into the water.

"Can you dive Marianne?"

"Yes, I can. I used to dive a lot at home in my local pool. I feel so free and alive when I swim. When I dive, I feel that I can fly. Can you dive?"

"Of course, I can." replied Leonard. Then he stood up, lifting his hands and dived into the clear blue sea. Leonard felt the cool surface of the water touch his skin and a surge of bubbles stream past his face. His body went deep and stopped close to the sandy bottom. With a strong breast stroke he pulled himself towards the surface, where the light streamed through. When he emerged, he found Marianne in the water and swum close to her. He kissed her warmly on her wet lips and saw her blue eyes flashing like star in the sky.

***

Leonard could see a young man in swimming trunks, bearded, and wearing glasses standing near the rocks. Leonard climbed the steps and grabbed the towel.

"Where are you from?" said Leonard.

"My names Steve Sanfield, I just arrived from Athens."

"Leonard."

"Pleased to meet you, Leonard," said Steve. sitting on a rock and wiping himself with a towel.

"You sound American," said Leonard.

"Amherst, Massachusetts. I was at university there - a student of English."

"I studied English at McGill in Montreal," said Leonard, sitting on a rock and putting his sunglasses on.

"Are you escaping America?"

"Yes, I was involved in a lot of politics over there. I was a freedom rider."

"Freedom rider, I have heard of you guys," said Leonard, wiping his shoulders.

Marianne climbed out of the water and Leonard introduced her.

"You're the guys that are fighting for black equality," said Leonard.

"Yeah, I was fighting against the segregation of blacks and whites in the southern states."

"Yes, that's so bad that this kind of racism exists," said Leonard.

"It is, even when the United States Supreme Court ruled that blacks could travel with whites on buses. It has been ignored. Blacks are outlawed in restaurants, waiting rooms in hospitals and buses and train terminals."

"You're a brave man," said Marianne.

"Well, someone has to make a stand against this kind of racism. Everyone is equal in America, but some are more equal than others. So, we challenged it. We started riding interstate buses in mixed racial groups."

"It was a dangerous game you played with the establishment," said Leonard.

"Yes, it was. We were beaten with truncheons by the police and tear gassed. I was arrested for trespassing and unlawful assembly, and violating local laws. We were attacked by white mobs. I spent a week in hospital. So, after I got out, I decided to head for Europe."

"Well, you found a good place to escape to," said Leonard.

"How badly were you injured?" asked Charmian.

"Well, I got a lot of bruises and cuts in a fight with the police."

"Do you write, Steve?" asked Leonard, lighting up a cigarette.

"Yes, I write poetry."

"Me too," said Leonard.

"That's so cool. I write a lot of poetry. I've been studying Zen poetry recently."

"Yeah, it's something that interests me.

I would love to study it," said Leonard, laying out on his towel, on the concrete platform near the rocks, beside Marianne.

"Let me see if I can remember a Zen poem." Steve looked out to sea, reflecting, engaging with his memory:

"Returning to my native village after many years I light incense and strained to sit in meditation. Poignant memories of those long years of pilgrimage. An old grave hidden away at the foot of a deserted hill. Once I was his pupil, in my youth. I try to pull away, but cannot. A flood of tears soaks my sleeves."

"That's beautiful said Leonard."

Steve had a black moustache that made him look like exotic.

"You look Latino," said Leonard.

"No, I'm Jewish."

"Jewish – me too.!"

"We should set up a synagogue here," said Leonard with a smile. As he drew on his cigarette, another figure appeared. At first, he could not make out who it was, as he was blinded by the sun. Leonard observed a man with a bald domed head with hair on either side. He wore glasses and had a camera hung on a leather strap. He wore a bright check shirt covered in stripes.

"Hi", said Marianne, looking at the camera. "We met before in Katsikas."

"That's a cool camera you got," said Steve, rubbing his hand through his moustache.

"Yes, it's a Leica M3. It was made in Easter Germany"

"Are you a photographer?" asked Leonard, resting on his right elbow.

"Yes, I am, I work for 'Life' magazine. I'm doing some photos on Hydra, on the artist colony. My names is James...James Bourke."

"That's us, a lost colony." Said Leonard laughing, and sitting up.

"This is Leonard and Steve," said Marianne.

"That's us," said Marianne with a smile.

"Can I take some photos of you guys?"

"Yeah sure," said Steve.

"What about you, Leonard?" asked Marianne, turning to Leonard.

"Are you trying to turn me into a celebrity?" replied Leonard, with a smile.

"Maybe a minor one," said James, lifting his camera and pointing it at them.

Within seconds their image was frozen in black and white – a moment in time captured forever. James told them that their photos would appear in Life Magazine across America.

"Do you know where George Johnson is? said James.

"He's not very well at the moment. He's has T.B."

"My God! When can I find him?"

"I will bring you to his house if you want'', said Leonard. His wife Charmian is looking after him."

"I owe my own life to George, he saved me." James sat down on the rocks and began to tell them solemnly of how George was his hero.

"It was in August 1945, and we were in Tibet. George was in search of Shangri-La. We went on a trek with ponies through the mountains and valleys. George was inspired by the novel 'Lost Horizon' by the writer James Hilton. We stayed in monasteries and temples. The locals guided us through the mountain passes. I got ill with a kidney infection. I was in a bad way, and mostly unconscious. He got me to an airstrip to catch the last plane out of there. Without George I was a dead man!"

***

Leonard returned that evening to the harbour after sunset. He was worried about Georges condition. If the TB got hold of his lung, it would kill him. The streets and lanes were illuminated by lights in the windows and occasionally a solitary oil lamp.

This time, Leonard walked and allowed Anthony to lead him on. He could hear some music in the distance as they approached the harbour. There they found some Greek men playing bouzoukis, the ancient instrument with a long neck almost like a giant mandolin. Leonard could see a man wearing a Greek costume with a red embroidered waistcoat. He wore a hat as well. Leonard recalled that he has seen it somewhere. He remembered the famous painting by Lord Byron. The romantic image of the great poet haunted his memory since he read his books of poems in university. He remembered the lines.

> *'He walks in the beauty like the night of cloudless climes and starry skies. All that is best of the dark and the bright met in her aspect and her eyes.'*

***

Chapter 17
Island of Hunger

Marianne said goodbye to Axel and Patricia at the port. She watched them sail away on a boat Axel had bought. Leonard came with her. He saw tears in her eyes. Life returned to normal and Marianne tried to forget about him. They began to focus on their own life together. Marianne moved with Axel junior, to Leonards house. She locked up her own place, until the divorce came through and it could be sold.

Leonard, with Anthony's help found some furniture for his house. He bought Greek chairs with straight backs and woven rope seats, and carved wooden, with classical Greek designs. Marianne made Leonard chicken stew that became his favourite. It was the cheapest dish that she could make. Her grandmother had made it during the war. She added olive oil, tomatoes, lentils and herbs. Leonard and Anthony drank retsina that tasted like pine resin, that was produced in Greece for three thousand years. It was stored in glass litre bottles and protected by wicker basket. She also baked fresh bread in Leonards oven, and covered it with butter and feta cheese.

Leonard and Marianne would also go to the port, to buy fresh fish that was stored in boxes covered in ice. The port that looked like a Greek amphitheatre, rose over six hundred meters to Mount Ere, the highest point of the island. On top, Anthony told him, there was a monastery that was dedicated to the prophet Elias, who had made many miracles. Anthony told him that the statue at the port was of Captain Kountouriotis, who led the Greek navy against the Turks, and became the first president of Greece. Leonard admired this statue of the great hero of Hydra, that looked seaward like a wise old man. Nearby was the post office, and the boatyard where the hammering and cutting of wood could be heard every day.

Leonard knew that he was part of the poorer ex-pats, living just above the poverty line. He had observed that there was a great difference between the rich and poor on the island, and its social inequality. Those who had little money like Leonard and Anthony rented as cheaply as they could. However, the houses were well looked after even in the poorer quarters. Every day Leonard could see women on their knees scrubbing the stone flagstones. Every Sunday the men and women would appear walking to church in their finest clothes. The children too also were dressed in the same manner.

Leonard's toilet was only a hole in the floor with a bucket of water to flush it. "It's not exactly the Ritz," said Anthony, peering down the hole. "The Greeks take no chances. Your bottom is suspended in the air. You have to practise squatting. They call it 'Greek yoga'. There is no way you catch the lurgy that way," said Anthony, laughing.

***

Leonard went to the post office one day. There was a letter from his mother. Inside was a cheque from her lawyer for $1,500. The letter read as follows.

> *'Your grandmother Rachel has died. We are all very sad here. I hope that you are doing fine in Greece. She has left you the sum of $1,500. Shalom, your dear mother Marsha.'*

Leonard was deeply saddened at the news and elated at the same time. $1,500 was enough to buy a small house on Hydra - somewhere to put his head down. He would no longer be a homeless poet. He met Anthony at Katiskas and told him the news. They shared a bottle of wine together. Anthony located the owner of his house and made him an offer to buy it. Leonard followed him over a mile along narrow laneways, to an old villa.

They greeted an old man with a white beard and moustache. He had a weather beaten face, that had seen too much of the Greek sun. He agreed with him the ptice of $1,500. He signed the contract and promised to deliverer a banker's draft within a week. The old man shook his hand with a smile and told him that he was not only a Hyroite now, but also a Philhellene. Anthony told him that meant he was now a friend of Greece. A priest, arrived to bless his house. He was dressed in black carrying a cross, and a servant boy in a white top, held the silver bowl with holy water. The priest said some sacred words raised his right hand and blessed Leonards house.

***

One day Leonard observed a funeral crossing the harbour. Six men carried a coffin. The recognised the same priest with golden robes carrying a tall brass cross that hovered over his head. Behind him, two altar boys carried a holy water bowl and an incense burner on chains. Anthony introduced him to an old man called Joseph who always walked at the back of the mourners. He had an arched back and struggled to follow the line of mourners. He wore a black suit with a crisp white shirt, black tie and a fedora hat. It was a Greek tradition to sell the deceased personal belongings as soon as possible. Anthony reminded him about the film called Zorba, when the Greeks mourners stripped the room bare in minutes, and removed from the room everything that belonged from the dead corpse in the bed. Joseph told them that on Hydra he always took part in every funeral and sold the dead person's belongings in the market. Joseph sold him a pair of a dead man's shoes. "Now, you're a dead man walking. It might bring you closer to heaven," said Anthony laughing.

"Yes, I have always wanted dead man's shoes." replied Leonard smiling.

"I was a rich man once, said Joseph."

Leonard enquired what he used to work at.

"I worked in America in a Greek restaurant, peeling potatoes and washing dishes; but they called me an Americano when I got back to Hydra. They called me a big shot, so I spent the money I saved on my friends and family. They needed it. It was after the war and we were all dying. That is how I started following coffins," said Joseph, with a sense of sadness in his eyes.

***

Leonard took the donkey with Anthony to a street called Kala Pigadia, with a large water well, that had protection from tall trees. Old men sat outside their houses with their wives dressed in black. The lanes were spattered in donkey shit, and even one of the lanes was called Donkey Shit Lane. The whole economy on the island was fishing, importing food and the hiring of donkeys. Leonard felt sorry for the poor donkeys, that were carrying water, wood, furniture, roof tiles and food up the narrow laneways all day. Anthony told him that he tried to complain to the Greeks but they had done nothing about it. Some of the donkeys collapsed on the streets, and one day he found one dying under a tree. Leonard went to find a vet, and when he arrived it was too late. One of the old Greeks put a bullet in its head, from a gun he had used in the war. Leonard saw blood flowing down the street.

The island Leonard had learnt from Anthony was recovering from famine and death. The second world war had only ended fifteen years before. There was a sense of foreboding here of hidden traumas and of loss and destruction. The Greeks had fought bravely against the Nazi occupation. Hitler had said.

> *'The Greek soldiers had fought with great courage and defiance, and scorned death.'*

Because of this, Operation Barbarossa - the invasion of Russia, was delayed until June 1941. As a result, the Germans died in their thousands in the Russian winter, when they were in retreat. The Greeks had saved the world.

This island was deceptive in its affluence, as many of the townsfolk had relatives that had died from this hunger. Anthony told him that Joseph Goebbels, Minister of Propaganda of the Third Reich had said that the Greek situation, was caused by a British blockade and not them. Goebbels said;

> *'I received a lamentable report on the situation in Greece. The hunger there has become a national epidemic. Thousands of people are dying on the streets of Athens, all a result of the brutal British blockade against a people who wanted to carelessly pick out of the fire the chestnuts for the English people. That's the gratitude of London.'*

Anthony told Leonard that Greece experienced widespread starvation during the occupation. The scarcity of food had already appeared in the first days of the German invasion for the whole population. Hunger had more victims than bombings, warfare and even reprisals, and was deeply engraved in the Greek collective memory. The most terrible period was the first winter of 1941–1942, where no less than 30,000 people died, the largest part of those in Athens. The famines in Greece were the most lethal in occupied Europe, during the second World War. It was estimated that the Greek famine killed close to five percent of the population. Even immediately after the Nazi occupation of the country, the food crisis was out of control and thousands of people died. The Germans were accused of genocide, and that they implemented a plan to starve the Greeks. Tens and thousands of people had to flee to other parts of the country, driven by the war and the confusion triggered from the occupation. The collapse of the transport links to the country had caused great difficulties to deliveries from one area to the other. Large stocks of potatoes, raisins, olive oil and other resources that were considered surplus products were exported to the German Reich. Greece had no imports of food for the duration of the war.

On September 6th, 1941, the rationing of food for the inhabitants of the Athens was fixed by law. At the same time, the black market had reached enormous dimensions. Most of the food crop was not delivered to the public, but controlled to speculators and middlemen and smuggling. The illegal market has been extended to all areas of the economy. Within a few months, food stores, shops and markets disappeared. Soup kitchens were organized by the church and the Red Cross, but the success was not consistent and inadequate.

Anthony told him that Princess Alice the mother of Prince Philip and husband of Elizabeth, Queen of England, organised many of these soup kitchens. Princess Alice had married Price Andrew and member of the Greek royal family, so their love of Greece and its people remained in their hearts. Although people from all classes died.

Anthony told Leonard that it did not obscure the fact that the majority of victims came from the lower classes. People collapsed in the street every day and it was reported that people were left lying on the road. The islands, were not agriculturally self-sufficient and the death rate was higher than in the poorest towns and villages. Piraeus, was amongst the areas that was also severely affected. The number of dead was not fully documented and statistics were very difficult to calculate. Hydra was one of the victims of this imposed Nazi genocide, and Anthony assured Leonard that the locals had not forgotten it.

Nick the owner of Katsikas cafe, told them that he remembered dead bodies in the laneways of Hydra, of those who had collapsed from hunger. The corpses had to be taken away from the houses on stretchers by the army. The faces of Greek children that were once fat were now bony. He recalled vacant eyes that looked at you in despair. So, this was how all those who wanted food credit obtained it from Nick, as he knew first-hand what starvation was all about. He agreed to open up a tab for Leonard. He told Nick that he would be getting a monthly payment from his father's estate. It was a small amount but enough to get credit for food.

Anthony told Leonard about Princess Alice the mother of Prince Philip husband of Queen Elizabeth. Princess Alice was a member of the Greek royal family. She organised soup kitchens in Athens during the war, where a thousand children died daily in Athens. These were the largest soup kitchens in Athens. The soup was cooked on large cauldrons over fires. The children were fed first then their parents. When she was visited by a German general, she proudly said; *'You can take your troops out of my country'*. She worked with the Swedish Relief Commission and Turkish Red Cross and the American Relief Committee, that brought in food.

The Princes had also been involved in hiding Jews from the Nazis. The Germans invaded Salonika in 1941, where the entire Jewish population of sixty thousand people were exterminated. A large number of Jews fled from norther Greece. The Jewish population in Athens expanded to six thousand. The Greek Orthodox community helped the Jews in whatever way they could. The Archbishop Damaskinos requested the chief of police, Angelos Evert, to issue 18,500 false identity papers to help them escape.

Anthony told Leonard that Princess Alive rescued and hid the Cohen family. The Princess had met Haimaki Cohen when she and King George 1st, Prince Constantine had stayed in his villa during a flood. Haimaki was now dead and his widow Rachel, daughter Tilde and sons Elie, Alfred, Jacques and Michael were hidden in the attic of the Princess house. "Maybe you are related," said Anthony with a smile.

■■

Anthony told him that the ferry arrived at 11;30 every morning, that brought the mail to the post office. All the expats arrived at this time and it was a meeting place for all the expats on the island. Leonard watched as the many parcels and a sack of letters were hoisted by a fishing net onto the harbour. The postman was always there to accept them. A wooden cart pulled by a donkey brought the letters and parcels to the post office.

Leonard cheque arrived from his grandfather's trust fund, and they were banked immediately. Anthony told him if the bank manager liked you, he would give you an advance. Katsikas was the haunt of the local bank manager, and wise travellers like Leonard and his circle. They always brought him a meal or a glass of ouzo at every opportunity. For this reason, the three most important people on the island, were the mayor, the bank manager and Nick, the owner of Kastikas. Many of the artists and writers that lived quietly and secretly on the island appeared there, and then vanished for another week. The foreigners, Anthony said were known as the 'hungry xenoi'.

***

Leonard and Anthony met with James Bourke and brought him over to see George and Charmian. George lay in bed and was pleased to see his old friend. They talked of old times and Georges search for Shangri La. George told them that some scholars believe that the Shangri-La was a place in Tibet called Shambhala, a mythical kingdom in the Tibetan Buddhist tradition, which was searched for by Western explorers. Shambhala in Tibetan Buddhism described a place of harmony between man and nature, that was also connected with the

Kalachakra or "wheel of time". George told them that philosophy behind this lost world, could be found the book called 'The Shambhala Sutra', that was written by the Sixth Panchen Lama; which describes some of the locations as being in Ngari, in western Tibet.

"That's where you will find Shangri La,"said George sitting up in bed.

"What is the philosophy of the Shambala text?'' enquired Leonard. George though for a moment.

"It's about cultivating a sense of holding dear all human beings. The main point is to develop an attitude that enables you to regard other beings as precious, much in the manner of precious jewels. You have to ask the question of yourself, why do we need to cultivate the thought that other beings are precious and valuable? In one sense, we can say that other beings are really the principal source of all our experiences of joy, happiness, and prosperity, and not only in terms of our day-to-day dealings with people. We can see that all they are desirable experiences, that we cherish or aspire to attain are dependent upon cooperation and interaction with other human beings.''

"It's a wonderful message,'' said Leonard, who was struck by its comparison with the life of the Canadian saint he so admired – Saint Catherine Tekakwitha. George continued.

"It teaches the concern of the cultivation of thoughts and feelings that cherish the wellbeing of others. One's own self-interest and wishes are fulfilled, by actually working for other people. The more one engages in activities; and thoughts that are focused and directed toward the fulfilment of someone else's' wellbeing. The fulfilment or realization of his or her own aspiration will come as a by-product. "That is the path of the Buddhism,'" said George gasping for breath. Georges words were music to Leonard ears – Buddhism was something that Hennessy and Ioannis had engaged in. Hydra seemed to be a home for those involved in the

Buddhist pathway. It was something he thought he needed to investigate further, perhaps it could bring peace into his life. Charmian served them all red wine, and raised George spirits as he lay in bed.

***

James Bourke enquired as to George and Charmian's plans.
"We abandoned civilization as we know it, many years a few years ago and escaped here, no cars, no electricity, no pollution or noise. I packed it in and escaped here, but with my tuberculosis, I think the game over here for me, it's time to return to Australia," said George sadly.

***

Chapter 18
Ramblin Jack

They all arrived at Dousko's restaurant – Leonard, Marianne, Anthony, Charmian, Steve and James. Douskos was only minutes from the harbour, up along a narrow laneway. There one could find a courtyard shaded by tall trees, that blocked out the intense summer sun. Leonard sat at a table close to the bar. That night a small stage had been erected in the corner. There was a pig roasting on a spit, and the skin began to bubble and crackle on a barbecue. As the flames were licking the pig's skin, it became brown with a golden tinge. The face of the pig looked calm without distress. Only the metal spike piercing through its snout gave one an indication that the pig was dead and now engulfed by the fire.

Steve Sandfield told Leonard that he had nowhere to stay, so Leonard offered him a place to crash. A young black man called Charles Heckstall joined them at the table. He was a friend of Steve's. He was tall, lean and muscular, and had short hair and glasses.

"Charlie, how are you?" said James, pouring out a glass of wine. He introduced him. "Charlie has an interesting story to tell. He was a paratrooper in the Korean war."

"Yeah, it was dangerous. I was injured badly by shrapnel. My back is covered in lesions, as if I had been whipped by a slave owner."

"Are you staying here?" asked Charmian.

"Yes, I've rented a place and I'm trying to write a book on black Americans. I was on the freedom ride like Steve. I know all about that as us blacks get a raw deal in America." said Charles passionately.

The stage lit up and lights beamed. A man dressed in a cowboy suit strutted forward. The boots were covered in an intricate inlay that looked like Mexican patterns. He wore red pants that were held up by a thick leather with a brass buckle. It had the head of an American eagle that flashed under the electric light. His shirt was covered in the stars and stripes of the American flag. Around his neck hung a guitar.

"My name is Ramblin Jack Elliot," he said in a deep southern American accent. "I'm going to sing you a song now by Woody Guthrie." Ramblin Jack's voice boomed across the restaurant. He sung to high heaven, as if he was greeting angels. Leonard was impressed. He wondered if only he could sing like that. Ramblin Jack was invited to join them along with his girlfriend June, a small, pretty, dark-haired girl with a sharply cut fringe.

Ouzo, retsina and wine began to flow, as souvlaki, the Greek dish of rice and roast chicken was served. Leonard soaked up the atmosphere. There was a smell of herbs, ouzo, and the smoke from the charcoal from the fire under the roasted pig.

Ramblin Jack regaled them with his travels, and his years as a busker and a travelling troubadour. He was an old friend of the great American folk singer Woody Guthrie and visited him in hospital; in his last days when he had Hodgkin's disease, when his mind, body and soul wasted away. Tragically a great American hero was snatched from life and into the realms of death. Ramblin Jack told them that he knew Bob Dylan in his years of struggle. He also hung out in New York's Greenwich Village with Jack Kerouac and the poet Allan Ginsburg and Gregory Corso. He told her had a telegram from Ginsberg in Athens, that he was on his way to Hydra. Dylan was billed on posters as 'The Son of Jack Elliot', such was Jack's reputation.

After Ramblin Jack sung a Dylan song, he took a break and another musician appeared on the small stage. His name was Oleg. He sang a song while playing his mandolin. He had blond hair and sang a beautiful lullaby. Oleg told him it was not a lullaby but rather a lament to the memory of the dead of world war two. The song was called 'Towards the Unknown' by Rod Mc Kuen. The song began with beautiful mandolin music.

The defeat of fascism Leonard pondered had only taken place twenty years before. It was known to the Russians are the Great Patriotic War. The war that saw over twenty-five million Russians dead. Six million were captured but most died until they numbered three million. The Russians were not unpatriotic and did not forget. He hoped he had remembered his own family enough with the phrase, 'burning violins' to reference the horrors of the holocaust. This all contributed to a war causality rate of a million losses a month.

He remembered seeing the film Doctor Zhivago about the Russian revolution and its civil war. He imagined the great vistas of Russia and how it was before the Bolsheviks and the Nazis destroyed its world. Leonard recalled his father's escape from Lithuania as eastern Europe when they were invaded by the Russian anti-Semite mobs.

***

Bill joined them later on that evening. They all retired to Leonard's house, where Jack and Leonard entertained them on their guitars. Steve rolled a joint and passed it around. The smell of marijuana wafted through the air and drifted across the room. "That's the best Moroccan I've had all year," said Steve, with a big smile. Leonard wondered where Anthony was. An hour later there was a knock on the door. When he opened it there was a man outside with him. It was Alan Ginsberg.

Alan and Leonard after some more wine got into a deep conversation, that continued late into the night. Alan told him that he saw the best minds of his generation destroyed by madness. He wanted to stop working forever and never work again, and write poetry. Alan told him about his mother's letter that he found when she had died. In it was advice to him on his future.

'The key is in the window; the key is in the sunlight at the window. I have the key. Get married Allen, and don't take drugs. The key is in the between bars, in the sunlight - in the window.'

It was a good metaphor about light getting through the bars, a metaphor about the light coming through the cracks. That's how the light gets in, he thought to himself. It was a metaphor that he wanted to use sometime in a poem.

***

The following morning the guest had left except Anthony, Steve and Ginsberg who were fast asleep on the floor. Marianne was also fast asleep in his bed. He made himself coffee and toast. He ate also some Greek yoghurt. Its creamy cool texture, comforted his throat after all the drinking the night before. Leonard wrote in his dairy.

'We sung our souls out at Douskos. We sat under the old tree where the roses climbed through the vines. In the night sky I can see the falling stars. There is always a place of wonder at the table there. There is wine for you, and apples to eat. There is a space to sing your songs. I felt that everywhere I had been was not my home, but Hydra was. What I found and have seen here is beautiful. I am blessed. I never had to remind myself, when I picked up a cup and held it close to my heart, handmade, natural and decorated in beautiful patterns. I could have been Ulysses with a gold cup of the ancient Greeks. The wine was ten cents a gallon. The people that I was meeting, I was meant to meet. I belonged here on this special island. From my house I have a dramatic view of the mountains, and the whitewashed houses. My rooms are cool in the summer and have thick walls with deep windows. Anthony tells me that my house is over two hundred years old, and an ancient sailor lived here.

Marianne with her hair like gold thread and a sweet smile, is an endless consolation to me. She has a good way with people. She is graceful and has a beautiful presence about her. She is always polite and unassuming. She keeps confidences and secrets, but most of all she is honest.'

***

That day Leonard went to Kamini beach with Marianne. Leonard dived into the water, when he saw the shadow of a dolphin. It's beautiful slender body swiftly sped past him; it's face smiling at him. It dived upwards, breaking the water's surface and made piercing sounds that dolphins make. For a moment he felt that time was suspended. He felt at one with nature and all his concerns and contemplations were forgotten in that moment.

As the summer progressed and the autumn winds started to rise. Anthony introduced Leonard to more islanders and their secret social world; especially those who were foreign and has emigrated there. One evening, Anthony invited him to the villa that was owned by Sam Barclay. Anthony told him that Sam was like Errol Flynn the Hollywood star, that he loved the good life, women and good food. Led by Anthony he walked to Sam's villa, which they found at the end of an uphill walk and many steps. Sam stood on the terrace and greeted them and led them inside.

Inside they found a table covered in bottles of wine and cards. Leonard was then introduced to the dark handsome Sam Barclay. Anthony informed him that since Christina his wife had gone to England; he had taken up the game of poker. He admitted to him that it was a separation and that she would not be back. Poker was one of the secret activities on the island and was a way of earning some extra cash. He wondered if Leonard could play. Leonard lit up a cigarette while Anthony poured him some wine.

He looked around the room as Sam spoke to them about poker and his life. He could see beautiful antiques and black and white photos of Sam on various yachts. He observed a beautiful blonde woman with Sam in a photo. At first thought it was Marianne, but he soon realized that she had different features.
"Who is that," said Leonard.
"It's Britt Ekland," said Sam, as he brought out a tray of champagne.
"She is a Swedish actress that I used to date. It was when she was making, 'The Happy Thieves' with Rex Harrison and Rita Hayworth. Scandinavian women are so beautiful."
"I agree," said Leonard smiling to himself.
"Would you like to join us for a game of poker?"
"What's is the raise like?" asked Leonard.
"This is little money at the moment, but it will increase after a few more games."

Leonard looked at Anthony for some reassurance. Anthony nodded approval. Leonard did join in the game, but pulled out after the bet went above $50. It became a late-night poker game. Leonard smoked many cigarettes as he observed the game. He had gotten accustomed to Greek cigarettes as the milder American ones were nowhere to be found. The tobacco has a certain bite to it, came from Turkey, from the region of Anatolia and Cappadocia. His cigarette smoke filled the room.

This he knew was part of Anthony's secret world. It was a way of making fast cash on Hydra that had its own treachery. Leonard saw the sweat on Anthony's brow. The fear and the expectation. His eyes rolled across the cards to the Queen of hearts, aces and fives. Anthony liked to joke about the Queen of Tarts, as his best card. He told him that he always looked for a royal flush. Anthony and Sam fought it out all night, in their attempt to win the sacred stack of notes in front of them. As the evening progressed the stakes were raised. Leonard drank more wine and smoked numerous cigarettes. So many that the stubs were warming his fingertips. Anthony won hands down and counted out the money. It was a tidy sum of $600. This kind of money could buy a small house on Hydra.

Sam looked at Leonard and Anthony unfazed. His reputation as a high stake's roller was certainly true. He was a man who lived on the edge. Hollywood stars and fast cars were part of his life. He was a man at home among the jet set. He boasted about the life he had led and the glamourous people he had met. He told him that he had known the Dominican diplomat, Porfirio Rubirosa. He was the one who also worked for the dictator Rafale Trujillo. Rubirosa was also a spy and an assassin. He also married one of the richest women in the world. Trujillo was assassinated and Rubi had to flee to Europe.

"Yes, he was a great lover, of women," said Sam, as he downed a glass of champagne.

"Who were his conquests," asked Leonard.

"The list is a long one," replied Sam.

"Dolores Del Rio, for one."

"There was also Eartha Kitt, Marlyn Monroe, Joan Crawford, Veronica Lake, Kim Novak, Judy Garland, Eva Peron, and Zsa Zsa Gabor."

"Well, that is a long list for sure," said Leonard.

"He was married to Doris Duke, the richest woman in the USA. He also was married to Barbara Hutton for a time; after their divorce she paid him $2.5 million after getting a divorce from her.

"He was reported to be hung like a mule!"

"What?" said Anthony breaking into laughter.

"They all married him for that, not the money!" "Why else, said Sam, breaking into laughter."

"Where is he now?"

"Well, we playboys work, live and die hard."

"He's in Paris living in a 17th century mansion that Doris Duke gave him. He races his sports cars between various night clubs across Paris. He is the last of the great playboys and a dying breed," said Sam in admiration.

***

He reflected back on the conversation that he had with Sam; the male bravado. the playboy lifestyle, the champagne, and fast cars. Why he wondered, why did he need to do this to attract women. Men were the hunters and the peacock of the species. Were women only attracted to money and not to love. He did not want this playboy life style. He knew that he was an idealist in an increasingly material world and there were many temptations. He had come to Hydra to live a simple life. He liked Sam, but promised himself that he would not be seduced by the playboy lifestyle, if he ever became a rich man.

***

Chapter 19
Priam's Gold

Anthony introduced Leonard to a Greek named George Lialio's. He was an educated young man and spoke many languages including French. Leonard liked to speak with him sometimes. He belonged to one of the old aristocratic families from Athens. He had an interest in philosophy, and had learnt to play classical piano from his father who was a composer. His family had a large estate on the Peloponnese, where they produced olive oil. They had bought a large villa in Hydra, above the harbour where many parties and grand receptions were held especially after their olive harvest.

One evening, Leonard, Anthony arrived with Marianne at one of the parties at his villa named after, Antonis Oikonomou a Greek naval captain in the Greek War of Independence; who build this villa and the church behind about two hundred years ago. He was married to Angelika a German artist, who created flower paintings, detailed garden scenes and watercolour miniatures of the Greek islands. The villa had gothic Venetian arches and inside lattice cedar ceilings. It had a grand terrace that looked down towards Hydra harbour and was a very fine setting to have a drinks party. The terrace was full of people when they arrived. Servants hurried about with trays of drinks and food.

Marianne wore a yellow dress with a pattern of white roses, a necklace, and her hair was held in a ponytail. Leonard was introduced to a beautiful Russian woman with long dark hair and deep blue eyes. She was called Lily Mack. He told her about his mother and her escape from Russia. Mack's parents had escaped also. He met her husband as well. He was called Christian Heidsieck who had inherited a champagne empire. Christian loved books too and spoke a lot about Ibsen, the great Norwegian playwright that Marianne loved.

Leonard recognised one on the guests. He had seen his picture before in a Montreal newspaper. It was the famous Greek millionaire, Aristotle Onassis, owner of a great shopping empire. Aristotle was not tall and had a balding head with coal black eyebrows, and sported a deep tan. He wore white trousers and a white shirt with gold cufflinks. Ari greeted them.

"We Greeks are always in search of the gold of Priam," said Ari to Leonard, Anthony and Marianne, as he handed them glasses of champagne from a passing waiter's tray.

"What is Priam's gold," said Marianne. Ari replied with a great smile.

"Well as you know, Priam's gold was found by the German millionaire Heinrich Schliemann in lost city of Troy. But it was taken to Moscow by the Russians after the battle for Berlin, and never seen again."

Behind Ari, a strikingly beautiful woman approached Ari and put her hand on his shoulder.

"Oh, Maria," said Aristotle, beaming a smile.

"May I introduce you to the greatest opera singer in the world - Maria Callas," said Ari.

'Ari is the greatest man in the world," said Maria smiling.

Maria was charming, and beautiful, but Leonard sensed her insecurity. She was a kind of trophy for Ari, who collected women like ships.

"Ari is always giving me compliments. I am just a normal woman with a big voice. My sister was slim and beautiful and my mother only loved her. I was the ugly duckling, fat and clumsy and not very popular," said Maria, sadly.

"Ugly duckling," your beautiful Maria said Ari.

"It is cruel to make a woman feel ugly and unwanted," said Marianne.

"I love my baby," said Ari, putting his arm around Maria's shoulder.

"I'll never forgive my mother for taking my childhood away," said Maria, filling her glass with champagne. Ari reflected for a moment, and looked out across the harbour to see the golden disc of the sun setting.

"You know I was a poor man once. God has been good to me. Luck was on my side. I was born in Smyrna in Turkey. But that was destroyed in a great fire in 1922. I was only sixteen at the time and we escaped by ship just in time, 100,000 Greeks and Armenians died there. Over 400,000 refugees escaped to the waterfront. We were nearly burnt alive. My father and my mother were close to death. No one was found responsible for the fire."

"You survived," said Leonard, philosophically.

"Yes, but only by the skin of my teeth. That is what my experience of life has been. I have come close to disaster many times and survived by a hair's breadth. I own the world's largest privately owned shipping fleet in the world. In a way I am like Ulysses who led a thousand ships to Troy. But I never forgot my past, the struggle, and the suffering of us Greeks, and what we endured during war and peace. We had a lots our property in Smyrna. We were rich, but after that night we became as poor as church mice."

Aristotle took up a piece of bread from a table covered in silver trays of grapes, olives and cakes. He lifted it up and looked at it. "We did not have not even have a piece of bread to eat, not one piece, now I am a rich man," said Ari with deep emotion. Leonard could see tears in Ari's eyes. He could see that there was pain and suffering inside him. Maria kissed him on his cheek and ran her hand over his forehead.

"Ari, don't be like this. You think too much of the past. Life is too short for all this pain. We Greeks are too sentimental - we love tragedy."

"We all have our troubles," said Marianne.

George approached them, "Maria, you promised that you would sing for us," he said. Leonard and Marianne felt it was good timing. The conversation had descended into sadness that he at times they had tried to avoid. Like a flash of lightening, Maria's mood changed and she stood up and became elevated, almost like a different person; enchanting like a Greek goddess from another age.

"Ok, this is from Donizetti. I am preparing for my performance of the opera called Poliutoi, in the La Scala theatre in Milan," said Maria, standing upright and expanding her chest, like a peacock.

Maria told them that it was an opera about Armenia, that was occupied by the Romans in 259 AD. It was decreed that all Christians be put to death. It was a tragic opera that begins in a secret sanctuary, where Christian worshippers assemble. Maria recited the chorus for them. "May a veil of secrecy still protect us from the ungodly sword, which threatens us." The words resonated on Leonard's mind. The Jews too had suffered under the Romans and the Nazis in this ungodly world. Somehow, he thought to himself we had to hold on to something. Religion was a crutch for mankind, but it was a good one. He remembered the lines from St Mathew. *'Faith love and hope and the greatest of these is love.'*

Leonard sat by Marianne and suddenly the party was silent. Maria's voice was like a nightingale. Her voice echoed across the villa and everyone stood still. It was a voice of an angel. Someone joined her on the classical piano. Leonard thought that the tone of her voice was warm, lyrical, beautiful, intense and profound. Her voice swirled and moved like a swarm of birds in the sky. It flared like a flame and filled the air with melodious vibrations. It was like a great choir and her voice shone with a certain refined brilliance.

Maria told Leonard and Marianne later that she had been a model student, and a fanatical perfectionist. She had dedicated her heart and her soul to her craft. She moved forward in her studies in great strides. She studied for six hours a day. Within six months she was singing the most difficult arias, in the international opera scene with the greatest musical excellence. Her technical training was of such brilliance, it assisted her voice that was like that an angel.

***

Aristotle invited them later to his large yacht called Christina, that was moored in the port. Anthony told him that it was his wife's name. Servants in white uniforms and gold lapels served them more champagne. Leonard could see that many young women had married older Greek men. Greece was a patriarchal society, and no one wanted to admit it. The men with the money found a trophy wife of a young age. There was no social security and no protection for women. If a woman had no family, a husband, or a job she had no income. Those who found jobs were usually held in contracts like servants. The women that were lucky to marry were showered with diamonds and beautiful dresses. Leonard observed these social contradictions. There was a social divide between the rich and the poor that as wide as the Grand Canyon. The women especially the young ones had to put up with these old men to survive. Somewhere charming while others were abusive or bad humoured.

***

Marianne received a letter from Axel. It was bad news. Patricia's car had been speeding along a road near Athens. When it turned to avoid a farmer's donkey and crashed into a bridge and ended in a riverbed, where the water had evaporated. She was thrown out of the car and broke many bones. In hospital she lay covered in bandages. The nurses did not provide her with antiseptic, so she developed gangrene in her fingers. One of her thumbs had to be amputated. Axel asked her to come to Athens. He wrote her words of desperation. Leonard told her to go there and see how he was. Axel abandoned her and now he wanted to console her and Patricia. What a terrible hypocrite Axel was she thought, but out of a sense of concern and damaged loyalty, she decided to go.

Marianne met Axel in the hospital and found Patricia in bad shape. Axel had lost a lot of weight, and was filled with emotions of guilt and despair. She could not feel anything for Patricia, the woman who destroyed her marriage. In the past weeks she had feelings of hatred and jealousy. There was no way back for her and Axel. She realised now it was all a terrible disaster.

Marianne returned to Hydra and lay in Leonard's arms. He kissed her sweetly. He touched her soft blonde hair. The bond with Axel was broken. She knew that and by a twist of fate she had ended up in Leonard's arms. Love and tragedy always seemed to be linked, Leonard reflected. Axel had pushed the boundaries of his desires and lost. Marianne lay with Leonard in the moonlight, while Axel junior lay near them.

Marianne spoke of Axel's egotism, and of his demands of forgiveness, and for her understanding. He admitted that he had broken a moral code between husband and wife. But his ruthless decisions had now brought him desperation and terrible emotional realities and its consequences. He had broken the vows of his protestant Lutheran religion, and because of this he had that now inflicted so much pain on her, and betrayed her. He told Marianne that he now suffered, and he still wanted her to feel for him, but realised that such now was impossible.

***

Chapter 20
Lorca's Ghost

Marianne cooked him a dinner from a Norwegian recipe, of dumplings, meatballs, spice, gravy ribs, and salmon. They exchanged many kisses, Leonard and Marianne spoke into the late hours. Marianne fell asleep in his arms as the clock sounded. He looked at her angel face. He wrote some lines about her.

> *'Her blonde hair and her blue eyes. I loved her in the morning. Her hair lay upon my pillow, blonde like silk. I see her in a golden light.'*

In the mornings, Marianne always gave him a sweet kiss before making a breakfast of fried eggs followed by oranges, cheese and scones, that were covered in honey that she had bought in Katsikas cafe. She also put an old disc on the record player of that Leonard had brought from Montreal.

Sometimes Leonard woke some night thinking of Marianne, as she lay beside him. He thought he had insomnia, or perhaps it was the cuckoo clock that he had bought in the market place, that struck ever hour. A little yellow bird always appeared by some articulated means; before it vanished behind two little doors that were painted with the Greek symbols of Alpha and Omega. At night, Leonard could see the moonlight casting shadows, that sometimes seemed to create outlines of some spectral figure. Was it his imagination or was it real he wondered? He recalled that this hour of the night, was known as the hour of the wolf. The hour between night and the dawn. The hour when most people die and when sleep is deepest, and nightmare and one's fears are the most real, and ghosts and demons are the most powerful.

***

One night he thought he could make out a figure standing in a shadow at the end of his bed, as Marianne lay asleep beside him. Was it the influence from the peyote, he wondered or the ghosts that Anthony had told him about? At first, he could just make out the outline but then a head appeared. He wondered if it was a figment of his imagination or was it real. He just could not tell. The face that appeared was a handsome one. It had features with deep-set eyes and dark wavy hair, round and pleasant features with high cheek bones, that could have been sculpted by Canova the Italian sculptor. The figure opened his mouth slowly to form words from his perfectly shaped lips. Leonard sat up in his bed nervously and saw the handsome man staring at him.
"Don't be afraid, I am only a spirit!"
"A spirit," said Leonard.
"Yes a spirit. My name is Frederica Garcia Lorca, I want you to rewrite my poem about Vienna, about love and loss and desire."
"So, you want to hear it."
"Of course,'' said Leonard nervously.
The spectral figure recited his poem; 'Viennese Waltz.'

> *''In Vienna there are ten little girls,*
> *a shoulder for death to cry on,*
> *and a forest of dried pigeons.*
> *There is a fragment of tomorrow,*
> *In the museum of winter frost,*
> *There is a thousand-windowed dance hall.*
> *Ay, ay, ay, ay!*
> *Take this close-waltz,*
> *Little waltz, little waltz, little waltz,*
> *Of itself of death, and of brandy,*
> *That dips its tail in the sea,*
> *I love you; I love you; I love you,*
> *With the armchair and the book of death,*

Down the melancholy hallway,
In the iris' darkened garret,
Ay, ay, ay, ay!
Take this broken-wasted waltz,
In Vienna there are four mirrors,
In which your mouth and the echoes play,
There is a death for piano,
That paints little boys blue,
There are beggars on the roof,
There are fresh garlands of tears,
Ay, ay, ay, ay!
Take this waltz that dies in my arms,
Can you create a song from my poem?"

"Yes, I would love to. I have always admired your work. You are an inspiration to me," said Leonard, looking at the spectre. "You opened doors for me to another world of emotions!"
"That is what we poets do. We hand the torch to a new generation." replied Lorca.
"I tried to open the doors of perfection to the human mind." said Lorca.
"I always will guide you, and be an angel standing at your shoulder," said Lorca.

The figure vanished into the blue shadow. He reflected on whether the spectre were real - he could not tell. He imagined a ballroom in Vienna. A ballroom in the Hofburg Palace and a ceiling covered with a painting of angels.

Leonard got out of bed and sat at his table and lit his oil lamp; and began to write and reinterpret Lorca's poem, that he found in his book. He wrote in his diary.

"There are women in long silk dresses, with pearl necklaces and diamonds rings. There is a long gallery

> *with nine hundred windows and Dorian columns, filled with white doves. He imagined a painting of a beautiful princess framed in gold. I can see Lorca as he dances with one of the ladies. They moved and danced about the gallery of mirrors, and across the green marble floor gracefully.'*

Leonard can see this magical scene. It was graceful like an image that belonged to another place and time. He reflected upon his visitation. Was it part of his imagination, was it real or not? He could not tell. Since he became a poet the line between his imagination and reality had become blurred. The true nature of the reality, of one's dreams and perceptions were questionable.

***

Leonard thought about Marianne during those dark hours as she lay sleeping. She was the most beautiful woman he had ever met. She was as an angel who had come to cure him of his loneliness and his longings. She was his guide through the darkness that he experienced at times. He knew he had to be with her for certain, and he felt that she understood the poetic mind. She too was in search of this world and understood it. They shared their deepest thoughts. In the morning Leonard lay back and took Marianne in his arms. He wrote in his diary.

> *'I wanted to be with you for a long time. But you know sometimes you want someone in your life, but you cannot belong to them. What you desire is not possible, but you know you can make it all possible.'*

He talked to her about Saint Catherine Tekakwitha, who Susanne had talked about. He told her how she believed in the value of suffering. She did not eat very much and she would lie on a mat of thorns. There was a custom among the native American people, to pierce themselves with thorns in thanksgiving for some good. Then knowing the terrible burns given to prisoners, she also burned herself.

   Leonard and Marianne shared their inner world and beliefs with each other. But Leonard never spoke about Lorca's ghost to her.

"You have to follow what you believe and show kindness to others," said Marianne looking at a bell hanging on the wall, with the image of an eagle carved on it.

"Where is the bell from Leonard?" said Marianne, quite curious.

"It's a sacred bell from Russia. It belonged to the synagogue where my father worshiped in Lithuania. Then Marianne looked at the small picture beside it.

"Who is the photo of?" said Marianne.

"It is a photo of my grandfather. He studied the Talmud and was a Russian Jew and escaped the pogroms. He was an expert on Jewish religious law, theology, and the foundation for all Jewish beliefs. He came to Canada in 1927.

"Why did they treat the Jews so badly?"

"Ignorance, stupidity and hatred," said Leonard laying back on his bed.

"As a child I was full of messianic beliefs. My father told me I was a descendant of Aeron, the high priest."

"Who was Aeron?"

"The brother of Moses. He escaped with him to Israel, the promised land. Aeron has the unblemished priest, and all the elders since have to be related to him, or they cannot administer in the Jewish faith."

Marianne lay in Leonard's arms and continued to ask about his past.

"Your love for poetry. Where did it all begin for you?"

Leonard was silent for a minute, then spoke quietly.

"I heard the singing in my local synagogue. I remember it so vividly as a child. The interior was filled with worshippers sitting in the pews and reading the Torah. At the head of the congregation in a dark cassock there was a rabbi, who wore a round skull cap. From his lips came the words from the Torah. The chanting of his phrases rang out across the synagogue, and they became embedded in my memory. It was a place of assembly and much prayer. My father told me that his ancestors were Ashkenazi Jews from Lithuania, and Poland but his mother's parents were Hasidic. They had spoken Yiddish that had its origins in Hebrew. They were persecuted under the Russian Tzar. So, one day with the help of the great Baron De Hirsch, they escaped across the fields and valleys of Europe, to the coast to catch the great liners to America.''

***

Leonard mind drifted to a song he had written about love. It was love that had preoccupied him. So, what was this love all about - a thousand kisses deep? He wondered could love have an endurance to it. Could it belong to a lifetime? Could love be really that deep? He recalled that his feelings at times had such a sensitivity, that it was like being exposed and naked. The feeling came back to him. The words about love came floating back, like tissues of memory once again.

There were words that he had scrawled in his notebook, with a blue ink pen that he had bought in a marketplace in Montreal from an old Jewish man. Leonard wrote lines about the vulnerability of love, of how some men did not match women's expectations. He felt that he had a second-hand physique that suggested to him his apprehensions, his insecurities about love that we all have sometimes. He thought about and reflected on this. How one sometimes we do not measure up to love and its great challenges.

He recalled he had read Dickens book, Great Expectations, at university. The image of Miss Havisham, who was jilted by her suitor on her wedding day, came to mind, and how she wore her wedding dress all her life. Leonard wrote in his diary.

> *'Many had loved before me. Love had smiled at us both. I hoped that they would not become too distant or ever have to say goodbye. I know that I am not looking for another. I will never have to wander in time or walk alone. My love goes with her and will stay with me, like the shoreline by the sea. I do not want to speak about the difficulties of our love, of the chains and the things that could unite us. I could see her eyes filled with tears and sorrow. I never wanted to say goodbye.'*

Marianne was an endless comfort to him. There was an emptiness, however, that came into his life at times. Momentary fleeting but perceptible. He fought against it. He filled his days with a routine of cooking, writing and dinner parties. Anthony brought him many fruits and cheeses. They were the largest grapes he had ever seen, and the oranges were also large like melons. There was something magical about them. Leonard sensed that it was because of the Greek sun. Here for hundreds of years a great civilization had flourished, maybe because of the food.

Perhaps this place would help him create great poems and great words of art. Lyricism was in the air, in the wine, food, the water and the landscape itself. It was inspiring. Perhaps it was the surreal enchanted landscape between heaven and earth, of a place bathed in liquid gold.

He felt complete in some way. He was Jewish and he still had a respect for his religion. He read the Torah as a boy and the rituals had seeped into his consciousness. The rituals and the prayers had a structure. The new poetry has evoked the past and the present. He recalled T.S. Eliot's "Mythical Method." He had read about it in university. In the present was the past and the imagery of the past belonged to the present. Where myth and reality were all layered into one. This was his own method that he used when writing his poems.

***

Leonard walked to the port every morning. His routine was to drink an American coffee and have fresh baked bread from the local bakery. He discovered it was run by Dimitri who sold white bread and brown loves. The oven for Leonard was a sight to behold and its furnace of flames. Now and then Dimitri would fling open the door and before the flames, one could see the crust of the loaves being cooked. With a wooden paddle he would remove the loaves of bread and put them on a freshly washed timber table top made from planks of wood sprinkled with flour. Dimitri would lay out his creations on its surface like new-born babies and wrap them in paper.

Leonard has bought a string bag to carry his shopping. He would make his way to Katsikas cafe. Nick had no objections to Leonard cutting slices from his warm bread. He even supplied a tray of fresh butter, made from goat's milk spices with herbs, that Nick said came from the mountains near Olympia.

Leonard loved the coffee beans from Africa. The brew was topped with cream of the richest kind. Leonard sometimes sat alone on a wicker chair at one of the small tables shaded by an umbrella. Anthony, George and Charmian would meet him sometimes, but it was difficult to make an appointment. He learnt that phones on the island were rare and it took months to install one. When they did meet at Katsikas, Leonard witnessed the arguments between George and Charmian, mostly when they became drunk; that sometimes would end in such fights, then Leonard and Anthony would have to separate them.

Anthony, however, told him that he knew a Greek called Alexander who kept pigeons. He had supplied pigeons to send message to the Greek army during the Nazi occupation. This was an idea he wanted to put to put to good use. Anthony brought Leonard to visit Alexander at his house above the village, where Leonard brought a pigeon in a cage. Anthony attached a ring to its foot which he could attach notes to. It was an amazing sight to see the pigeons fly in and land in Leonard's window. Before the month was out, George, Charmian and Timothy had bought a pigeon too. Making an appointment would no longer be a problem.

***

Leonard read Lorca poem,' The Wounds of Love.'

> *'This light, this flame that devours this weight of the sea breaks on me. This scorpion that lives inside my breast. They are a garland of love, bed of the wounded, where dreamlessly, I dream of your presence among the ruins of my sunken breast, and though I seek the summit of discretion that your heart grants me a valley stretched below, with hemlock and passion of bitter wisdom... it is the wounds of love."*

***

Chapter 21
Pain and Pleasure

Hydra for Leonard was unfolding to them like layers of an onion. It was enchanting but it could be treacherous at times. Those that came to Hydra escaped many conflicts and the pollution of the city they lived in. The Greeks seemed to accept all those who sought refuge there. But for Leonard, the outside world always protruded into his. He had bought an old radio in the market and Anthony rigged it up for him with an aerial on the roof. He picked up the Voice of America. There were reports of the deaths in the Vietnam war, and the racial unrest in America, and the heroic efforts of Martin Luther King.

More drama emerged on Hydra that Leonard could not have imagined. He continued to record it faithfully in his diary, and all these events. Sometimes reality become more extraordinary than fiction. For Leonard, Hydra was becoming a paradise lost. He could feel the pain and the inequality.

The island was raw and savage at times. It only appeared now and again. It had its handicapped and poor hidden behind closed doors. It had its suffering sad donkeys, kittens with diseased eyes and fur with sores. It had thumb sized scorpions that could kill you, braying donkeys and viper snakes that crawled into your bed at night. There were drunken neighbours, long suffering wives, and women in black mourning their dead husbands forever. There was infidelity, and wives screaming at idle husbands playing games of backgammon. There was the sound of an owl at night, bed bugs. There was the smell of unclean toilets, charcoal, frying meat, perfume, and hair oil. There was thunder and lightning, and rain on roof tops. There were violent dangerous storms, that brought sand on winds from the Sahara. Between the sea and the mountains of Hydra, there was a port that was like a theatre whether you liked it or not. He had to take part in this theatre every day. There was just no escape. It was a place that created a drama, among the people who lived there.

***

As always there was Marianne and Axel problems. "Drugs had driven him crazy," said Marianne, looking despondent. Marianne told Leonard that she was filled with a sense of defeat after the breakup. She had followed her heart like most women, and it had become a disaster. She had been abandoned. The great achievement of having a son together had it seems meant little to Axel. Why did men engage in such liaisons with women she asked Leonard? Why were men guilty of such transgressions?

She had heard of a Norwegian girl who had married a man and left him for another, after the wedding reception. The final insult was she took all the wedding presents with her. It was painful, demeaning and degrading what Axel had done, in his in pursuit of his ego; and in the investigation of the outer reaches of his mind. Leonard for her was like a wise old owl. Patient and understanding. Alex was impulsive and aggressive in contrast to Leonard's calmness, good manners, great courtesy and empathy.

***

Within all these struggles there were some small pleasures that Leonard indulged in. Leonard and Marianne spent enchanting evenings together, drinking ouzo and retsina. They danced to Mikis Theodorakis or to some beautiful Greek ballad. They regularly went to Kamini beach together. Leonard always wore a sun hat, that made him look like Al Capone, while Marianne wore a wide straw hat. Sometimes they would walk there together. Marianne pulled along Axel in a children's pram that had large wheels, made in the 1930's. Sophia had sold it to her.

One day when Leonard and Marianne were swimming in Kamini beach, a film crew arrived that were making a movie called Phaedra. It was the story about the wife of shipping tycoon who falls in love with her husband's son, from his first marriage. It was an unusual retelling of the Oedipus mother and son love story - a love that is doomed. Leonard and Marianne met the director Jules Dassin, and its stars the Greek actress, Melina Mercuri and the American Anthony Perkins. Leonard had seen Alfred Hitchcock's film, psycho and was surprised to meet the star, of Hitchcock's murder story, on the beach. He did did not look like the psycho Norman Bates at all.

There they sat admiring the many fishing boats tied up and painted white and blue. They always had lunch in a yellow painted café, run by an old Greek man named Thanos. He had a beard and a bald head, and he spoke with a stutter. Leonard wondered was it because of his lack of English or a childhood trauma. The yellow cafe had walls with old Greek photos of bygone days. Thanos' grandfather and his relatives peered down at them.

There was a photo of Spiros Louis, the winner of the Greek marathon in the Athens Olympics in 1896; giving a bunch of flowers to Hitler at the Berlin games. Leonard thought it would make a good title for his new book of poems – Flowers for Hitler. They sat looking at the sunset while Axel junior lay sleeping under an umbrella to block out the sun. Leonard wrote in his diary.

> *'Everyone was so beautiful and talented on Hydra. They had the Gods protecting them. They were involved in acts of love and creation. Everyone in our world seemed special and so perfect. We all lived with our dreams and with the illusions of youth.'*

Marianne and Leonard went to the post office as usual one morning at 11:30. There was a letter there from Axel. She opened it slowly in Katsika's café and read it to Leonard.

'Please forgive me Marianne. I have been brutal towards you and insensitive. I realise now I have an egotistic nature. I am unable to beg you for forgiveness; or even ask you for understanding about what I have done to you. It is far beyond common morals. My behaviour has its consequences and has made me feel that I am in a trap. I am deeply sorry for inflicting this suffering on you. I believed in my conviction that one can live by one's desires. But I have discovered that breaking the rules is not moral. My decision to live with Patricia has made me lonely, not happy and I am dealing with that. My heart bleeds deeply for you. I feel sad for you. There are a thousand voices in me that scream at me for my terrible mistake. The voices say leave Patricia, to go back home to your wife and hold her close in my arms. I wish that you could feel for me in the way I feel for you. But I know that it is all not possible now. I must accept my fate. Think of me, but believe me, I love you more than ever. Leaving you has made me a victim of my own ego. Our marriage hangs on a thin thread. I am going to travel to Mexico with Patricia, to discover the secrets of the Mayan prophecy - that will bring about a new age for us all - the age of Aquarius.''

Marianne handed the letter to Leonard.

"He's realized he has made a mistake. It's too late. He has lost me," said Marianne.

"That thread is broken," said Marianne. She placed Axel's letter over a burning candle. They watched it burn.

***

Anthony arrived at the beach in Kamini one day, and dropped a bombshell that he was sleeping with Charmian Clift. Leonard was surprised. He told them that George was impotent, and

Charmian had enough of his drunken binges. Marianne could not reproach him as she understood his dilemma.

"You are married, Anthony. What about Christina, your wife and Emily your daughter?" said Leonard, challenging him.

"Nothing is forever…you both know that. I need your love, Leonard not your morals?" said Anthony.

"I know nothing is forever," replied Marianne sadly. She knew only too well what that meant.

***

Many weeks later another letter arrived from Axel, informing Marianne that he had arrived in Mexico with Patricia, to investigate the Mayan prophecy. Leonard assured Marianne that the Mayan calendar was just a cycle in time like the Julian calendar that the Vatican had created; and that there would be no end to the world on the appointed date of 2012. Axel had experimented with LSD in Mexico, and got infected by malaria from a mosquito bite. He had a fever and was vomiting for ten days while Patricia nursed him. Another letter arrived from him.

> *'Dear Marianne; I don't want to see your tears. I cannot comfort you. I know you will think it cruel of me. Try and accept that there was never a complete relationship between us. If it is not a perfect one, I don't want it. I know that I have given you a lot of pain. You should liberate yourself in the arms of another man. I am in a rat trap that I cannot escape from. Can you investigate immediately how we can get a divorce quickly as possible as I want to marry, Patricia.'*

This was the final betrayal for Marianne. She thought that maybe the relationship with Patricia would just fall apart, but this letter was 'the straw that broke the camel's back'.

***

Leonard remembered about the introduction to the painter Ghika by Barbara Rothschild, who wanted to become his third wife. He told Anthony about it. He arrived with two donkeys and the headed up the hills to the house. Anthony told him that it was an eighteenth century forty room mansion, perched on a steep hillside. Many famous artists, writers and photographers had stayed there, like Henry Miller, Lawrence Durrell, Norman Mailer, Henri Cartier-Bresson, Le Corbusier, John Craxton, Rex Warner and Cyril Connolly. Ghika himself, was greatly inspired by the island's unique scenery, in his paintings. Anthony told him that the American writer, Henry Miller, wrote 'The Colossus of Maroussi', on Hydra in Ghika's villa. Miller travelled to Greece in 1939, after the Nazis invaded France in September 1939.

The villa appeared with archways and many windows. It looked like a large imposing building, more like a palace than a villa. They made their way with their mules up along steep tracks, that were shaded in places by trees. Anthony came to a halt at a row of steps that led up to a patio. There were many earthenware amphora. Beyond the terrace was a large door. They dismounted and tied up their donkeys and climbed the steep set of steps. They crossed the patio and stood in front of the large door. They could see a brass knocker with a lion's head. Leonard lifted it and made three raps on the door.

They waited a few minutes and it slowly opened. It began to creak on it hinges. A figure of a woman appeared. She had grey hair, and wore glasses, a white apron and a blue dress covered in white flowers. She had weathered skin deeply tanned by the Greek sun.

"I am looking for Mr Ghika, is he here?" said Leonard.

"I am afraid he is not here. He is in Crete at the moment."

"I have an introduction from Barbara Rothschild, who I met in London. When he comes back will you tell him that Leonard Cohen called to see him."

For a moment the woman looked at Leonard up and down, with disgust.

"We want no more Jews here in this house." Before Leonard could reply, she slammed the door in his face. Shocked, Leonard turned to Anthony, who lifted his eyebrows. It was the first time that he had directly experienced anti-Semitism. It made him feel angry, sad and confused. They climbed back down the steps and sat there. Anthony gave him a bottle of water to help calm his thirst and his nerves.

"There has to be a good reason for this. It is possibly related to the fact that Ghika is marrying Barbara Rothschild and the housekeeper thinks she's Jewish. Greek women do not take kindly to infidelity and men marrying women from other countries or races, remember that woman with the knife, 'said Leonard on a state of shock.

"I am beginning to find out how jealous Greek woman can be. Have you heard the lines, hell hath no fury like a woman scorned?"

"Shakespeare," replied Anthony.

"No, everyone thinks it's Shakespeare. It from the play 'The Mourning Bride', a tragic play by the Anglo-Irish playwright William Congreve," said Leonard.

"We have learnt a hard lesson here today, Anti-Semitism is alive and well in Greece, even after the Nazis left Greece."said Leonard drinking heavily from the bottle of water and pouring it over his head. He felt the cold liquid streaming down his face and it consoled him.

***

Chapter 22
Ghika's House

Leonard lay in bed with Marianne and woke in the middle of the night. He was awoken by crackling noises and the smell of burning wood. Suddenly the night sky flared up in flames of crimson, yellow and orange. Leonard leapt out of bed and put his clothes on quickly.
"What is it?" asked Marianne, sitting up in bed.
"It looks like a fire." Leonard could hear the crackling of wood in the flames. Marianne got up quickly and got dressed also. Minutes later they were standing in the laneway. They could see some men running up the street, along with Anthony.
"What happened?" asked Leonard.
"It's Ghika's house. Let's get up there and see if we can save some paintings," said Anthony. After his bad experience there, Leonard was not so sure.
"What about the fire brigade?" he said.
"Leonard, there is no fire brigade. You forget there's a water shortage on the island." For one brief moment a cold hard reality came home to him that Hydra still belonged to the 19th century. Leonard and Marianne ran after Anthony up the laneway. They followed Anthony as he frantically made his way up the narrow laneways, until they reached a rocky outcrop. Before them lay a tragic sight. Ghika's house was engulfed in flames.
"We've got to try and save the paintings. They are priceless," shouted Anthony. They walked further on to find many of the locals carrying furniture. Anthony spoke to them in Greek. Anthony cast his eyes to the ground and then looked at Leonard and Marianne.
"The old lady we met was injured when the roof collapsed on her," said Anthony. Was it deliberate, Leonard wondered?
"Where is she?" asked Marianne, quite concerned.

Out of the darkness appeared four men carrying a stretcher. On it lay the Greek caretaker. He head was covered in bandages and her hands also. The bearers of the stretcher stopped and observed her condition.

"It looks like third degree burns," said Anthony. Then they watched the old lady disappearing into the night. Then they headed on upwards towards the house. They could feel the heat of the flames, that had spread from the house like a furnace. Ashes and small pieces of wood floated in the breeze. Marianne held Leonard's hand and watched the inferno. In the surrounding landscape they could see men carrying paintings. It was a large house on a slope, whitewashed, surrounded by rocks, almond and fig trees, marble busts and Greek vases.

"At least they saved some things," said Anthony, his face flickering in the flames.

"Where is Ghika?" asked Leonard, holding Marianne tightly.

"He's in London. I will call him and tell him the sad news," said Anthony, looking dejected.

"The house had forty rooms full of antiques and paintings. It's a national treasure."

"Get them to take the paintings down to my house," said Leonard.

"Yes, I agree there could be looting. Remember some of these Greeks are descendants of pirates."

Anthony gave the men Leonard's instructions. When they returned to the house, their sitting room was filled with Ghika's paintings. Sophia their housekeeper arrived. She came to check on them, and made them all some tea and served them some buns with jam and butter. Sophia looked at them intently.

"It's a woman's revenge," said Sophia, lifting her finger and pointing it at a painting of Ghika's wife that lay against the wall. Leonard sat mystified.

"What revenge?" said Leonard, casting his eyes at Marianne and Anthony.

"I know Ghika's housekeeper. She told me the story. He left his Greek wife and wants to marry an Englishwoman." Leonard, Marianne and Anthony recoiled in shock.

"It can't be true," said Leonard, with his eyes wide open.

"No one is angrier than a woman rejected in love," replied Anthony. "I have seen this before."

"In Norway we say 'If you cannot make a man treat you right, you can make him wish he did," said Marianne. She knew what this anger was all about.

***

The following day Leonard, Marianne and Anthony were invited to Katerina Paouri's house – the richest woman on Hydra. She was a close friend of Ghika's. One of her servants called Leoni arrived at Leonard's house, with a message from her. They followed her along the back laneways to her villa overlooking the port.

Leoni told them that Katerina's family were one of the oldest families on the island. Her ancestor was Lazaros Coundouriotis. She was a patron of the arts and bought many of the artist's paintings on the island, including Ghika's.

They were greeted by a distinguished woman with a large frame, with blonde hair and large blue eyes. Katerina wore a traditional Greek dress and was introduced by Leoni, who disappeared into the kitchen to prepare afternoon tea. They were ushered into a sitting room that was painted in pink, and had walls covered in old oil paintings. There were many antiques there also.

"Please take a seat. I am wearing the traditional dress of Hydra. They are putting me on the thousand drachma bank note. I have the engraver coming later. Thank you for saving his paintings?"

said Katerina sitting in a large armchair covered in red and yellow silk with peacock feathers.

Leonard observed Venetian chests, mahogany tables, gold-framed oil paintings of old sailing boats and sailors. The mirrors were exquisite. They had Baroque elaborate ornamentation of intricate gold. Beneath one window there was a model of an old sailing ship.

"It is a tragedy! I called Ghika. He is very depressed. Will you make a list of the paintings?"

"Of course," said Leonard.

"Ghika is our most important living painters. We must preserve our culture and his work."

Leoni entered the room with a tray holding a teapot and tea cups and served them tea.

"I have heard the rumour that it was Ghika's servant who may have caused the fire. His first wife was not happy. It's all a terrible conspiracy to destroy him, " said Katerina

Leonard looked at Marianne and smiled.

"I am trying to save Hydra and its past. Costas is coming soon. He has been diving in the search for gold, that is located on an ancient Greek ship that was sunk by the Turks."

A well-built muscular man entered the room. He sported a moustache and long hair held in a ponytail. In his hand he carried a leather bag.

"Costas, thanks for coming," said Katerina, pouring him some tea, in a porcelain cup.

"I was lucky today, I found some gold on a sunken ship." Costas opened the case and took out a bag of gold coins and spread them on the table. They shone in the evening sun.

"They look like they are from the 18th century,'' said Katerina lifting one of the coins.

"When the Greeks launched their War of Independence in 1821, Hydra was as a leading naval power. The harbour, with its two forts had plenty of cannon, to protect the fleet of one hundred and thirty ships. The Hydriot's leader was Andreas Miaoulis, who led them and their ships in destroying the Ottoman navy. Lazaros Kountouriotis, a wealthy shipping magnate donated his fleet of ships to the cause. I can see his face on this coin, and his name. Greece won its independence, but it was at a great cost to Hydra, which lost many of its military ships in the conflict, causing an economic disaster there. During those lean years, Hydriot's again found salvation in the sea, farming the sponges that lived below the surface. Divers here used the diving suits. gathering sponges kick started the local economy and kept Hydra afloat. How many coins Costas?" said Katerina.

"I think about two thousand."

"I will contact the national museum in Athens. They are worth millions of dollars, but belong to the Greek people. Leonard, I will send my workmen to bring Ghika's paintings here."

Leonard agreed. Katerina enquired about Leonard writing and invited him there again. Leonard wrote in his diary that night.

> *'It was a terrible moment for Ghika to have lost his family home, that had been built many hundreds of years before, and now lay in ruins. Precious paintings have been destroyed, and antiques that were valuable to the people of Hydra. All because of one man's love for another woman and his rejection of his wife. Like me, Axel and Marianne, three in a relationship is a crowd. What can be salvaged from the ruins of Ghika's house and our dreams, I wonder?'*

***

Chapter 23
The Stormy Seas

Anthony informed Leonard that his card playing friend Sam Barclay had finished repairing his boat 'The Stormy Seas', in Athens, and he would be arriving in Hydra soon. He was planning on a trip with a few friends to the Greek islands. Maybe Leonard and Marianne would like to come on this trip. Marianne agreed Maria could come too and look after little Axel.

Leonard told her about his poker game with Sam and Anthony. Marianne told Leonard one of her secrets, which was that she knew Sam, and that he was once in love with her. She had not seen him in years. She told him that Sam had proposed to her once before, but she had turned him down. She was in love with Leonard and she did not want to make a bad decision. She told him that she loved Leonard, and they could only be friends and he agreed.

He arrived from Athens in his sail boat, 'The Stormy Seas'. Sam told her that he wanted her to come along on a sailing trip with some of his friends and new acquaintances. All the guests boarded the beautiful two-masted schooner early one afternoon. Sam gave the orders to the hired hands to hoist the sails. They bought enough food supplies were bought for three weeks, including wine, cheese, bread and grapes.

Leonard learnt more about Sam's life. Maybe he was a kind of playboy, but he was also a war hero. He told them that he had escaped to Greece from his banking family. His grandfather was the founder of Barclay's bank. Like Leonard, he had rejected the world of suits. Instead, he preferred to stand barefoot on his ship's deck. Sam stood erect, looking like a Viking warrior, six-foot tall, blond, athletic and with a deep tan. Sam arrived with his Scots-Irish girlfriend called Eileen. She was a tall, beautiful woman with dark hair and beautiful green eyes.

Sam laid a map out in the boat's deck and pointed out the route. The plan was to sail to Spetzes nearby and then on to the island of Skopelos, Sounion, the gulf of Euboea, and the Sporades islands, before they returned home via Mytilene and Kos. The great red sails billowed in the wind and the boat headed out of Hydra harbour. It was a wonderful majestic sight and many in the harbour watched its departure.

Sam took the till, but later a deck hand took over. On the beach on Spetzes that night they lit a camp fire and roasted meat, along with some sweet potatoes. Sam served them red wine and ouzo. Around the camp fire, Sam told them of the dark past he had led as a spy fighting the Nazi occupation of Greece. The 'Stormy Seas' was involved in a lot of secret operations. He also told them about his secret operation to overthrow the fascist regime in Albania, and how he escaped death, but his other commandos were executed.

Under the flickering light of the fire all their faces danced in the night, and above them lay the vast and clear Greek night sky. Leonard sang a song and played his guitar and people joined in the singing.

Later, Leonard and Marianne stole away and kissed in the sand dunes. Leonard could feel her warm lips; her skin so soft like silk, and for a moment all his desires of love seemed realised.

The following morning, they had breakfast in the village café. Marianne and Eileen agreed to take care of the cooking. They laid out on the galley table, grapes, cheese, meat, eggs, coffee, wine and freshly baked bread.

"Spetzes is the island where the novel 'The Magus' was written,' said Sam, explaining that the English writer John Fowles had lived there in the fifties. " It was a mysterious novel about myth and reality."

"He is still here," said the waiter.

'What do you mean?' enquired Leonard.

'Mr Conchis is still here. Do you want to meet him?'

'Why not,'' said Leonard looking at Marianne. An hour later the waiter took him after the café was closed to meet the infamous Maurice Conchis, that the book; 'The Magus', was based on. Was the book real or unreal? Nobody knew. Leonard was curious. They arrived at a large white villa, with statues of lions and Greek heroes along the pathway, that had a line of ancient trees.

Marianne and Leonard are greeted by an old man, elegantly dressed in a white suit. He had a well-trimmed grey beard and wore glasses. He had a walking stick made of the finest cedar wood, that had a silver handle that had a shape of a lion, with an open mouth. He wore a white straw hat with a gold bandana. Maurice Concis told them that he used to practice as a psychologist, but was now retired. Marianne told him about her dreams and studies and he offered to help her. He had studied Carl Jung.

Conchis had a beautiful villa with Roman columns and mosaics floors. The walls were covered in paintings of ancient Greek nymphs, the Sybil at Cumae, and the Delphic Oracle. Conchis was a man of tastes, and an aesthete of sorts. He continued to talk about the fascination that the Nazis had for Greek culture and how the first Olympic flame was taken by relay runners from Athens to Berlin in 1936. Leonard became nervous of him when he said he was an admirer of Hitler, and admitted that he assisted the Nazis when they occupied Athens. He told him he was Jewish, and it seemed to him that his blood drained from Conchis face. Leonard was disappointed and disgusted by Conchis rantings and made an excuse to leave with Marianne, who could see that Leonard had grown angry.

***

They sailed north towards the Sporades islands. The sky was illuminated by a liquid light tinted with gold and cobalt with a touch of yellow ochre; the kind of light that only one finds in the Mediterranean. Leonard felt elated in this light that reflected onto the pale blue sea, that was covered in millions of sparkling lights. He realised that it was in this sea that Ulysses had sailed to Troy with his thousand ships. It was in this sea that Jason had crossed in search of the Golden Fleece, that Leonard had read about at university. This sea conjured up for him the extraordinary world of ancient Greece. Anthony had given him a book of poems by Cadafy that morning. It was a very old book that Anthony had bought in a second-hand bookshop on Hydra port. The famed poet Cadafy he had heard about, but had not read his poems. He opened the book and read the poem 'Ithaca' to Marianne.

> *'Keep Ithaca always in your mind,*
> *Arriving there is what you're destined for,*
> *But don't hurry the journey at all,*
> *Better if it lasts for years,*
> *So you're old by the time you reach the island,*
> *Wealthy with all you've gained on the way,*
> *not expecting Ithaka to make you rich,*
> *Ithaka gave you the marvellous journey,*
> *Without her you wouldn't have set out,*
> *She has nothing left to give you now,*
> *And if you find her poor, Ithaca won't have fooled you,*
> *Wise as you will have become, so full of experience,*
> *you'll have understood by then what these Ithaca's mean.'*

On the island of Skopelos, Leonard and Marianne went swimming with turtles and dolphins. They gracefully swam among the fish that parted in many directions. Leonard felt closer to Marianne. All the troubles of her marriage seemed so distant now, for a moment in time. Like all wonderful moments, time stood still, suspended in this liquid light and the glorious waters; that were part of an eternal, joyful spirit, where all their trials and tribulations vanished.

On the island of Delos at the amphitheatre, they went to see the play in the setting sun called Hecuba a tragedy by Euripides. It takes place after the Trojan War, but before the Greeks have departed Troy. The central figure is Queen Hecuba, wife of King Priam. It depicts Hecuba's grief over the death of her daughter Polyxena, and the revenge she takes for the murder of her youngest son Polydorus. He was sent to King Polymestor of Thrace for safekeeping, with gifts of gold and jewellery. But when Troy lost the war, Polymestor treacherously murdered Polydorus, and seized the treasure. These events haunted Hecuba's dreams, and she raged against the brutality of such actions, and wants to take revenge.

***

Leonard met a young man called Redmond Wallis from New Zeeland, who lay on the foredeck alone, deep in thought. He was an old friend of Sam's. Leonard engaged in conversation with him. He also wanted to be a writer, and was attempting to complete a novel titled 'Unyielding Memory', based on a phrase by the German philosopher Friedrick Nietzsche's, from his book 'Beyond Good and Evil'."

Leonard had read a book by Nietzsche, 'Twilight of the Idols'. The book criticizes German culture of being decadent and nihilistic. Nietzsche explores morality by the church who fail at their goal of improving man. A priest converts a man to Christianity, in order to make him 'moral'. However, like all men they eventually fall into the basic human instinct such as lust, hate, desire, avarice and greed. He is seen as a sinner and is full of hatred for them and is isolated in his own town. Because of this the man's life miserable.

Leonard recalled Nietzsche's original line *'What does not kill me makes me stronger.'* He quoted these lines to Redmond, and explained to him what he thought that these lines meant, and that suffering, is an inevitable part of life. Because of this we have developed many ways to try to ease it. Suffering, Leonard thought can be transformative and can strengthen one's resolve to fight the great struggles ahead of us in life.

Redmond explained to Leonard that for Nietzsche, memory had many forms, and was responsible for moral illusions which Nietzsche wished to challenge, that people do not tell the truth. They manipulated memory as a limited resource, and is convenient to use it as a lie and a falsehood that requires invention, deceit, and memory. Nietzsche tells us that memory is the place in which acts are given their moral interpretation. The witnesses of a deed often only measure the morality or immorality after the fact, depending on what version of the truth they want to present to the world. Even the memory of the deed is clouded by false motives. Memory can be presented as a cover-up of a good conscience. Nietzsche believed that morality is not absolute and beyond question.

"We are all guilty of manipulating our memories," Redmond said.

"It's an ambitious book," said Leonard. "I'm writing one, too."

"I've got over sixty characters in mine," said Redmond, with a smile.

"I've got about five."

Charmian came up behind them.

"How is George?" asked Leonard.

" I have a Greek woman looking after him. He is still coughing up blood sometimes, so we are all returning to Australia soon," replied Charmian, as Anthony walked up the deck.

"Anthony!" she said looking at him sadly.

"Its bad news – you win some you lose some," said Anthony laughing.

"We are talking about our novels," said Redmond.

"You got to edit your novels. Run a hot knife through the text, like butter," said Charmian.

"That's not easy, every line is precious to me" said Leonard.

"If you're going to be a writer, you have got to be critical of your own work. It's a craft, not an indulgence." said Charmian.

"Maybe us writers are too obsessed with our own ego and our own destiny," said Leonard, lying back on deck and resting his head on a coil of ropes.

"Yes, some psychologists call it a narcissistic complex," said Charmian.

"I don't think all writers are obsessed with themselves. Some books have changed the world and how we see it. Some writers are the prophets of their generation. One meaningful poem can change the world," replied Leonard. At that moment Anthony stepped forward.

"Do you think you will write that poem?"

"I hope so. I want to try. If I knew where the great poems are, I would be so grateful to find one," said Leonard.

"It's worth a try. Most men go in search of the money. I want to just try find the honey," replied Anthony, laughing.

***

On the beach the following day Leonard could see the silvery surface of the afternoon sun, light up the sea like a thousand candles. The blue waters sparkled. They could see the fish in tropical colours as they darted about at speed. Marianne dipped her hand in the water and it was warm. She wore a bikini that morning in the harbour shop. Leonard and Marianne's feet touched the warm sands on the beach. They soon entered the water. Its warm waters enveloped them as did its pale blue translucence. They dived beneath the surface. Leonard could see Marianne's body move as if she was a mermaid. The light penetrated from above and danced around them. Leonard held Marianne and her sweet lips touched his. They lay on the beach together on their woollen towels.

"I love you Marianne," said Leonard, holding her in his arms.

"Me too... you will always be a part of me," replied Marianne, kissing him warmly.

    Leonard spent the night with Marianne on the beach in sight of the camp fire in the sand dunes. There was love, sweet kisses, and unfulfilled desires and unchartered passions between them. Marianne's eyes were no longer filled with sorrow, but a sense of joy. He touched her straw-blonde hair, her breasts, and kissed her lips, and love seemed possible.

The boat returned via Piraeus on the Greek mainland. They took a taxi to Athens, where they went shopping, for clothes, shoes and books. Leonard had bought a locket attached to a necklace. Inside he placed a photo of Marianne and himself, that they had made in a photo booth. Then they visited the famous Zonar cafe for coffee. Little Axel ate some ice-cream. All the great and the good of Athens society went there.

They stayed at the Niki Hotel in Piraeus. It was a hotel that had not changed much since the nineteenth century. It had pictures of the old port of Piraeus with pirate ships. There they spent the night in the pleasures of love. They walked along the harbour and watched the boats sail by. They shopped for food in the open-air market and the antique shops and bookshops. Leonard thought to himself lucky, that he lived an independent life and was with a beautiful woman, and he was blessed with the gift of writing.

They returned to Hydra on Sam's boat that sailed gracefully into the harbour. Leonard sat on his terrace with Marianne, and observed the beautiful magenta flowers bloomed from the trees.

Life was simple. There was a joy to this simplicity as they watched over little Axel as he lay wrapped in a blanket on a rocking chair. Leonard sometimes read Marianne a poem that he was working on to get her opinion. They drank Greek wine under the vast starry night that they could see out beyond the harbour. Sometimes he would watch Marianne sleeping under moonlight. Leonard reflected and whispered to himself "You are so perfect. I won't ever hurt you." Then he kissed her while she was sleeping.

***

Chapter 24
Boy on a Dolphin

Even with all the dramas and struggles on Hydra, Leonard at times was enchanted by life there. He lay in the sun, and felt its rays on his skin. It was as if the effects of the cold, freezing winters of Montreal had vanished from his body. He soaked it all in and cooled off by diving into the blue waters, with its surface reflecting many shades of light. He felt liberated. Greece was a place where one's mind could find a closeness with nature, that he had not found before. Leonard continued to meet Anthony almost every evening in Katsikas café. They spoke about the latest news, or the ongoing gossip and emotional dilemmas they all faced.
"Do you think you will ever live in Montreal again?"
Leonard drew on his Greek cigarette and exhaled some smoke. He looked intently at Anthony' and then across the Hydra harbour, and reflected for a moment.
"Yes, sure this island is a kind of paradise, but like all paradises, we can lose it. So someday I am going to get out of here, maybe on a boat or in a coffin. I'm not sure," said Leonard.

From the corner of his eye, Anthony could see a beautiful woman with dark hair walking with a man near the harbour. A smile appeared on Anthony's face. It was Sophia Loren, the star of the movie made on Hydra called 'Boy on a Dolphin'.

Anthony hurried over to her. She recognised Anthony as she met him before. She greeted Anthony and Leonard warmly. She was with an Italian bodyguard named Giuseppe. Nick the owner of Katiskas served them some wine.
Sophia told them about the movie and its plot. Sophia played a woman called Phaedra, who was a poor Greek sponge diver on the island. She works on a boat of her boyfriend Rhif, an

immigrant from Albania. She accidentally finds an ancient Greek statue of a boy riding a dolphin on the bottom of the sea. The statue has been lost for over two thousand years. Her efforts to sell it to the highest bidder lead her to two men. Dr. James Calder an honest archaeologist played by Alan Ladd, who wanted to give it to the Greek authorities, and Victor Parmalee, played by Clifton Webb, an unscrupulous dealer in historic artefacts. The sculpture of the boy riding a dolphin, is said to have the magical power to grant wishes.

"Sophia, can you sing us that song from the movie," said Anthony.

"Of course, it's called 'What is this thing they call love," replied Sophia. Everyone in the restaurant looked on as Sophia began to sing.

> *'There's a tale that they tell of a dolphin,*
> *And a boy made of gold,*
> *With the shells and the pearls in the deep,*
> *He has lain many years fast asleep.'*

Leonard thought that Sophia sung with the voice of a nightingale. They spent some time together talking about her days on Hydra. Leonard felt he was talking to a great legend of the screen, where a movie fan meets their idol in the flesh.

***

Marianne was lying in bed with little Axel when Leonard got home. He told her about his meeting with Sophia. But she looked worried. Marianne had heard some gossip from Charmian about her relationship with Leonard. She lay in his arms and he talked late into the night. Only the clock disturbed their thoughts and the cat moving about the house. Leonard wrote in his diary.

> *'It has been an extremely difficult time for Marianne, little Axel and me. The rumours are already buzzing*

around, that unavoidably people have been gossiping about us. Due to irresponsibility, our relationship hangs by a thread. Time will tell whether or not that thread will snap. People are saying that the whole thing is my fault. That I am a thief and I have stolen Marianne from her husband, when that is not the case. The moralists have come out to hang me in Hydra square. Marianne is slowly being pushed over the edge, into the dangerous world beyond conventions. The process has been painful for her. At times it's also true for me too. I wrote about this kind of pain.'

***

The following morning Marianne spoke to Leonard.
"I still miss Axel, even though he did this to me - abandoned me and betrayed me," said Marianne.
"Betrayal is part of love," replied Leonard.
"Why can men not be faithful to just one woman?" said Marianne.
"Why can they not be monogamous in marriage?"'she said.
He remembered that the poet Lorca wrote about love and recited the lines to her.
"I see him sometimes in my dreams. I remember the words. It's true that it costs me pain to love you as I love you. For the love of you it hurts!"
"Why was there so much pain in relationships?" said Leonard, kissing her softly. "We are all searching. We are all beautiful losers. Sometimes we win, sometimes we lose. I think everyone has that experience. That sense of defeat that either makes embitters you or makes you stronger. If they get it, some are still not happy either. The object of our desires continuously escapes us," said Leonard softy - almost whispering. Leonard continued and Marianne listened intently.

"It is by the grace of God that I met you, Marianne. We were always in a ceaseless search for a companion. No one wants to be alone," he said. His words echoed in the room.

"It terrifies me to be alone, it's an empty place. Humans are not designed to be alone," said Marianne.

"Remember the lines from St Paul. Three things remain, faith, hope and love, but the greatest of these is love," said Leonard. "We want too much. People think there is some wisdom, like some path to take. If you can embrace all these aspirations, you search for another life. But there is suffering in all this!"

"That is so true Leonard," said Marianne, sitting up in bed.

"There is always the thought that another life would be better. The idea that there is something more to grasp,"replied Leonard.

"I think Axel is suffering in this way. He wants too much and he thinks life could be better. We can all become victims of this. We have longing and we have disaffection. Everybody suffers a sense of something that belongs to the west. It is our disease," said Leonard.

"That's true, so true. We want too much and don't appreciate what we have," replied Marianne kissing him on the side of his cheek.

"If you leave me Leonard, half of me is going to die."

"Don't worry, you will always be in my heart," replied Leonard.

"Love is all forgiving, and we need to forgive each other. Please forgive me if I ever hurt you," said Leonard.

"I hope you ever hurt me like Axel did!"

"Love is simple to understand."

"What is it, tell me?"

"It's the sweetest thing. The Japanese say, I go your way and you go my way. Husband and wife drink tea, your smiles are my tears. The Japanese also say that when you name the bird, you no longer experience their song, so just live in the moment."

He knew that he would be always be thinking of Marianne and her beauty. That evening they walked home from Katsikas cafe. They walked home across the harbour. Marianne kissed him and put her face against his, and held him tight and closed her eyes as she walked. He never felt so moved by such an act of trust. She held him like he was a crucifix, as they walked through abandoned empty laneways.

Leonard looked at Marianne as she slept her face, her hair and thought of her tenderness, her sweet words and her wisdom. He remembered the lines from Shelley's poem, his ode to love.

"Love's Philosophy'.

'The fountains mingle with the river and the rivers with the ocean. The winds of heaven mix forever. With a single sweet emotion nothing in this world is single.''

***

Leonard visited the cathedral of the Assumption with Marianne that Anthony told him about. He had been curious to visit it. It had an imposing tower that was cut in beautiful Portland stone. At the top of the church, there was a great bell that sounded when mass was on.

Outside they met an old priest wearing a black cassock and a grey beard. He told them that the first church on this site was built by a nun from Kythnos in 1643. It was dedicated to Saint Charalamisos. His name meant 'glowing with joy'. He was from the city not far from the famed city of Troy, where the legend of Ulysses was born.

In the courtyard there were statues of some of the heroes from the Greek war of independence. They admired the statue of Admiral Lazoros Kooundourotos and his tomb. He was a hero of the Balkan war. The old priest told him that the Easter feast of Pascha, Assumption of the Mother of God was celebrated on Aug 15. It was the most important event of the religious calendar in Greece. The monk told him that the Hydroites held a special reverence for the sacred icon of the Mother of God; which the Bishop carries in a ceremony to the church for the virgin's blessing.

The original structure was destroyed by an earthquake in 1774. It was rebuilt by a Venetian architect. The monastery came to an end in 1833, and the monks left. Leonard and Marianne entered. Inside they marvelled at the Byzantine frescoes of gold, deep reds and yellow umber. Light streamed through the stained-glass windows. There was a white marble alter and gold icons decorated its walls. They knelt in front of the Virgin Mary, below a golden chandelier that was lit with candles. They smelt the air filled with incense. It was a place of peace, devotion and the spirit. Leonard lit a candle for his father and felt his presence. Leonard spoke to Marianne about the different beliefs of the Catholics and the Jews. They all had one focal point, Jesus Christ who was the messiah for the Jews and the son of god for the Catholics. Leonard thought for a moment and turned to Marianne, as she lit a candle.

"You, I and Axel are like the trinity in a triangular relationship; the Father, Son and the Holy Ghost," said Leonard. Leonard and Marianne lit a candle and said a prayer for their lost ones, that now belonged to the ranks of death.

***

Marianne and Leonard woke up one morning to read the headlines in the London Times that Marilyn Monroe was dead. They read that Marilyn's housekeeper Eunice Murray was staying overnight at her home. She had woken at 3:00 a.m. and felt that something was wrong. She saw light from under Monroe's bedroom door, and found the door locked. Murray then called Monroe's psychiatrist, Dr. Ralph Greenson, who arrived at the house shortly after and broke into the bedroom through a window to find Marilyn dead in her bed. Monroe's physician, Dr. Hyman Engelberg, arrived at around 3:50 a.m. and pronounced her dead at the scene. At 4:25 a.m., the Los Angeles Police were notified.

The toxicology report showed that the cause of death was acute barbiturate poisoning. The possibility that Monroe had accidentally overdosed was ruled out because the dosages found in her body were several times over the lethal limit. Monroe's doctors stated that she had overdosed several times in the past, possibly intentionally.

Due to these facts and the lack of any indication of foul play, deputy coroner, Thomas Noguchi, classified her death as a probable suicide. Monroe's sudden death was on the front-page in the United States and Europe. The article stated that the suicide rate in Los Angeles doubled the month after she died. French artist Jean Cocteau commented; *'that her death should serve as a terrible lesson to all those, whose chief occupation consists of spying on and stalking film stars'*.

At her funeral, hundreds of spectators crowded the streets around the cemetery. Marianne and Leonard spoke about her death. She had an old book on Marilyn and had underscored her comments about life and love. Marianne read them to Leonard that night as they lay in bed together.

> *"I don't forgive people because I'm weak. I forgive them because I am strong enough to know people make mistakes. Sometimes good things fall apart so better things can fall together. Do you know a girl doesn't need anyone who doesn't need her? Always remember to smile and look up at what you have got in life. A wise girl knows her limits while a smart girl knows that she has none. Just because you fail once doesn't mean your gonna fail at everything. That's the way you feel when you're beaten inside. You don't feel angry at those who've beaten you. You just feel ashamed. Boys think*

*girls are like books, if the cover doesn't catch their eye, they won't bother to read what's inside. You believe lies so you eventually learn to trust nobody but yourself. When you're young and healthy you can plan on Monday to commit suicide, and by Wednesday you're laughing again. Dreaming about being an actress is mor*e exciting than being one.

***

Chapter 25
The Venetian Ball

Some nights, Marianne and little Leonard observed the moon that always hung in the sky like a giant disc. Sometimes he would write late into the night, while Marianne slept. He struggled with his poetry and prose. Some nights, it would come easy to him. Other times it was difficult. He continued to work on his novel, 'Beauty at Close Quarters', that had changed to a new title of 'The Favourite Game'.

He continued to type his novel, on the old Remington typewriter. At times he would run short of paper that had to be ordered from Athens. On some days he would sit in his sunlit terrace and type. The chapters emerged as the keys clattered across the pages and the red and black ribbon, was slowly pulled onto two spools from left to right. He was not an accomplished typist, but regardless he made progress. His only distraction was a cat walking by, or even a stray dog.

Hydra, he learned was where many cats were looking for a home. Before long he adopted one. It had white fur with black spots on its tail. He named the cat Byron after the poet. Every time he heard Byron's meow he would think of the great poet's lines. A few weeks later he located an old battered photocopier the only one on the island, that Nick Katiskas rarely used, and made a copy of his novel. Then he posted it to his publishers in Montreal.

***

One morning Leonard woke while Marianne was sound asleep with Axel in her arms. The light was always so clear and bright, in the early morning it cast shapes with distorted angles across the wall's surfaces. It was so peaceful in his room at that hour. He heard footsteps and the hooves of a mule. He heard the brass knocker rap on his door, and he knew for certain that it was Anthony.

Leonard threw on his night gown and made his way to the door. He was right. Anthony stood there with his donkey and a straw hat. He had a large smile on his face. A smile of mischief that he sometimes had. Anthony had a coffee with him in the kitchen. Leonard told him about the gossip.
"Don't worry about the gossip; everyone is having affairs these days. Look Hennessy is having a masked Venetian ball at his villa tomorrow night. It is the countess' birthday." They all agreed to go.

Anthony brought them to a clothes shop on the port. Leonard bought Marianne a beautiful long dress covered with a print of a peacock's feather. She wore a belt of gold and a Venetian mask. Leonard bought a mask too and dressed up like the poet, Lord Byron from the famous painting of him. He wore an Albanian waistcoat in red and gold and a turban of deep red, with a belt made of leather. The shop owner told them that the secret on Hydra was that most of the population were Albanian, not Greek. They were the Albanian refugees that had arrived from the mainland four hundred years ago. Albanian costumes were worn by many of the local population. Anthony dressed up as a Venetian pirate with a blue shirt and a bandana that covered his forehead. Marianne wore the Greek national costume.

Anthony told Leonard that Lord Byron visited Albania in 1809 while he was on his Grand Tour with his friend John Hobhouse. There he found much inspiration, writing his epic poem Childe Harold's Pilgrimage based it partly, on his experiences there. At that time, it was a wild land on the fringes of Europe. Byron also acquired a traditional Albanian costume, which he wore in the famous painting of him.

In Albania, Byron met with Ali Pasha an Albanian warlord, who was a hero for fighting the Turks. Ali Pasha is mentioned in

Byron's epic poem, Childe Harold. Leonard recited it to Marianne and Leonard as his costume was fitted.

"I talk not of mercy; I talk not of fear;
He neither must know who would serve the Vizier;
Since the days of our prophet, the crescent ne'er saw
A chief ever glorious like Ali Pasha."

Anthony told him that Ali Pasha was a bandit, who fought against the Ottomans. He ruled the territory that covered parts of southern Albania and northern Greece, known as Ioannina. Ali Pasha admired Byron, and Ali made a lasting impression on the poet. In a letter to his mother, Byron described his meeting with Ali.

> *'He told me to consider him as a father whilst I was in Turkey, and said he looked on me as his son. Indeed, he treated me like a child, sending me almonds and sugared sherbet, fruit and sweetmeats twenty times a day. He begged me to visit him often, and at night when he was more at leisure. I then after coffee and pipes retired for the first time.'*

Byron heard later that Ali Pasha would meet his end in 1822, fighting the Turks. His head was cut off and presented to the Sultan Mahmud II. His body rests now in a mausoleum next to the Fethiye Mosque in Ioannina on the Greek mainland.

***

Hennessy's villa was lit up with lanterns and candles. Everyone was there, including; Timothy, George, Charmian and Bill. They were served with champagne by two waiters on silver trays. A small orchestra was made up of a violin player, a cello and a piano playing Mozart. A young Greek woman with a sequined blue dress sung Moon River. The Henri Mancini's song that everyone knew and loved.

"Moon river, wider than a mile. I'm crossing you in style. Two people off to see the world. There is such a lot of world to see. "
Waiters in black suits and dickie bows served trays of champagne.

Hennessy was dressed as a Venetian doge with a long gold and deep red cassock. He wore a head dress with a lion, the symbol of Venice. The countess wore a gold Fortunay dress with many pleats, the signature design of such a dress. The gold thread glowed in the lights. The champagne flowed. George and Charmian were there. They got quiet drunk. George turned to Leonard.

"How are you Leonard?" said George.
"I am fine, but I will be leaving this damm island soon. "
Peggy Guggenheim appeared in a beautiful blue dress covered in red flowers. She had dark silken hair and fine features.
"Meet the great Peggy Guggenheim!" said Hennessy.
"Your reputation precedes you," said George.
"This is the woman who has saved the art world," said Hennessy.
"You flatter me," replied Peggy, sipping on her champagne.
"This is the poet
Leonard Cohen, also, George and Charmian Johnson,"said Hennessy.
"You must come and visit my museum in Venice. I am putting on a Salvador Dali exhibition. Do you know what Dali said to the Surrealists, when he was kicked out of their group?"
"No," replied Leonard.
"The difference between me and Surrealists is that I am a Surrealist."

***

The countess' mother had arrived from Venice. She had the grand title of the Duchess of Marcello. At least that is what

Anthony thought her title was. She looked frail, and used a walking stick. She wore an elegant silk dress which has a beautiful pattern of Peacock's feathers. Around her neck she wore a long pearl necklace, so long so long that it had two loops, like the Victorians who always wore them in this way. She had a long aquiline nose, deep brown eyes and lips covered in lipstick. Even at her advanced age she looked glamorous, elegant, dignified and beautiful. She could have belonged to a Gainsborough painting or a Proust novel.

The duchess was greeted by the countess. Timothy introduced her to everyone. Although she was Italian, she spoke good English. When Leonard spoke to her, she always replied, 'Morte Bene." She was a woman of some sophistication. She loved the film of the neorealist like Victoria De Sica and Luchino Visconti and Roberto Rossellini. Her favourite film was Visconti's 'Death in Venice', based on the German writers Thomas Mann's book. She loved his film 'The Leopard,' based on the Sicilian aristocrat Giuseppe Tomasi di Lampedusa's novel. Leonard was impressed by her intellect. He could see she was an aristocrat with a refined education.

Among the guests that Leonard was introduced to there was Lady Dorothy Lygon, a beautiful young woman, who was an English socialite. She was known in the London social scene, known to be part of the 'Bright Young Things' of the party set. She told Leonard that she was an old friend of the English novelist Evelyn Waugh, the author of the novel Brideshead Revisited, and the inspiration for Cordelia Flythe in the book. She worked now in the British Embassy in Athens, but planned on moving to Hydra. She revealed to him the secret scandal behind the creation of the book, that Waugh never spoke about. There were rumours that Waugh had been bisexual and had a love affair with Hugh Lygon, who was depicted as Sebastian Flythe in the novel.

Leonard and Marianne listened intently to Dorothy's story. She told them about the scandalous behaviour of her father, William Lygon, 7th Earl of Beauchamp. He engaged in a homosexual affair's mainly with his butlers. At one dinner party someone overheard him whispering 'jet adore', to the Butler. When he was questioned by one of the guests he replied, nonsense, I said shut the door. But when they looked around the door was shut.

Her mother's brother was the duke of Westminster called Bendor Grosvenor, who took it upon himself to destroy her homosexual father. Bendor was a secret member of 'The Right Society Club', that was a right-wing anti-Semite organisation, with British aristocrats and politicians as its members. Bendor threatened to expose her father and informed King George about his behaviour. As a result, he was forced to give up his position as member of parliament and move to Venice. Dorothy believed that Waugh had avoided direct reference to the anti-Semitism and bisexuality in Brideshead, as it was a too controversial a mix to engage in at that time. When Brideshead was published in 1945 the horrors of the concentration camps had just been published and homosexuality was still illegal. Leonard hoped that the cracks in this new era would be exposed.

Another woman at the dinner table was a friend of Ioannis. Her name was Zina Rachevsky. She was tall with peroxide blonde hair and large blue eyes and high cheekbones. Leonard thought that she looked like Anita Ekberg, who starred in Fellini's movie called 'La Dolce Vita'. She had just returned from Nepal, where she had been one of the first foreigners to study with Tibetan lamas. Leonard told her that he was fascinated by Buddhism and wanted to study it. Anthony told him later that she was from the Straus family, who were fabulously wealthy. He had painted a portrait of her, and got a large sum of money for it. He told him that 1921, Simon William

Straus, Zina's grandfather, founder of SW Straus & Co, held loans on new buildings across America, worth over $150,000,000. He built the Metropolitan Tower, in Chicago, the Ambassador Hotel in Los Angeles, New York and Atlantic City. Zina inherited some of his wealth. She was an actress, socialite, who knew the Beat Poets, like Ginsberg, who Leonard had met recently on Hydra.

Zena's father had Russian nobility, and her grandfather were German Jews, who had emigrated to the United States; and had made their money first as peddlers, then bankers and developers. Zina was called a Russian princess. Leonard told them that she did not think of herself as a Russian Princess, and not a drop of royal blood was in her veins. But it was useful when creating a name for herself as an actress and a showgirl. Nina had bought land and founded a retreat and study centre at Kopan in Nepal. She spoke to them about this world of lost ancient wisdom.

***

There were so many people at Hennessy's party that it was impossible for Leonard to meet them all. One other couple he did meet was the writer William Gordon Merrick, a former Broadway actor. He was a best-selling author of gay-themed novels. He was one of the first authors to write about homosexual themes for a mass audience. He was interested in Leonard's novel. Gordon told him it was the gay sex that sold his last book; 'The Strumpet Wind' an autobiographical novel about a gay American spy in France during World War II. The spy's director is a handsome, sadistic, and bisexual. Leonard told him that his book had been rejected because it was too explicit about sex. They both laughed at the thought. Gordons told Leonard about gay love.

"Beauty is an important part of gay life. Men aren't spending all those hours at the gym just for the cardio-vascular benefits. This obsession with the muscular look, has its roots in our core definition. We are gay because we find men beautiful. Beauty has its dangers, of course. That's part of our complex response to it, and it is in fact this complexity that makes beauty a valid subject for our literature."

Leonard asked Gordon about Thomas Mann's novel 'Death in Venice', that the Duchess was talking about. Was it a bisexual novel he wondered? Gordon told him about the Greek philosophers Plato's, who wrote a manuscript called 'The Phaedrus'.

"Plato believed that beauty, was the most radiant thing to see beyond heaven, and on earth it sparkles through vision, the clearest of our senses. Some have not been recently initiated, and mistake this reminder for beauty itself and only pursue desires of the flesh. This pursuit of pleasure, then, even when manifested in the love of beautiful bodies, is not divine.''

***

One morning Leonard woke up and turned on the radio. Marianne was there too when they heard the news, that President Kennedy was assassinated in Dallas. It was at 12:30 pm, Friday, November 22, 1963, while traveling in a motorcade through downtown Dallas, he was shot once in the back, the bullet exiting via his throat, and once in the head. President Kennedy was taken to Parkland Hospital for emergency medical treatment, where he was pronounced dead thirty minutes later. Everyone gathered at Katsikas to watch the funeral on TV.

A requiem mass was celebrated for Kennedy at the Cathedral of St. Matthew the Apostle in Washington. Not since the funeral of King Edward VII in 1910, had there been such a large gathering of presidents, prime ministers, and royalty at a state funeral. The honour guard to turned around and move back from the coffin. The flag was carefully folded, and the coffin lid was raised. Jackie Kennedy saw the president lying there, with his eyes closed peacefully just like he was sleeping,

Weeping, Mrs. Kennedy turned to one of the generals, and asked if he would bring her a pair of scissors. He quickly found some in the drawer of the usher's office across the hall, and placed them in her hands, with tears in her eyes she clipped a few locks of her husband's hair. President Kennedy's coffin was placed on an artillery carriage and led by a team of horses. Directly behind, Mrs. Kennedy rode with the children, the attorney general and President and Mrs. Johnson.

They headed out the northeast Gate of the White House, the procession moving slowly, at the pace of the marching horses, and turned onto Pennsylvania Avenue. Thousands of people stood, ten and fifteen deep, on both sides of the street. Tearful, faces grieving the president they had loved. The only sounds you could hear, were sounds that would remain forever in Leonards memory; were the clip-clop of the horse's hooves and the repetition of drums, all the way to the capital. There was a heavy security presence, for the dignitaries who marched; because of concerns for the potential assassination of so many world leaders, the greatest concern was for French President Charles de Gaulle, who had threats against his life.

President Kennedy was interred in a small plot, in Arlington National Cemetery. The honour guard at Kennedy's graveside was the 37th Cadet Class of the Irish Army. The president favour poem was publisher in a newspaper. 'I Have a Rendezvous with Death', by Alan Seeger, who was killed in action in World War I in 1916; was one of the president's favourite poems and he often asked his wife Jackie to recite it. He read it slowly to Marianne.

"I have a rendezvous with death,
At some disputed barricade,
When spring comes back with rustling shade,
And apple blossoms fill the air,
I have a rendezvous with death,

When spring brings back blue days and fair,
It maybe he shall take my hand,
And lead me into his dark land,
And close my eyes and quench my breath,
It maybe I shall pass him still,
I have a rendezvous with death,
On some scarred slope of battered hill,
When spring comes round again this year,
And the first meadow flowers appear.
God knows twere better to be deep,
Pillowed in silk and scented down,
Where love throbs out in blissful sleep,
Pulse nigh to pulse, and breath to breath,
Where hushed awakenings are dear,
But I've a rendezvous with death,
At midnight in some flaming town,
When spring trips north again this year,
And I to my pledged word am true,
I shall not fail that rendezvous with death.

    Leonard was in shock so was Marianne. They whole of Hydra spoke about this terrible tragedy for many nights. The world had changed and like Yeats poem, that Leonard remembered; *'All changed utterly a terrible beauty is born'.*

***

    Leonard also received more bad news. A letter arrived at the post office. His novel, 'The Favourite Game' was rejected by his publisher Jack Mc Clelland. He rejected it because of its autobiographical content and found the novel to be 'tedious and preoccupied with sex'. He sent Leonard a list of revisions, without a promise of publication, even if the revisions were made. He felt dejected. Maybe novel writing was not his forte and he should focus more on poetry he wondered. He decided to try send it to English publishers, and made changes.

He felt dejected and decided to write another novel and give it one last shot. He would return to the spiritual story that had always haunted him, and what Susanne had told him about. He would write a novel located in the Canadian province of Quebec. It would be a story about the saint Catherine Tekakwitha, intertwined with a love triangle, similar to the one he was in between Marianne, and Axel. One of the characters would be leader in the Quebec separatist movement. It would refer to mysticism, radicalism, sexuality, and drug-taking that was part of this era and his life in Canada.

***

Chapter 26
I Loved You in the Morning

Leonard realised that love has a price. He had set off on this journey to find love and had found it. Marianne was not free, but he wanted to be with her. He knew that divorce could be a tortuous route to take. He knew that there was a mountain to cross. He had experienced the storm of emotions that were unleashed by Marianne, that would hang like a cloud above them. Like many men he had found something, but in Marianne it was tainted by a cloud of complications, that painful and insecure in its possibilities. She lay nightly in his arms with her hair upon the pillow. He loved her, and her kisses were sweet and warm; and her hair always lay golden in her sleepy golden slumber. He thought of Marianne and the situation he now found himself in.

"I feel so good in your arms Leonard, I feel protected," said Marianne. Then she thought for a moment about Axel.
"Axel is so explosive, but you are a traditional Jewish gentleman with such good manners."
"My father taught me to place my shoes in a row under my bed. I was thought how to follow rules and have respect for others."
"What is going to happen to us, can we survive on this island?" said Marianne.
"Someday we will have to return to the real world. I am going broke fast," said Leonard. He lay back and looked at the ceiling in thought, before he spoke softly to Marianne.
"You know; it was a pity the way he treated you. I know you can't forgive him. The ending was so ugly. But you once loved him. But you love me now. He's used up all his chances, and I am sure you will never take him back. Could you hate him less? It is a shame and it is a pity, that you can't forgive him now."

Marianne gave Leonard tenderness and hope, there was love that he had never experienced before. She belonged to him now. She had reached out to him, when they were strangers in the night. She had filled his loneliness with love. She had opened up to a world he never knew existed, but now had found. It was precious like a diamond, that had lain there forever waiting to be discovered.

Leonard saw the way she looked at him and smiled and her grace took on a new meaning for him every day. He had hope, and she gave it to him. She gave him the will to go on. She was his muse now, and he wanted her to be with him. She understood the life of the poet. He was more in love with words than material things. Out of the ashes of her past, they had found each other, and he knew that life would never be the same again

***

Leonard was visited again by the ghost of Lorca. Leonard was not nervous, and this time he had wanted to speak to him and connect with Lorca's spirit. His deep dark eyes looked at him. The spectre in the moonlit night spoke to him warmly.

"I met a woman once, but she had a husband, but she was unfaithful to him," said Lorca. I wrote a poem called, The Unfaithful Wife, about her. Do you want to hear it?"

"If it be, you will," said Leonard, philosophically. Lorca spoke softly.

> *"So, I took her to the river thinking she was a maiden, but it seems she has a husband. It was the night of St James and it almost was a duty. The lamps went out and the crickets lined up by the last street corners. I touched her sleeping breasts, and suddenly they blossomed like hyacinth petals. The starch of her underskirt crackled in my ears, like a silk fragment that was ripped apart by ten daggers. We passed the tree by the river, past the hawthorns, the reeds, and the brambles. They were not as*

smooth as her skin, that had crystals in the moonlight, that were shining brilliantly. Her thighs slip from me like fish. One half was half full of fire while another one was half full of coldness. That night, I galloped on the best of the roadways on a mare without stirrups and without a bridle.

As a man, I cannot tell you the things she said to me. The light of understanding has made me discreet, smeared with sand and kisses. I took her away from the river. The blades of the lilies were fighting with the air. I behaved as what I am, as a true gypsy. I gave her a big sewing basket with straw coloured satin. I did want to love her, for although she had a husband, she told me she was a maiden when I took her to the water and touched her sleeping breasts. Under the moonlight I smeared her with kisses. For although she has a husband, she told me she was a maiden when I took her to the river."

As soon as he finished, the spectre vanished into the night and Leonard reflected on Lorca's poem.

***

Leonard told Marianne about Lorca's ghost. Marianne told him that it was just a dream he had experienced. She had become fascinated by dreams. It was Axel who had first introduced her to dreams and their interpretation.

"You know that I write my dreams down in a secret diary," said Marianne.

"My diary is called - Once Upon a Dream."

Marianne told him that she had read a book that Axel had given to her about dreams by Carl Jung. It spoke about the archetypal collective unconscious made up of symbols, that one can find in the tarot cards. The tower, water and tree of life. Marianne bought a pair from Anthony who said that they were designed by the occult leader, Alistair Crowley, who said; *'in dreams and fantasy symbols appear'*. Anthony was fascinated by Crowley as they both had a connection with Hastings. Anthony was born there and the great magician had died in a boarding house there.

Leonard remembered the poem by WB Yeats, "The Second Coming." It was a poem, like a dream full of symbols. He recited it to Marianne.

> *"A vast image of Spiritus Mundi troubles my sight somewhere in sands of the desert. A shape with a lion's body and head of a man. Things fall apart and the circle cannot hold. Mere anarchy is loosed upon the world. The blood dimmed tide is loosed and everywhere the ceremony of innocence is drowned."*

"What does Spiritus Mundi mean?" said Marianne.

"The poet W.B. Yeats talked about the collective soul of the universe, containing the memories of all time. From 'Spiritus Mundi,' Yeats believed, came all poet's inspiration. I always look for it."

'I want to explore my dreams but, not through drugs.' Marianne told Leonard.

'Marianne told him that Jung believed that dreams were messages from the unconscious. They were dream images of symbols; that were part of our darkest dreams that contained imagery, that illustrated our internal conflicts. These dreams explored our fears and other emotions. Jung described his dreams as terrifying encounters with his unconscious, which often threatened to destroy him.

Leonard bought a picture by Salvador Dali and hung it in his house Marianne told Leonard that the Spanish painter Dali had painted many images of dreams. Dalí and García Lorca met in Madrid in 1923, along with the filmmaker Luis Buñuel who made the surreal dreamlike film with Dali, called Un 'Chien

Andalou' or 'An Andalusian Dog'. The bond between Dalí and García Lorca, had been rumoured to be something more than just friendship. Their relationship lasted, until Lorca's assassination in 1936. Marianne had been given a book by Axel on Dali, that had his dream paintings. Axel had told her that *'dreams, especially, are the diamonds mined from the unconscious.'*

Dali was the father of the Surrealist movement. Dali's dreams, visions and symbols supplied fantastical images for his work. Marianne and Leonard looked at his painting that was titled; 'Soft Watch at the Moment of First Explosion'. Dali described his paintings as *'hand-painted dream photographs.'* One of his favourite images, was bent watches, that look as if they're made of wax, melting away on a hot summer day in the desert.

Another painting that Marianne found in a Dali book was 'The Persistence of Memory'. It was inspired by Einstein's theory that time is relative, unfixed, and fluid. This was illustrated by a piece of cheese melting in the summer heat. The constraints of time and space are shattered; and time travel and impossible scenarios, and infinite opportunities become possible.

Marianne was fascinated by Dali's ideas that when we dream, the conscious brain disappears, and the unconscious takes over. Images from myth and reality, morph into something fantastic. Dali was able to harness his dreams and hallucinogenic imaginings, without the use of drugs. His images were of the dreamer, dreaming the surreal dream; and the waking world is far off in the distance, just an echo of his memory.

***

Anthony called to see Leonard one evening at Katsikas cafe. He wanted to talk to him urgently. Leonard knew that something was up, as his dear friend only asked for urgent meetings, when he was under some financial or emotional stress. Anthony told him that a Frenchman had arrived on the island, and he had found Charmian kissing him. His name was Jean Claude and he was an artist. He looked like a bum and a 'clochard,' said Anthony. He wore sandals, and had patched jeans that were covered in holes. His shirt looked like a torn rag, and he wore a gold ear-ring and a chain around his neck. He carried a canvas on his back with a cat in it. Leonard began to laugh.

"That's every woman's dream,' to have an affair with a man that dressed like Van Gogh, or a playboy. He is playing you at your own game Anthony," said Leonard smiling.

"Seriously Leonard…this is not a joke."

"Sorry Anthony," replied Leonard.

Leonard tried to console him, but he knew like Marianne, that once a woman made a decision, there was nothing a man could do to reverse it.

"Your just not rich enough, Anthony," said Leonard looking at him intently. Then then they both began to laugh and Leonard poured him some ouzo.

"You win some and you lose some. You're a betting man you can understand that," said Leonard with a smile

***

Chapter 27
The Seventh Seal

One afternoon when Leonard was typing his new novel – Beautiful Losers, Anthony arrived. Marianne was cooking in the kitchen. She made them some drinks.

"Ioannis is visiting a monastery in the hills", said Anthony, drinking a cold beer.

"I am going with him with some donkeys, if you and Marianne want to come."

Marianne agreed to come with them. She told him that Maria could look after Axel junior for a few days. The following day they visited Ioannis at Hennessy's villa. He greeted them on the terrace.

"I am so happy you came. I am going to meditate and pray at the monastery. Are you coming?"

"Yes, we will come," said Leonard.

"Marianne must wear a veil in the monastery and she must sleep in a separate room. The festival of Easter will be on the same weekend. The bells will ring throughout Hydra. Tsouereki bread will be baked, and eggs will be dyed red. It is a sacred time for all Greeks."

The monastery Ioannis told them, was dedicated to the prophet Elias and was built close to Mount Eros. It could be reached in two hours from the port of Hydra. One had to take the cobbled path that began from the Church of Saint Constantine. They then had to pass the nunnery of Agia Efpraxia. The monastery on the island, was established in 1813, by thirteen monks who arrived on the island from Mount Athos in northern Greece. They constructed the monastery on the site of another chapel that had been built in 1771. The prophet Elias obtained the money from donations. The monks were involved in the Greek Revolution, in

1821. The Greek revolutionary figure Theodoros Kolokotronis was kept a prisoner in the monastery cells for four months.

***

The sun rose in the sky. Anthony had brought four mules that were all roped up together. Marianne mounted one. Leonard helped her onto her saddle. Ioannis led the way, looking like a Christlike figure in his black garments and beard. There were cacti, scrubs and rocky outcrops on the way. One had to be careful as the road narrowed at times near a cliff, that headed upwards like a snake to the top of the island. The landscape became sparser. There were rocks and outcrops, and the sun beat down on them. They wore straw hats and sunglasses. Anthony provided them with water bottles that once belonged to the Greek army. After two hours the white facade of the monastery appeared. It had a white painted dome, and on top a cross. It looked like an image from the bible.

The monastery was Byzantine in design, with an octagonal bell tower. Ioannis told him that the monastery had fallen into disrepair, and the monks have only recently returned there to begin the process of repairing and repainting it. The last priest he knew there was Fr Vetins, who had died there. The monastery was surrounded by cypress trees. Their branches waivered in the wind due to the high location.

A tall priest dressed in black and with a white beard stood in the doorway, that was a semi-circular stone arch. The way he was framed in the arch made Leonard think he looked like a Greek sacred icon. They dismounted from their mules and were greeted warmly by this monk who introduced himself as Fr Nikolai. He looked like a wise old man. He wore a large chain around his neck, that made him look like a man of great importance.

"Ioannis, how are you?"

"Welcome, please come in," said Fr Nikolai, warmly.

"This is Leonard, Marianne and Anthony," said Ioannis dismounting from his mule.

A young monk appeared and took hold of their reins, and guided the mules away. They entered the great arched doorway and walked through the long hallway, and finally entered a courtyard. On each side there were Roman arches. At the end of the courtyard there was a small church that was surrounded by the monastery walls.

They entered the beautiful doorway and found the church covered in Byzantine icons, with religions figures of angels and saints. Fr Nikolai told them that he had some food prepared for them. They retired to the monastery dining room where a priest called Fr Papos served them. The cedar table was covered in plates of ham, olives, cheese, boiled rice and lamb. Leonard, Anthony, Ioannis and Marianne savoured the meal. After their long trek they felt they deserved it. Fr Nikolai looked at them intently. His wise eyes looked at them, as if searching for their souls.

"You have come in a search for peace. Many have believed in the Greek ideal of our civilization and our love for democracy, and also, our love for liberty and freedom," said Fr Nikolai.

Then Fr Nikolai brought them to a library filled with ancient books, and valuable manuscripts. He talked about Greece, and its biblical theology. Fr Nikolai opened a beautifully gold bound book, and translated the Greek title for them; 'The Book of Revelations'. He told them that it recorded the second coming of Christ. Leonard told him that as a Jew he also believed in the second coming. Fr Nikolai told them that it was written on the Greek island of Patmos by St John. It was St John who had been with Jesus in the garden of Gethsemane. Fr Nikolai read the words from this book; *'You will find the word of God and the testimony of God.'*

Fr Nikolai told them that Saint John was banished there by the Roman authorities as a punishment for his preaching. At that time, one could also be banished for practicing magic or astrology. Saint John's Christianity was a threat to Roman beliefs, as they worshipped many gods. He was tortured and was plunged into boiling oil but survived. He did not appear to have suffered from that terrible experience. John, in his 'Book of Revelations' had described the seven seals of God, that he saw in an apocalyptic vision.

Fr Nikolai explained to them that the opening of the seven seals marked the second coming of the Christ, and the beginning of the apocalypse. The seven seals contained secret knowledge only known to God. Fr Nikolai told them that the only one worthy enough to open the seals, was the Lion of Judah and the lamb with the seven horns.

When the first four seals are opened four winged horsemen were released. The first was a great white winged horse so loved by the Greeks, called Pegasus. Each horse was red, white, black and grey. These were mounted by angels that had been sent by God to patrol the earth. The first horse had an angel carrying a bow, and his mission was to conquer pestilence. The second was a red horse and its angelic horseman was a creator of war. The third angel on a black horse brought famine, while the fourth angel on a green horse was a bringer of death.

Fr Nikolai told them that God has given these angels the authority to rule over the earth. They may kill by the sword, or through plague and by means of the beast set free on the earth. Nobody was protected from these seals once they were opened and released. If man did not change his ways, the seals would be opened.

***

Leonard woke the following morning. The bells were ringing in the church tower. It was Easter morning. Fr Nikolai informed them that the ceremony to venerate the sacred shroud of Jesus known as the Epitaphio's would take place at noon. They observed it as it lay in a gold lined case. It was a shroud that was carried out by the monks from the monastery, down to Hydras port. Fr Nikolai told them that this shroud had the image of Jesus after the crucifixion. It was a sacred Christian religious icon, consisting of a large, embroidered richly adorned cloth, bearing an image of the dead body of Christ. The icon depicted Christ after he has been removed from the cross, and being prepared for burial. The scene was a depiction of the Gospel of St. John. Beside him was the Blessed Virgin Mary, St John, Joseph of Arimathea, Mary Magdalene, and many angels.

In the evening, they went inside the church and found some other worshippers. The statue of the Virgin Mary shone in the lamplight. Fr Nikolai in his finest robes of gold and silk entered carrying a tall staff, at least eight feet tall, with a gold cross. An altar boy carried a gold flask that held a relic of St John. Ten altar boys dressed in white cassocks and black coats followed them. Around their waists they wore a belt embroidered with a cross of gold thread. One held an incense bowl suspended on four chains. He blessed the statue of Mary, with the incense by motioning the chains back and forth. The smoke rose and enveloped the statue of the virgin. Leonard inhaled the sweet perfume of the smoke. Fr Nikolai spoke biblical words in Greek. His voice filled the dome above him and echoed across the church. Leonard looked around him and could see the reverence on the people's faces. The Greeks were believers, and this was the evidence of undying faith.

***

That night as Leonard lay in bed alone, in the darkness. Outside through the small window he could see a blue moon that was bright in the sky over Hydra. This sacred world had been a revelation to him. There was some truth he felt in the parable of the seven seal, and a great chastisement would befall mankind if such did not change its ways.

***

After breakfast they said goodbye to Fr Nikolai. The route was much easier as they headed downwards to the white strip of sand, that appeared like a mirage against the shimmering blue Aegean Sea, on the other side of the island. Two hours later their feet touched the warm sand of Vlycho's beach. Soon they were swimming in the sea where the heat of the water cooled their bodies. The light penetrated the water and danced across their skin. Leonard and Marianne dived beneath and kissed each other. Then a dolphin appeared. He was friendly and seemed to smile at them, beckoning them to join him. Their bodies followed him.

***

One morning Leonard heard men outside his window talking in Greek. He opened his window and looked outside. There he could see men digging a hole and installing a tall timber pole over twenty-foot high. Anthony told him later that they were installing the telephone system and the electricity for light to everyone across the island. Later that day he saw a bird sitting on the wires and started to write a poem about it. It had a mix of the many emotions and images he felt at that time, after his visit to the monastery. He had though much about the virtue of humility.

He saw a drunk in a midnight choir in Hydras church of the Assumption. He had come to this island and had, tried in my way to be free. But sometimes he felt that he was, like a worm attached to a hook, or a knight in an old book. He hoped that there would never be any misunderstandings with Marianne. He wondered if he had been unkind to her. He hoped if he was that she would - just let it go by. If he was ever- untrue he hoped that she would understand that it was never towards her. He swore to himself if he ever done anything wrong that he would make it all up to her.

He had always tried to be graceful and humble in his feelings towards Marianne. He was reminded of the necessity for humility one day when he saw a beggar at Hydra harbour one-day leaning on his wooden crutch. He said to him don't ask for much. Then one day he saw a pretty woman at night in a door way, who wanted him to ask for more.

***

Chapter 28
The Queen of Persia and America

Marianne met a tall glamourous woman named Magda Tilche with Leonard. She had beautiful long red hair, that looked like flames around her face. Her dresses were covered in many colours with beautiful images of leopards, peacocks and parrots. She wore jewellery made from amber, the kind that held insects inside that were over two million years old. She wore silver bangles and necklaces around her neck. Marianne liked her jewellery, so Leonard bought her a lock with his photo inside. He also bought her a necklace with an Egyptian sacred beetle.

Magda became like an older sister to her. She consoled her and they confided in each other. She told her that her husband was ten years younger than her, and he was a sort of Italian toy boy. It was becoming more fashionable for woman now in the sixties to do so; to turn the tables on the advances of age, and to bring in a new kind of feminism.

Magda had fled from Prague after the Nazi invasion. She told Marianne that she had escaped by the skin of her teeth, and moved to Paris where she met a French man. There she opened a small jazz club. Her husband died and, in his will, she was granted a small fortune. Then one day she met Paolo, who swept her off her feet. Was it for love or money, Marianne and Leonard wondered? Paolo was introduced to them one evening.

He was tall, dark and handsome with a dark beard and a muscular body. He had a quiet aggression about him. Magda had come up with the idea of a bar and restaurant on Hydra called the Lagoudera. It was a town that Magda had once visited. It had a church with Byzantine icons in Cyprus. Magda spoke about the mural of Saint Simeon holding the Christ child with St John the Baptist, written on a scroll held by St John. The words on the scroll read; *'Behold the lamb of the God who takes away the sins of the world.'* Magda laughed with Leonard and Marianne when Paolo would appear. She told him that she would say to herself; "Behold, Paolo, who takes away my pain and loneliness in acts of sin."

Then she would laugh hysterically until it was painful and she could laugh no more. Magda's club's name in Paris was called the Rose Rouges, in Saint-Germain des Pres. It was the home of jazz players and was frequented by the existential writer, Sartre and the feminist Simone de Beauvoir. But she sold this bar and moved to Hydra. She had not much left after paying back her creditors.

Her new plan for the Lagoudera bar, had much support on Hydra. Many gave funds for the creation of the bar, and within weeks it was underway in one of the old building's workshops. They fitted timber floors and painted and its walls blue and pink. An old sailing boat was hoisted underneath the rafters to pay homage to its past. It was a new place for Leonard and Marianne to listen to Greek musicians. There was also pop and jazz on an old juke box that Magda had bought from an old Greek. Magda and Leonard would sing old Jewish songs together late at night to the chosen guests.

One day Magda told them that she saw Paulo sitting, with a rather elegant looking woman in a light blue dress with gold treads. She wore gold braids in her hair, and on her right hand was painted in henna of beautiful geometric shapes, that looked Arabic in design. Paolo seemed to be engaged in deep conversation with her. Leonard and Marianne were introduced to her as Princess Farina. She said she was the cousin of King Farouk of Egypt. She spoke English fluently and spoke of her palace with servants and vast wealth that came from oil. Magda could see that Paolo was enchanted and seduced by her. She was much younger than his wife Magda, and a better catch for Paolo's roving eye and love of vast wealth. It was all too much for him to ignore. Anthony joked with Leonard and Marianne later, that it was a *'launch pad relationship'*, and Magda was only the platform of his *'rocket engine'*. Paolo had now climbed on board the 'rocket' and his trajectory into the world of vast wealth was now assured. Leonard knew that Italians had a reputation as great lovers like Giacomo Casanova, but Magda and Pablo were married. Surely, he could not be seduced by the disease of infidelity, that had swept across the island, and was the virus that everyone had caught.

***

One evening Magda came frantically looking for Leonard, who was talking to Anthony at Katsikas cafe. She looked very frightened and worried.

"He's gone," said Magda.

"He vanished with the princess," said Magda, distraught. The safe was open too.

"All our money is gone."

Leonard was not surprised. As he finished his words, two police officers approached them. One showed her some papers from the Bank of Greece, where Pablo had forged a cheque for five thousand dollars with Magda's signature on it. The bank had cashed it against the security of the deeds of the bar. But the bar had been sold to a Greek the week before by Paolo. There was fraud and forgery involved, and Magda pleaded her innocence, but they ignored her pleas. She was handcuffed and led to the local police station. Marianne and Leonard followed them and sat with the chief of police, a large fat man, who smoked a cigar and had a large round head and bushy eyebrows. Magda was locked in a cell and Leonard tried to negotiate for her release by offering bail money. But the fat Greek refused to listen. She would have to sit it out in jail, in Athens until the court case.

Weeks later Marianne received a message that Magda, that she had got six months in prison, and could she and her friends look after Lagoudera, while she was away. Because of this Marianne took over as a manager and Leonard was a regular there with Anthony helping out.

***

One day, Leonard arrived at the bar to see Anthony sitting with a very beautiful dark-haired woman. She looked sad, with lipstick of pure red crimson. She wore a headscarf. Behind her at the bar stood two men, with dark moustaches that looked like bodyguards. Anthony greeted Leonard.
"Leonard, we were waiting for you. This is Queen Soraya of Iran." Leonard was intrigued. What was the Queen of Iran doing on Hydra?
"Your Highness, I am pleased to meet you," said Leonard respectfully.
"This is Leonard Cohen – poet, and novelist," said Anthony.
"Pleased to meet you," said Queen Soraya, almost whispering.
"What brings you to Hydra?"
"I have divorced the Shah of Iran, so I am sailing my yacht around the Mediterranean, to find some peace!"
"I recall seeing photos of your amazing wedding," said Leonard.
"Yes, it was amazing, I received many gifts, and donations for the poor."
"Tell us about your gifts," said Leonard, looking into her deep dark eyes. Queen Soraya thought for a moment.
"Joseph Stalin sent me a Russian mink coat. King George VI and Queen Elizabeth sent me a silver Georgian candlestick. The Shah ordered one and a half tons of orchids to decorate the palace, sent all the way from Holland. We had a circus from Rome. But for all the presents and good wishes it was not to be. I was a German Catholic in a country, that I knew nothing of; its legends, its history, or the Muslim religion. So, I am sad."
   Shortly after the Queen left their table, Leonard thought to himself, there was proof that even with vast wealth and privilege,

one could fall out of love and could lose everything. Privilege and wealth did not necessarily bring happiness. In a moment, escorted by two bodyguards, Leonard watched as the former Queen of Iran vanished into the night.

***

More and more Hydra became a magnet for celebrities from around the world. Hydra was becoming less isolated. Leonard read about Jackie Kennedy's visit to Greece. She had become romantically involved with Ari Onassis. It seemed to him that Maria Callas affair was over. She too had seen the film 'Boy on a Dolphin', and was captivated by Hydra and Greece. There was 'Greek fever' that had reached its peak. The Greek Prime Minister Constantine Karamanlis ordered the highest level of security for her. She was greeted at Athens airport with a major reception.

A group of U.S. Embassy employee wives assembled in a straight line, and greeted her, as if she were a queen, chanting "Jackie! Jackie!" Leonard went to the port with Marianne with Gordon Merrick that he had met at Hennessey's villa party to see her. Gordon had met Jackie before at a publishing party in New York. So, when she arrived, Gordon greeted her.

Leonard and Marianne were introduced to Jackie, who greeted them warmly. Leonard and Marianne looked on as the crowds gathered on the promenade beside the ship. The moment she set her foot in the port, every single church in town began ringing its bells, and it seemed the entire population of two thousand Greeks rushed down the streets to greet her. She was led down the alleyways by the mayor and all along the way, people were applauding, smiling at and waving at her. Many threw roses and fresh flowers at her. When she learned that locals had organized a festival just to honour and welcome her, she cancelled her plans for other excursions, and stayed on Hydra. Leonard and Marianne sat at long wooden tables, and local women brought long trays of food of freshly caught fishes, lamb, cheese pies and other traditional cuisine. Local restaurant owners donated bottles of ouzo, wine and beer. Musicians gathered and began playing traditional Greek music. Jackie joined hands and took part in traditional dancing, raising her arms, clapping her hands, kicking her legs and turning her feet as she followed the steps of each dance move.

"I want to have a home here someday," she said to the Greek reporters. "I want to return and bring my children here," she said.

***

Leonard read the following day about her trip to Hydra, and her visit to the Parthenon in Athens. She reported that she would *'...like to see the Elgin Marbles returned to Greece.'* Anthony told him that this was a reference to the marble sculptures, that were removed from the site of the Acropolis and taken to England by the Scottish peer Lord Elgin, and eventually become part of the British Museum's permanent collection in 1815. Jackie Kennedy's public exposure and her opinions, began a movement that would soon gain global attention, to return historic artefacts to their original sites, from the colonial or invading nations, which had been plundered by them.

Jackie ascended into the hills about fifteen miles from Athens for a formal dinner with King Paul, Queen Frederica, Princess Sophia, Princess Irene and Prince Constantine at their summer palace. She then joined them on the lawn to pose for reporters and photographers. Jackie Kennedy showed reverence and respect for her host nation's culture and history. Her respect for the Greeks of all classes, won her the nation's respect and affection. Leonard reflected that she had shown extraordinary bravery after her husband's assassination.

***

Chapter 29
Peal Me A Lotus

Leonard's novel, Beautiful Losers was progressing. He tried to type three pages a day on his old Remington typewriter. He would sit out on the terrace and type away on his old machine, that had seen better days. Sometimes the ribbon would get stuck and he had to wind the spool himself.

George and Charmian invited Leonard and Marianne over for dinner. Leonard brought over his unfinished book. He placed a bundle of pages into his leather satchel, and Marianne walked across the harbour to George's house. They found George and Charmian there drinking wine before dinner. Charmian came in from the kitchen with a plate of food. Charmian placed the dishes in front of them. It smelt of fish and vegetables that Charmian prepared, with garlic, onion, bay leaves, and rosemary. She also brought in an earthenware dish with grapes and fruit. Charmian asked Marianne about Axel's books. Marianne searched in her bag and pulled out a book with the title called 'The Girl I Knew', by Axel.

"I think it's about me. It's very racy," she said. "Axel had written about our sex life and some papers in Norway said it was immoral. Some papers refused to write about it, and a library wants to ban it."

"Censorship is a terrible thing, they did it to James Joyce,'' said Leonard turning to George.

"How many have you written?" said Leonard.

"Nine novels," replied George.

"That is a lot of writing. I am struggling with mine," said Leonard, pouring a glass.

"That why I have grey hair. Have you got it with you?" said George with a searching look. Leonard took the manuscript out of his satchel. "What is it called?"

"Beautiful Losers," replied Leonard.

"Let me have a read," said George taking the manuscript, and reading it quickly.

"Do not to be so precious about your writing. Be ruthless and critical in your edit. What's it about?" said George in a confident manner.

"It's about a love triangle. A Canadian academic, an Indian saint called Saint Catherine Tekakwiitha, and a member of Quebec separatist's movement."

"Sounds like an interesting mix," said Charmian, drinking her glass of wine.

"What is this Quebec movement about?" asked George.

"They seek the independence of Quebec from Canada. Quebec was discovered by an Italian named Irrazzano, who was sent by King Francis of France to Canada. They were looking for a route to China in the 17th century. The explorer named Cartier arrived carrying a catholic cross and planted it on the mouth of the Saint Lawrence river. So the Quebecian's see themselves as French and Catholic, not Canadian." said Leonard.

"You know a lot about the history," said Charmian, smiling at him.

"Not really. My friend Susanne Verdal told about the history of the place."

"It sounds like a good idea for a novel. What about the saint?" said George.

"She became Canada's national saint, her life was one of poverty, chastity and obedience to God."

"Chastity, I don't think it's a vow for Charmian." said George condescendingly.

"George…behave yourself…we have company," replied Charmian rolling her eyes.

They heard a knock on the door. Charmian hurried into the hallway and opened it. It was Bill. She invited him inside. He looked quite distressed and he was sweating, as if he had been running. He entered the sitting room and addressed them all.

"Bill, I was not expecting you, what's up?" said George.

"It's the Duchess, she is dead!"

"The Duchess Marcello, Hennessey's mother-in-law," said Leonard.

"Yes, she is dead. There is a rumour going around that she was murdered," said Anthony looking dejected.

"Murdered, said Leonard. That can't be possible, by who?"

"Don't know, Anthony called into my bar and told me," said Bill. Everyone looked at him in shock. Leonard gave him some water. Then he told them the story. The countess has been found in the garden of the villa. She collapsed in the midday sun, possible from a heat stroke. Maybe it was not murder.

***

The funeral was in the church of the Assumption and was a sad occasion. The coffin was blessed by the priest with incense. Hennessy asked Leonard to read Shelly's poem. Elegy on the Death of Adonis. Leonard read the words in the ancient church. His voice echoed across the packed audience.

> *"Peace, peace she is not dead, she doth not sleep, she hath awakened from the dream of life."*

The coffin was covered in the Venetian flag. It was then carried by six strong Greek men to the boat, that would take the Duchess to Venice. Leonard and Marianne offered his condolences to Hennessy. He could see that he and the Countess Adriana were deeply upset.

***

Leonard found George outside the church smoking a cigarette.

"How are you, Leonard?"

"Not great. It's a sad situation," said Leonard, lighting up one too.

"How are you Marianne?" said George.

"I'm good George. Hope you're ok."

"We're leaving soon," said George putting on his sunglasses.

"Australia?" said Leonard.

"Back to the old sod, Australia," said George, walking with them towards the harbour. There they watched as the boat with the Duchess' coffin sailed away.

"Death of a Venetian," said George, philosophically.

***

Leonard thought about the old Duchess. How she had been snatched by the jaws of death. One moment she was with him and next she was gone. At these times he always questioned life and death asking of its meaning and its purpose and was there a God? He had begun to walk this knife edge between reality and unreality. Perhaps it was the path between life and death - a path of no return. This was the life he had chosen. The life of a poet - a pathway filled with certain dangers.

Leonard, Marianne and Anthony stayed on the port that night. A jazz band had come in from Athens called the Cotton Club. They were playing in Bill's bar. The place was packed with Hydroite's and expats. A black man in a white suit played the trombone. It was some ragtime tune. One played the cello and another the piano. A blonde girl in a white satin dress with a feather in her hair sang.

> *"I am blue,*
> *It was a morning, long before dawn,*
> *Without a warning I found he was gone,*
> *How could he do it,*
> *Why should he do it,*
> *He never done it before,*
> *Am I blue,*
> *Am I blue,*

Ain't these tears, in these eyes telling you,
How can you ask me am I blue?
Why, wouldn't you be too."

Anthony sat with Leonard and Marianne.
"What's up Anthony? " said Leonard, looking at him intently.
"I'm ok, but I have been hearing rumours last night in Katsikas cafe."
"What rumours?" asked Leonard.
"Greece is a kind of paradise, but if you live here a long time like me, you have got to know how the clock ticks," said Anthony, drinking a beer.
"What do you mean?" said Leonard, looking a little puzzled. Then Anthony leaned forward.
"In 1951 we had an attempted coup by the army. I have heard a rumour that there will be another one."
"What does that mean. Who told you?" said Leonard, looking concerned.
"I know an old coronel, who lives here. His son is high up in the army. I met the old man last night."
"Who runs Greece now?" said Leonard, leaning back in his chair.
"It is called a constitutional monarchy. It has a king and parliament," replied Anthony.
"What is the king's name?" asked Marianne.
"King Constantine."
"Can I meet the coronel?" said Leonard looking concerned.
"Yes, he has a little bar up one of the backstreets. The old coronel runs it. He has got one of the few TV's on the island. He has got a phone there too. His son calls every night with the news from inside the army."
"It sounds all very interesting," said Leonard, not sure what to believe.

"Maybe you are just paranoid, Anthony," said Leonard, with a smile.

"You don't know Greek politics. There are always tensions, under the surface between the army and the parliament. Come and meet the old colonel. He will tell you what is going on. He has the best ouzo in town."

Then the blonde girl began to sing a song by Duke Ellington, the Mooche.

> *'Hey, moocher,*
> *See the cat on Cienega Blvd,*
> *Hey, he's the moocher,*
> *Listen here mooch,*
> *Why you always comin' round my crib,*
> *Your borrowin' my cow boots, squeezin' my dame,*
> *What's the deal moocher,*
> *That's the mooch,*

***

Leonard pondered that night on what Anthony had said when he got home with Marianne that night. There were storm clouds appearing on the horizon. Was this the end of the beginning of this paradise? They lay in bed talking.

"I hope this is not the end for us on Hydra," said Leonard.

"What can the military do to us? " said Marianne consoling him.

"A lot. Look what they did to Lorca. The first thing they do is lock up or shoot the writers, the intellectuals and then the poets."

***

Charmian, George and their children were leaving for Australia. Maybe Leonard thought that it was because of Charmian's various affairs, that George wanted to put an end to, or because of his illness he did not know. Leonard went with Marianne to the Katsikas to say goodbye. Anthony did not go for obvious reasons. Charmian made the usual excuse that she felt that the island that she had escaped to, was now becoming a jet set tourist attraction. She had come there to get away from civilisation, now it was overrun by tourists and the famous. Regardless of all the reasons, it was certain that George, was very ill with tuberculosis, and needed serious medical care that he could not get in Athens.

Many of the island's expats came to say goodbye. Among the list were James, Timothy, James, Steve, Gordon, and the Countess Adriana. They drank wine and ate souvlaki. They stayed there late into the night. At the time the harbour had a surreal quality about it. There were few lights that cast shadows on the promenade. The boats bobbed up and down and make a clicking noise from the various chains and masts that swayed in the light breeze. The water lapped against the boats. It was surreal and magical to see the boats silhouetted against the moonlit sky. Even the villas shone with a blue glow like a De Chirico painting. George turned to Leonard as he drank some red wine, and told him that he was saddened about their departure, and he felt that he would never see Leonard again.

"The game is over! We have lived the bohemian life, but it is time to return to civilization. We have books coming out in Sydney, and have to sell some soon or we will all starve to death," said George. "What about your novel?" said George.

"I'm struggling with it. Maybe I'm not cut out to be a novelist like you. If the second novel does not work out, I'm going to stick to poetry or maybe song writing."

***

There were tears and laughter and talk of old times. Leonard had warm words to say about George and Charmian and their friendship. Leonard got up and told him about the song 'Waltzing Matilda', that he wanted to sing to them. It was

Australia's best-known ballad, and the country's unofficial national anthem. He told them that the title Waltzing Matilda, was Australian slang for travelling on foot, with one's belongings in a bag called a matilda slung over one's back. The song was the story about a travelling homeless worker, known as a 'swagman', making tea in a billy can in a bush camp and capturing a stray sheep to eat. When the landowner, and three troopers and mounted policemen hunted down the swagman for theft, he committed suicide by drowning himself in a nearby watering hole, after which his ghost haunted the site. He played its tune on his guitar and began to sing.

> *"Once a jolly swagman camped by a billabong,*
> *Under the shade of a Coolibah tree,*
> *And he sang as he watched and waited till his billy boiled,*
> *You'll come a Waltzing Matilda with me,*
> *Waltzing Matilda, Waltzing Matilda,*
> *You'll come a Waltzing Matilda with me,*
> *And he sang as he watched and waited till his billy boiled,*
> *You'll come a Waltzing Matilda with me,*
> *Down came a jumbuck to drink at that billabong,*
> *Up jumped the swagman and grabbed him with glee,*
> *And he sang as he shoved that jumbuck in his tucker bag,*
> *You'll come a Waltzing Matilda with me.''*

It was a sad occasion for Leonard to say goodbye to George and ~~Charmain~~ Charmian. They had been very supportive to him. Léonard and Marianne walked to the ship the following day. They said goodbye to their children Shane, Martin and Jason with much waiving. Leonard felt too that he would never see them again. George and Charmian had been such an inspiration to him in his own struggles. They had a quiet bravery about them to live the life that they had led; but he knew that they had paid a certain price for it.

***

Charmian 30
Rimbaud's Words

One day Leonard and Marianne went to the beach with some of Hydra's local women and their children. They brought with them picnic baskets of bread, feta, cheese and grapes. The boatman named Mikilis brought them there. Marianne watched Axel junior play on the beach with their children. Mikilis son Alex helped him tying up the boats.

They heard Mikilis shouting and found his son tangled in the ropes, and he was dead. They carried him onto the beach and tried to give him the kiss of life, but he could not revive him. The funeral was a deeply sad one, and Leonard attended it with Marianne. It was in a small church near the cemetery. That was where he was buried. The coffin was blessed by the priest with incense. They followed the cortege of the coffin, that was placed in the glass case and wooden hearse. It was pulled by black mules and a coachman.

Leonard had never seen a Greek cemetery before. There were extraordinary graves with a marble carving of Greek figurine's, and beautiful urns graced with olive leaves and drapes. Also, around the graves he could see wild cats roaming. It was a surreal eerie sight. Some of the graves had carvings of faces of the deceased in framed photos covered in glass. Inscribed on them were their names in Greek. Leonard offered his condolences to Mikilis. Leonard flicked his cigarette into the sand, and placed his foot over the burning cigarette end, and slowly he said the epitaph from Yeats' grave; "Cast a cold on life and death, horsemen pass by."

***

Leonard continued to struggle on with his novel, Beautiful Losers. As he wrote, Leonard listened to the American Forces

station playing county music. He listened to Ray Charles' songs on his battered record player. He loved the song, Hard Times;
"My mother told me before she passed away.
She said son when I'm gone don't forget to pray."

He wrote in the midday sun in blinding light. He put everything he believed in and felt about at that time. Then he took a religious ten day<u>s</u> fast, to try and understand what the Saint Catherine Tekakwitha had suffered. He hallucinated and had extraordinary dreams. Marianne realised that Leonard was on the verge of collapse, or a nervous breakdown. She called the doctor and Anthony. He was taken on a stretcher by four orderlies, who took him down the back streets to Koulouris hospital. The doctor put him on a drip. But the hallucinations continued. After a week he recovered. Anthony visited him with Marianne. Then he was sent home and Marianne took care of him. The doctors considered if he was suffering from manic depression or some mania.

Was it due to him pushing the limits of his imagination, that dealt with the saint Catherine's sacrifice? Had this novel pushed him to the edge of madness and induced in him a messianic complex? Leonard's obsession had reached a point of expression that he felt like his Jewish ancestors, that he wanted to 'save the world'. One morning he woke up in the darkness. His psychosis was gone. He walked out on the terrace and held Marianne's hand. He could see doves flying from their place of rest in the church nearby. It was a sign that peace and calmness in his life was restored.

Leonard had written intensely as if his life was ending. It was as if the sands of time were running out. It was as if that he understood that the universe did not listen to one's command, and that once one's voice was not heard, one would die in obscurity. Leonard felt that for him now it was a kind of torture writing his novel. He had come to realise, that he was a man of the great one liners but not of endless prose.

He had struggled on, and felt emotionally drained in his writing efforts. This he knew was a long-distance race, not a sprint. He felt he was losing the battle with his book and that each page he felt was a loser in a losing battle. He was wiped out with the struggle. But he wanted to go on and finish it whatever the cost. He thought of Rimbaud's words.

> *'I mean that you have to be a seer, mould oneself into a seer. The poet makes himself into a seer by a long, involved, and logical derangement of all the senses. Every kind of love, of suffering, of madness; he searches himself; he exhausts every possible poison so that only essence remains. He undergoes unspeakable tortures that require complete faith and superhuman strength, rendering him the ultimate invalid among men, the master criminal, the first among the damned, and the supreme savant! For this he arrives at the unknown!'*

He felt, however, that he should not give up regardless of the pain. His novel 'Beautiful Losers' was a long prayer of sorts; about his discovery of sainthood, and of the transformation of the soul and one's redemption. Leonard felt the book was written in blood. He had spent sometimes, ten hours a day and tortured himself in the creation of every sentence. It was too much of a sacrifice.

Marianne posted the book to the publishers and waited. His housekeeper, made Sophia nettle soup with herbs, that were boiled in olive oil and kelp that she had harvested from the sea. Slowly, Leonard recovered with their love and affection, of these two wonderful women. One evening she brought her two orphans to see him. The little boy could walk better now.

Leonard marvelled as he walked towards him and held his hand. The little girl smiled at him.

***

A month later, after Leonard had recovered, Marianne went to the post office. There was a letter there for Leonard. She brought it home to Leonard and he opened it slowly. It was from his publisher. Leonard read it carefully and looked at Marianne with tears in his eyes.

"My book was refused. All the reader's reports were unfavourable. This makes me strangely happy. I feel that I can be free again. Nobody knows me and nobody has ever heard of me. I can experiment again, and just focus on writing poems and songs. It does not matter. I can be alone with myself and my words. It will be a joy to be a bum. I want to write only songs and poems; I will never write a novel again.''

***

Chapter 31
The Death of Lorca

Anthony took Leonard to see the old colonel. They found him watching TV, in a small cafe on a side street off a small square behind the harbour. The walls were covered in old prints and photos of a bygone age of King George, and Prince Constantine, at the opening of the first Olympic Games in Athens dated 1896. There was a large photo of the Olympic stadium with a runner heading to the finishing line. "That was Louis the winner of the first marathon," said an old colonel sporting a moustache, a shock of grey hair and bushy eyebrows. "Leonard, this is Costas," said Anthony taking a seat with Leonard.

"Welcome, take a seat," replied Costas, as he pointed to a table covered in bottles of wine. Leonard and Anthony took a seat. They smelt an aroma. "My food, I left a pizza in the oven," said Costas, hurrying into a small kitchen and returning with a pizza. He lay it on the table in front of them. He grabbed a large knife and began to cut some slices. Leonard took a slice and tasted the olives, ham and the feta cheese.

Then Costas poured them some wine. "It's from Thessaloniki, the wine there is the best."
"I wanted to ask you about the politics in Athens," said Anthony.
"I was a coronel in the army. I was there when the last military coup took place in 1951."
"Tell us about the rumour that there were planning another one," said Anthony.
"Well, my son is high up in the military in the Greek army. He tells me they are planning on taking over, and kicking out the parliament and the king," said Costas gulping down a glass of wine.
"My God." said Anthony.

"Yes, the king of Greece. Look, I am Greek. My grandfather was a friend of the king. Our family have always been royalists. I have no time for dictators or communists. I believe in a constitutional monarchy," said Costas, raising a glass of wine. "Long live the King. He is on TV soon, talking about the future of the Greece. You want to see him?"
Costas switched on the TV, and the image flickered, and the words appeared Greek News' in Greek - Ελληνικά Νέα.

The king appeared handsome, young and dignified. He spoke in Greek. "What is he saying?" said Leonard.
"He talks about the future of Greece, the economy and the birth of democracy."
The phone rang, Costas turned down the tv. It was Costas' son from Athens. He spoke to him in Greek in an old phone, then Costas put the phone down.
"He said the coup is on."
"What does that mean?" said Leonard, looking a bit alarmed.
"They will be watching our every move. If we are known to be too liberal. You could be arrested," said Costas.
"We will be all thrown in jail, if we are not careful," said Leonard, drinking some more wine and trying to remain calm.
"What do you expect. That is what dictators do? My advice to you is to get out of Greece before the shit hits the fan," said Costas with a grin on his face that worried them.
"When?" said Leonard leaning forward in his chair and peering into Costas' eyes. "I'll let you know," said Costas, scribbling down his phone number and handing it to Anthony.
"I will let you know, if I have any news. But not a word to anyone," said Costas, lifting his glass and gulping down his wine as if it gave himself some consolation.
"My friends in Athens are trying to save the king and his throne. Let's hope he doesn't lose his head!" said Costas with a laugh. Then he turned on some Miklis Theodorakis music on the radio,

and began to dance in front of them, lifting his hands in an ancient rhythm that Leonard knew the Greeks had been performing for hundreds of years.
***

A few days later Marianne went to Athens with Sophia and her children to see a doctor. Maria looked after little Axel. Leonard stayed on in Hydra. Leonard met Anthony at <u>Katsikas</u> cafe. Anthony looked quite pensive as he greeted Leonard. "What's up, Ant?" said Leonard grabbing a seat. "Costas rang me, he wants to see us," said Anthony, looking worried. "Where is Marianne?''
"She went to Athens with Sophia to see a doctor. They should be back on the ferry today.''
***

Twenty minutes later they arrived at Costas' Cafe. Costas looked a bit rough. He had not shaven and his hair was ruffled.
"You have news? said Anthony?"
"I have been up all night. My son rang me at four in the morning. The coup is on. If you don't believe me, watch the news."
Leonard glanced at his watch. It was 2:58. Costas banged on the top of the film set and switched on the TV. It flicked into action. There were images of tanks on the streets of Athens and outside the Greek parliament building. Colonel George Papadopoulos spoke to the Greek people. Costas translated.
"He says that due to the extraordinary circumstances, the military have taken over. Papadopoulos says that he planned to restore the press to its national purpose. He felt he had a serious mission within the framework of a true democracy. Freedom of the press does not mean irresponsibility, shamelessness, in this current communist press reporting, and the betrayal of all national values.''
My son tells me that the military have complete control of the city. Leading politicians and citizen with left wing views have

been arrested. Spandidkis, the commander and chief of the Greek Army has been arrested also. The train stations and the airport are under their control. The royal palace has been surrounded. 10,000 people have been arrested. I think it is time you boys got out of Greece, before they close the borders.''

***

Leonard told Costas about Marianne, Sophia and her children, and how now he was deeply worried. They hurried over to the ferry port and waited. Two hours later, the ferry appeared and he could see Marianne and Sophia waiving to them. He embraced Marianne as she got off the ferry and greeted Sophia and her children.

The police approached them and instructed them to register at the police station the next day, as they were regarded as 'foreigners' now in Greece. They were required now to prove that they had a residence permit; and were not employed and received money from abroad. They were instructed to give knives and guns to the police also.

They could see police everywhere, as they walked to Katsikas cafe. Marianne told him of the events in Athens, and how she and Sophia had heard shots in Syntagma square. They ran up the stairs to the roof of their hotel. From there they could see that the streets and squares were empty. They could see military tanks advancing and shots were fired from the rooftops. They were scared and did not sleep that night. They watched the TV for updates until early morning; then they found a taxi driver that took a risk in driving them to Piraeus, via the backstreets of Athens.

***

The following morning, Marianne and Sophia rushed up to their terrace, and heard the roar of plane engines, and went out on their terrace and saw military planes flying over Hydra. The planes speed over and dipped close to the harbour, and then climbed towards the top of the island. On their radio they picked-up the BBC in London. Then they heard the announcement.

> *"A group of right-wing army officers have seized power in a coup d'etat in Athens. The coup leaders have placed tanks in strategic positions across Athens, and gained complete control of the city. A large number of small army units were dispatched to arrest leading politicians, authority figures and ordinary citizens suspected of left-wing sympathies. The whole of Greece is now in the hands of the Colonels."*

***

Leonard thought to himself. It was time to escape Greece. Leonard and Anthony went to visit Costa, who told them in great detail about the coup. The coup leaders led by Colonel George Papadopoulos, met with King Constantine at his residence in Tatoi Palace; which was surrounded by tanks to prevent his resistance. The king argued with the colonels. He went with them to the Ministry of National Defence, where all coup leaders were gathered, and had talks with the leading generals. He agreed to swear in the new regime only when they agreed to include a number of civilian politicians.

Panayotis Kanellopoulos, the last prime minister of Greece before the coup, was arrested by soldiers with machine guns and brought to the palace to meet King Constantine. He urged the king to use his status as commander-in-chief of the Greek military to order loyal officers to crush the coup.

Costas told them that he had a call from his son. He told him that, Constantine had a plan to escape to the north of Greece, to the city of Kavala, east of Thessaloniki. There he wanted to organise a counter-coup. The plan was to form an army unit that would advance to Thessaloniki and take it. Constantine planned to install an alternative government there. With two governments the King felt that this would, force the military junta to resign, so he could return to Athens. Costa told them that he would contact Anthony if he had any news.

***

Leonard lay back in bed <u>with Marianne</u> and lit up a cigarette. He had come in search of paradise, but he was discovering that this could become a nightmare too. He would have to get out of Greece immediately. The country was paralyzed by this new dictatorship. He wrote in his diary that; *'there was an almighty reckoning coming, and democracy would appear through the cracks once day again. He could see the future and he knew that he had the gift of prophecy.'* This he felt was a wakeup call, and a reminder of the great burdens and social injustices that the Greeks lived under.

***

Leonard met with Anthony in Katsikas cafe. It was his last night of Hydra. Leonard and Anthony drank ouzo together the night. Anthony told him that he had decided to stay and wait it out. He had no money to go anyway.

Marianne was asleep when he got home, Axel junior lay beside her. They looked like the–Madonna and child. Leonard reflected on that time Greece was an enchanting one. He read by the moonlight and observed Marianne's beautiful face. He would never forget this love of his life. There were days of shared love that had its pain and tears. He would always remember Marianne's love as a special one.

Leonard, had made up his mind. He was leaving his beloved island not just because of the military situation, but also because of Marianne and Axel's safety. Liberals, intellectuals, writers, expats could become a target in this dictatorship. He was certainly could end up on that list. It would be only a matter of time that the police could come knocking on his door. The borders could close any day now. If they could not make it to Athens, they could buy a car and head northwards. Leonard had one last glass of wine with Marianne on the terrace and watched the sunset. He knew that the situation was very grave, and the game was over for this lost paradise.

***

He read from Lorca's book that described how he was murdered, in Spain under Franco's military dictatorship. Along with three friends that had been taken from a lorry, and were locked up for ten hours. At midnight, Lorca was taken by a car to the village of Vizwar, five miles from Granada, and over three thousand feet up the Sierra De Huetor mountain range. It was just a few miles behind the front line of Spain's civil war. The car arrived at a building known as the Colonia. It was a place for those to be executed and housed the men, that executed and buried them.

One of the young men on guard was Edwardo Aurioles. Their mothers knew each other, and Lorca as a boy had saved him from drowning. At 11;13 Lorca, a school teacher and two bullfighters who were known anarchists, where taken out and driven along the Alfacar road, past the Vizwar ravine. Here they were forced at gunpoint to walk two hundred feet to their place of execution.

The firing squad had a young man who boasted later that he had shot two bullets at Lorca's head. Lorca lay beneath an old cedar tree. This was how and where Lorca had died. Leonard reflected that Lorca had died before his time was up; and how he was murdered in cold blood, without a trial he was a victim of the fascists. His songs were about love, not war. Like Lorca, he could be executed or imprisoned like him.

***

Leonard heard from Anthony that the composer Theodorakis went underground and founded the "Patriotic Front" to liberate Greece. On 1 June, the Colonels published "Army decree No 13", which banned playing, and listening to his music.

Theodorakis was arrested on 21 August, and jailed for five months. It was the day the music died and freedom in Greece.

***

Chapter 32
King Constantine

Costas contacted Anthony, and he and Leonard hurried over to his café that evening. He told them that in the early morning hours, the king had boarded a plane together with Queen Anne-Marie of Greece, their two young children, Princess Alexia and Prince Pavlos, his mother Queen Frederica, his sister Princess Irene and Premier Kollias.

King Constantine arrived in Kavala under the command of generals loyal to him. The air force and navy, where royalist and supported him. Constantine's generals cut all communication between Athens and Thessaloniki. The king wanted to avoid bloodshed, even if the junta attacked them.

Pro-junta officers were arrested in Thessaloniki, and royalist generals took command of their units. However, pro-junta forces also advanced on Kavala to arrest the king. Costas told them that the counter-coup had failed, and Constantine fled Greece on board the royal plane, a few hours ago, taking his family with him to Rome. Costas turned on the TV. They could see King Constantine's final speech to the Greek people. Costas translated.

> *"I consider myself King of the Hellenes and sole expression of legality in my country until the Greek people freely decide otherwise. I fully expected that the military regime would depose of me eventually. They are frightened of the crown because it is a unifying force among the people. God save Greece, and God save the Greek people!"*

***

At Katsikas' cafe there was a farewell party for Leonard and Marianne. Everyone came and the partied the night away. Leonard and Marianne packed his suitcase with his typewriter and his rejected novel. Marianne put a wool coat on Axel junior, and a pair of new boots. Leonard gave his cat to Sophia and said goodbye to her children along with Marianne. She agreed to look after the house while they were away. Hopefully he would return some day.

They had one last drink in Bill's bar with Anthony. Later he walked with them to the port, carrying Leonard's suitcase. Then they boarded a ship leaving for Athens.
"Be careful in Athens, the army is on the streets," said Anthony.
"Don't worry about us, we will be ok."
"Goodbye dear friend. I hope to see you soon again. I will come back to Hydra someday. You are like the wind, Leonard. You breathed poetry into all our lives."
Marianne kissed Anthony on the cheek and said goodbye. Anthony smiled at Axel and shook his little hand.
"Take good care of him, won't you," said Anthony.
"Don't worry, we will," said Leonard sadly.
Leonard sat on the rear deck and looked at the harbour as Hydra receded in front of him. The ships horn sounded and slowly pulled away from the harbour, as the ropes were cast loose by the sailors.

They waived to Anthony. To the left he could see Hennessy's villa, up above on the steep hill. He could make out the figure of Hennessy standing beneath the archway with the Countess Adriana. They waived at them. Leonard's heart was filled with mixed emotion. Hydra had been his home for many years, and this landscape of white houses, under a glorious sun had nurtured him. He had discovered himself and his limitations, on this glorious island. Hydra at this time of day was bathed in a golden light, and before long Anthony and Hydra drifted into the mirage of the early morning sun.

When they arrived at the harbour in Piraeus, there were many soldiers and police carrying guns. They checked Leonard's and

Marianne's passports. They took a taxi to the Niki hotel near the port, that they had stayed in before.

Leonard discussed the political situation with the hotel receptionist, who advised him to get out of Greece as soon as possible. In their room, Marianne and Leonard discussed their escape plan with a sense of urgency. They would stay the night in Piraeus, and buy a car from a local garage they knew, that was run by a man called Dimitris. Their plan was to leave Piraeus by night. Then would drive around Athens and avoid the main streets. They would also have to buy enough petrol to take them to Thessaloniki and enough food supplies for at least five days. They would also need camper a gas burner to heat food and boil water.

The following morning, Leonard bought an English newspaper about the generals taking over Greece, with the headlines; *'Regime of the Colonels.'* They located an old garage where the owner Dimitris sold them a French Citroen 2cv car and filled up the tank. In the boot they put more cans of petrol. Marianne sat in the back seat with little Axel.

By early morning, they had reached the west of Athens, and took a small road that passed through the Greek countryside; over hills and mountain passes parched by the sun. Leonard glanced at Marianne from time to time, her blonde hair was blowing in the breeze, and little Axel, was sleeping on the back seat. He felt exhausted, but he had to keep driving.

Two hours later he could see a giant viaduct ahead called the Gorgopotamos bridge. A memorial sign in English and Greek informed them that during World War II, one hundred and fifty Greek partisans, and a group of British SOE officers, blew up this railroad bridge in 1942. It was part of an operation to cut off the Nazi controlled route between Thessaloniki and Athens. The blast destroyed two of the six piers of the bridge. In an act of reprisal, the German occupation forces executed sixteen Greek locals. Leonard and Marianne could see the viaduct in the distance. It was majestic sight.

Their car headed northwards and for a period of time hugged the coast. The sun descended and they found an inn where an old woman gave them a room for the night.

The following day they arrived in Thessaloniki. Opposite the station they found a hotel. They lay their heads on the pillow and looked at a map of Europe. He could see the route ahead of him.

They passed over the border into Yugoslavia with a sense of relief. The soldiers at their post asked them about the coup. They slept in small inns on the way.

After a week they reached Trieste. Leonard remembered that it was in this city that Irish writer, James Joyce had once lived. Trieste was situated towards the end of a narrow strip of land between the Adriatic Sea and Italy's border with Slovenia. Leonard and Marianne could see that Trieste's coast had a broad gulf, with numerous tiny bays, and the beautiful Miramare Castle, located on a cliff by the sea. Near there they found a cheap hotel for a few days. They were exhausted after this road trip of over fifteen hundred miles.

They drove on towards Venice and reached the Mestre on the mainland, that is connected to the city across the Liberty bridge. They found a place to stay near the Piazza Ferretto that had many frescoes and coffee shops and trattorias. They lay there together while little Axel slept. Leonard, could see the moon out over this great city and he thought to himself, that Marianne had filled his emptiness in his life now. He thought about their love. Happiness was all he knew from her and the simplicity of that moment. He had made a commitment to her, and there was no way back for him. He wondered if she felt the same way.

The following day in the magical city of Venice, they walked among the pigeons in St Mark's square. They visited St Mark's Basilica on its eastern end. The church's western facade had great arches with marble decoration, and Romanesque carvings around the central doorway. Inside they found a great altar and with a sculpture of four horses, that displayed the pride and power of Venice.

Leonard took Marianne and little Axel to the Café Florian, where he had been before. Leonard told her that almost nothing happens by accident, and that Axel was now re-examining what they have done to her. He told her that she was important to him, and that their times together gave him courage for many things.

By the emerging light at dawn as the sun rose over the bay of Venice, they began their journey across the wide-open expanse of the plains of Lombardy. The plan was to reach the French border. They had to drive on to the town of Bordighera on the French border.

This trip took them via Verona, where Shakespeare's famous play was located. This play explored the story of Juliet Capulet, the only daughter of the head of the House of Capulet. She fell in love with the Romeo, a member of the house of Montague. But the Capulets have a blood feud. In order to deceive her parents when they want her to marry; she comes up with a plan to take a drug that will put her in a coma. Juliet visits a friar and he offers her a potion that will put her into a deathlike coma for forty hours. The friar promises to send a messenger to inform Romeo of the plan, so that he can join her when she awakens.

On the night before the arranged wedding, she takes the drug, and when discovered they think Juliet is dead, and she is laid in the family crypt. The messenger, does not reach Romeo, and instead, Romeo learns of Juliet's death from his servant, Balthasar. Heartbroken, Romeo buys poison from him and goes to the Capulet crypt. Still believing Juliet is dead, he drinks the poison. Juliet then awakens, and discovering that Romeo is dead, she stabs herself with his dagger and joins him in death. The families are reconciled by their children's deaths and agree to end their feud. The play end with the words; *'For never was a story of more woe, than this of Juliet and her Romeo.'*

They drove on to Menton, where the Irish poet Yeats that Leonard admired had, died in 1938 at the Hôtel Idéal Séjour. His body was taken back to Ireland after the war. Her remembered his lines.

'Come away, O human child: To the waters and the wild with a fairy, hand in hand, For the world's more full of weeping than you can understand.'

They drove on past Monte Carlo to the beautiful town of Beaulieu-sur-Mer's, with it Belle Époque architecture. They visited the Villa Ephrussi de Rothschild, and it beautiful gardens in Cap Ferrat. It was there that the great benefactress Béatrice de Rothschild had once lived. They passed along the winding road by the coast and on to Cannes and Avignon. Then they took the road to Paris.

***

After two days driving, exhausted, they decided to stay in a cheap hotel in Saint-Germain-des-Prés. They had dinner at the café Flore, and the Deux Magots, where many French writers and artists frequented.

Marianne, realised that at times she was filled with a sense of despair at because of her situation. One night after too much wine they went to bed. Leonard woke up in the moonlight and Marianne was not beside him. He found her at the French windows trying to climb out. He grabbed hold of her before she could jump. She told him that she wanted to end it all, as Axel's separation had disturbed her so much.

Leonard consoled her and she cried in his arms. It was joy and sadness, for them both in that moment. The woman he loved could have been lost. He contemplated this as the early morning light appeared above the spire of Notre Dame, and he heard the bells toll. Marianne recovered and visited the Louvre with him. There she saw the Mona Lisa, and her enigmatic smile enchanted them both, and later they sat in cafe Flore on the Left Bank and talked late into the evening.

They drove North through Belgium, then on to Antwerp and stayed the night there. The next day they travelled over the border into Germany and on to Copenhagen. From there they crossed into Sweden and drove through Malmo, and on to Gothenburg. The following day they arrived in Norway in the town of Sarpsbor, south of Oslo.

Marianne had a smile on her face. Leonard could see the great vistas of lakes ahead of him and majestic mountains. Norway was indeed a dramatic place. It was a revelation to Leonard. He could see the valleys, fjords, cliffs, and the drama of the landscape, that the composer that Grieg had written about. Marianne moved the radio dial to Norway's classical channel and he heard his music for the first time. This was the landscape of the Vikings and ancient rune stones. They passed through beautiful deep forest, where the light cast shadows through the trees flickering across his face.

Oslo appeared in the evening light. An hour later they arrived at her house, and hurried inside to find her mother. They felt a sense of relief, they were home at last, and their escape from Greece was over. Leonard met Marianne's mother. Little Axel fell fast asleep. They had dinner together. Marianne's mother told them that her grandmother has once predicted, that she would *'...meet a man with a golden voice'*, and Leonard she felt was that man.

***

Leonard stayed in the Viking hotel in Oslo. Her mother was a strict Lutheran, and did not allow men say at her house unless they were married. Leonard wrote in his diary about Marianne in his hotel room.

The following day, Leonard went with Marianne to the Theatre Café, where she used to go with Axel. They then went to see a film called Elvira Madigan.

It was a film about a Swedish girl called Elvira, who was born in in 1888. She joined joined a circus with her parents. On one of the circus tours she was seen by an army lieutenant Sixten Sparre. He was married and had two children, but fell in love with Elvira, who was very beautiful, with almost meter-long, blond hair. They wrote to each other, Elvira tired of his writing, tried to end their relationship. Sparre, tried to persuade her to leave her family, and the circus to marry him. Sparre threatened to shoot himself if Elvira did live with him. He also lied about being divorced from his wife, and lied to Elvira that he was rich. After considerable emotional pressure, Elvira finally agreed, and secretly escaped with him.

The two went on to Stockholm, where Elvira's mother, tried to catch the couple. They lived a few weeks in Svendborg, at the city hotel. When the hotel director gave them the bill, and they fled.

They travelled to a forest in Denmark, where Sixten shot Elvira and then himself on the morning of July 19, 1889. The bodies were found three days later. In Elvira's dress pocket was found a paper with a poem, which she had written herself just before Sparre killed her with his revolver. They poem reads as follows.

> '*A drop fell into the water,*
> *faded out slowly,*

And the place where it fell,
surrounded from wave to wave.
What was it that fell?
and where did it come from?
It was but a life,
and but a death that came,
to win itself a track,
Now the water rests once again.
Hedvig.'

Leonard knew what suicide was all about he had come across it so many times in his life, as he contemplated Elvira's loss.

***

When they came out of the cinema it began to snow, and it reminded Leonard of Montreal. Marianne started to feel at home in Oslo again. Her mother wanted her to wear a Persian lamb's wool coat. The kind that rich Norwegian woman wore, and to get a perm in her hair like Marilyn Monroe, to make her look more sophisticated. The social scene in the theatre café had moved on and many of her friends were married. But Marianne longed for her barefoot days on Hydra. Leonard wrote in her diary.

> *'Marianne is sad, but is full of love for me. I wish I could hold her tightly and tell her not to worry. I will take care of her, and her son. Everything will be fine, but these are promises that are hard to make. Marianne, is my beautiful woman, I don't ever want her ever to experience being left alone again. I wish she was with me now, as I lie her in my hotel room. I will be with her always – and admire her beauty!'*

***

Leonard had only three hundred dollars to his name and no book deal. Things were becoming more desperate. He had to find some way to get back to Montreal as flights there were too expensive. He thought too that a break from Marianne would help them both think about her situation. They met again at the Theatre Café.

"I dreamt about you and Axel last night. I do not understand why you want to give up so quickly with Axel," said Leonard softly.

"I was waiting for you to say that," replied Marianne.

"I did not want to stand in the way of reconciliations. Whatever happens now, let see if your divorce is going to go through. I do not know what will happen to us, but I know that we are joined together and will not be taken apart. I will always want to talk to you and touch you."

Marianne admitted that she was filled with confusion and admitted that she wrote secretly to Axel, and suggested they live together again. But when she received a negative reply from him, she confessed to Leonard and showed him Axel's reply, saying she would never do so again. Leonard was disturbed by Marianne's changing moods, of love and hate for Axel. What could he do but ride out the storm and express it in his poetry.

***

Chapter 33
Jesus was A Sailor

Leonard wanted to return to Montreal as soon as possible to see his publishers about his novel that was rejected. Maybe there was a possibility that he could re-write it. The trip from Greece had exhausted his money. He had an idea; he would go to Oslo harbour by taxi, and see if he could find a fishing boat sailing for Nova Scotia. He took a taxi there and stopped near the medieval castle and the royal residence. It was called Akershus castle, and included several magnificent halls, a church, government reception room and a banquet hall.

Leonard found a captain of a cargo ship from Nova Scotia in a café. He was sailing there in a few days. He agreed to take him on board the next day. He was sailing for Nova Scotia. He hurried back to Marianne. She looked elegant in a red dress, that was covered in small white flowers. She wore lipstick and her hair was held back in a ponytail. She had followed, it seemed to Leonard, her mother's advice. He told her of his plan and promised that as soon as he could raise some money, he would invite her to Montreal. They stayed and had drinks and talked about the future. The divorce she assured him could be through soon. There were tears in her eyes when he said goodbye to her, her mother and little Axel.

***

His cabin was simple and comfortable, with shared toilet and shower, one single bed, and a desk with a porthole to see the ocean. It had twenty-five crew members. They were a mix of Filipino and eastern European men who were warm and friendly. It was all-male company for his transatlantic voyage. Leonard wrote in his diary.

'I am always thinking of Marianne, and her beauty. She has changed me deeply. Maybe I should let her continue with her life and not intrude on her uncertainties. I will always remember our work of love. It is late at night when I write this. You are probably asleep. I am thinking about you and your son, like a Madonna and child. There is so much joy to seize. My love for her fills my heart. It does not matter what happens. We have made this union already. All my love is for her. It is strange to leave her. Marianne is a beauty. I got to confront her mystery and she has touched my heart. When I am with her, there is harmony and life is simple. There is a spiritual order to the world. I must see what happens to us when we are together again, perhaps everything or nothing. Anyhow, we shall speak and touch. If there is nothing left, I shall go on with my life and leave her.'

Leonard was the only passenger. The crew was welcoming, respectful, and polite from the moment he arrived on board. Leonard was struck by the hospitality of the crew, who seemed genuinely happy to be there, despite being thousands of miles from home. The food was good. Leonard was served fluffy buttermilk pancakes, with maple syrup. He had dinners of hemp-crusted trout, roast veal chops and fresh vegetables that were delicious. The atmosphere among the crew was jovial, with communal mealtimes and a noisy bar where he swapped travel stories. Leonard wrote again in his diary about Marianne, he had begun to miss her.

Leonard went out on deck to see the vast Atlantic ahead of him. He observed the great expanse of waves. He knew that his life as a novelist was not one for him. He had spent seven years in Greece, and he had sold only a few hundred books, with each publication. He felt that he would become another obscure poet, penniless with a voice that was crying in the wilderness. He knew that there were thousands like him, that would never have an audience. He knew too that it was only a few poems that were remembered among the famous poets.

Perhaps he should try to compose a song, after all a song was a kind of poem. It just had a chorus added. Perhaps he could begin to write a ballad that would somehow get his voice out there, and his message to the world. The world it seemed was not interested in his poems and his novel writing was a disaster. The reviewers had been savaging his first book, and the publisher had rejected his second one. He was indeed a beautiful loser.

Could a song save his literary career he thought to himself. He would have to think of lines for a song that meant a lot to him, and maybe to the world. He thought of Susanne and her spirituality, and his beloved Saint Catherine Tekakwitha; her beautiful sacrifice; and the eight hundred women that had come to-save the colony of Montreal. There was a meaning to all their sacrifice. He began to write a poem about Susanne and then later added a chorus to it.

***

The shipped docked in Novia Scotia. He took a train to Montreal. It crossed New Brunswick, and very soon he could see the St Lawrence river. He could see the endless forests, reflecting under the winter snow. A blazing sun hung over the white Quebec forests. Montreal city appeared on the horizon - he was home at last.

He took a taxi to his house, where his mother greeted him warmly. She cooked dinner for him and they talked for hours. He went with his mother and sister Ester, to their synagogue. He remembered this place so vividly. The interior was filled with worshippers sitting on their pews and reading the Torah. At the head of the congregation in a dark cassock, stood Rabbi Solomon, who wore a round skull cap. He welcomed Leonard back. He was greeted warmly by everyone. The rabbi read some words from the Torah. His words rang through his ears and they became embedded in his memory, in this place of assembly and prayer.

It was a place of refuge for him now. Leonard could smell the incense and he saw his Jewish community huddled together from the snow outside. He remembered sitting close to his father there, who always wore woollen gloves in the winter months. He remembered how his face had felt cold, and when he breathed a little fog appeared beyond his lips. The chanting of the rabbi comforted and consoled him. He was pleased to be back home in the place that had nurtured him in his youth. Maybe Leonard thought he could re-examine now the reasons why he had left in the first place, and re-evaluate his life.

***

Mort came by the following morning in his Cadillac, and they cruised over to see Susanne at her cafe. She was gracious as always. She told them that she was now seeing a sculptor called Armand. Mort went with Armand to see his sculptures, in his workshop, while Susanne and Leonard had tea together. They engaged in their traditional ritual of tea and oranges. Leonard asked her where the tea was made. She told him that it was a flavour called Constant Comment made by the Bigelow Tea Company. It was a black tea flavoured with orange rinds and sweet spices. The recipe was developed by Ruth Bigelow in 1945; from an old colonial tea recipe for making orange and spice flavoured tea.

Susanne had the picture of the Saint Catherine Tekakwitha framed on her wall. It all came back to him again; the sacrifice of this saint, and the spiritual connection he had with Susanne.

He lay in bed that night and began to think again of a song about Susanne, the mystery of life, the saint, the bible and the sacredness and the dignity of that relationship. He knew that there was a spiritual beauty between Susanne and him, that no one could not touch, remove or destroy. They could almost hear each other thoughts sometimes, it was a delight to them both. She sensed a deep philosophical side to Leonard, that she understood.

Susanne told Leonard that she was moving to San Francisco and would try and keep in contact with him.

'Why did you leave Hydra? said Susanne, pouring him some more tea.

"I escaped from the military takeover. When things get too much, we all escape, - ware are all like escaped prisoner. Some men do it in other ways, when life backs them into a corner. They become heroic warriors against life, to try and outmanoeuvre their problems," said Leonard in his usual philosophical way.

"It's something men don't talk about, failure is something they don't want people to see, or what they perceive as failure," replied Susanne.

"Most men can't show that their heart is shredded. That they are filled with high hopes and despair. So, men chose the hangman's noose rather than face it. I have been filled with those moments of despair also. Some men want to throw themselves off a cliff, but they cannot do it. Maybe its cowardice not heroism that saves us. Now I toil in the tower of song, I hope I can find a song that can save me!"

"So, what's the plan Leonard?" said Susanne.

Leonard paused for a moment and lit up a cigarette.

"Canadian cigarettes are not the same as Greek," said Leonard thinking about Susanne question and smiling.

"I am thinking of writing a song, about you. But it takes so long."

"Is it really that hard for you?

"Yes, it takes me a long time. Dylan can write a song in ten minutes, while it takes ten me weeks. You know Susanne, you have to take what cards you're dealt with. I search for the beautiful lines all the time - the poetry and the meaning – but it is hard for me to express it."

"What's your favourite song?" enquired Susanne, handing Leonard a plate of cakes.

"It's a song by Fats Domino - Blueberry Hill. I found my thrill on Blueberry Hill. The moon stood still - that's poetry."

"Where does the inspiration come from?"

"I am sometimes touched by some illustrious spirit. But we are up against the great poets you know; Shakespeare, Homer, Shelley, and Byron, who we are trying to share the room with."

Susanne paused for a moment and looked at Leonard intently as if she was reading his mind.

"So how is Marianne?"

"I was doing fine until her husband and Patricia turned up."

"Where does that leave you?"

"I don't know. I am confused, she's confused, it's a classic triangular relationship."

"My God, what a terrible situation."

"I love Marianne. You know you have always had to depend on the kindness of women. It's women who chose the men. It not the other way around. You know men don't accept this, but they cannot do a single thing, without the understanding of a woman. You know our free will is exaggerated, we all end up doing something we don't like in order to survive."

Leonard looked out on the St Laurence river. He could see a boat with its sails billowing in the breeze, as it sailed past. Susanne's eyes followed his. Then Leonard spoke softly.

"If men's hearts stay hardened, if we lose touch with our spiritual selves, then that is the end of civilization. If men continue to have hearts of stone, then we are all doomed. Only women's love and compassion can save us.''

"We all need redemption; we all need to be saved!" replied Susanne.

"Susanne, I know you understand my vision of the world. We give each other so much comfort. There is too much to tell you right now. You will always be special to me."

***

Chapter 34
My Indecision is Final

Leonard met with his publishers Jack Mc Clennand, who gave him a list of revisions that he wanted. Leonard worked day and night over many weeks to make the changes, but for him now it was a pointless exercise. When he got home on night, there was a letter there from Marianne.
"Dear Leonard, don't worry I miss you and love you too. But there cannot be three in any relationship. I have filed for a divorce with Axel. He isstill with Patricia despite this, he continues to still say he loves me. He can't make up his mind and his indecision is final. With love Marianne."
Leonard sat down at his kitchen table, while his mother slept and replied to her.

'My dearest Marianne,
I was happy to get your letter. I have never read anything so simple and beautiful it moved me very much. You are a rare and lovely woman, and what a privilege it is to be close to you. The thought of you never answering me made me worried, although I think sometimes, I have no right to be part of your life. I never have been so happy as when we are together. I say this always because the comfort you gave me is still with me and I long to have it renewed. I am doing a difficult revision of my novel. It is so dam slow that sometimes I think I want to abandon it all together. I am working on a song about Susanne and St Catherine, I hope their vision of the world will save me. I hope you can come soon to Montreal. I believe you will be wise enough to live with me again. I sleep alone. But please understand, that I did not want to stand in the way of reconciliations with Axel. I want to talk.to you and touch you. I do not know what will happen to us, but I

know that we are joined together, in a wonderful journey. My dearest Marianne, you have all my love. I never have been so happy as when was are together. Love Leonard.'

***

Beautiful Losers was finally published, but it sold no more than three thousand copies. The book was distributed Simpson's and W. H. Smith refused to carry the book. Jack McClelland's gave them the reassurances, '...that most of the people interested in pornography, would not begin to understand either Cohen's purpose or his accomplishments.' Leonard felt dejected, this was his second novel and its sales were not very high. He took the book one night and threw it into the fireplace, and vowed that he would never write a novel again. This book had exhausted him, and brought him close to death, like Saint Catherine Tekakwitha - the sacrifice was too much. Leonard wrote another letter to Marianne.

'My darling Marianne. Your letters are full of love. I wish I could hold you tightly. And tell you not to worry. I will take care of you and your son Axel, and everything will be good. These are promises that are hard to make. I just want to give my heart to you. I have only two hundred dollars to my name that my mother gave me. Now Marianne my beautiful woman. I am worried that you are lonely, something I think that I have not given you the things you needed. I don't ever want you to the experience of being left alone again. It would be so simple if you were with me. I would brush your hair, and love you. To hell with all the glories of loneliness. I am with you. I want to be talk to you now. This letter is part of our mysterious enduring love. I have given up plans for revolution, and redemptive visions. I hope that we will see each other soon. I don't like the ocean between us. I sleep in a very empty bed. I wish you were lying on it,

waiting for me to come to bed. I miss you so much nothing has changed about the way I feel about you. Love, Leonard.'

***

Leonard began to listen to the music of, Ray Charles, Edith Piaf, Nina Simone, Charlie Fox, and Sylvia Vartan. He began to think about a song again about Susanne and the spiritual beliefs still preoccupied him. He contained to draft it and put the lines together. He wrote late into the night. It was not the finished draft, but it was a start.

He wrote about Susanne, and about their meeting in the café by the river. There they watched the boats nearby, on the St Lawrence river. At first, he wanted to sleep the night beside her, but they both knew it was spiritual love between them. At first, he thought that she might be crazy, and unusual. But that's why he wanted to be there. She always served him tea and oranges, that came a long way from China. There was so much love between them. She was on his wavelength. He had a dream once to be her lover. He really did trust her, because she touched her perfect mind with his. It was Susanne that had told him about St Catherine, who had once believed in Jesus, the sailor that had walked upon the sacred waters. He had spent a long time searching, from his lonely ivory tower. When he knew that, only drowning men could believe in him. He knew that all men would be sailors, until he could free them. She told him that Jesus himself was awoken them, to the message of freedom and when the heavens did open. He was forsaken, but not forgotten. Suzanne sometimes took his hand as they walked by the St Lawrence river. She wore clothes and feathers from the Salvation Army. They watched the sun pouring down on the Lady of the Harbour, that was the statue of the Virgin Mary, on the top of the Notre-Dame Chapel. Then he knew for certain that she would always be with her, that she had saved him, and he was not forsaken, like so many before him. Susanne had believed in his poetry and that's all that mattered.

He changed the lines many times and wrote for days. The song started to take shape, he put a melody together and played his guitar in his bedroom. After a few days a song emerged.

Leonard decided to go to Nashville and play his song to a few producers there. Leonard met with his friend Robert Hershorn and told him how desperate his financial situation was. Robert agreed to provide him with the money for his trip there. Robert shared his love of poetry with him, He gave him a book of poetry by the eleventh century Persian Sufi poet Attar of Nishapur. It was a collection of lyrical poems in the philosophical tradition of Islamic mysticism, and sayings of famous Muslim mystics. It had text from his book. 'The Conference of the Birds'. Leonard opened the book and read his poem.

'In the valley of the quest, where the wayfarer begins by casting aside all dogma, belief, and unbelief.
In the valley of love, where reason is abandoned for the sake of love.
In the valley of knowledge, where worldly knowledge becomes utterly useless.
In the valley of detachment, where all desires and attachments to the world are given up. Here, what is assumed to be 'reality' vanishes.
In the valley of unity, where the wayfarer realizes that everything is connected and that the Beloved is beyond everything, including harmony, multiplicity, and eternity.
In the valley of wonderment, where, entranced by the beauty of the beloved, the Wayfarer becomes perplexed and, steeped in awe, finds that he or she has never known or understood anything.

In the valley of poverty and annihilation, where the self disappears into the universe and the wayfarer becomes timeless, existing in both the past and the future.'

For Leonard it was a last-ditch attempt to save his career as a writer. He, knew he could not sing but he thought to himself that many ballad singers did not know how to sing either, but still had a big audience. He said goodbye to Mort, Susanne, Ester and his mother and took a train south to Nashville. Leonard hoped and prayed that his song Susanne about his muse and his inspiration Saint Catherine, Jesus and the sailors of the St Lawrence river, would somehow find a producer and an audience.
Leonard wrote a letter to Marianne.

> *'Marianne you are beautiful. I could tell you that over and over, your hair must be getting long now. Send me pictures, I have never had such pleasure from a human face as yours I worry that you have trouble sleeping. It's a terrible affliction. I hope you didn't catch it from me. I hope I am not the cause of it. I sleep in my bed and it's very empty. I wish you were lying on it. Waiting for me to come to bed. I miss you so much nothing has changed about the way I feel about you. I received your letter this morning. I have never read anything so beautiful and simple. It moved me very much and brought to me again. whit know so well, that you are a rare and beautiful woman, and what a privilege it is to be close to you.'*

***

Chapter 35
Rivers of Memory

Leonard boarded the train to for Nashville. Leonard sat in a café and had a coffee before departure on his journey of over fifteen hundred miles to Nashville. It was his last shot he knew and some kind of recognition and he was nervous.

Leonard hurried down the platform and jumped onto the train with his guitar and his suitcase. The train cross Maryland and very soon he could see forests the George Washington and Jefferson National Forests; and land stretching across the Appalachian Mountains of Virginia, to Kentucky. The train past Johnson and Knoxville city. Leonard saw a tall man in a sharp haircut and dark sunglasses.

Leonard stepped off the train in Nashville and took a taxi to the producer's office. It was supposed to be the home of country and western music, but he saw a lot of men in well-cut suits and women in neat dresses, and men in cowboy hats and boots. It was a town he realised for insurance and bible reading. He could see rows and rows of religious bookshops. The area of music publishing and recording was called music row and had neat lawns outside. It was the heart of Nashville where Elvis Presley first recorded. He passed a sign that read 'The Country Music Hall of Fame'.

It was home of the grand old Oprey. It was full of wannabe songwriters coming from everywhere. Leonard knew that he was another hopeful. The bars there were full of men that had come with a song leaving their decent families, and ended up with the hookers and alcohol. It was full of cafes, diners and 'last chance saloons'.

Leonard found the producer's office that Robert had told him about. Leonard saw a tall man in a sharp haircut and dark sunglasses, sitting behind a desk.
"Jake Williams," said to Leonard,
"Yes, that's me."
"I have come a long way to find you."
Jake poured him some water into a glass, and pulled a contract from his drawer.
"What can I do for you sir?
Leonard took his song titled Susanne out of his jacket pocket and handed it to him,
"I wrote a song called Susanne, I am looking for a record deal," said Leonard shyly.
"I'll get to the point. Jake takes some pages from his drawer and places a contract on the table.
" I get songwriters in her every day. They are two a dime. It may be good or may go nowhere."
"What is this?"
"It is a standard writer's contract."
"How much?"
"Ten dollars' advance and will get royalties too."
Leonard paused and then signed it.

   Leonard returned to his hotel and met an old songwriter in the bar. He told him that Jake was a con-artist and that he would never see a penny or a deal from Susanne. Leonard felt depressed, that song meant so much to him. He returned to his hotel room and wrote in his diary.

. *'I signed that contract and now I fear that my song Susanne is gone. I will never did see any royalties - not a cent. I felt very good about this song as it was a song that people loved. The rights have been stolen from me, and I think this was justified. This song belonged to the world not me. It would be wrong to write this song and get rich too? I am happy for that person who put that piece of paper in front of me.'*

He recalled Marianne and her son Axel and he would watch her in her sleep. He watched her in the moonlight and under the lamp. It was his destiny. Like the poem it was so precious to me in these moments. He sometimes waited until she woke at dawn; and lay beside her and kissed and caressed her hair. He thought of Marianne. The words came to him and he thought of Yeats poem '. Leaning on my shoulder where she laid her snow-white hand. She bid me take life easy. But I was young and foolish and now a full of tears.' Then he pondered if he was a naive young man and foolish to fall in love with a married woman.

Marianne had become a kind of obsessive love an enigma. The kind of love that grips the human mind. That was uncontrollable at times. Love he knew was a kind of madness. He did not want to find another? Leonard had been under this spell of love for some time now. There was much to talk to Marianne about.

***

Chapter 36
By Grand Central Station I Sat Down and Wept

Leonard took the train to New York. A journey of over twelve hours and six hundred miles. He slept for many hours and was awoken by the announcement that they were close to the city. He could see the skyline opening up before him. The lights shimmered across its skyscrapers as if dancing in the night. He saw the signs for Easton and Newark. He felt a certain apprehension about this city. He had heard so much about it. It was a meeting place; a mecca for artists, writers and musicians.

Leonard searched in his coat pocket where Robert had scribbled down a name on a cigarette packet. On it was written 'The Chelsea Hotel'. This was a famous place for artists of all persuasions to stay. The train ground to a halt in New York's Grand Central Station. Leonard entered the main hall; it was vast. He had not seen such a giant space before.

In the station he stopped for a coffee and a sandwich. It also sold paperbacks and newspapers. He bought a book of the novel titled 'Grand Central Station I Sat Down and Wept', written by fellow Canadian author Elizabeth Smart. It was written in beautiful poetic prose. The book was about Elizabeth relationship with the poet George Barker, who was married man. It had many parallels with his own triangular relationship. Elizabeth had discovered Barker's poetry in a book shop in London, and later met and started a relationship with Barker. It took three years for them to meet him. They first met at a bus stop in Monterey in California. The relationship lasted eighteen years, and Smart had fifteen children with him. It was an extraordinary about how two people had met through poetry, not unlike his relationship with Marianne. Her book too had a similar fate as his. It sold only two thousand copies. Elizabeth's mother campaigned with government officials to have its publication banned in Canada. She bought up as many copies as she could, and had them burned. Leonard read from this book, Elizabeth's beautiful words and lyrical prose.

> *'Oh, canary, sing out in the thunderstorm, prove your yellow pride. Give me a reason for courage or a way to be brave. But nothing tangible comes to rescue my besieged sanity, and I cannot decipher the code of the eucalyptus thumping on my roof. I am unnerved by the opponents of God, and God is out of earshot. I must spin good ghosts out of my hope to oppose the hordes at my window. If those who look in see me condescend to barricade the door, they will know too much and crowd in to overcome me. The parchment philosopher has no traffic with the night, and no conception of the price of love. Moon, moon, rise in the sky to be a reminder of comfort and the hour when I was brave. No, my advocates, my angels with sadist eyes, this is the beginning of my life, or the end.'*

Grand Central station was quite run down, with it beautiful architectural detailing dirtied and covered in grime, largely from cigarette smoke; on the ceiling murals, of the stars. There was blackout paint from World War II on the windows. Leonard drank hid coffee listened to the radio playing in the café.

Leonard took a yellow cab to the Chelsea Hotel. Irving had told him about this place that many writers, and poets had staid some for long periods of time; like Allen Ginsberg, Jack Kerouac and Gregory Corso. The Welsh poet, Dylan Thomas, had stayed in room 205 and died there a few days after he became ill with pneumonia. Arthur Miller lived there, and also the writers Mark Twain, Brendan Behan graced its rooms. It seemed like a perfect place for him to stay. Perhaps these great writers would inspire him by their ghostly presence, like Lorca had on Hydra.

The red brick façade loomed up in front of him and the sign 'Hotel Chelsea' he could see clearly. It was built in the golden age, located between the Seventh and Eighth Avenue. Leonard entered the building. The floor had tiles that looked like marble. The walls were covered in paintings. It had a certain enchanting beauty about it warm and inviting. Leonard was greeted by a man with a large domed head, framed on the sides with grey hair. He had deep set eyes and a large curved nose.
"Greetings, can I help you?" the man said.
"I need a room...a bed, whatever you have."
"My name is Stanley. I'm the manager here," he replied in a sharp New York accent.
"My name is Leonard."
"Nice to meet you, Leonard," replied Stanley, who flicked through an old leather-bound ledger on a desk covered in papers and receipts.
"Let me see, I have a small room at the top for thirty dollars a night." Stanley looked at him intently. "How long for, Leonard?
"Maybe for a week. I'm heading for London."
"That will be ten dollars a night…surname?"
"Cohen," said Leonard.
"I think Andy Warhol, or one of his crew, crashed there when he was making that movie here, called the Chelsea Girls," said Stanley, looking at Leonard with a smile,'' and giving him a key to his room.
"It sounds like you run a fun place," replied Leonard.
"I took a lot of abuse on that film. I think the artists who come here think it's a place to perform, and experiment on how not to sleep. Okay Leonard, take the elevator to the fifth floor."
Leonard looked upwards to the great atrium of the hotel that had a great glass ceiling. He observed the beautiful wrought iron stairs that belonged to a lost gilded age; the Gatsby age of Scott Fitzgerald, that was an era of elegance. Leonard pressed the lift

button. He smelt the perfume of a woman and looked around. It was a familiar face he had seen somewhere before. She had a wild look about her; long dark curly blonde hair that was held together with a ribbon. She wore many bangles around her wrists that were made of many colours. She had exotic rings on her two right fingers. In her hair were feathers attached to her flowing locks. She had black beads in her hair also. Around her neck she wore a necklace of shells. She also wore a red t-shirt with an image of the famous rock star Jimi Hendrix. Her belt was made of rope and she wore pants of red velvet. She certainly was a child of the sixties, Leonard thought. She also wore large round sunglasses. Everything about this woman had an energy about her, and something enchanting about her.

"How are you?" Leonard said, beaming a smile as the lift opened.

"I'm doing fine," she replied, as they both stepped into the lift, and Leonard, pressed the button.

"Have I seen you somewhere before?"

"Maybe, I travel a lot."

"You look like Kris Kristofferson," said the young woman with a smile, clutching her beaded hair.

"It's your lucky day. I am Kris Kristofferson," said Leonard, as the lift ground to a halt. They both stepped out into the corridor covered with prints of old New York.

"Do you play that guitar?" the woman asked curiously.

"Yes, I do. Do you want to hear me play?" She looked at him intently.

"Yeah, sure."

"Come with me, I've got an apartment here," said the young woman with an invitation that surprised him.

"What's your name?"

"Janis."

"Joplin?" said Leonard.

"Yes," she replied.

"I've heard one of your records."

"Yeah," said Janis, as she turned the key in the lock.

Inside, Leonard observed a beautiful apartment filled with antique furniture. The walls were covered in framed prints by Warhol, Rotko and Pollock. Leonard took one of her guitars and sung her a Dylan song. Janis listened to him. He felt that she understood him. Theirs was a meeting of minds, and of souls. Janis was a free spirit like him. She understood his poetry and his songs.

Janis told him about how she felt she was bullied at school. She was overweight then and had acne. She was taunted by kids in school and was called a 'pig', 'freak' and a 'nigger lover'. Maybe it was because she met some teenagers after school that loved the old black singers like Ma Rainey, Leadbelly and Bessie Smith. The delivery of the black female singers she loved the most. The big notes that climbed to the top of a mountain, was the note she wanted to reach; that expresses pure raw emotion.

Leonards meeting with Janice was a short lived. He knew that if he stayed on at the Chelsea, that he would eventually run out of funds He had to find a recording deal fast, or he would have to return to Montreal. He would need to check the if the rights were lost on Susanne lyrics, and if it was true that the publishing rights were stolen. Leonard wrote to Marianne.

Leonard called Mary Martin a music agent, that Robert Hershorn had given him the-number of. He told him that she was from Toronto. She had worked as a hostess in a folk club and as an assistant for Bob Dylan's manger. Now she acted as a music agent, searching for new songs and performers. She arranged to meet him at Café What, in Greenwich Village. Leonard woke late, and pulled his shirt and trousers on and buckled up his belt. He put on his leather cowboy boots that he had bought the day before. He quickly shaved and combed his hair. All the late nights had given him dark rings beneath his eyes. He could see how bloodshot they were. New York was taking a toll on his health. He pulled on a velvet blue jacket he had bought in a Salvation Army shop, in Montreal and headed down the long flight of stairs of the Chelsea Hotel, with his guitar.

Leonard took a yellow cab. He peered out through its window, as it cruised along down New York streets illuminated by lamplight. At times he could see great tall buildings looming up before him; some modern, while others looked like they belonged to the batman comics of Gotham City.

Leonard arrived on MacDougal Street, a jumble of comedy cellars, theatres and cheap cafes and basement bars of the folk scene. He located Cafe What, where Jack Kerouac was performing. It was here that Bob Dylan made his New York debut. Leonard found a notice on the door listed a few of the famous names who played there: Jimi Hendrix, Ritchie Havens, Jerry Lee Lewis, Little Richard and the Velvet Underground.

Leonard entered the cafe and found it filled with people. Mary turned up at the café with another woman named Judy Collins, a singer from Seattle. She told Leonard about her own journey to New York and her struggles there as a musician. She had trained as a classical pianist, and later fell in love with folk music. She had arrived in New York at the age of twenty-two in 1961 and stayed in a cheap hostel, costing two dollars a night. Within a few weeks she got a record deal with Electra records who launched her first album, 'A Maid of Constant Sorrow'.

She wanted to hear him sing Dress Rehearsal Rag, his song about suicide. She had tried to commit suicide when she was only fourteen. He understood her sense of despair. The darkness that had enveloped him after Pablo's suicide, that had filled him with darkness at times too. It had begun to creep into his mind, and created anxieties. Somehow, he had developed a maturity to handle it. The winged angels had come through the cracks and saved him, and snatched him from the jaws of death many times. Leonard lifted his guitar and sang the song for them both. Then he sang Susanne. Judy agreed to record his song on her next album. They would include songs also by, The Beatles, Bob Dylan and Richard Fariña. Judy wanted to sing Susanne too.

Later they listened to the guest artist at the club for the night, playing some country and western music. A new song was announced called 'Gentle on My Mind', and the singer was John Hartford. It a song about friendship, loneliness, poverty and long distances between loved ones. The song refers to a door that is always open, and that you can leave and return any time; and a sleeping bag can always be left behind your friend's couch. There are no shackles in their relationship, even though there were forgotten words and bonds; that were recorded in letters that were ink stains, that have dried upon some line. The connection and the love with his loved one, kept him on the back roads by the rivers of my memory, and were ever gentle on my mind. It was a beautiful song. He wondered if the song about Susanne and how special she was to him would evoke the same emotion.

***

Leonard stayed at the Chelsea hotel and continued to jam with Janis. He slept and wrote many poems. A few weeks later Mary called him to tell him that he got a call from Mary. He was now totally broke, and packing his suitcase_to go back home to Montreal. She told him to turn on his radio and that is that his song Susanne, was been sung by Judy, and broadcast across New York. Leonard listened to the crackling waves of sound, and he could hear the words of Susanne. Finally, his voice had been heard to an audience of millions. Later he would learn what an important moment it was for him, as this song would save his career and his life, and open up a new world for him in - the tower of song.

***

Leonard wrote a letter to Marianne, that night.

> *'My dearest Marianne. My song Susanne has finally been recoded and was broadcast on radio today in New York. All I want to tell you is that you are important to me. Our time together gave me courage for many things. The closeness with you despite our distance has not diminished. When we are old, I will be your shadow. I think of you with all my heart. You are the woman who released me from my pain. We used to watch the moon together on that island of dreams. You loved me without hesitation, you love me tenderly, and we danced the waltz together. You welcomed me into your heart. You touched me with your love, and with your mind, that was a thousand kisses deep. You were like a thousand candles in the wind. I was born again and I loved your beauty, that you shared with me. All my Love, Leonard.'*

Leonard returned to Montreal to rest and tell his mother, his sister Ester, Robert, Mort, Irving, and Susanne the good news. Before he took the train north, he knew that there was one final thing he had to do. He took a cab to St Patricks Cathedral. The great granite façade shone proudly in the evening light. Nearby he bought a bunch of white lilies, in a flower shop and entered this majestic building. He entered and walked down the aisle to find the statue of Saint Catherine Tekakwitha. There he said a prayer to the saint and lit a candle to her. As he finished his small ritual, an organist began to practice and Leonard paused for a moment to listen and reflect. He cast his eyes towards the great stained-glass window and watched the rainbow colours stream through. He thought to himself, that it was faith that had gotten him through his struggles and his darkness. Saint Catherine had inspired him with her heroic faith, virtue, and love, in the face of adversity and rejection. He remembered the words from Saint Catherine.

> *'I am not my own. I have given myself to Jesus. He must be my only love. The state of helpless poverty that may befall me, if I do not marry does not frighten me. All I need is a little food and a few pieces of clothing. With the work of my hands I shall always earn what is necessary and what is left over I'll give to my relatives and to the poor. If I should become sick and unable to work, then I shall be like the lord on the cross. He will have mercy on me and help me, I am sure.'*

***

Susanne was a big hit all around the world and established his name as a recording artist. He days as an unknown poet were over. He rented an apartment down near the St Lawrence river, close to the church where the statue of Saint Catherine was. He sent plane tickets for Marianne and little Axel, to fly to Montreal. There they lived for seven years together, until their lives took them in other directions.

Epilogue
The Innocent and the Beautiful.

43 Years later;
Hotel Carillion, Paris 2012.

Leonard woke from his sleep. He was lying now in the hotel room. It was early morning and the light entered at the edges of the curtains. Outside the bells of Notre Dame were ringing. Leonard thought about Saint Catherine, Sister Marguerite and Susanne Verdal. It was their inspiration that had inspired his song Susanne. It was the song that saved his career and his life.

The St. Lawrence river had a poetry and beauty about it. The river tied them together. It was a spiritual union. They could almost hear each other thinking. Susanne would always light a candle and we would be quiet for several minutes, then we would speak, about life and poetry, and prayed to Saint Catherine. She had given him a beautiful song. It was a sweet moment. He had stayed true to art for art's sake. Leonard had stayed true to the cause like Susanne. They time they shared together, in that moment was eternal and it deeply touched him. They had gone their different ways and lost touch. Some of my most beloved friends have departed. Susanne, he knew always held dear, and close to their hearts this time together. The song was played now all over the world and listened too by millions. But many people did not know the meaning and the inspiration behind this song. He hoped someday a writer would remember its truths and write about it.

The past now came flooding back to him. He thought to himself of how none of the relationships on Hydra survived. But in a sense, he continued to honour them. He recognized the richness of those experiences. The island was magic and tragic and there was laughter and pain in all of it.

***

29 July 2016, Los Angeles. Hotel Chateau Marmont.

Four years later, Leonard sat in another hotel Chateau Marmont in Los Angeles. Its beautiful architecture was inspired by a French chateau in the Loire valley. This hotel that was part of the old part world of Hollywood. A place where stars had come to party and where some had died. Its classical façade shone in the evening light. Leaves swayed in the early morning breeze. Leonard looked out his window down towards Sunset Boulevard that looked like, like a snake winding into the distance.

Leonard had booked in for a few days. He had come down from the monastery at the top of Mount Gabriel where he was studying Zen Buddhism with a monk named Roshi. It was this Buddhism he recalled that he had first discovered on Hydra. He had booked into a room at the rear of the chateau overlooking the gardens. He found some peace there.

He opened a letter from Oslo. The stamp had a face of it of as old man with the name of Ibsen. Yes, it was the man who wrote the play; 'The Enemy of the People', that Marianne had loved so much. The letter was from a man named Jan Christian Mollestad, a friend of Marianne.

Memories of Marianne came floating back to him, like the breeze that ruffled and came through the curtains. It was a memory like a ripple in time, evoking his past with Marianne. Flashes of memory appeared, her smile, her crimson lips; her blue eyes were surrounded by blonde hair; long dark and curved cheekbones, and skin stretched over the perfect curved of bone and muscle. Her dress was covered with colourful patterns of flowers. Around her perfectly formed neck she wore a gold chain, with a simple cross that hung about her neck. Her hands were graceful, with long fingers and nails painted in the colour of magenta. Yes, this was Marianne. Why had someone contacted him about her. He refocused on the letter and the words moved across the page, as if written in calligraphy, that all seemed so balanced and perfect.

> *'My name is Jan Christian, a friend of Marianne Ilhen. I am writing from Oslo, Norway. I am afraid I am the bearer of bad news. Marianne is dying - she has leukaemia. She always speaks fondly of you. I just thought you should know. Marianne asked me to send this letter to you.'*

Tears appear in Leonard's eyes. Then he sat at his desk and began to write a letter to Marianne. The thought of losing Marianne - his precious Marianne worried him. It was the inevitability of time. That had always haunted his poems. Now the angel of death had appeared. He continued to write.

> *'Well Marianne, it has come to this when we are really old and our bodies are falling apart. Know that I am close behind you and that if you stretch out your hand, I think you can reach mine, and you know that I have always loved you for your beauty and your wisdom, but I don't need to say anything more. I just wish you a very good journey. Goodbye old friend, endless love, see you down the road. Do you remember when we first met? We were so young.'*

They had lived together for eight years in Montreal. He had written a song about her many years ago called; 'So Long Marianne' to her. He wrote in his diary the feelings attached to the creation of that song, that took so long to write.

> *'We met when we were young. I remembered standing at the window with her, at my house in Hydra looking out at the sunset. She held on to me like a crucifix. I was in love*

with her, and she was my little darling. I held her hand and read her palm. She had a long life line. In those days I lived the life of a travelling troubadour. I used to think I was a gypsy boy, but then she let him take her home. I loved to live with her. I am old now and forget so very much. I forget sometimes to pray to the angels. So, so long, Marianne, it's time to remember and laugh and cry, and laugh about it all again.'

He also dedicated his poetry book 'Flowers for Hitler' to her. A photo of her appeared on the back cover of his second album, 'Songs from a Room', that was taken in his house on Hydra. Marianne sat typing on Leonard's old Olivetti, at a rickety wooden desk, wrapped in a towel; the hot sun streaming through gaps in the shutters. He remembered how she's turned and smiled fondly at him as he took the photo

He thought about love, loss and memory, and one of one of his favourite poets William Butler Yeats, who had written about such things. He had visited Lisadell House in Ireland, in 2010. It was there that Yeats, used to meet the sisters Eva and Constance and wrote a poem about them; ' In Memory of Eva Gore-Booth and Constance Markiewicz'. Like these two sisters Marianne and Susanne had made a profound impact on his life; Eva and Constance – Marianne and Susanne they seem to merge into one. He began recall the poem as he lay there in his bed. His lips moved slowly and he whispered softly.

> 'The light of evening, Lissadell,
> Great windows open to the south,
> Two girls in silk kimono both,
> Beautiful, one a gazelle,
> But a raving autumn shears,
> Blossom from the summer's wreath;

The older is condemned to death,
Pardoned, drags out lonely years,
Conspiring among the ignorant,
I know not what the younger dreams,
Some vague utopia and she seems,
When withered old and skeleton-gaunt,
An image of such politics.
Many a time I think to seek,
One or the other out and speak,
Of that old Georgian mansion, mix,
Pictures of the mind, recall,
That table and the talk of youth,
Dear shadows, now you know it all,
All the folly of a fight
With a common wrong or right.
The innocent and the beautiful.
Have no enemy but time.

***,

Postscript
In Search of Lost Time

1. Marianne Ilhen Jensen died in 2016, in Oslo, at the age of 81.
2. Axel partner the American painter Patricia Amlin became a film director and writer, known for the; Popol Vuh, The Creation Myth of the Maya, The Five Suns: and A Sacred History of Mexico.
2. Irving Layton became an important poet in Canada. He died of Alzheimer's disease, at the age of ninety-three on January 4 2006.
3. Axel Jensen had a distinguished career as a novelist writing twelve in total. In the last ten years of his life, Jensen was severely disabled from amyotrophic lateral sclerosis. He gradually became paralyzed, losing all his motor-coordination abilities. He later, relied on a breathing-aid to breathe. In his final years he could neither write nor speak. He died in Oslo on 13 February 2003.
5. Mary Martin continues her work as a music agent and finding new songs and talent.
6. George Johnson died of tuberculosis in Sidney in 1964 before the publication of his novel 'Clean Straw for Nothing', that exposed his wife's affairs on Hydra.
7. Charmian Clift died in 1969. On 8 July 1969, the eve of the publication of Johnston's novel 'Clean Straw for Nothing', exposing her various affairs. Clift committed suicide by taking an overdose of barbiturates before the publication of her husband's book.
8. Shane Johnson (Charmain's daughter), committed suicide in 1974.

9. Martin Johnson (Charmain's son) became an important poet in Australia. He returned to Hydra in 1980. He died of alcoholism in 1990, at the age of forty-two.

10. George Lialios died in London in 2013. His wife Anjelika lives and Greece today and continues to paint.

11. Anthony Kingsmill returned to London and lived with the author. He died in Islington in 1993. His daughter Emily lives today somewhere in America.

12. Stanley Bard manager of the Chelsea Hotel, died in Boca Raton in Florida in 2017. He became famous as the Robin Hood of hotels, because he *'nurtured talented writers, artists and tolerated assorted deadbeats.'*

13. In early 1967 John Starr Cooke formed the Church of One, and took part in 'The Council for the Summer of Love'. In early 1976 Cooke became the basis of a film 'Prophecy of the Royal Maze', which showed him doing a New Tarot reading for the Aquarian Age. By this time, he was in great pain from a swollen hand caused by the cancer in his shoulder moving down his arm. Cooke died of skin cancer on August 21, 1976, at the age of 56.

14. Olivia de Haulleville today lives near the Joshua Tree National Park in California, and write books about Buddhism. A quote from her Facebook reads; 'If I were given a wish. To be what I wish. I would wish to be
who I am – myself!'

15. Elizabeth Smart died in London, in 1986 of a heart attack at the age of 72. She was buried in St George's churchyard, Saint Cross South Elmham, Suffolk.

16. Rubert Nurse retired to the town of Arima, Trinidad, and continued to mentor musicians there and write arrangements for them. He died there in 2001, at the age of 90.

17. Bill Cunliffe owner of Bills Bar, died in 2011. After a farewell ceremony his daughters Carolyn and Kathy scattered his ashes in Kimini Harbour, Hydra in 2012.

18. Alan Ladd died on January 29, 1964, at the young age of fifty years. His death, was caused by a cerebral edema. It was alleged in the press that the cause was related to an acute overdose of alcohol, barbiturate, and two tranquilizers. His death was ruled as accidental. Ladd suffered from chronic insomnia and regularly used sleeping pills and alcohol to induce sleep. Suicide was ruled out.
19. Clifton Webb never married, and had no children. He lived with his mother until her death at age 91. Noël Coward remarked: *'It must be terrible to be orphaned at 71'*. Clifton spent the last five years of his life as a recluse at his home in Beverly Hills, California. On October 13, 1966, Webb suffered a fatal heart attack at the age of 76. He was interred in crypt in Hollywood Forever Cemetery, alongside his mother.
20. King Constantine remained in exile for almost forty years after the vote in favour of the republic. He returned to Greece on February 1981, when the government only allowed him to return for a few hours, to attend the funeral of his mother, Queen Frederica, in the family cemetery of the former Royal Palace at Tatoi. Constantine sued Greece at the European Court of Human Rights for €500 million in compensation for the seized property. He received the compensation of €12 million for his lost property. Constantine, announced the creation of the Anna Maria Foundation, to allocate these funds back to the Greek people for use in '*extraordinary natural disasters*', and charitable causes. In 2013, King Constantine returned to reside in Greece.
21. Princess Alice died at Buckingham Palace on 5 December 1969. She left no possessions, having given everything away. Her remains were placed in the Royal Crypt in St George's Chapel at Windsor Castle. Before she died she had expressed her wish to be buried at the Convent of Saint Mary Magdalene in Gethsemane on the Mount of Olives in Jerusalem, near her aunt Grand Duchess Elizabeth Feodorovna, a Russian Orthodox saint.

On 3 August 1988, with the initiative of Prince Philip her remains were transferred to Israel. On 31 October 1994, Princess Andrew's two surviving children, the Duke of Edinburgh and Princess George of Hanover, went to Yad Vashem, the Holocaust Memorial); in Jerusalem to witness a ceremony honouring her as "Righteous Among the Nations" for having hidden the Cohens in her house in Athens during the Second World War. Prince Philip said of his mother's sheltering Jews;

> *'I suspect that it never occurred to her that her action was in any way special. She was a person with a deep religious faith, and she would have considered it to be a perfectly natural human reaction to fellow beings in distress.'*

In 2010, the Princess was posthumously named a Hero of the Holocaust by the British Government.

22. In September 1972 Leonard received the news that Robert Hershorn had mysteriously died in Hong Kong. His son Adam was born the same week. He departed immediately to Montreal to see his son and bury his friend. Leonard shovelled the dirt on the coffin in the Shaar Hashomayim cemetery, a Jewish custom of the living and honouring the dead, Leonard wrote an epitaph to him;

> *'Hershorn is now gone. He was a partner in spirit, and love, He was the lion of my youth, the eagle of experience, the grizzly bear of our forest and the highest leaping deer of our imagination. He was my pupil in music, my teacher in war, addict of God, original as an explosion, murdered by mid-wives in Hong Kong, buried in Montreal snow weeks later, black and bloated, under Hasid supervision.'*

23. Ramblin Jack Elliott the American folk singer is alive and well and continues to perform his songs.

24. Steve Sanfield died in California in 2015. He published over thirty books during his lifetime. The University of California Davis library holds a collection of all his books.
25. Redmond Frankton Wallis returned to New Zeeland with his wife Robin and died there in 2006. He never published his book - The Unyielding Memory. The unfinished manuscript is deposited in National Library of New Zealand's -Turnbull Library.
26. Muriel Belcher the founder and owner of the private drinking club The Colony Room, died in London, in 1979.
27. Ian David Archibald Board, became the successor to Muriel Belcher as the proprietor of the Colony Room Club. He died in London, in 1994.
28. George Whitman the proprietor of Shakespeare and Company, died in Paris in 2013. His daughter Sylvia named after Sylvia Beach who first published Ulysses, continues to run the bookshop.
29. Gordon Merrick died of lung cancer at the aged 71 in Colombo, Sri Lanka, on 27 March 1988. He was survived by his partner of thirty-two years, Charles G. Hulse.
30. Magda Tilche remarried again, and died in a care home in Hydra in 2015.
31. George Melly the English jazz and blues singer, died in London, in 2007.
32. Timothy Hennessy died in Avignon in 2015, in a large villa behind the Bishops Place, at Rue De La Croix. He had fallen and remained in bed for over two years. He was buried in an undisclosed location by his executors. The author visited him before he died and but did not attend his 'secret funeral', that his executor refused to disclose. His son Sebastian lives in Paris today.
33. Countess Adriana Marcello, Timothy Hennessy his first wife lives in Italy today.

34. His second wife Isabel died tragically in Ireland in 1996. Timothy informed the author that he could not bear to put her name on her tombstone. She lies in the cemetery at Sallin's, Co Kildare.

35. Baroness Barbara Judith Ghika (Hutchinson) died in Westminster, London at the age of 78, in 1989.

36. Patrick Leigh Fermor suffered from a cancerous tumour, possibly from smoking over one hundred cigarettes a day. In June 2011 he underwent a tracheotomy in Greece. His last wish was to return to England. He died in England, at the age 96, on 10 June 2011, the day after his return. His funeral took place at St Peter's Church, Dumbleton, Gloucestershire, on 16 June 2011. A guard of honour was provided by serving and former members of the intelligence Corps. A bugler from the Irish Guards sounded the last post. Leigh Fermor was buried next to his wife in the churchyard at Dumbleton. The Greek inscription on his tombstone is a quotation from Cavafy, that can be translated from Greek that read; 'In addition, he was that best of all things, Hellenic'.

37. In 1979, Soraya the Queen of Persia, wrote to the Shah of Iran, as he was dying of cancer in Panama, saying she still loved him and wanted to see him one last time. He wrote back saying that he also still loved her, and wanted to see her also before he died. This meeting never too place. In 1991 her memoir, was published its title was; 'The Palace of Loneliness'. Soraya died on 26 October 2001 in her apartment in Paris, France.

38. Porfirio Rubirosa died in the early morning of July 5, 1965, at the age of 56, when he crashed his silver Ferrari 250 GT, into a tree in the Bois de Boulogne after an all-night celebration, at the Paris nightclub 'Jimmy's', in honour of winning the polo Coupe de France.

39. Ioannis Cardamatis, went to live with Timothy Hennessey in Avignon. He died there in 2010. They had one final art exhibition in Athens in 2015, that Timothy attended.

40. Anthony Perkins was diagnosed with HIV during the filming of Psycho IV: The Beginning, and died at his Los Angeles home on September 12, 1992, from AIDS-related pneumonia at the age 60. His urn that was filled with his ashes, was inscribed with the words, 'Don't Fence Me In'. It was located in an altar on the terrace of his former home in the Hollywood Hills

41. Lady Dorothy Lygon (1912-2001), died in Oxfordshire, in 2001.

42. Ari Onassis died at age 69 on 15 March 1975 at the American Hospital of Paris in Neuilly-sur-Seine, France, of respiratory failure. Onassis was buried on his island of Skorpios in Greece, alongside his son, Alexander. Onassis' will establish a charitable foundation in memory of his son; The Alexander S. Onassis Public Benefit Foundation.

43. In December, 1993 Jacqueline Kennedy Onassis was diagnosed with non-Hodgkin lymphoma, a type of blood cancer. In March the cancer had spread to her spinal cord and brain, and by May to her liver was deemed terminal. She made her last trip home from New York Hospital to Cornell Medical Centre on May 18, 1994 The following night at 10:15 p.m, she died in her sleep in her Manhattan apartment at age of sixty-four.

44. Rod McKuen's songs sold over 100 million recordings worldwide, and sixty million books of his poetry. He died of respiratory arrest, a result of pneumonia, at a hospital in Beverly Hills, California, on January 29, 2015.

45. John Hartford, who has died in June 4, 2001, of cancer aged 63. His last soundtrack was the fiddle tune Indian War Whoop, heard on the soundtrack of the Coen Brother's film, O Brother, Where Art Thou? (2000).

46. Susanne Verdal lived on Venice beach, in her truck after she became homeless due to a back injury. She has since found a permanent place to live. She met Leonard again many years later and he thanked her for giving him such a beautiful song.

47. Sister Marguerite Bourgeoys, the French nun and founder of the Congregation of Notre Dame of Montreal in the colony of New France, now part of Québec, Canada; was canonized in 1982 and declared a saint by the Catholic Church, the first female saint of Canada.

48. Ekaterini Paouri died on Hydra in 1986.

49. Mikis Theodrakis Following was released at end of January 1968, and was banished in August to the town of Zatouna with his wife, Myrto, and their two children, Margarita and Yorgos. Later he was interned in the concentration camp of Oropos.

An international solidarity movement, headed by Dmitri Shostakovich, Leonard Bernstein, Arthur Miller, and Harry Belafonte demanded to get Theodorakis freed. On request of the French politician Jean-Jacques Servan-Schreiber, Theodorakis was allowed to go into exile to Paris on 13 April 1970. Theodorakis's flight left secretly from an Onassis-owned private airport outside Athens. He arrived at Le Bourget Airport where he met Costa Gavras, Melina Mercouri and Jules Dassin. Theodorakis was immediately hospitalized, as he suffered from tuberculosis. His wife and children joined him a week later in France, having travelled from Greece via Italy on a boat. He lives in Greece now and is ninety-five years old.

50. On December 19, 2011, the Congregation for the Causes of Saints certified a second miracle by Saint Catherine Tekakwitha, through her intercession, signed by Pope Benedict XVI, which paved the way for pending canonization. On February 18, 2012, Pope Benedict XVI decreed that she be canonized. She was canonized on October 21, 2012, by Pope Benedict XVI.

51. Leonard Cohen died on Nov 17, 2016, at the age of eighty-two at his home in Los Angeles. According to his manager, Cohen's death was the result of a fall at his home on the night of November 7, and he subsequently died in his sleep. His body was flown back to Montreal where he was buried on November 10. As was his wish, Leonard was laid to rest with a Jewish rite, in a simple pine casket, in his family's plot. The city of Montreal held a tribute concert to Cohen in December 2016, entitled 'God is Alive, Magic Is Afoot', after a poem from his novel Beautiful Losers. A memorial also took place in Los Angeles. Cohen was survived by his two children Adam and Lorca, and his three grandchildren.

***

Photo Album

1. Marianne (Ilhen) Jensen, Charmian Clift, Ioannis Wolfgang Kardamatis, Timothy Hennessey and George Johnson, Hydra 1958

2.Hydra Port, 1960. Photograph by Redmond Wallis.

3.Nikos Hadjikyriakos-Ghika in Hydra, 1960. Benaki Museum – Ghika Gallery, Athens. Photo: Suschitzky. (1912 – 2016).

4.Jackie Kennedy, Hydra, Hydra. 1961.

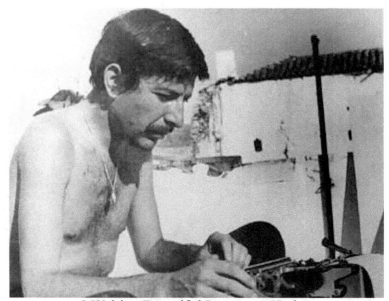
5. Writing Beautiful Losers on Hydra.

6. Nelly van Doesburg, Timothy Hennessy, and Peggy Guggenheim Venice, early 1960's.

7.Marianne Ilhen Jensen, at the port of Hydra in 1962, two years after she met Leonard Cohen.

8. Charmian Clift and George Johnson, circa 1962.

9. Hennessy's Villa, Ioannis Kardamatis, Hydra 1986.

10.Axel Jensen. Photographer Unknown.

11.Leonard and Marianne on a donkey ride Hydra 1960.

12. Interior Katerina Paouri's villa, Hydra, George Johnson Charmian Clift and Katerina.

13. The tapestry of Kateri Tekakwitha hangs from the St. Peter's Basilica, at the Vatican, Friday, Oct. 19, 2012.

14.Marianne Ilhen Jensen.

15. Cover The Favourite Game, design by Barry Trengrove. Published by McClelland & Stewart Canada 1970.

16.Beautiful Losers. Novel by Leonard Cohen, New York: The Viking Press, 1966.

17. Gordon Merrick o cover of his novel, The Good Life, Alyson Publications, 1997.

18. Susanne Verdal.

19. Mary Lygon, Evelyn Waugh and Dorothy Lygon.

20. Ghika's House Hydra.

21. Victor Rothschild, 3rd Baron of Rothschild (1910-1990) and his first wife Barbara Hutchinson. She later married Nico Ghika the Greek artist.

22.Olivia de Haulleville, Kathmandu, Kopan Monastery.

23.Peggy Guggenheim in Paris.

24.Sophia Loren with Ekaterini Paouri.

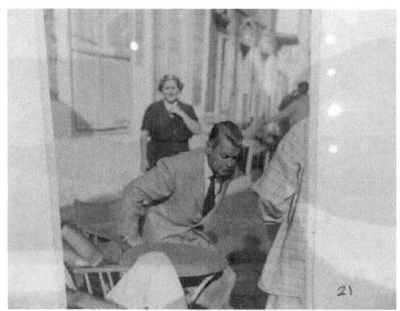
25.Ekaterini Paouri with Alan Ladd.

26.Muriel Belcher.

27.Federico García Lorca. 1898-1936.

28. W.B. Yeats. 1865-1939.

29.Lord Byron, 1788-1824.

30. George Whitman, Shakespeare and Co Bookshop, Paris.

31. Sylvia Whitman

32.The house where Cohen lived on Hydra, in November 2016.

33.Portrait of Shelley.

34. Painting;The Death of Shelley.

35. Princess Alice of Greece, (1885 – 1969)
Prince Philips mother.

36. Sixten Sparre and Hedvig Eleonore Jensen (1867- 1889), better known by her stage name Elvira Madigan.

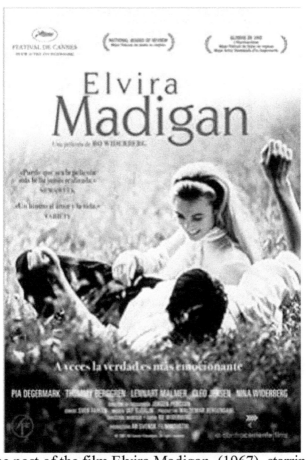

37. The post of the film Elvira Madigan, (1967), starring Pia Degermark and Thommy Berggren.

38. Gabriel Murray. Author,
A Thousand Kisses Deep.

Picture Credits;

1. Marianne (Ilhen) Jensen, Charmian Clift, Ioannis Wolfgang Kardamatis, Timothy Hennessey and George Johnson, Hydra 1958, Photographer unknown, Johnson and Clift Collection.

2. Hydra Port, 1960. Photograph by Redmond Wallis. Photo, Dorothy Wallis collection.

3. Nikos Hadjikyriakos-Ghika in Hydra, 1960. Benaki Museum – Ghika Gallery, Athens. Photo: Suschitzky. (1912 – 2016), © The Estate of Wolfgang Suschitzky.

4. Jackie Kennedy, Hydra, 1961. Photographer unknown.

5. Writing Beautiful Losers on Hydra (pic Axel Jensen Jnr).

6. Nelly van Doesburg, Timothy Hennessy, and Peggy Guggenheim Venice, early 1960s. © Solomon R. Guggenheim Foundation. Photo Archivio Cameraphoto Epoche.

7. Marianne Ilhen Jensen, at the port of Hydra in 1962, two years after she met Leonard Cohen. Photo by, ECW Press.

8. Charmian Clift and George Johnson, circa 1962, Photographer unknown, The Australian Newspaper. News Corp Australia.

9. Hennessy's Villa, Ioannis Kardamatis, Hydra 1986, Photo, Bjorn Saastad

10. Axel Jensen. Photographer Unknown. Public Domain. Arbeiderbevegelsens Arkiv og Bibliotek

11. Leonard and Marianne on a donkey ride Hydra 1960, From Life magazine archive. Photo by James Burke.

12. Interior Katerina Paouri's villa, Hydra, George Johnson Charmian Clift and Katerina. Photographer Unknown.

13. The tapestry of Kateri Tekakwitha hangs from the St. Peter's Basilica, at the Vatican, Friday, Oct. 19, 2012. (Photo AP / Alessandra Tarantino)

14. Marianne Ilhen Jensen. Photographer Unknown Getty Images.

15. Cover The Favourite Game, design by Barry Trengrove. Published by McClelland & Stewart Canada 1970.

16. Beautiful Losers. Novel by Leonard Cohen, New York: The Viking Press, 1966.

17. Gordon Merrick o cover of his novel, The Good Life, Alyson Publications, 1997.

18. Susanne Verdal, photographer unknown.

19. Mary Lygon, Evelyn Waugh and Dorothy Lygon.

20. Ghika's House Hydra, Photographer unknown.

21. Victor Rothschild, 3rd Baron of Rothschild (1910-1990) and his first wife Barbara Hutchinson. She later married Nico Ghika the Greek artist.

22. Olivia de Haulleville, Kathmandu, Kopan Monastery.

23. Peggy Guggenheim in Paris, photographed by Rogi André, ca. 1940 Copyright

24. Sophia Loren with Ekaterini Paouri. Photographer unknown.

25. Ekaterini Paouri with Alan Ladd. Photographer unknown.

26. Muriel Belcher. Photographer unknown.

27. Federico García Lorca. 1898-1936. Photographer unknown.

28. W.B. Yeats. 1865-1939. Photographer unknown.

29. Lord Byron, 1788-1824. Photographer unknown.

30. George Whitman, Shakespeare and Co Bookshop, Paris. Photographer unknown.

31. Sylvia Whitman, Photographer unknown.

32. The house where Cohen lived on Hydra, in November 2016. Photograph:

Louisa Gouliamaki/AFP /Getty Images.

33. Portrait of Shelley, by Alfred Clint (1829).

34. The Death of Shelley by Louis Edwouard Fournier, 1889.

35. Princess Alice of Greece, (1885 – 1969), By Philip De Lazlio.

36. Sixten Sparre and Hedvig Eleonore Jensen (1867- 1889), better known by her stage name Elvira Madigan.

37. The post of the film Elvira Madigan, (1967), starring Pia Degermark and Thommy Berggren.

38. Gabriel Murray. Author, A Thousand Kisses Deep.

39. Arnold Bocklin, The Isle of the Dead. 1880.

Copyright;

This book is a work of fiction. No quotes have been made of material from Leonard Cohens poems. This book only makes reference to his three songs Susanne, Bird on Wire, and So Long Marianne The words of lyrics are not quoted. There is only a prose interpretation. All the letters between Leonard and Marianne are fiction. The quotes listed below are out of copyright. There are quotes by Garbo, Cohen, Marianne and Prince Philip that belong to the public domain, as they are not creative works. There is also the rule of De Minimus that applies in this case. The Berne convention regulations on copyright have been observed.

Quotes; Poems, Quotes, Out of Copyright
1. Quote. Susanne Verdal.
2. Quote, Saint Catherine.
3. Rimbaud. Letter 1871.
4. Oyfn Pripetchek, (On the Hearth"), by M.M. Warshawsky, 1875.
5. Down by the Sally Gardens. W.B. Yeats, 1889.
6. Under Ben Bulben by W.B. Yeats, 1939.
7. Mack the Knife by Kurt Weill, 1928.
8. The Morning Market. Frederica Garcia Lorca. 1934.
9. The Truth Goes Marching On, Julia Ward Howe, 1861.
10. Bound for Glory, Woodie Gutherie.
11. The Second Coming. W.B Yeats. 1920.
12. Guantanamera,
13. The Song of Hiawatha, Henry Longfellow, 1855
14. Its True. Frederica Garcia Lorca. 1927.
15. Ode to a Nightingale, by John Keats. 1819.
16. Teddy Boys, Lord Kitchiner.

17. South of the Border Down Mexico Way. Jimmy Kennedy and Michael Carr,1939.
18. The Wounds of Love. Fredricka Garcia Lorca.
19. Le Vie En Rose. Edith Piaf. Louis Louiguy and Marguerite Monnot, 1945.
20. The Second Coming W.B.Yeats.
21. Being Beauteous, Arthur Rimbaud.
22. Fleur Du Mal, Au Lecturer by Charles Baudelaire,1857.
23. White Rose of Athens, Nana Mouskouri.
24. For All of Us, Anthony Kingsmill.
25. Dust to Dust. Shelley
26. Quote, Greta Garbo,1955.
19. The Unfaithful Wife by Frederica Garcia Lorca, 1929.
20. Percy Bysshe Shelley; 'Love's Philosophy', 1819.
27. Greek resistance, Joseph Goebells.
29. Vieneese Waltz. Fredericka Garcia Lorca.
30. Ithaka, Constantine Cadafy, 1911.
23. Death, Land, Spirit, Percy Shelly.
24. She Walks in Beauty by Lord Byron.
31. Beyond Good and Evil. Fredrick Nietche.
10. Teddy Boys. Lord Kitchiner,1959.
To My Native Village by Taigu Ryokan 1758-1831. Zen poet. John 1:29,
32. What is that Thing Called Love, Sophia Loren.
33. Childe Harold, Lord Byron.1812.
34. I Had a Rendeverous with Death, Alan Seeger.
35. Elegy on the Death of Adonis, John Keats.
36. Am I Blue, written by Harry Akst and Grant Clarke, 1929.
37. The Mooche, Duke Ellington.
38. Waltzing Matilda by Banjo Paterson, 1895.
40. Quote, Arthur Rimbaud.
42.. Conference of the Birds; by Attar of Nishapur, 1177. AD.
44. Quote, Saint Catherine.

45. Letter from Marianne, 1981, Public domain.
45. Letter from Leonard, 1981, Public domain.
46. In Memory of Eva Gore Booth and Constance Markievitz, by W.B. Yeats, 1933.
40. Quote Prince Philip, Public domain. 1994.
41. Quotes from Interviews;
Susanne Verdal. You Probably Think This Song Is about You, BBC Radio 42. FM, June 1998. Interviewed by McCallister interviewed by Kate Saunders. Transcription from tape by Marie Mazur.
43. King Constantine speech Toronto Star: Curley, W.J.P. (1975). Monarchs in Waiting. London: Hutchinson & Co Ltd. pp. 39–41.
45. Hennessy Home for Visual Ritual; St. Louis Post-Dispatch from St. Louis, Missouri, 1970, April 3, 1970, pg 40.
46. Quotes, Marylyn Monroe.
47. An Iroquois virgin, Catherine Tekakwitha, Lily of the Mohawk and the St. Lawrence, 1656-1680, by Eìdouard Lecompte, 1932.
48. Kateri of the Mohawks by Marie Cecilia Buehrle.
49. Bradshaw's Guide, by Lindsay John Bradshaw, 1939.
50. Hitler speech about the Greeks.

***

37. The Isle of the Dead by Arnold Bocklin, 1880.

A Thousand Kisses Deep.

Copyright. © Gabriel Murray

Printed in the USA
CPSIA information can be obtained
at www.ICGtesting.com
LVHW020003171024
794045LV00006B/161